# THE PAWS OF HOPE

# THE PAWS OF HOPE

LAURA NAPOLI

To my bestie, SulisDracarys,
Have I told you I've written a book, or four?
Seriously though, thank you for putting up with my
hyper-focus for the past few years and supporting me at every turn!

Now, go sit down...and read the book.
Also, purple.

# CONTENTS

# CHAPTER 1

# Marsee: Jump

The domed roof of the shuttle bay spiraled open to reveal Ellie's ship hovering above, gleaming in the early morning sunlight.

Unable to help herself, Marsee started bouncing from both excitement and nervousness. "Mama, are you sure you don't need me here to help with Little Flower and Hope?"

"For the last time, I'm positive. Even your sister says you should go. We'll be fine. Little Flower and Hope will be fine. I promise. The only one who won't be fine will be you, if you don't get your furry little behind on that ship before the Senior Guild Master demotes you again."

Laughing, Marsee gave her a hug, and then ran for the ship the moment it landed and the passenger door slid open. Once inside, she hit the switch for the door and flopped down in the jump seat Ellie indicated. Marsee grinned her thanks as it was the window seat Ellie normally took. She normally sat across from Ellie, but she wouldn't be able to look out the window during takeoff from that seat.

"Ready?" Ellie asked her, as she began buckling the safety harness.

"I think so. I've got my hearing aids and my tablet. Do I need anything else?" Marsee asked. She hadn't brought anything else, since nothing she had was really waterproof and her father had said nothing else would be needed.

"Nope. Everything else will be provided for us in our suites when we get there, and if not, we can always pick it up," Ellie replied.

"Then I guess I'm ready," Marsee said, unable to keep the shiver of excitement and nervousness out of her tail, although thankfully, it hadn't completely embarrassed her and gone fully poofed from fear yet. She was sure the thing had a mind of its own, as it betrayed her emotions all the time.

This would not only be her first trip to another planet, but her first extended trip with her new mentor. She'd attended a few guild meetings at Ellie's request, but those had been short visits in Council City, where she'd been able to return that same evening or the next day at the latest. They would be gone for several weeks this time. The day after they arrived, they planned to attending a resource allocation meeting with the Local Council. After that, they would travel around the planet, meeting with the various guild masters and touring several of the bigger guild halls, before ending up back at Council Platform in time for the Full Council, and then hit up a few more guild halls afterwards. She was really glad she'd had Little Flower teach her to swim, because most of their time would be spent underwater.

Ellie leaned over and tugged on Marsee's harness and made an adjustment, and then pulled it far tighter than Marsee normally wore it. "Remember to keep your head against the seat and facing forward during the initial takeoff."

"Yes, ma'am," Marsee replied, far too nervous not to go all formal on Ellie.

Ellie snorted but didn't comment as she hit the comms built into the armrest of her seat. "Petra, we're ready to depart."

"Yes, ma'am," came the quick reply and the engines hummed back to life.

The ship slowly rose into the air and flew away from New Hope before pivoting, such that they were practically laying on their backs. The force of the engines as they broke free of the planet slammed them back into their seats, before the ship's gravity systems compensated and the pressure eased. Once she could lift her head from the seat, Marsee's eyes were glued to the window beside her as the ground quickly fell further and further away.

"Orbital velocity has been achieved," came Petra's voice again. "Are you ready to begin the jump to the Water World?"

"Not yet. Please maintain orbit for now," Ellie replied.

"Yes, ma'am."

"So, what do you think?" Ellie asked. "I remember the first time I ever saw the planet from space. It's something few people ever get to do."

"It's just...wow..." Marsee said, completely blown away at the sight. No picture she'd ever seen did it justice. "It seems so small from here, like how can it support so many people?"

"Kind of makes you feel insignificant? Doesn't it?" Ellie asked.

Marsee nodded.

"It's something to keep in mind. People tend to get so wrapped up in their own day to day problems that they forget the big picture, or the impact that they have on others, but we're all sharing that one tiny little planet, and have to find a way to co-exist."

Marsee nodded again, not taking her eyes off of the widow.

"Would you like to try zero-g before we jump?" Ellie asked.

Marsee spun to look at Ellie, bouncing slightly in her seat. "We can do that?!"

Ellie nodded and grinned at her enthusiasm. "Petra, would you please disengage the gravity systems so that Marsee can experience zero-g for the first time?"

"Yes, ma'am. Have fun!" came the quick reply.

An alarm blared and a slightly mechanical voice called out. "Warning, Gravity systems will disengage in thirty seconds. Please ensure all items are secure. Warning, Gravity systems will disengage in ten seconds. Nine, eight,.."

Marsee silently kept count along with the warning system, barely able to contain her excitement.

"Gravity systems have been disengaged. You are free to move about the cabin."

To Marsee it felt like the ship suddenly started falling out from under her, and she yelped as she was lifted slightly out of her seat and pressed against the safety harness.

Ellie picked up her tablet and let it go. It just floated in front of them.

"Oh! That's so cool!" Marsee exclaimed.

"Go ahead, unbuckle your harness. Take it slowly though. Your actions will be magnified." Ellie un-clicked her harness, gave a small shove, and twisted to face Marsee, her fur sticking out in all directions.

Marsee unhooked her harness, but as she was taking her arm out, she moved too quickly, and ended up spinning herself across the room. "Ack!" she yelped, followed by an "oof" as she bounced off the wall, and came tumbling back.

Laughing, Ellie hooked a foot under her seat, braced against the roof with one hand, and caught her with the other. "Easy there. It's best to hold on to something until you feel comfortable. That's what the bars along the walls and ceiling are for."

Ellie floated her in the general direction of one of the bars which she thankfully managed to grab.

Once Marsee secured herself and slowly turned around, Ellie flipped over so that she was now standing on the roof of the ship, completely opposite of Marsee. She felt positively green.

"Are you feeling alright? Trust me, you do *not* want to throw up in zero-g," Ellie asked.

"Yeah. I think so. That just hurts my brain to look at," she replied.

Ellie's tail spiraled. "Well flip around, or pick a different direction entirely. It's important to learn that in space there is no up or down until you're close enough to a planet or object big enough to have a noticeable gravity. You'll feel much the same in the water with the mask you'll need to wear. It's very different from swimming in the pool."

Marsee carefully flipped herself upside down. "Woah" she said. "That's just weird."

"Try giving yourself a push off of the wall. You'll need to learn how much force you need to make it to your next hand hold. The last thing you want to do is end up in the middle of the room without anything to grab ahold of."

Marsee followed her instructions, and almost made it across the room before air friction slowed her down. She tried reaching for the railing, but just ended up spinning in a summersault.

"Ugh!" she groaned.

Ellie laughed and pushed off, grabbing Marsee upside down on the way by, and landing them both on the other side.

"Thanks!" Marsee said, but felt greener than before. She swallowed hard. "I think I'm going to have to stop now or I'm going to be sick."

"I'm impressed you've made it this far. The last three people were sick before they took their harness off." Ellie helped her back over to her seat, ensured she was safely buckled in before grabbing her tablet, and then buckled herself back in. "Petra, we're safely back in our seats. You can restore the gravity again.

"Yes, Ma'am! How'd she do?" came Petra's reply.

"Her stomach contents are still safely in her stomach," Ellie replied.

"Oh excellent! Well done!"

This was followed by the thirty second warning that the gravity systems were turning back on. When they did it was a gradual return, so that even if people were caught out of their seats, no one would get hurt.

Once gravity was fully restored, Ellie flipped open the table in front of her and pulled out a packet. "Take this and put it under your tongue. It'll help settle your stomach."

Marsee took the dissolvable tablet gratefully. "That was so much fun! I want to try that again sometime, but maybe not after I've just eaten breakfast."

Ellie grinned at her and activated her comms again. "Petra, we're prepared to jump."

"Yes, ma'am!"

The same thirty second warning blared and suddenly the universe shifted. Marsee felt like she was pulled in every direction at the same time, and then squashed into a tiny ball before bouncing back to her normal size. Outside the window the planet and stars disappeared and a rainbow of light took their place.

"Jump velocity achieved. E.T.A. to our arrival above the Water World is three days and twenty-one hours. It's now safe to move about the ship."

At those words, Marsee unbuckled her straps and bolted for the waste room.

Ellie sat in her chair and chuckled, knowing full well what would happen. Marsee had done well making it through her first experience with zero-g, but no one *ever* made it through their first jump without getting sick.

"Feeling better?" Ellie asked her when she made it back to her seat.

"Define better?" Marsee grumbled, which caused Ellie to laugh again.

"Stomach contents remaining in your stomach?" Ellie qualified.

"There's nothing left in my stomach to remain there," Marsee muttered in reply. "How are you not sick? That was awful."

"I did throw up my first few times too, but I've been doing this for well over a century now. You'll get used to it."

"I doubt it. I don't know how anyone could get used to that," Marsee muttered, and leaned her head up against the cool side of the shuttle to watch the mesmerizing colors of the universe.

Ellie handed her another nausea tablet. "Trust me, eventually you'll come to welcome jump as it signifies several days of peace and quiet, where the universe can't easily get a hold of you."

"That may be, but my *father* is going to hear from me," Marsee growled. "He could have warned me, and not brought such a big breakfast this morning. Why does no one mention how awful jump is, in *any* of the stories?"

Ellie chuckled. "I think your father's been hanging out with Wind Rider too much, but it is a bit of a right of passage. Everyone gets sick their first time, and if people knew what it really felt like, they'd never do it."

"Fair point, well made. Now please excuse me while I curl up and die."

Still chuckling, Ellie picked up her tablet to get some work done and left Marsee to her misery.

It took her over an hour for her stomach to fully settle, even with another one of the tablets Ellie had given her. She thought about going to her room to lay down, but she couldn't pull herself away from the window. Finally though, she sat up and unclipped her tablet to read.

"If you're feeling better, I've sent you several documents to read through. If that doesn't put you to sleep, I have several requisition forms you can fill out," Ellie said, without looking up from her own tablet.

Marsee pulled up the documents that had been shared with her, and groaned. There were detailed descriptions of each of the major guilds on the Water World, the current guild masters and other high ranking members, the crafts they specialized in, and what each guild had produced for the past year, along with reviews and any complaints that had been logged against each. In addition, Ellie had provided her with the list of items each of the guild masters wished to discuss with them when they arrived, along with notes that Ellie had made indicating areas that she wanted Marsee to research before they arrived. *This is going to take days to get through! So much for being able to finish reading my book,* she thought, miserably.

Several hours later, her eyes were starting to cross on her, so with a massive yawn, she set her tablet down and stood. Her spine snapped and popped audibly as she stretched. "I'm going to find something to eat. Do you want anything?" she asked the Guild Master.

"Something to drink would be nice. Thank you," Ellie replied, without taking her eyes off her own screen.

Padding over to the small onboard kitchen, she examined the offering. Meals had been pre-packaged in reusable stasis canisters to keep the food fresh, and prevent them from shifting during takeoff or floating off in zero-g. Each was labeled although she only recognized a few. Grabbing one that sounded interesting, she turned to examine the available beverages and grabbed a large thermos of bosa berry juice, wondering what it was, and two clear cups, figuring that the ship would only be stocked with the foods Ellie liked.

"I picked something called bosa berry juice. I've never heard of it. If you don't like it I can grab something else," Marsee said, as she set the items down on the large table in front of them, and then sat on the other side, swiveling the seat around so she could face Ellie.

"Bosa berry is...interesting. I'll be curious to know what you think of it. It's Petra's favorite, which is why we carry it," Ellie said, setting her tablet down.

With that somewhat nebulous response, Marsee poured out a cup for the both of them. It was an intense blue and bubbling. Marsee lifted the cup to look at the bubbles. "Is it supposed to do that?" Marsee asked.

"It is," Ellie said, taking her cup and wrapping her paws around it before taking a sip.

Marsee sniffed at her cup and the bubbles tickled her nose. She had to twitch her whiskers furiously to keep from sneezing. It smelled like the air during a thunderstorm, which made her flick her ears back in surprise. She took a look at the Senior Guild Master, who was watching her with an innocent expression.

*Too innocent,* Marsee thought, but she was the one that picked it out. With a slight glare at Ellie, she tentatively took a sip and then gasped. It felt like she'd been struck by a million tiny lightning bolts, as it ran down her throat, and made her fur stand on end.

"So? What do you think?" Ellie asked, unable to keep the smile off her face any longer, or her tail from curling.

"If you call drinking a lightning bolt 'interesting', I hate to see what really excites you," Marsee replied, trying to smooth her fur down, which was crackling with static electricity. "How under the three moons did you drink that without reacting?" Marsee asked.

Ellie held her cup up, showing it was just as full as before. "I didn't," she replied, and then burst out laughing as she finally took a drink, and her own fur poofed out with static electricity.

"I knew you were hiding something!" Marsee said. Her tail curled at the practical joke, even if she'd been the recipient. She'd set herself up for it.

"It is Petra's favorite, though. Apparently it doesn't affect the Flyers like it does us, but then they don't have fur. If you don't want to finish it though, you don't have to." Ellie spun the meal around to see what Marsee had picked. "Ooh, good choice on the meal too! This is considered a delicacy on the Water World. The texture takes some getting used to, but the taste is good. Better you familiarize yourself with it now. I expect we'll be invited to dinner by many of the guild masters, and likely the Senior Councilor the night we arrive, if not the night after. Clear Seas regularly invites me over whenever I'm visiting Council Platform, and I'm sure he'll want to get to know you better. I had them stock the ship with a wide selection of foods from the Water World so you could try them out before we arrived."

"Me?" Marsee asked. "Why?"

Ellie just rolled her eyes and shook her head, as if it should be obvious, and nodded towards the food.

Marsee tilted her head in confusion and shrugged before opening the small stasis container, revealing a platter of strange foods. She reached down to pick one up.

"Not with your fingers," Ellie said. "Use the sticks. While they know we don't use utensils to eat, it's considered rude to handle your food with your fingers before eating." Ellie picked up the two sticks that had been included with the meal and showed her how to use them.

"It's just like Little Flower did when we first learned they liked their food cooked, although her sticks were a lot smaller," Marsee said, as she fumbled to get the sticks to open and close, and then tried to pick up the food. She managed to get the piece halfway to her mouth before it fell into the paw she'd placed under it just in case. "Oops!"

"Keep practicing," Ellie said with a chuckle, and then stood to retrieve her own meal, deciding she was hungry after all.

Marsee managed on the second attempt, but her fingers were cramping from the effort. She chewed slowly. *Ellie's right about the texture,* she thought. It was tough and kind of chewy, but tasted pretty good.

"So what is this anyway?" she asked when Ellie returned, carefully picking up another piece.

"Some sort of giant sea crawly, from what I understand," Ellie replied, picking up her own sticks and popping a piece in her mouth.

Marsee paused, mouth open, and food almost in her mouth. "What!?" she exclaimed. "It's a bug?"

Ellie nodded, and grabbed another piece and popped it in her mouth.

"They eat bugs?" Marsee asked again, horrified and slightly terrified of another hunting instinct flare-up. "You're not pulling my tail again are you?"

"Not about this I'm not. Now eat up. I had to trade a commission to get this. It's almost impossible to find off-world." Ellie popped another piece in her mouth and sighed in obvious enjoyment.

Marsee looked at the piece of creepy crawly in front of her, and swallowed hard. "I don't know if I can," she said finally.

Ellie nodded. "That's why I insisted on getting some. You're going to be exposed to all sorts of new foods, many of which will taste horrible, or will go against everything you've been taught about what is moral and right to eat, but just like the Hue-mans, the other species have different dietary needs than we do, and don't always have the luxury we do around avoiding foods that come from creatures. They'll usually try to make sure to provide us food we can and do enjoy, but some foods are traditional, and refusing can or will insult your host. Not only will you need to eat it, but you're going to need to pretend to like it. This is one of those foods, and if you can forget that it comes from a crawly, it's actually pretty good."

"The taste isn't the issue...," Marsee started. Ellie looked at her curiously, so she explained. "Little Flower's fried fish was a major trigger for me. I haven't had meat of any kind since then. Well, not that I know of anyway. It's hard to tell with some of the creations that Jordan makes, but everything is usually well labeled unless I'm sneaking it from the kitchen."

Ellie nodded her understanding. "That's partly why we're doing this now. To give you time to deal with any issues you might have. How are you feeling?"

"I'm still firmly in control. I have been since that day in the garden. I'm scared about what might happen more than anything," Marsee admitted.

Ellie nodded her understanding. "I won't push you to eat more if you're not ready, and if you truly can't, then I'll have your mother add this as a food allergy. That way you'll have an excuse your hosts will honor and understand. You'll just need to let them know when they invite you to dinner, but hiding from your problems only made things worse for you before. It might be better if you tried facing them, and seeing if there's even anything to worry about. I'm not particularly worried, if there was going to be a problem, it would have happened by now."

"Are you sure?" Marsee asked.

"Unfortunately, yes," Ellie replied with a sigh.

Marsee looked at her Mentor hard and saw the edges of grief in her expression. *Who did she lose to psychosis?* she wondered, but didn't ask. She nodded, swallowed hard, closed her eyes, and then ate the piece, eventually getting it down.

*It's okay but nothing I have any intentions of chasing down. Now if those chocolate chip cookies suddenly developed legs and ran away, we might have a problem,* her instinct teased.

Marsee had a hard time keeping a straight face. The last thing her Mentor needed to know was that she was talking to herself.

*Well who else am I going to talk to?* her instinct muttered. *Ungrateful fur-ball. If you don't think your mentor speaks to herself, you're sadly mistaken.*

Marsee's brow lifted at that thought, but Ellie just nodded her approval, and then pointed to another item on her plate.

"This is a form of seaweed and this is a sea fruit. It kind of tastes like yellow fang."

Marsee tried the others. They weren't bad, then deciding to face her fears, took another piece of the sea crawly, only hesitating slightly this time.

# CHAPTER 2

# Little Flower: Useless

Little Flower lay in her swinging bed, thinking, but didn't open her eyes. Today would be exactly two months since she'd woken up from her coma, or six excruciatingly long months in Earth time. Marsee had left the day before on her trip to the Water World, and she was both happy and excited for her, and thoroughly depressed without her. It had taken her hours to fall asleep without being wrapped in Marsee's protective embrace, and the swinging bed felt cold and empty without her. Not only that, but the others would soon be following Marsee to the next Full Council meeting, and she wouldn't be there. Her mother had already indicated that she wasn't fit for interstellar travel yet, and frankly, her mother was right, and that infuriated her to no end.

She hadn't even been cleared for Local Council meetings, which made her even angrier. There was no reason she couldn't attend, but her mother refused to take her off of medical leave, stating that if she did, she would be limited in what she could do for treatment. Which further infuriated her. Just because she couldn't speak well, didn't mean she didn't understand what was going on, and she could use her tablet well enough, if slowly, to vote.

The last two months had been one grueling day of pickle torture after another, as her physical therapy sessions had come to be called, by everyone. She felt like a limp pickle most days, so it was apt. They were thoroughly exhausting and painful, and the thought of another session made her want to cry.

Her mother never backed off, and if she managed to do something once, her mother refused to accept anything less than that afterwards, even if she was sore, tired, or sick, and no matter how often she asked for a break or even just a nap, her mother refused, and continued to push her.

After all this time she'd only made the barest of progress, at least from her own perspective. Her mother seemed pleased though, but maybe that was because they lived for three hundred standard years, so a couple of months didn't seem like very long.

At this point, she'd progressed to being able to sit up unassisted, but still couldn't walk on her own. Her speech had barely improved, although the others seemed to understand her better, since she routinely made the same mistakes, and she could sign, but it was limited. Her fingers didn't have the fine motor control necessary to make many of the signs, and tended to cramp up on her.

She'd flat out refused to even try drawing, even though everyone had tried to make her, including the Senior Guild Master in one of her many visits to see Marsee. She'd only grudgingly agreed to work on translations with Marsee because Ellie was one of the few people who didn't act like she was an invalid around her, but watching Marsee sketch, when she couldn't, was depressing. She'd probably be jealous if she had the energy.

Hope was far more mobile than she was at this point, and was even signing quite regularly, and saying dozens of words in both Saber and English according to the others. A week before, they'd determined that she was managing well enough on solid foods to be weaned. Little Flower had cried herself to sleep every night for the past week at that loss, and the pain in her breasts as they dried up and she'd gone through two large tubs of nano cream to treat it.

She'd reached her limit, emotionally and physically. She was exhausted and in pain all day, every day. She provided no value to Hope, now that her daughter could survive on her own, and saw little in the way of improvement to make her feel like she was ever going to be a valued member of society again, or any indication that she was ever going to be allowed to be. She couldn't even watch her own child without assistance, and could barely play with her.

She felt like a burden to everyone, and was just trying to figure out a way to end it all, and wondered if she could crawl out the door during the few moments she was left alone, and whether or not the fall would be far enough, or just hurt her more.

*What's the point of living like this?* There was none as far as she could tell.

She felt a touch on her leg and opened her eyes to find her mother looking at her. "The monitors said you were awake. Do you need to use the bathroom?"

Little Flower sighed and nodded, not looking forward to the effort that would take, and frustrated that she couldn't even pretend to be asleep.

Her mother lowered the bed so that it rested on the legs, giving her a stable platform, and then helped her to sit up. By help, that meant her mother just gave her a tail to hold onto, as she pulled herself up into a sitting position. Thankfully the dizziness that had plagued her for the first few weeks had finally gone away.

Once she was sitting up, her mother attached the harness that Marsee had crafted for her to help her walk. Little Flower called it the Pinocchio belt because there were straps that her parents could hold on to to help her walk without having to bend over. That she couldn't walk on her own, didn't stop them from making her try, and she had to shuffle her feet along. Her feet never ended up where she wanted them to on the first, or even the second try.

They'd tried a walker, but she didn't have the upper body strength yet to even hold herself up, and her mother flat out refused to allow her a wheelchair, saying that would only slow her progress. They had fought over it for days. She just wanted even the slightest sense of freedom again. She couldn't go anywhere without someone carrying her, and there was no way she was going out in that moon's forsaken belt, so she refused to leave the room instead, even though she was absolutely sick of the room, and they never left her alone for more than a few minutes.

Thankfully she didn't have to rely on them to hold her up when she went to the bathroom anymore. Those first few weeks had been horribly degrading and traumatic for her, and GrandFather hadn't been able to help. The first time he'd tried, she'd completely lost it, and started screaming, completely trapped in a flashback and panic attack. He'd tried hugging her to calm her, but that had only made it worse, and she'd flailed, trying to escape, and attacked him thinking he was her rapist, and ended up breaking his nose, when head-butting him was the only thing she'd been able to do in her weakened state.

Marsee had been upstairs in her room, heard her screaming and came running, pushed GrandFather aside, and carried her off. She'd only calmed down when she was safe in Marsee's purring embrace. GrandFather had left to treat his nose, and when he came back she'd apologize profusely. She still felt horrible about it, but GrandFather had understood and never mentioned it again.

When she was done making use of the throne of muck, she leaned up against the wall for several minutes, not wanting to repeat the journey back out, but she knew if she waited too long her mother would check on her. Sighing, she pulled the call string they'd added, and her mother entered to helped her back out.

"Chair or bed?" her mother asked before helping her to stand.

"Chair," Little Flower replied, and began the long slow tortured shuffle out to the rocking chair.

Once there, her mother unhooked the straps and tied the belt to the chair. She'd fallen asleep on more than one occasion, and had even fallen out of the chair twice before someone could catch her, before they worked out the strap. Hope was still sleeping. She watched her baby sleep as she gently rocked in the chair amazed that her daughter was already a year and a half old by Earth time. She was growing so quickly!

She was honestly surprised her mother hadn't started the pickle torture right away, and she looked over to find her mother watching her with a sad expression on her face, before it vanished behind her mask.

Out the window behind her, the sky was just starting to lighten, which explained why the pickle torture hadn't begun. It was still really early.

Little Flower sighed, and turned her head to watch Hope again. *What kind of mother am I ever going to be to her? She can already do far more than I can at this point.*

She felt a paw on her shoulder and turned to see her mother looking at her with concern. "What's bothering you?" her mother asked.

Little Flower just shook her head.

"Talk to me, Little Flower. I can't help you if you don't."

"Don't want," she finally signed.

"Don't want what?" her mother asked, confused, "to talk about it?"

*Pickle torture, pretending that I'm ever going to get better. I'm exhausted Mama. I can't do anything by myself. I can't even take care of my own cub. I'm just a burden to you and everyone else,* she thought, unable to articulate what she really wanted to say. Without Marsee or GrandFather there to translate for her, she was less able to communicate than her own daughter.

"Live," she finally forced her fingers to sign. She couldn't stand the look of grief on her mother's face and turned her head away.

Her mother touched her shoulder again. "Little Flower, you can't give up. You've made so much progress in the past two months."

*It may only be two months for you, but it still feels like half a year for me. There's hardly been any improvement in weeks. I'm not going to get any better and you know it. Hope doesn't need me anymore, and frankly, Marsee should be living her life, not stuck here caring for me.* "No. I'm useless," she signed. "No get better."

Her mother frowned, and then walked away, confirming her suspicions. She watched as her mother walked over to the window and looked out, absently twisting her tail, and then sat down at her desk and called someone on her tablet. A few minutes later she was surprised to see Healer Ammond walk in. *What's he doing here this early in the morning?*

"Good morning, Little Flower. It's nice to see you again," he signed after sitting down so she didn't have to crane her neck so much to see him.

She just sighed. There was nothing 'good' about it.

"Your mother called me saying that you were frustrated about your progress."

She sighed again, but nodded, and rolled her eyes at the understatement.

Ammond's tail curled slightly at her expression, but his face was the calm mask of a healer. "How much have you been told about what happened to you?"

"Died - holes - useless," she slowly replied.

"You are not useless, you're injured. And yes, we drilled holes in your skull. It took us a long time to figure out why our treatments weren't working on your species, and eventually we ended up having to inject the nano's directly into your brain. It was a very risky procedure, but everything else we'd tried failed to wake you, and it worked, to an extent. Your mother and I have been talking for the past week that we think it might be time to try another treatment, but it comes with a significant amount of risk. If something goes wrong, we could make your situation far worse than it is now, and it could kill you. Your mother thinks we should wait another month until you're stronger, but I agree with your statement that you've stopped making progress. So if you want to try this, I'm willing to perform the operation."

*I can't live like this. I can't walk, go to the bathroom on my own, or care for my cub. I can't talk or sign without difficulty, and I can't even hear my own cub laugh or cry. What's the point of living like this?* she thought and slowly signed "Better I die than this."

"I'll take that as a yes. If I do this though, you'll have to promise me something."

"What?" she asked with a glare.

"That you'll give it time to work. It took almost a week for you to wake up last time. And, if it doesn't work or you get worse, that you don't give up. We'll both keep trying to find a way to make things better. I vow to you we won't quit trying, but we'll need time to be able to find a solution."

She nodded, willing to agree to anything at this point. If there was even the slightest chance they could fix even some of what was wrong with her, she'd take that risk. "When?" she asked.

"I'll need to run some tests first, but maybe today, if you're ready."

She nodded that she was.

"Have you had anything to eat this morning?"

She shook her head no.

"Good. Shall we head to the Trauma Center then?"

She shook her head no. "Mama Hope?" she asked instead.

Her mother nodded and walked over, waking the sleeping toddler, and bringing her over.

She gave her sleepy child a hug, and then handed her back to her mother after a few moments. With heavy sigh, she nodded to Ammond, and he carefully picked her up and carried her down to the Trauma Center.

It was strange being carried by him. She'd only ever been carried by her parents or Marsee, and she'd flat out refused to leave the room for the past two months, so she was not prepared for the changes she was seeing. The stone floor of the corridor had been replaced with a large water filled tunnel where the occasional Water Sprite swam underneath, and while Marsee had told her about all of the new buildings, it was still strange to see them, and she wondered what they all were.

When they arrived at the Trauma Center, she didn't even recognize it. Ammond carried her through a waiting area, down several long halls, to an examination room where there were all sorts of equipment, including what looked like the helmet she'd worn when she'd had her hearing tested all those months ago.

"Fix ears?" she asked, wondering if he could fix her hearing at the same time.

"Some, but not all," he signed back. "Now, I'm going to have to shave your head again so I can get a better scan of your brain while you perform various tasks. You're going to have to try as hard as you can at everything I ask you, so I know for sure what parts of the brain you're using for each task."

She nodded and he quickly shaved her head. It had only grown back a few inches since she'd woken. She didn't particularly mind as she'd always liked having short hair, and it was less of a hassle to deal with now. She ran her hand over her bald head marveling at the feel of how smooth it was. She wondered what she looked like, but he didn't have a mirror in his office, and she didn't ask.

Once he was done he applied some sort of stretchy hat on her head, not the bulky helmet she'd been expecting, and then had her run through all sorts of tests, from physical tests, like moving in every way imaginable, to signing, to speaking, to watching video recordings. She did everything he asked up until he handed her a piece of paper and a pencil.

"Write your name," he signed.

She just stared at the paper, and the pencil she could barely hold. She'd been terrified to find out whether or not she could still draw.

He waited, and looked at the pencil and paper pointedly after a few moments. "I know you're afraid, but I can't fix it, if I don't know how badly it's broken."

"Language?" she finally asked.

"Both, if you can."

She sighed and tried hard to write her name. She couldn't grip the pencil hard enough to hold it in place and it fell out of her hands.

After a few tries, he picked up the pencil, tapping it absently on his other palm and left the room. He returned a few minutes later with bandage putty and the setter tool.

"Put the pencil where you want it," he signed.

She did, awkwardly, and then he slathered a bunch of the putty on her fingers and ran the setter tool over it. When he was done, she now had a solid grip on the pencil and tried writing her name again. Her letters were ragged and shook. When she was done, he told her to draw a stick figure, so she did. It was even worse. She couldn't get the pencil to go where she wanted, and she would have thrown the pencil if it hadn't been stuck to her fingers. It was far worse than she feared, and she swallowed hard to keep from crying.

He then drew several shapes on the paper and made her trace them, then did the same with several words. At that point he must have had what he needed because he used the setter tool again and wiped off the putty.

"Have you always flipped your letters, or is that something new?" he asked, once she was cleaned up.

She nodded. "Always."

He flicked an ear back, but then handed her a small cubs book written in Saber. "Sign to me what you read."

It was hard and she couldn't make several of the signs, but they were close enough that he seemed pleased. When she was done, he took the book back and removed the hat.

"It's going to take me an hour or so to review everything. Do you need anything before I start?" he asked.

She shook her head and he left the room, leaving her alone for more than a few minutes for the first time in months. After a few minutes of looking around the room, she closed her eyes and napped. She was woken some time later when Ammond returned. Her mother was with him.

"Are you sure about this?" her mother asked.

She nodded yes, so her mother picked her up, hugged her tightly, and then darkness pulled her under, as her mother sedated her.

# CHAPTER 3

# Marsee: Translator

The next three days passed quickly. After Marsee had read through the initial set of documents and looked up the items requested, in the information Ellie had downloaded before they took off, Ellie quizzed her on what she'd read, and then had her study a guide on manners and etiquette unique to the Water World. They practiced for hours so that she felt reasonably comfortable she wouldn't make a complete fool of herself, and anger everyone in the process.

There were just so many things to remember that before long she was feeling rather overwhelmed. She had no idea just how different their culture was. None of the Water Sprites she'd ever interacted with had seemed all that different. For the last few hours before they came out of jump, she'd hidden in her room with her hearing aids in, listening to her favorite music and trying to relax. She'd asked Ellie to come find her before they exited, since she intended to shut everything off, and knew she probably wouldn't hear the announcement.

She missed her swing and its soothing motions, but the music was calming and blocked out the hum of the ship. She'd had to wear her hearing aids for most of the trip, even to sleep, and hadn't slept well because of it. Well it hadn't helped anyway. She was missing her sister and Hope fiercely. *I wish they were here with me. It feels so strange to be away from them for so long. Maybe when Little Flower is better I can ask if they can come along on another visit.*

By the time Ellie came for her, her nerves were mostly under control, and she'd taken two anti-nausea tablets in preparation for exiting the jump.

"Warning! We will be exiting jump in thirty seconds. Please ensure your items are stowed and you are strapped in."

Marsee double checked her harness and waited for the countdown. When the universe imploded and then expanded out again on her, she breathed hard trying not to lose the contents of her stomach. It was touch and go for a moment, but she managed.

"We've safely exited jump velocity," Petra called out over the comms. "I've received permission to begin our descent. Please remain in your seats until we've landed."

After sending a quick text to her mother that they'd arrived, Marsee looked out her window at the blue and white world below her.

Except for a few small uninhabited islands, the Water World was entirely under water. The world vanished as they hit the planet's atmosphere, and the heat from reentry flashed around the ships outer shields. Even with the shields and the thick insulation of the ship, Marsee could still feel the heat. It didn't last long though, and soon the ocean appeared below them again. They would be landing at Council Platform, the only landing platform designed for the massive transport and cargo ships, and the only community currently designed to adequately support the needs of off-world visitors.

As they flew over the ocean towards Council Platform, a massive creature launched itself out of the sea, and tried to swallow their ship whole.

Petra swerved and lifted the ship higher up.

"What was that?!" Marsee exclaimed, as she jerked back away from the window.

"I believe that's what the Sprites call a Leviathan," Ellie said, as two ships flew past them and dove into the sea after the creature. "Don't worry, they'll chase it off. They rarely approach the platform, so you don't need to worry about them. This ship is well equipped to avoid them, even if Petra wasn't paying attention. If by some miracle they do get a hold of the ship, the shields will feel like bosa berry juice to them, only a million times worse, and they won't hold on for long."

"Has that ever happened to you?" Marsee asked.

"Thankfully no, and I'll be honest, that's the closest I've come to one of those behemoths too. I didn't realize they were so big, but then they are called Leviathans."

Marsee nodded, and tried to smooth out her poofed fur as she watched their approach. The platform turned out to be a collection of platforms, but to her surprise, rather than landing on one of the platforms, where she could see several of the massive public transport and cargo ships being loaded and unloaded, the center of the platform below them opened, and their ship slowly descended inside. They passed through several levels before there was a slight jolt and the ship was suddenly below water. They continued to descend through several more levels before the ship rotated and there was another small jolt as the ship docked.

"Welcome to the Water World and Council Platform. It's now safe to walk about the cabin." Petra's voice came over the comms again, and a few moments later, "The docking port has been attached, and I've received clearance that it is now safe for you to disembark. Enjoy your visit!"

All Marsee could see now was a wall, and she peered behind her to see that a walkway had been attached outside of the shuttle door.

"Thank you, Petra, for another uneventful trip. We'll see you in a few weeks. Enjoy your vacation!" Ellie told the pilot.

"You're very welcome, and I intend to!" Petra replied.

"Well, come on then. Let's go meet the delegation that I'm sure is waiting for us," Ellie said.

Unhooking her safety harness, Marsee patted some ruffled fur back into place and followed her mentor out.

They exited the ship through the short walkway into a long tunnel that surrounded the platform. The entire outer wall was transparent, and Marsee found herself completely surrounded by the ocean and strange creatures swimming by. A railing ran along both sides of the tunnel, only breaking where there was another docking port. Marsee gingerly walked out onto the tunnel, and up to the curved wall, to look down at the city around her in amazement.

Smaller shuttles darted in and around the various buildings. Water Sprites of a variety of sizes, and other strange creatures, that seemed completely unfazed by the crafts, swam everywhere.

She'd only ever seen the older adult Sprites, and so was surprised at how small their children were. Many weren't much bigger than her sister's cub, and she remembered that unlike her species, they never stopped growing. The oldest of the Sprites were far longer than her mother was tall, but it was hard to tell with the way their tentacles bunched and flexed as they swam.

Ellie let her sightsee for a few moments, and then motioned for her to follow. "Come on, we don't want to keep our hosts waiting," she said, and then wrapped her tail around Marsee's arm, dragging her along, when Marsee didn't immediately respond.

Marsee followed, hardly able to watch where she was going. If it wasn't for the Guild Master guiding her, she'd have probably run into a wall. They followed the perimeter of the landing platform until they arrived at a wider tunnel that connected over into another massive building and into the terminal. Half the tunnel was a Water Sprite tunnel that wrapped around the other side of the landing platform.

Marsee blinked in surprise as they entered the terminal. The space was split neatly in half with off-world seating and tables on one side, and the types of furniture the Sprites used on the other. A massive static shield separated the two, giving everything a slight shimmer, and reminded her of the Senior's conference room.

As massive as the room was, it was nearly empty. Floating in a booth on the far wall, between the two sections of the room, was a single Sprite. Signs that read 'Visitor Check-in' in all six languages hung above it, with a walkway or tunnel access on either side. There was also food and drink available and clearly labeled waste rooms for visitor's use.

The only other people there were a small group of Water Sprites that were lounging around a table when they entered, their skin flashing in conversation while they waited, but they stopped their conversation and floated up and over to them the moment they entered the room.

Ellie approached the contingency, leading Marsee behind her. She managed to pull her attention back, just in time to see the introductions.

"Welcome Translator Chenzira, Senior Guild Master Khihar. It's an honor to have you both on our world. I sincerely hope you enjoy your stay here," the head of the contingent signed.

Ellie gave her a little squeeze with her tail before letting go, and she recovered her manners. She'd been addressed first, and so should respond first, but she had no idea why they were using her translator title instead of journeyman. While she was still an official translator for the Council, she hadn't done anything for the Council for the last few months, and as she was with Ellie as part of the Guild, they should have used her guild title. She shrugged internally, dismissing it.

"Thank you! It's an honor to be here. What little I've seen of your world so far is stunning, I can barely look away long enough to keep from walking into the walls. If the beauty I've seen so far is any indication, I am sure I will have a wonderful stay," she replied, in sign as well.

Several of the Sprites flashed the blues and greens that indicated their pleasure at her words.

"I trust your journey was uneventful?" the head of the contingent asked.

He looked very familiar, as did several of the others, but she couldn't place them, and it was considered rude to ask. That they didn't give their names indicated that they believed she should already know who they were.

*Maybe he's one of the Guild Masters in the report Ellie had me read,* she thought to herself, still half distracted by the sights around her, and nervous around unexpectedly being acknowledged first. She'd expected to just follow Ellie around for this trip.

"Our journey was safe, but far from uneventful, at least from my perspective anyway. This is my first trip off-world, and so everything about our journey has been both new and exciting," she replied.

"I remember my first trip off-world fondly. What was your most memorable experience?" he asked.

She thought about it for a moment. "It's hard to pick just one. Entering and exiting jump is something you can't even begin to describe, although my stomach was not at all impressed."

Several of the contingent flashed their humor at that statement.

"I had a brief opportunity to try zero gravity before we jumped, which I'm looking forward to trying again, and seeing both our worlds from space is so much more awe inspiring than can ever be captured by a video or picture, but if I had to pick just one, I'd have to say it would be all the wonderful samples of your foods my mentor introduced me to on our journey. Growing up in the desert as I did, I was limited, for the most part, to what we could grow in our garden, up until the past few months. Imports of your food never made it to our part of the world either, and what we get in New Hope from here is still being reserved for the Hue-mans and our Water Sprite guests. I'm looking forward to trying and experiencing everything your world has to offer, or as much as I can in our limited time here."

More blues and greens followed her words.

"I do remember my first few jumps. Thankfully, you do get used to it, *eventually*. We are approaching the evening meal. I'd thought we might take the scenic route on the way to your rooms, so you could see a little of the city, and perhaps stop and try some different foods from the vendors in the market, but if you need more time to recover from your trip, we can reschedule for later this evening or tomorrow. If you'd like a tour, that is."

Marsee glanced over at the Senior Guild Master, who twitched her whiskers forward, with a slight nudge of her head, in an indication that Marsee should decide.

"I am quite recovered, and if it's not a bother, I would really love a tour. Thank you!" she replied with enthusiasm. She wasn't lying. She wanted to see everything.

He smiled and nodded before motioning for her to follow.

To her surprise, they followed the contingency out of the terminal, completely ignoring the gate attendant, who just nodded at them as they passed, and exited into a large open atrium. The walkway continued on either side, with the Sprite's tunnel circling along the outside, and up and over where she and Ellie exited.

She walked over to the railing on the outside of the walkway to take a brief look, overwhelmed by the sheer size of the building. Below her, was an underwater garden where Sprites and others swam, but above her was a clear shot all the way up to the top of Council Platform, where a massive domed skylight let in the sun.

Several banks of clear elevators were transporting people to various levels, while others sat or strolled about. It looked like there were several floors of shops and restaurants on the first few levels, but the rest all appeared to be apartments.

She pulled her attention back to the contingency who was patiently waiting for her on the other side of a bank of doors leading to the outside.

"I've never seen a building with so many floors before," she signed. "It's incredible!"

"The original platform was designed to support fifty thousand off-world visitors. Until this past year, it was more than adequate to support our needs. We're in the process of finishing a second residential building on the other side of the platform, that can support up to twice that, including housing designed specifically for the Hue-man Council. Council Platform is not only the largest residential building on our planet, but on any of the planets. Only Council Cavern comes close in size, although there is some debate if that counts as a single building or not, as it runs leagues through the inside of a mountain and connects several communities."

Ellie chuckled beside her. "I've had numerous heated debates with Apakna over that. While Council Cavern can support twice as many people, much of that is in separate buildings or wings off of the main cavern. A few years ago, we decided that it was a complex of buildings, and only the main cavern counted as a single unit. It can only support about twenty-five thousand people, so both this, and the new wing, are far bigger, and at risk starting an interplanetary incident, I would much rather visit here. I'm personally not a big fan of the ice and snow, and while it's heated, it's never quite warm enough for me."

The head of the contingent chuckled, his skin rippling with humor. "I promise not to tell her," he replied, but Marsee had a feeling he was lying.

Ellie apparently thought so too, as she snorted and glared at him.

Further humor rippled across his skin at her glare, before he faced her again. "Translator, if you place your electronics and anything else you don't want to get wet into the compartment over there, we'll make sure they're delivered safely to your rooms."

Ellie placed her travel harness and tablet in the indicated compartment, so Marsee followed suit with her own harness, tablet, and hearing aids. She wasn't sure if they were waterproof or not. Once they were safely inside, the compartment closed, and they were transported up a long tube and out of sight.

Ellie grabbed one of the masks that were hanging on the wall beside the door, where the contingency waited for them, and showed Marsee how to put it on.

Once it was around her neck and snapped into place, an invisible shield expanded and wrapped around her head, and then continued to expand to wrap around her entire body. While she couldn't see it, she could feel it. Her fur stuck out from the charge and it tickled.

"This will both provide oxygen and counteract the pressure of the ocean as you change depths. It'll be a lot like being in zero-g with the mask on, but you'll be able to use your body to push against the water to move in whatever direction you want to go," Ellie explained.

Marsee could still breath, see, and hear through the mask, and once in place, she could barely feel it, except for the slight pressure of the band around her neck, and the tickle of her electrically charged fur.

Once properly equipped herself, Ellie hit the switch on the door and it slid open, revealing another static shield that kept the water from spilling into the room. Ellie stepped through and pushed off the floor to bob a few feet away, her fur going from sticking straight out to drooping like she'd just come out of the pool.

Marsee held her breath and carefully followed through, not sure what to expect. The water was warm on her fur, like the pool, and she felt wet like she was under the water without anything on, and started to panic, afraid to breathe thinking the shield had failed. She turned around to go back in the terminal, but couldn't find the button to reopen the door that had closed behind her.

"It's okay Marsee, just breathe. I promise you won't drown," Ellie said after seeing the look on her face. "Trust me." Ellie took several very large breaths to prove it, even so much as opening her mouth wide open when doing so.

She was running out of air and took a small breath. When no water entered her nose and she didn't choke, she took a bigger one. The water smelled of salt and other scents she couldn't identify. *How odd that I can smell through these masks,* she thought.

"Better?" Ellie asked, and she nodded back.

"Can you swim?" the delegate asked, politely not commenting on her near panic at thinking she was going to drown.

"Some. Little Flower taught me, but we only have a small pool. I've never swum very far before, or underwater like this at all," she replied.

The delegate nodded and handed her a drone. "This will allow you to keep up with us. Hold on here. To go forward, rotate this control here. To stop, release."

Marsee gave it a gentle try and was pulled forward. She released and came to a stop. A second drone was passed over to Ellie, and they took off at Marsee's pace, letting her get comfortable with the device, and take all the time she wanted to look around. The shops and restaurants all had water entrances and seating inside for the Sprites, as well as dry areas for the off-world residents. They didn't go in any of them, but there were many she wanted to check out later.

Eventually they came to the other side of the platform and exited the building to explore the city.

"This is Council Square," the head of the contingent signed. It was a large beautiful park where families were swimming and children playing. "Directly across is the Council Building," he pointed out. "Hence the rather uninventive reason for the name. On the north side of the park, you'll find the Trauma Center, and to the south, what I imagine, you'll be far more interested in, if you're anything like your uncle, the public archives."

Marsee grinned and her tail spiraled with enthusiasm, but before she could say anything, Ellie spoke up.

"You probably should have kept that information to yourself. Now that she knows where the archives are, I'll never get any work out of her," Ellie muttered.

Marsee frowned. "I'm not that bad."

"Uh huh. Tell me again how many books you read on the journey here?" Ellie teased.

"Only three," Marsee replied. "You had me working almost the entire trip."

"Only..." Ellie said, causing the others to chuckle.

Marsee glared at Ellie's teasing, but this just seemed to amuse the others even more. "And just how many books did you read while I was busy doing all of *your* research, hmm?"

Ellie pursed her lips and scratched at her ears, but didn't answer.

"As I thought," Marsee muttered, and everyone else burst out laughing, their skin rippling with humor.

Her guide led them across the park, past the council building, and down what appeared to be a main thoroughfare with additional shops and restaurants. He pointed out the Guild Hall, and several museums and attractions she might be interested in visiting if she had the time, and eventually they arrived at what looked like a large open air or rather, open water market. Dozens, if not hundreds of vendors were set up scattered randomly throughout another large park, with even more restaurants and shops around the outside.

"Welcome to Market Square," her guide said.

Marsee stopped and spoke with many of the vendors, admiring their work. It would take hours to explore them all. Her guides pointed out several of their favorite booths, and explained the purpose of many of the strange objects she found if something caught her eye, and made suggestions of foods she should try. Apparently she could easily eat with the mask on as well.

*I really need to bring a set of these back to the compound. Little Flower and the others would love them,* Marsee thought. *Maybe it would get her out of the tower.*

At every booth though, the vendors seemed far more overwhelmed than she was, that she was talking with them and examining the wares in their booth. She heard "Translator, it's an honor to meet you. Welcome to our world," from everyone. Only a few even acknowledged the Guild Master's presence, and then only the crafters who apparently knew her personally. Her guides were completely ignored, which frustrated her to no end, since she was hoping to figure out who they were through these interactions.

From what she could discern from their body language, at least one member of her tour guides was just as frustrated, or possibly bored. She wasn't sure which, as they kept their feelings firmly under control, and never slipped with their color when they spoke to allow her to confirm her suspicions. She wasn't as comfortable discerning their body language as she was her own or Little Flower's people, simply from lack of exposure.

She was examining a set of beautifully made baskets carved out of a translucent rainbow colored stone, on the far side of the market, when she felt a slight tug on the fur at her side. Looking down, she saw a tiny Water Sprite looking up at her. By her size, she couldn't have been more than a few years old. In the distance, she could see what was probably her mother frantically swimming over to fetch her, and then stop, unsure if she should approach.

Marsee floated down so she was face to face with the child. "Hello there, little one! My name is Marsee, what's yours?"

"I'm Coral," the child signed. "Are you really the Translator? My brother says you're not, and that the Translator wouldn't bother with visiting a simple market like this."

Marsee saw the yellow and red that indicated the other's surprise and anger at the child's statement, which surprised her. The question made her smile, and she was confused by their reaction. She was used to the direct nature of small children, having spent so much time with the rescued cubs of Little Flower's species, and she'd seen nothing that would have given her offense. Since everyone else seemed to think she was this Translator, she decided to go along with it, and ask questions of her mentor later, when they were in private.

"It's very nice to meet you Coral. You can tell your brother that I am, and that I think your market is one of the most amazing places I've ever had the honor of exploring. Like this vendor here, everything I've examined has been the work of master craftsmanship, and frankly pure works of art. Even your food is exceptional," she signed back.

The tiny Sprite flashed a beautiful blue in happiness, and she saw a flash of white and blue flash in her peripheral vision from the vendor, which indicated her shock and happiness at her compliment.

"I knew it! I just knew it was you!" Coral signed, and then swam up and gave Marsee a hug.

Surprised, Marsee carefully hugged the child back.

"Thank you, Translator, for giving us a way to speak to the others!" Coral signed afterwards, and then darted off before Marsee could answer.

Marsee just watched her swim up to her mother and brother, the colors of her skin flashing in their natural language, as she told them all about what she'd learned. She could only see part of the conversation but she did see 'She is the Translator' and 'You're an idiot, Rock Face.'

This last bit made Marsee struggle to keep from laughing, but she smiled after the group, and her soggy tail curled with amusement.

Her mother signed "thank you" to her, and when Marsee signed "you're very welcome" back, she turned and dragged her children off, scolding Coral for swimming off like that.

Marsee turned and glanced at Ellie who tilted her head and raised an eyebrow at her, but didn't comment.

*What's that look all about?* Marsee wondered.

"Come, let me show you the Arboretum now, and then I'll take you up to your rooms so you can rest from your long journey," her guide said, once she'd turned her attention back to him again.

She nodded to her guide, but then turned back to the vendor. "Your baskets *are* very beautiful," she signed and swam off before the shocked Sprite could answer. They were led back to the platform, but instead of returning to the exit they'd been through before, he led them through a massive arched entrance at the bottom of the building, and into the Arboretum.

"Oh wow!" she signed. "If my mother saw this place, she'd never want to leave!"

*This garden makes our oasis back home look like a root bound potted plant that had been left in the sun too long,* she thought.

Her guide wandered the garden showing her the different plants, and the variety of creatures that made their home there. They spent nearly an hour exploring, and had only seen a tiny fraction of it. Her guide explained that it ran the entire width of the three massive buildings that made up the landing platform and housing for off-world guests, and took up the first three floors entirely. Eventually though, they made it to one of the shafts that ran the length of the building, and followed their guide up to the very top before stopping at a locked door.

"Translator, if you would, please place your paws on the scanner. The room has been keyed to your entrance."

She did as requested, and the door opened, revealing a large open room filled with several couches, chairs, and tables that surrounded one of the biggest monitors she'd ever seen, mounted on the far wall, above what looked like an actual gas fireplace.

They entered into the small water foyer, hung up their drones on the hooks provided, and then swam through the static shield and into the room, their fur instantly dry and sticking straight out again as they walked through the shield.

Marsee stumbled as the weight of gravity returning hit her, but thankfully managed not to embarrass herself by falling flat on her face. Ellie showed her how to release the masks and they hung those up next to the door before turning to face the delegation that waited for them in the foyer.

"Thank you so much for the wonderful tour! I enjoyed every second of it!" Marsee signed.

Blues and greens flashed with their happiness. "It was our pleasure! Please make yourself at home and feel free to explore at your leisure. Until tomorrow?" her guide asked.

"Until tomorrow. Thank you," Marsee signed, and their guides turned and left, the door swishing closed behind them.

Marsee's shoulders slumped from weariness and stress the moment the door was shut, and she dragged herself over to the chair nearest the fire. Flopping down in it with an exhausted sigh, she closed her eyes and enjoyed the warmth of the fire. The water had felt warm at first, but she'd been starting to feel chilled towards the end of the tour. She was surprised to see a fireplace in an underwater dwelling, but she was very thankful for the unexpected source of heat.

"Well done, *Translator*," Ellie teased, as she began exploring the suite they'd been given.

"Moons! Not you too!" Marsee cried out after her.

"Well I'm certainly not the one that snagged us the penthouse suite. If I'm not mistaken, this is the one typically reserved for your uncle. I wonder where they've moved him. He's apparently been bumped down a notch or two and apparently so have I, or maybe I've been bumped up due to association. I suppose it's possible they're being moved to the new building, but either way, works for me," Ellie called back from one of the other rooms.

"What?!" Marsee squeaked.

Ellie returned from the room she was in, leaned up against the door frame, and just looked at her. "I'm usually housed several floors down, more if the Full Council is in session, and my suite is usually half the size of this. The fireplace is a nice touch though. If I'd known that was an option I'd have requested a room with one decades ago." At Marsee's look of astonishment, Ellie squinted at her. "You didn't recognize who was giving you the tour, did you?"

"No, I didn't, but you said it was impolite to ask if they didn't tell me first. Weren't they guild masters?"

"Not even close," Ellie laughed, and then pushed off to go check out another room.

"So who was it then?" Marsee yelled after her, getting very annoyed that Ellie was having so much fun at her expense.

From some distant room, Ellie called back, "That was none other than Senior Councilor Clear Seas, and the others were the highest ranking councilors, Spotted Trout, Snapping Turtle, Rip Current, and Crystal Cove. If I'm not mistaken, I'm pretty sure they were all at the Hallowed Eve festival as well."

"What?!" Marsee squeaked again, absolutely horrified that she hadn't recognized a member of the Senior Council. Not just any member but the senior councilor that she'd stood beside for several days straight, the same councilor she'd shared meals with in her home, and who had congratulated her on her promotion, when he'd visited New Hope. "Three moons! I can't believe I didn't recognize him."

"It's okay. It took me a long time to be able to tell them apart too. The easiest way is to look at their ear fins and scale patterns around their face. They all have different shapes, colors, and patterns there, and unlike the rest of their body, they don't change color when they speak,"

Ellie reappeared and entered another room. "Oh Marsee, you need to see this!" Ellie called out a few moments later.

Marsee stood and followed her mentor's voice, through a massive bedroom suite that made her room back home look small and dingy, and out onto a balcony overlooking the ocean that was lapping right below them. A gentle breeze ruffled her fur as she stepped out. The sun was just setting and the sky lit up with a sunset that rivaled anything she'd ever seen before.

"Oh wow! I didn't realize we were above the water!"

There were two seats on the balcony so they sat and watched in silence for a long time.

"Like I said, penthouse suite," Ellie murmured, as she watched the show before her. Off in the distance some creature leapt out of the water before crashing back down.

"What was that?" Marsee asked.

"Not a clue," Ellie replied.

Finally as the sunset dimmed and the first few stars started to peek out, Marsee turned to her mentor. "Okay. Explain it to me like I'm the idiot that I clearly am. What's with all the 'Translator' stuff? I haven't done that in a while. Why are they all treating me like I'm royalty?"

"Because you are," Ellie replied.

"What?!" Marsee squeaked yet again.

Ellie swiveled her chair to face her and looked at her with complete seriousness. "Marsee for three days straight, you were the public voice of Little Flower and her people. Everyone watched as you interpreted not just her words, but her intent and her feelings, but more importantly, especially for the people of *this* world, you gave them a voice too."

"But Sina is the one who came up with the language?" Marsee said. "The Senior Councilor even named it after her."

"She may have, but you're the one that took what she created and turned it into something that everyone could use with ease, not just our species. Not to mention the thousands of signs that you added to the language to prepare for the trial, and continue to add on practically a daily basis. You did all of the hard work of translating those signs into the other languages, not to mention your efforts in recording the various Charters into sign. You saved the people of this world a lot of effort there. And, you're the one that showed them that it was possible to be able to communicate with the rest of us on equal terms, and without decades of hard work and intense training to speak more than the basics of our spoken languages. I still don't know how you managed to learn as much as you did in only a month. It wasn't just Sign, I know you were just starting to learn Water Sprite when Little Flower came to live with you, yet by the time of the trial, you were easily translating for those councilors that couldn't speak our language, even before their personal translators spoke. I've never seen anyone learn their language that fast, even with a personal tutor like you had, ever. For most of my tenure as Senior Guild Master, I've barely been able to communicate with the masters and guild masters here. I'm not even close to fluent in their visual language, and I've never once been able to speak to one of their children like you did today. Their bodies aren't capable of making all of our sounds until they're fully grown, and even then it would be like learning to speak without a tongue. It's clear to me from their interactions tonight and from the fact that the Senior Councilor addressed you first, *and* the fact that he personally guided the tour, that you are about as close to royalty as exists. Certainly, they all knew who you were, even the children. You've completely changed their world Marsee, more so than anyone probably has since they joined the Consortium. As for your title, that wasn't just for the trial. You are an official translator for the Council now, and will retain that title forever. That being said, based on the way everyone was using it today, I wouldn't be surprised if you outrank Clear Seas in the eyes of the people at this point. "

Marsee sat completely dumbfounded at her words.

"Honestly it was kind of nice to not be recognized for once," Ellie mused.

"You might have liked it, but I don't think some of the other councilors were happy," Marsee replied.

Ellie frowned. "What makes you say that?"

"I'm not really sure how to explain it. I was hoping the vendors would give away who our guides were, but they completely ignored everyone but me. And after the fourth or fifth 'Translator, what an honor' from the vendors, several of the councilor's body language changed. I wasn't sure if they were upset or just bored with how much time I was taking to look at everything, but they didn't say anything or let anything slip with their colors, so I just figured I was reading them wrong."

"I didn't notice that at all, well, except for when you spoke to Coral. I've never seen them that angry before, certainly not Clear Seas. He's very careful about what emotions he lets slip in public. You know, you probably saved that poor mother and her small fry their very lives by not getting offended at her children's words, and by responding with such kindness."

"What!? What did she say that was so offensive? It was just an inno-cent question. They were just cubs! Would they really have hurt them?" Marsee asked.

"First off, she interrupted what was clearly an official tour. If you noticed, no one else approached us the entire time, although everyone was watching. And she didn't wait for you to finish what you were doing before speaking to you, which is considered very bad manners here, and then, she, or rather her brother, insulted both you, the coun-cilors, and every one of those vendors there, and no, their age wouldn't have mattered."

"I don't understand. She just asked who I was. What made that so insulting?" Marsee asked, completely befuddled.

Ellie sighed and scratched the back of her head. "I'll try to explain, but there's a lot of nuance here. First off, she called the market simple, which insulted the councilors by insinuating that they'd brought you to see something that wasn't of value. That also insulted the vendors, who are all very talented in their chosen fields. Then by stating the belief that you wouldn't visit something so simple or common, she insinuated that you thought you were so much better than everyone else. If this were one of the Hue-man stories, she'd have said something like 'My brother said you couldn't possibly be the Queen if you're here eating pig slop with the peasants.' The customs and culture of this world are very different from ours, and while they agree to the Charter, there are a lot of things that have been allowed to slide over the centuries, simply because we've had so little contact, and those that we do interact with are careful to abide by our culture when we do. But instead of being marched off to be disciplined, she'll have a story to tell of your kindness and benevolence, and how she was there when you promoted an entire market of crafters to master."

"I did what?!" Marsee yelped. "How could I have possibly done that? I'm just a journeyman."

"I told you, in their eyes, you outrank me. It doesn't matter that I'm your mentor or the Senior Guild Master. If I can promote anyone at my whim, so can you. You know, the whole 'Poof you're a master' bit. By now, I'm sure word of your comments have made it back to Agate, and the certificates are already being written. If I know her, she'll be highly amused, and tease me about it the first moment she has a chance."

"But I didn't say 'poof you're a master'. *How* did I promote them?" Marsee asked, thoroughly confused.

Ellie sighed, trying to figure out how to explain. "You need to remember that this society is still very rooted in its feudal history. They've only been part of the Consortium for what, five hundred years or so? They're nearly as long lived as we are, and it takes more than a generation or two for culture to change. I publicly claimed that I was hoping you'd succeed me as Senior Guild Master when I die or retire. In this society, I made you my heir. Yes, I was technically voted into that position, and a vote will be held as the Guild Charter requires, but I would be shocked if any Water Sprite voted anyone else in but you, unless you publicly turned down the position. That's just how things work here. Junior councilors are the named heirs of the other councilors. While they have to hold a vote, per the Charter, it's incredibly rare for someone else to be elected. As far as I know, it's only happened once. It's that way even in the case of a senior councilor. Clear Seas hasn't named his heir yet. Everyone expected Temperate to be named, but then he joined the Sea Patrol. His daughter is a healer, and Stormy is too young. If Clear Seas dies, it'll be the first real vote for senior councilor since they joined, and likely would be chosen from one of the other's you saw today. So when the Translator and future Senior Guild Master says something is master quality, who is any other master or guild master to argue? In their eyes, the only reason you aren't a master yet is for the same reason I haven't promoted you, and that's just your age and lack of life experience, but for the Water Sprites, that's just a formality. If I were to die today, they would still vote for you, just like a large portion of the population would vote for one of Clear Seas children, even if they weren't actively running for the position."

Marsee slumped back in her chair and put her paws over her face. "Really? Moons! I'm sorry. I had no idea."

"Don't be. You were right. Every one of those vendors were exceptional, and I would have put my recommendation in when we met with Agate anyway. Now though, they have the honor of being the first people promoted by the Translator and future Senior Guild Master."

Marsee lowered her paws enough to look at Ellie to judge her seriousness.

"On the plus side, it looks like I get to sit back and relax for the next several weeks, while you have to do all the work, *Translator*." Ellie grinned wickedly as she stretched, and then stood and walked back inside without another word, her tail spiraling in humor behind her.

"Don't you dare walk away from me after a statement like that!" Marsee growled after her.

Ellie immediately returned, but didn't say anything, just raised an eyebrow at her, clearly trying to keep a straight face, although her tail was now curled so tightly, it must have hurt.

"What under the three moons did you mean by that?" Marsee asked. "Are you pulling my tail again?"

"Not in the least. As I've told you at least half a dozen times now, you outrank me, *Translator*, so they're going to expect you to lead, just as you did today. Now may I please go use the waste room, or do you need something else from me that can't wait a few minutes, *Translator*?" Ellie asked.

Marsee just groaned and slid further down in her chair.

"Thank you for your benevolence, *Translator*. I'll take that to mean I'm free to go," Ellie replied with barely controlled humor and disappeared into the other room again.

"Enough with the translator bit already!" Marsee called out after her mentor. "Keep it up and I'll demote you!"

Ellie roared with laughter from the other room. "As you wish, *Translator!*" came her reply.

"That's it! Poof! You're an apprentice now!" Marsee yelled back.

Ellie whooped from the other room. "Yes! Finally!"

Marsee slid deeper into her chair. "What a mess," she groaned, burying her face in her paws.

After several minutes, she heaved herself out of the chair to use the facilities herself, and figure out where her hearing aids went, so she could put some calming music on. She had a feeling it was going to be a very, very long night.

She wasn't wrong.

# CHAPTER 4

# Petra: Broken Wings

etra groaned as she took off her headset and carefully stretched her wings, trying hard not to bump into the equipment, or her two co-pilots. Ellie's ship was nice, but it wasn't built for adult female Flyers, and she was growing fast. *Too fast,* she thought with a frown.

"It's not going to be much longer," Leaf said, echoing her thoughts. "When are you heading back to Flyer?"

Petra sighed. "Sooner than I'd like, I think. You're almost starting to look attractive," she teased.

"Ha, ha," Leaf replied, and playfully snapped at her wing. She pulled it back and whacked him upside his head instead.

"I work with weyrlings," Willow muttered under his breath.

"Says the person who stayed up late playing with toy ships," Petra teased.

"They're models, not toys," Willow replied with a glare.

Petra grinned at her friend. Willow spent a lot of his free time working on his model ships, and they were detailed enough that he could have been in the Guild if he'd wanted to, but he rarely sold them.

"Seriously though, this might be my last trip," she said. "I was hoping I'd get another year or two but I doubt it. My wingspan has increased by several feet in the last month alone. In another month I might not fit through the door. Be glad you don't have to go through this. My wings ache and my scales itch something fierce."

The male flyers were smaller in general, as they didn't have to grow to support the massive clutch of eggs the females of her species would produce after each mating flight, and her wings didn't fold back as much as the males did, an adaptation used to protect her clutch while sleeping, if she were personally hatching them, like they used to do before they developed the incubators. She could fly longer and higher than them too, but it had its disadvantages, and getting through door-ways was one of them.

"Well, then we'd better make the most of this vacation," Leaf replied. "Before you're too big to fit through the Jeweled Caverns, and too pampered to want to leave your weyr."

Petra snorted. "I'd rather be flying, and you know it. I've had enough pampering to last me a lifetime. It may seem all glamorous, but you didn't have to go before the Council to get permission to leave the planet. I won't be able to leave home again for decades. Not until I've hit my minimum quota anyway."

"Have you found out where you're going to nest yet?" Willow asked as he finished shutting down his systems and took off his headset.

"Mother wants me to stay in Council Weyr with her," Petra said, rolling her eyes. "But Sea Cove has been putting a lot of pressure on the Council to have me move there. Their nest mother only had a dozen eggs with her last clutch. She's probably only got another clutch or two left in her."

"Sea Cove? That place is beautiful and you can float on those warm up-drafts for hours without the slightest effort. That would be my vote," Willow replied.

"Mine too," Petra said. "I put in my preference weeks ago, but that's up to the Council. Council Weyr doesn't need another nest mother. The only reason they're even considering it is *because* of Mother. She doesn't like the idea of me being on the other side of the planet."

"Well, I think you should tell your mother to go jump off a cliff. It's your life to live and just because your mother is Senior now, doesn't mean she will be with the next vote," Leaf said.

Petra snorted. "Her and the rest of the Council. They all follow her lead anyway. No one even put their name in for consideration to run against her for the past two votes. My mother will be senior for as long as she wants to, just because no one else wants it. It's too much work. As for where I end up, I should know soon. Mother said it was planned for discussion in today's meeting. Yippie."

Petra flicked her wings in frustration. *Why should the Council have any say in what I do for a living or where I live, just because of my sex? It's just not right.* Everyone thought being a Nest Mother was glamorous and a life of luxury, but it wasn't the life she wanted, and the closer it got, the angrier she got about it.

A light flashed on her monitor indicating the ship's door opened and closed. "Well come on. It looks like Ellie and Marsee have left, and I need to get off this ship and spread my wings."

She maneuvered her awkward and growing body around, and made her way out, tucking her wings in as close as she could to squeeze through the doors, barely fitting. After a quick use of the facilities, and ensuring everything was in order, they made their way out of the ship, and into the terminal.

The one good thing about being Ellie's pilot was that they rarely had to clean up after her. Today was no different. It was usually only when they had guests that there was more work, but Marsee's room was spotless as she'd expected. Even the bedding had been switched out already. They didn't even have to bother with restocking the kitchen, since Ellie usually put in a special order before they departed, and rarely left in a hurry. Plus they still had more than enough of the standard supplies if they did have to leave in a hurry.

They arrived in the terminal just in time to see Marsee and Ellie walking away with the contingent that had arrived to meet them.

Petra stretched her wings with another groan and flapped them a few times to get the kinks out. *Oh that's so much better.* There wasn't enough room to fly in here but it felt good to open them fully and stretch anyway.

"That's unusual," Leaf muttered quietly.

"What is?" Petra asked.

"Look who came to meet Ellie and Marsee," Leaf stated. "Those are all the highest ranking members of the Council, if I'm not mistaken. I thought this was a Guild trip."

"That's not surprising at all," Petra replied. "It's probably because of Marsee. She is related to two of the other Senior Councilors, and it is her first trip off-world. I'm sure if they realized I was Ellie's pilot, they'd have done the same to me on my first trip here."

"Perhaps, but Saber doesn't elect based on family, like they do here," Leaf countered. "I'd expect Clear Seas, or Guild Master Agate perhaps, but not the others."

"No, but she will be Senior Guild Master some day, and she'll have as much power as them. I expect they want to get her on their good side now, for when they have to negotiate in the future," Petra replied.

"I don't know about that," Willow said. "A lot of people are unhappy about Ellie's little stunt. It gives Marsee's family too much power."

Petra fluttered her wings in a shrug. She'd seen a few of the comments online, but they'd mostly been directed at Ellie, not Marsee. "That won't matter in a few decades, once they get to know her. It's unlikely her father will get another term as Senior. He won't be able to run again according to their charter, although he could get a write-in vote. It all depends on how many of the Hue-mans want a council position by then. They still don't have a full council, and Marcus has said he plans to step down at the end of his term as well. At a minimum, he won't run for the South District, and his replacement in the South Plains district is doing a good job so far. I don't think Marcus will run against her. Marsee's a good kid too."

"For now," Willow muttered.

Petra looked over at him with confusion. "What do you mean?"

"It's one thing to earn that kind of rank, but another to grow up expecting it. Look how much she's changed since we first met her. That shy little cub is long gone. What's she going to be like by the time Ellie gets done with her. She could be just as bad as you some day," Willow replied with a roll of his eyes.

Petra snorted at his usual teasing. Unlike most of the females of her species, she honestly had no real desire for the power that came from being a nest mother, or the work involved in being a councilor, like her mother wanted. She loved being a pilot, especially Ellie's pilot, and wasn't looking forward to giving up that life, as much as the others teased her about it.

They never believed her though. It was unusual enough for a female to leave home. The risk to their species was just too high. The females of her species were pampered and protected their entire lives because of how few there were. It had taken a council edict to allow her to travel off world, and the only reason they'd finally agreed was because Ellie agreed to take her on as her pilot.

Her mother had made the argument that being around Ellie would be a good experience for her as a future councilor, as it gave her exposure to the various guilds and councilors on all five planets, and the rest of the council had bought it, thankfully. It was true, to an extent, although not nearly as much as the Council thought. Ellie did bring her along on special occasions, and she did get to meet many of Ellie's guests, but most of the time when not on active duty, she curled up on a sunny rooftop to read or floated in the currents to strengthen her growing wings.

She needed to be close enough to return to the ship quickly if Ellie called, but Ellie understood her need to stretch her wings, and almost always gave ample warning before heading out somewhere, especially off planet. Those trips, like this one, were often scheduled days, if not weeks in advance. Ellie was a competent pilot, and often took the ship out on her own too. Being Ellie's pilot was honestly one of the easiest positions in the Ship's Guild simply because of Ellie's consideration. She'd heard more than a few horror stories from other pilots, and knew she was very lucky to have this position, even if it was only for a few years.

Once the contingent had left the building, they made their way to the lifts and took them down to shuttle rental. She and Leaf waited while Willow signed the ship out, as he still had the hours needed to legally fly to the Crystal Caverns, but Petra quietly groaned when she saw the shuttle they'd been given. It was an ancient Water Sprite model, and far too tiny.

"Sorry Petra. They were out of the bigger shuttles," Willow said.

"It's alright. I'll manage. You're the ones that are going to suffer when I whack you accidentally with my wings," she teased, and started to squeeze her way inside. "They never make the personal shuttles big enough here, but then most of their rentals are from Sprites that are far more flexible than I am." She ended up having to wiggle in diagonally to get her wings through the door. Once inside it wasn't too bad though.

Willow made his way forward to the pilot's 'seat' and fumbled his way into the net. "Stupid fish net," he muttered. They didn't use seats either, but it took time to configure the harnesses to properly fit their bodies, and even then the Sprite's design still wasn't ideal.

Petra chuckled. "They are a miserable design, I'll give you that, but better that, than ending up fish food. Did you see the size of whatever that thing was that tried to eat the ship on the way in?"

"I think that's what they call a Leviathan," Leaf said with a snort.

"Well I doubt they call it tiny," Petra snarked back, and settled into her own fish net. "I hope this thing has shields too. It's old enough I'm betting it was built before the Sprites joined the Consortium."

"The attendant said they all do," Willow said, and examined the controls. "Ugh, it's all in Sprite, and there's no built-in translation program. That shouldn't be allowed."

"You want me to fly?" Petra said. "I still have a few hours left." She was more than capable of reading Water Sprite, but it was the hardest to learn, next to Hue-man, and one they didn't often get a lot of practice with.

"No, I've got it," Willow muttered, and then snorted as he dug through translations on his tablet. "There's not even an auto-pilot on this thing. Guess I'm doing this the old fashioned way. But it does look like there are shields."

Willow hit a button and the view outside the window shimmered as the shields activated. It took him twice as long as normal to complete the pre-flight check and confirm all the controls, but after a bit of additional muttering, they were off.

Once they were in flight, Petra pulled out her tablet and opened the book she was reading, one recommended by Marsee on the trip, and soon lost herself in the story.

Some time later, Willow pulled off in a small canyon and parked the shuttle.

"Where are we?" Petra asked, looking around as she hadn't expected to be stopping so soon.

"The middle of nowhere. I need to pee," Willow said.

"Where?" Petra teased. "We're in the middle of nowhere. I doubt there's a waste room around here."

"Where do you think?" Willow muttered, rolling his eyes. "It's not like the fish swim up to the nearest public waste room to go."

"I might as well too," Leaf said and followed after. "Are you coming Petra?"

"And swim in your pee? No thank you," Petra said with a disgusted shudder. "I'd need to see a healer afterwards."

Leaf rolled his eyes and exited the shuttle.

She went back to her book with a chuckle. When the shuttle door opened, she didn't even bother to look up, so she was completely surprised when pain suddenly wracked her body, and she was knocked unconscious with a wordless cry.

~~~~~

Petra woke slowly to find herself locked in a cage with her hands and feet bound tightly and something wrapped around her neck.

"Ah look who finally decided to wake up?" a voice crooned.

She looked over and recognized the Sprite floating in front of her with Willow and Leaf floating behind him, and blinked in confusion. "You?"
~~~~~

"Ah so you remember me? I'm honored," he said.

"Why are you doing this? I've never done anything to you?" she asked.

"True, but I can't have you messing up my plans, and you'll make a convenient distraction," he said absently as he tapped away on a tablet.

"A distraction for what?" she asked.

"Oh nothing much. I just intend to blame you once I've killed the Senior Guild Master and her little kitten. Thank you so much for your tablet. By the way, you really should find better friends. These two are kind of sketchy. Seems they don't like you very much, and the Guild Master even less. I wonder why?"

Petra looked at the other two, who just fluttered their wings in a shrug.

"Why?" she asked. She'd thought they were her friends. They'd worked together for years.

"I'm not about to let another Chenzira gain power," Willow said. "They have enough as it is. As for you, well, you get to spend your life mating and living in the lap of luxury, while the rest of us have to work. Even your stint as a pilot is just for fun. Besides, an awful lot of us are tired of nest mothers having all the power, just because they lay the eggs. They don't bother raising any of the weyrlings half the time, or doing the hard work, and get all the benefits for it."

She looked over at Leaf and he just shrugged. "I was Ellie's pilot and ship master for decades before you showed up, and not once has she taken me to an event like she does with you. Then you show up and suddenly you're the ship master, and we have to stick around while you get to play. You're a good pilot, but you haven't put in the time or effort in, like the rest of us, and you never once questioned that you didn't deserve that rank. You're only a ship master because of your mother, and because you'll be a nest mother someday."

Petra looked at the two that she'd once thought were friends in shock, unable to even find the words to respond to their betrayal.

"Like I said, pretty sketchy. Fortunately for you, I don't like sketchy people either," her captor said, and then before either of them could move, he shot two of his tentacles back and shocked both of them, killing them instantly. Not even fazed by his actions, he reached back and grabbed their tablets, after unlocking them using the thumbs of her dead co-pilots, and fiddled with all three tablets for a while.

As he did, her tablet dinged with a message from her mother.

"Ah look at this, dear old Mummy says hi, and wants to know how your vacation is going. She'll be glad to know you're having a fantastic time." Another ding came in. "Oh how wonderful. It looks like you got your wish, future Nest Mother of the Sea Cove. Let's see, how excited should you be about this?" He scrolled through her messages for a bit. "Ohh, Mummy wanted you to stay with her, how sweet." He began typing. "Sorry Mummy, I know just how much you wanted me to stay in Council Weyr, but I promise to come visit often. There, that should do it." He set the tablet aside and looked up at her again. "Now, if you want to see your dear old Mummy again, I'm going to need you to do one little thing for me."

"What's that?" she growled.

"Oh nothing much, just record your confession, once I've killed the Senior Guild Master and her kitten," he said. "Oh, and tell everyone how your dear old Mummy made you help, so you could get your preferred assignment."

"What?!" she asked, horrified, and started struggling to try and get out of her restraints. "Never. Leave them alone."

"Never is a very long time, but I'll give you some time to think about it while I deal with your sketchy friends. Enjoy your stay," he said, and swam off.

The moment he left the cave they were in, she tried biting the chains and when that failed, tried yanking them out of the wall where they were secured.

"Save your energy," a tired voice called out from behind her, and she flipped around, to see a cage full of other people. All of which were chained to the wall like she was. "You can't break the chains. We've all tried. Do what he wants. Trust me. If you don't, you'll regret it. Do what he wants and he'll kill you quicker."

"Who are you?" she asked.

"It doesn't matter," he said. "I'll be dead soon anyway. When he shocks you, scream. It's what he wants. He'll keep at it until you do."

Several hours passed before he returned and unlocked the cage. "Have you changed your mind?" he asked.

She said nothing.

"Ah perfect! You want to play that game. It's one of my favorites," he crooned with a wicked grin, and swam over, shocking her, just like she expected.

She did everything she could to keep from screaming, knowing that was exactly what he wanted. She wasn't going to give him the pleasure of that, no matter how much it hurt.

"How about now? Ready to change your mind? I can do this all night, ask them. They'll tell you."

She just glared up at him. He shocked her again and again, but while her muscles seized with pain, she refused to give him the satisfaction of her screams.

"Huh," he said after a bit. "I've never had the pleasure of a Flyer in my workshop, I suppose those lovely purple scales must provide you with some protection. I wonder how hard it would be to take them off." He reached over and yanked one off before she could stop him.

She tried hitting him with her wings, but the water slowed them down, and he easily moved out of the way.

"Now, now, behave," he said. "We can't have you doing that."

Before she realized what he was going to do, he reached up and snapped her wing as easily as if it were a twig. The pain of it was so much worse than the shocks had been, and she screamed. She couldn't stop herself.

"Ah, that's better," he replied. "Now, are you going to confess to your crimes or shall I break the other wing?"

She swore at him. "I hope you're swallowed by a Leviathan."

"I won't be, but your friends will, before too long," he said, and snapped her other wing. "Oh I'm sorry, I didn't realize just how fragile your wings are. I hope for your sake they can be repaired."

He floated there waiting until she stopped screaming and asked her again. "No? Still no confession? Well then I guess we'll have to do this the hard way." He pulled a knife off of his harness, grabbed one of her broken wings, twisting it hard to make her writhe in pain. and then proceeded to tear her wings to shreds, slowly.

When the water was thick with her blood and her wings in a tattered and broken mess he asked her again.

"You might as well just kill me," she growled at him.

"Oh, I already have. I wonder though. How long will you survive with these injuries," he whispered, "or before something swims in here and starts to nibble on you." He left with a chuckle. The light of his skin disappeared as he swam off, leaving them in darkness.

It wasn't long before she felt the first of the fish begin to nibble at her and she screamed in fear. None of the others said anything, but the one who had spoken to her before, lit his skin up dimly so she could see.

"Don't be afraid of the fish," he said weakly. "The bigger predators can't get in here, and the smaller ones aren't strong enough to break through your shield."

She calmed and watched. While it hurt when they bumped against her shield, he was right, they weren't actually eating her.

His light started to flicker. "I'm sorry, I'm not strong enough to keep the light on for much longer." Moments later the light of his skin flickered and went out.

# CHAPTER 5

# Nightmares

She found herself floating in the sea again, although unlike before, this one was full of light and color and exotic plants, and swarming with strange creatures. Ahead of her in the distance was her sister admiring a large bush of vibrantly colored flowers.

From where she stood, she could see a dark swirling mass approaching from behind her sister. She tried to call out in warning but her sister didn't hear her. She frantically tried to swim to her, but the sea was thick like molasses, and she couldn't make any progress. Her arms and legs were weak and useless.

Screaming, she watched in horror as the darkness swallowed her sister whole, and then turned its vile face in her direction, and started stalking her.

Little Flower bolted awake, sitting straight up with a scream, panting in fear as she tried to figure out where she was.

Her mother, half dozing in a chair, bolted awake and ran to her side, looking frantically at the monitors and back at her.

"What's wrong, Little Flower?" she signed.

There was just enough time for her to realize that she'd been having a nightmare, that she was in one of the recovery rooms, and that her head was throbbing in pain, before the room spun and she collapsed back down on the bed with a groan. The room kept spinning, and she grabbed the sheets to try and stop the room, but it didn't help.

"I'm going to be sick," she signed and started to roll over. Thankfully there wasn't much in her stomach, but it didn't stop her body from trying.

Her mother helped her roll over and shoved a bag under her mouth. When she was done, her mother tossed the bag, washed off her face, and then popped one of those nausea tablets in her mouth. The horrid taste nearly made her throw up again, but it eventually calmed her stomach. It did nothing to stop the room from spinning.

"Head hurts. Room is spinning." Hoping her mother was looking at her, she signed the words carefully, trying to move as little as possible without opening her eyes, open it was even worse. She lay there, pantingand a few minutes later, she felt something pressed against her arm and darkness pulled her back under.

---

She was pulled right back into her nightmare, the swirling darkness looming ahead of her. She turned to run but there wasn't anywhere for her to run. She was stuck on a ledge with nothing but a dark, stormy sea in front of her.

She looked behind her but now there was nothing but a wall of swirling darkness. It was nearly on her. She leaped into the sea and tried to swim away, but the water was so cold it numbed her limbs almost instantly. She was so cold she started shaking. She couldn't keep her head above the water, and the darkness pulled her down until there was nothing but a pin prick of light above her.

---

She woke gasping for oxygen as her body shook. She was awake but she still couldn't breathe and she was so *very* cold. She couldn't remember ever being this cold before. Her head throbbed as the room spun around her. Her mother placed something over her nose and mouth, and then something was pressed into her arm again. The last thing she saw was her mother's worried expression.

This time, she found herself in the wilderness, bound so she couldn't move. She looked around and saw her grandfather next to her in the same situation. On her other side was Hope, sitting in the dirt, oblivious to the rattlesnake that slithered behind her.

She screamed, frantically trying to escape her bindings, when someone walked over and grabbed her grandfather, dragging him over to a tree that hadn't been there moments before, a rope carried in his other arm. She couldn't see who he was though. In the place of his face was the face of the swirling darkness, but she recognized the hate symbols tattooed on his arms.

Her grandfather struggled to get away, but he was bound just as tightly as she was, and she couldn't do anything but watch as both her grandfather and child were killed in front of her.

She screamed, and screamed, and screamed.

She woke screaming again to see her mother's concerned face, and it took her a long time to realize it had just been a nightmare.

"Shhh, You're okay," her mother signed. Her mother looked exhausted, like she hadn't slept for days. "You're safe. It was just a nightmare."

Little Flower calmed her breathing as her terror subsided. Her mother asked how she was feeling and she considered it for a moment before replying. Her head still ached but not as bad as before, and the room was only spinning a little, but she was freezing. "Better, but really cold," she signed.

Her mother nodded and left briefly, returning with a blanket and covered her in it. The blanket had been heated and was gloriously warm. She sighed and snuggled in.

"Better?" her mother asked,.

She carefully nodded. The room only spun slightly faster which was manageable as it was no worse than what she'd dealt with for weeks after waking from her coma. "How long was I out?" she asked, sticking her hands out briefly to sign, before covering them up again.

"Four days. You had complications from the surgery, but I think you're through the worst of it now," her mother signed.

"Did it work?" she asked.

"It's too soon to tell, but you do seem to be signing much easier. How does your head feel?"

The comment surprised her, and she realized her mother was right. It was much easier to get her fingers to do what she wanted them to. She'd forgotten for a moment that she'd had difficulty signing before. "My head still hurts, but not like before, and the room is only spinning a little," she answered, and then buried herself back under the blanket.

"Good. I need to run you through the same set of tests we did when you first woke up from your coma," her mother said.

She nodded her understanding, not really wanting to move out from under the warmth. Moments after her mother was done and she'd snuggled back down in the blanket, Healer Ammond walked in.

"Ah, you're finally awake!" he signed. "How are you feeling?"

Sighing, she pulled her hands out from under the now cooling blanket. "Better than before," she stated.

Her mother said something to him which he nodded to.

"So I see!" Ammond said with a smile. "You're signing much better. Now, I was able to repair your eardrum and the fused bone in your inner ear. The vertigo you've been experiencing was likely caused by the injection of nano's in your inner ear. We've had some success with the others, so I'm hoping it will work with you, but it'll take time. Your ear is still very swollen and we have a patch over it so you won't be able to hear much of anything out of that for at least another day or two, so don't worry if you're hearing less than you did before. As for the nano's we injected into your brain, we are seeing some improvements, but you had a seizure caused by swelling. We were able to treat that, and I'm not seeing any additional signs of damage, but I'd like to keep you here for at least another day for observation. I don't want you to even attempt walking until the dizziness passes, as a fall could be very dangerous for you right now, and if you feel anything off, if you feel sick to your stomach, or the pain in your head increases, let us know immediately."

"Okay," she signed. "Mama, can I have another warm blanket? I'm still really cold."

Her mother nodded and left to fetch another blanket, but Ammond frowned and placed his palm on her head and then uncovered her foot and touched that as well.

"Can you feel my touch?" he asked.

"Yes," she replied.

"Good, wiggle your toes."

"Mama just did all of that," she signed.

"Humor me," he replied, so she did, and he went through all of the same tests her mother had just finished performing, plus several others. Her mother returned with the warm blanket and tucked it in around her once Ammond was done with his examination. He said something to her mother again, and left.

"Are you hungry?" her mother asked.

She shook her head no. She was too dizzy to even think about food. "Just cold."

Her mother carefully picked her up and carried her over to the chair next to the bed and sat down, wrapping her snuggly in the blankets and her warm furry arms.

She leaned her head against her mother's soft warm body and sighed as her mother started purring. She was asleep again in minutes. When she woke several hours later, she found herself back in her bed, with several blankets tucked in around her, and her mother asleep in the chair.

"Mama," she called out, hoping that she might at least hear her, but her mother didn't wake. Instead GrandFather came around to that side of the bed.

"Hey there. Nice to see you awake finally. How are you feeling?" he asked.

"Hungry," she signed. This earned a huge grin from him.

"I'll see what I can find. Let your mother sleep though. She's barely slept since your surgery."

She nodded and he left, returning a few minutes later with a bowl of fruit and a glass of juice. He helped her to sit up and eat, propping a pillow behind her. When she was done eating, he set the empty dishes aside and glared at her.

"What?" she asked.

"Next time you decide to go in for brain surgery, do you think maybe you could let me know first? When I showed up to visit, everyone was gone. I found Hope in Jer's office, and he didn't even know what was going on. Your *mother* apparently just showed up, asked him to watch her for the morning, and disappeared. When she didn't answer our calls, we both showed up here to find out you were in the middle of surgery."

"Oh, sorry. I didn't exactly expect it to happen so quickly either. One minute I was in Ammond's examination room, and the next Mama picked me up and sedated me."

He growled at her, but then pulled something out of his pocket. "I should just eat both of these," he signed, holding up the package.

"Please tell me that's a chocolate chip cookie," she replied.

"Nope, even better. Brownies," he replied, and carefully unwrapped the package revealing two glorious, slightly squished brownies. He took one and bit into it, showing his evident delight.

"Hey! Share!" she said back with a mock growl, holding her hand out.

He smiled and handed over hers after pretending to think about it for a second. She yanked it out of his hands with a glare and took a huge bite and groaned in absolute delight. GrandFather finished his quickly, but she took her time, savoring each bite. She was about halfway through when she stopped, and frowned.

"What's wrong?" he signed.

"It tastes funny. Bitter," she replied.

"Mine tasted alright. Maybe something didn't get mixed up thoroughly," he signed back.

"Could be," she replied, and frowned her way through the bite and took another tentative taste. The next bite tasted normal so she shrugged. *He's probably right*, she thought.

When she was done, she sighed and lay back in contentment. Jordan had outdone herself. "Can you hand me my drink?" she asked her grandfather a few moments later. He reached over and grabbed it off the table and handed it to her. She reached up to take it but her arm started shaking.

He quickly set the glass down and signed. "Are you feeling okay?"

She couldn't answer as pain exploded throughout her entire body, and her body seized on her, as everything started to shake.

~~~~~

James bolted for Myra's side and shook her hard. "Myra, wake up!" he yelled. She opened her eyes just as the alarms started to blare. Myra shot out of her seat, and frantically started examining the monitors trying to figure out what was going on.

"What happened?" she asked him as Healer's Brice and Ammond came running into the room.

"I just gave her something to eat. She was doing well, said she felt pretty good, and was making jokes and talking better than ever, then her arm started shaking and a moment later this."

"What did she eat?" Ammond signed.

"A bowl of mixed fruit, half a glass of star fruit juice, and a brownie."

"What's a brownie?" Brice asked.

"A Hue-man desert, like a cookie. Someone left Jer a basket of them this morning. I'm assuming it was Jordan," he signed.

"Another seizure?" Ammond asked, as Myra tried to figure out what was wrong, flipping through brain scan after brain scan not finding anything, and then flipping back out to the more generalized body scan.

"No, something else must be going on. This looks more like she's having an allergic reaction. Her airways are starting to close up."

At this Brice bolted out of the room.

"GrandFather, do you know if Little Flower has any food allergies?" Myra asked him.

"Not that I..." He stopped as his hand started shaking too. Myra's eyes went wide and he started to sign something else, but before he could, pain wracked his body, and he collapsed.
~~~~~

~~~~~

Myra caught him before he could hit the floor, and placed him on the bed next to Little Flower. As she was doing so, Brice came running back into the room.

"GrandFather too?" Brice asked, as she applied the hypo to Little Flower's neck, dialed in another dose, and applied it to GrandFather.

"It must be something they ate," Ammond replied.

Myra started running a tox scan trying to figure out what was triggering a response this severe.

"Myra, somebody, help! There's something wrong with Hope!" Jer yelled from the hallway. Myra looked up in fear at Ammond for a brief second, before bolting out the door to find Jer standing in the hallway looking lost as Hope shook violently in his arms. As soon as he saw her he started running towards her.

"What did she eat?" she asked him as she grabbed Hope from his arms.

"The usual, although she had a piece of my brownie," Jer said, running right behind her.

"It's the brownie," she told the others as she bolted in the room. "Jer, are there more, and how much did you both eat?"

Brice handed her the hypo and she applied it. On the monitor she could see that Little Flower's stats were showing her airway was clearing up some, but she was still shaking violently.

"The hypo should have stopped an allergic reaction by now. Why are they still shaking?" she asked Ammond.

"I don't know," Ammond replied. "I'm not seeing anything that would account for it."

"Yes, there's a whole basket of them. Someone left them at my office this morning. I had most of one, except for the small piece Hope had, maybe this big," Jer said at the same time, indicating the size, and watched in horror as the others continued shaking.

"Where are they?" she demanded.

"In my office," he replied.
~~~~~

"Brice, go find them. I want to know everything that's in them. Jer, sit down. If you start to shake or feel sick, speak up," Myra ordered.

Brice bolted out the door, and Myra waited impatiently for the tox screen to come in. She watched as the results started to display, and then the monitors started flagging several identified chemicals in Little Flower's blood stream. She and Ammond both gasped with matching looks of ears back horror, neither one of them trying to hide their fear behind their masks. She bolted out of the room towards the locked supply room, slamming her palm against the lock, and started scanning the shelves looking for what she needed, but the box was empty. Growling in fear she bolted out of the Trauma Center and onto one of the waiting Trauma Ships.

Tabor was there. "What's wrong?"

"I need Sand Spinner anti-venom immediately," she ordered. The healers on the ship bolted to their feet and dug through their supplies, handing her the box. She turned and bolted back to Little Flower's room, grabbed the hypo, swapped the canisters, injected it into all four of them, and waited.

A few minutes later Little Flower, GrandFather and Hope stopped shaking, and Little Flower's vitals started to return to normal, and then finally the alarms stopped blaring.

Myra breathed a sigh of relief. As she did, her tablet dinged with an incoming call from Brice. She pulled it off her harness and answered.

"The brownies have all been laced with sand spinner venom," Brice said.

Myra nodded, holding up the hypo. "Tox screen showed that as well. They're responding to treatment."

"Sand Spinner venom?!" Jer asked in horror. "Are you saying what I think you're saying?"

"I am Jer. Someone tried to kill you."

# CHAPTER 6

# Marsee: Protest

It was well past midnight before Ellie called it quits and ordered them both to bed, after spending the majority of the evening giving Marsee a crash course in what to expect at the Council meeting the next day, and while she was still horrified and overwhelmed by her new status, she at least felt slightly prepared to handle what the day would bring.

The next morning, Ellie woke her up, far too early for her liking. The days were nearly half the length of her own world, and it felt like she'd just gone to bed. They shared a breakfast out on the balcony as the sun rose behind them. It was a calm day and the sound of the water lapping against the side of the building was peaceful, and probably would have lulled her back to sleep if she hadn't been so nervous about the upcoming meeting.

They'd found a fully stocked refrigeration unit with a wide variety of foods. Marsee chose several foods she was familiar with, deciding her stomach was far too unsettled to try something new. The last thing she wanted to do was throw up in the middle of the meeting.

As they were eating, her tablet dinged with a message from the Senior Councilor, indicating he would be arriving in half an hour to escort them to the meeting. She relayed the information to Ellie, who frowned.

"What? Are you still upset that you've been demoted, and he contacted me instead of you?" Marsee teased.

"No, I'm surprised at the escort. I've never needed one before," Ellie said, still frowning.

"Is this just a courtesy?" Marsee asked.

"No, I don't think so. If you were by yourself, then maybe, but Clear Seas knows I know how to get to the council building, and he showed you where it was last night as well. It's not like it's all that far away. Something else is going on, and I don't like it." Ellie went back inside and retrieved her own tablet. When she returned to the balcony she was scrolling through local news articles, frowning.

"Find anything?" Marsee asked as Ellie sat down again.

"Unfortunately, yes. It looks like there was a protest yesterday before we arrived, and the Sea Patrol had to be called in to control the crowd, as they wouldn't let the councilors leave. It doesn't look like anyone was hurt though," Ellie replied as she finished reading the article, and handed it over to her to read.

"The Sea Patrol?" Marsee asked, taking the proffered tablet.

"Those were the ships chasing after the Leviathan yesterday. They patrol the currents and swim lanes to keep people safe from predators," Ellie explained.

"That's not what I meant. Why would they be called in and not the Honor Guard?" Marsee asked.

"I don't know. Numbers maybe? The article doesn't say how many protesters there were. I also wouldn't have expected protestors to act that way either. That's dangerously close to sedition."

Marsee nodded as she finished reading the article and handed the tablet back. "We had a long discussion about protesting, and what was allowed by the Charter with Little Flower and GrandFather. Apparently violent protests happened all the time on Earth. It wasn't uncommon for people to die on either side. From what I could understand most of those protests occurred when those in power overstepped their authority, or when people were trying to gain the rights being denied to them. GrandFather said he's been to many protests where violence occurred in his life, as did his father, and he's both been injured and arrested for doing nothing more than showing up at a protest. He's working on a history book and I've translated a few chapters. I'll send you what I've completed so far. It's horrifying what his people went through, and I can understand why they reacted with violence. They had no other method to stop what was happening to them."

"GrandFather was arrested? I can't believe it. They couldn't vote those people out?" Ellie asked.

"He was, but thankfully not convicted of any crime, and no. For a long time people with dark skin like GrandFather didn't have the right to vote, and could even be owned by others. They were traded like wares at Market Square. Even when they finally earned their freedom and the right to vote, their system was rigged to keep them out of power. One of the latest challenges they were facing was against their version of the Honor Guard. Their justice system was heavily biased, and people with different colored skin would often have vastly different punishments for the same crime. It's one of the reasons why they insisted on a fixed limit to the number of terms a councilor could have for their people, and why they've refused to set up their own Honor Guard. They don't even trust themselves to act without bias, even though they're trying hard not to introduce them into their own laws."

Ellie's ears flicked back in surprise, but pondered for a moment before answering. "I had no idea those issues were so recent. Little Flower said they happened over a hundred years ago."

"No, that was one of their great wars you're thinking of, and it was a hundred of their years, so only thirty or so of ours. GrandFather's grandfather was born a slave." When Ellie indicated she wasn't familiar with the sign she'd used, Marsee explained. "It means he was owned by someone else. He had no rights. Was not even considered Hue-man or sentient, and there were no laws against what could be done to a slave. They could be traded, forced to mate to make more slaves, and have their children traded away. It's what my sister feared we were doing with her. They could be beaten for not working hard enough. They weren't educated outside of doing whatever work was required of them, and if they even remotely tried to fight back or escape they would be beaten or killed. Even the amendment to their charter that outlawed slavery didn't do away with it completely, and would allow it if convicted of a crime. It's one of the reasons why their justice system was so unbalanced."

"Are you saying GrandFather would have become a slave if convicted for protesting to protect his own rights?" Ellie asked.

"I am, and owned by their government. Several of his friends were, and spent years locked up and forced to work for basic necessities until they were released. It was one of the reasons he moved to the district where we rescued him. It was safer for him there, and not just because of the color of his skin. GrandFather prefers to partner with men, which was seen as unnatural, and even illegal in many of their districts, for much of his life."

"Dark moons. How does he even trust us after we held them in quarantine for so long?"

"I honestly don't know. He was sedated for the first several months though, as they figured out how to replace his damaged heart. He was a healer on his own world and they'd just been through a pandemic where millions of people died too. Perhaps he recognized the risks of two species interacting with each other for the first time, where Little Flower didn't." She checked the time and frowned. "Clear Seas should be here any moment and we should probably get ready."

Marsee picked up their breakfast dishes and brought them into the kitchen to wash. By the time she'd finished, Ellie had followed her in, carrying both their tablets.

"I'm going to send these over to the Council Chamber. Do you want to send your hearing aids too?"

"No. They can stay here. I should be fine. It's so much quieter here. The electronics don't buzz like they do back home, or at least nothing in this suite does. If I start to feel overwhelmed, I'll ask for a break," she replied, after considering it. "Besides, it can't be any worse than the trial."

Ellie nodded at her approvingly. "If you do need them, we can also send a runner up to get them, but I expect you'll be having a harder time trying to stay awake than getting overstimulated. Resource allocations meetings are rarely fun or exciting. Although there have been fights a time or two."

"Actual fights?" Marsee asked.

"Once, that I witnessed anyway. The councilor who hit first was kicked out of the Council immediately, but it was rather entertaining, and to be honest, if he hadn't hit the other councilor, I would have. Fortunately, that particular councilor was voted out a few months later. He was a real pain in my tail."

Before Marsee could ask more, the door chimed with Clear Seas arrival, so they made their way out to the foyer and let him in. "Good Morning, Senior Councilor," Marsee said when he entered. Several members of the Sea Patrol remained outside as the door slid shut behind him.

"Good Morning to you as well, Translator, Senior Guild Master. I trust you slept well?" Clear Seas asked.

"We did. Thank you," Marsee lied. It had taken her a long time to fall asleep, but that had nothing to do with the accommodations. The bed was the softest she'd ever slept in, but she was anxious about the coming day, and she didn't have Little Flower to use as a pillow.

"Excellent! Are you ready to head down to the council meeting?" he asked, but before she could reply, Ellie interrupted.

Ellie nodded towards the sea patrol outside. "Between old friends, Clear Seas, how concerned should we be that we need an escort, both this morning and the one we had yesterday?"

Clear Seas visibility slumped. "I had hoped you hadn't noticed the guards yesterday, but I should have known better. I assume you saw the news reports?"

"We did," Ellie replied. "I know you've been having protests. That's half the reason we're here, but why the need for the guards?"

Clear Seas sighed. "They're getting worse. There has been violence at a number of protests over the past several months. Two weeks ago there was a fight and one of the junior councilors was injured. Her injuries were minor, and the person who hurt her was...dealt with. Everything had been relatively quiet until yesterday when word got out that you and the Translator were coming for a visit. Thankfully, no one was hurt yesterday, but based on what I saw on my way here, a crowd is already forming."

"Is that why locks have been added to the suite?" Ellie asked.

Clear Seas nodded. "We have honor guards positioned discreetly as well, for your protection."

Marsee frowned at this conversation. Ellie hadn't mentioned any of her other observations, and she would have words with her mentor about that later. She also wondered what Clear Seas meant by having the protester's dealt with. If the child's comment the night before would have caused severe punishment, she wondered what someone would get for harming a junior councilor. Surely he didn't mean they'd been executed. That seemed excessive, but then she remembered what her mother's punishment would have been. She didn't dare ask him, reserving that for her conversation with Ellie later as well, but she did have questions she felt comfortable asking.

"Senior Councilor, forgive my ignorance, but help me understand what has the protesters so upset they'd harm someone over it? The article we read only stated they were upset by the increase in visitors to the planet, and I know others are upset about the new construction, as that's part of the reason we're here, but I don't understand why they'd be willing to hurt someone over it."

Clear Seas didn't answer for nearly a minute, the colored lights of his skin completely blank. It was all she could do not to glance over at her mentor while she waited, but she was used to her father and uncle choosing their words carefully before they spoke.

Finally he responded. "People fear what they do not know. Most of my people have never even met someone outside of their own species. In the last year, our world has seen incredible change, and we are now more a part of the Consortium than we have ever been before. For most of us it's been a good thing, but for some, the change is both terrifying and unwanted. They fear their way of life will be lost, and that our world will be overrun by visitors and the demands of the Consortium.

Many are scared of the new creatures from Earth, even though our own species are far more dangerous." He paused and then looked at Ellie. "And while it has not been reported to the public, there have also been two deaths."

Marsee gulped and looked over at her mentor. Ellie leaned in and wrapped her tail around Marsee to comfort her.

"How much danger are we really in?" Ellie asked Clear Seas.

"I honestly don't know. I am afraid the darkness Little Flower spoke of has infected my people, and I don't know how to fight it," Clear Seas admitted, a little of his fear, seeping through his skin as it flashed a faint white. He locked his emotions firmly under control quickly though.

"That's what I was afraid of," Ellie said.

"Have you met with them to discuss their demands?" Marsee asked.

"We did initially, but once the protests turned violent, we stopped. I won't discuss demands with people who are willing to hurt others," Clear Seas stated.

"I'm assuming you...dealt with those individuals," Marsee stated, using his words back at him.

"The ones we could catch, yes," he qualified.

"So as far as you know, those remaining did *not* act out in violence. Shouldn't they have their voices heard?"

Clear Seas flashed a brief color of surprise at her words, before bringing his emotions under control again. She didn't wait for him to respond.

"My sister and I have had many conversations about the darkness that infected her world. She fears its return, and it continues to infect her nightmares to this day. I've been woken by her screaming in terror from her dreams on many occasions. One thing I've learned is that ignoring people, and denying them their say or place at the table just spreads the darkness. It breeds resentment and anger, and responding with violence never seems to accomplish anything. If there's time before the meeting, I would like to meet with these protesters, and hear what they have to say. If they're upset about the Habitat, then it's my responsibility on behalf of my sister and her people to get involved. Either way, it's what my sister would do."

Clear Seas flashed his astonishment for several seconds before bringing himself back under control. "Please forgive my emotional outbursts. I should not be so surprised. It's clear that Little Flower's courage has rubbed off on you, or perhaps it was the other way around. I don't recommend it, but I will not stop you. Frankly, what we've tried has not worked, and as you state, has only made things worse. Come then, let me call in the Honor Guard, and we will go speak with the protesters."

"No," Marsee heard herself say, absolutely flabbergasted at her own audacity to tell a Senior Councilor what to do. "If we approach showing that we expect violence, violence is all we'll get in return. I'll approach alone. That way, if anyone gets hurt, it'll just be me, and it'll be entirely my own fault. If there are members of the Guard around, keep them hidden until the situation escalates and I call for assistance."

Clear Seas seemed just as surprised, although he kept his emotions off his skin. He blinked at her, then glanced at Ellie, who said nothing, just raised an eyebrow. He turned back to her again and tilted his head in approval. "As you wish, Translator." With that he turned and swam out the door.

Marsee looked over at Ellie, who just handed her a mask without saying a word, and followed out after the Councilor. Marsee put her mask on, stepped through the static shield, grabbed her drone and followed behind, praying to the Ancient Gods that she was doing the right thing.

A few minutes later, they stopped. In the distance a crowd of at least several hundred flashed their anger in rhythmic oranges and reds towards the stream of councilors making their way inside. Several Honor Guards floated motionless by the entrance, the only sign of guards, that she could see. She couldn't make out what the protesters were saying though, as they were facing away from her.

"Are you sure about this?" Ellie asked her quietly.

Marsee turned and looked at Ellie. "You're the one that told me I needed to step up and lead. If my tail wasn't soaking wet, it would be poofed straight out right now, but I'm sure. I have to try something." Then, before she could second guess herself, sped off in the direction of the crowd. She noticed the moment they saw her coming and realized who she was.

Curiosity rippled through their skin, and several people signed or said, 'It's her!" or "It's the Translator!"

She pulled up in front of the crowd and hovered about ten feet from them. They all looked at her expectantly, but she saw no sign of hostility from them, only curiosity, and perhaps a hint of hope. Taking a deep breath, she began signing.

"Good morning! As many of you have already figured out, my name is Marsee Chenzira." One of the Water Sprites flashed the words of their people, repeating what she said for those who didn't know sign.

"It's my understanding that you're here protesting the changes that have occurred following the rescue of my sister and her people. I sincerely wish to thank you and your people on behalf of my sister and hers for the care you've given to the creatures of her world. I know that this has been a monumental undertaking, and that change can be hard, and have many unforeseen consequences. So, for any harm that I or my sister may have caused you, whether directly or indirectly, I am truly sorry."

Waves of astonishment pass through the crowd. They obviously hadn't expected her apology.

"I would like to better understand those challenges and the pain you've experienced, and see if there's a way I can help you, as you've helped my sister. Is there someone among you who would be willing to join me for a swim in the Arboretum, and help me to understand the changes you desire. I promise to take your concerns to the Council, and try to find a solution we can all agree to."

Several of the Sprites turned to look at a male in the center of the crowd. He swam forward. "Translator, my name is Deep Current. The Council has not listened to us in the past. What makes you think they would listen now?"

"Because I have the ear of both Senior Councilor Clear Seas and my mentor, Senior Guild Master Khihar," she said, pointing back in their direction. "Between the four of us, I'm sure we can come to a solution. Please, let me be your translator as I was for my sister and her people."

Another wave of astonishment, as well as several conversations flashed through the crowd, most far too fast for her to read.

Deep Current thought for a moment, and then turned to his people and spoke something to them that she couldn't see. Surprisingly they all swam away. He turned back to her. "I've asked everyone to disperse as a show of good faith. Whatever happens, I thank you for listening, and trying, when so many have turned their backs to us."

Marsee nodded, and then tilted her head in the direction of the gardens. "Shall we?"

He nodded and swam off.

She glanced briefly in the direction of her mentor, who signed her a quick 'good luck', before she sped off after Deep Current. She followed him to an unoccupied area of the garden and stopped when he did.

"You picked a beautiful location to talk," she said, when he turned to face her. "I've been completely overwhelmed with the beauty of your world, and I've barely seen any of it."

He looked at her with a wry smile. "With your first words, you come to the very heart of the issues we've been trying to bring before the Council."

"How so?" she asked, curious.

"We wish to keep our world beautiful, but the most recent changes have brought both death and destruction in our districts, and we only wish for it to stop."

Marsee frowned with confusion. "That's not what I was expecting to hear at all. Perhaps you should start from the beginning, and explain as if I've been told nothing. I don't want there to be any misunderstandings between us."

Deep Current flashed both surprise and perhaps a hint of admiration at her words, but continued. "When word of the Cataclysm reached our world, we of course wanted to help, and many of the people you saw earlier, including myself, helped to build the specialized holding tanks needed to support the rescued creatures for their time in quarantine. Others hunt for the sea creatures of our world, which the scientists deemed both safe and necessary for the survival of your sister and her people."

It was Marsee's turn to be surprised. "Then I wish to thank you for saving my sister's life. She would have died without the food you've provided. They can't process the protein sources of my world, and she was nothing but skin and bones when she came to live with us. Even still, maintaining her weight proves to be a constant challenge."

He flashed his gratitude at her words, but then paused. "Were you aware that several of my people have died in that effort? The preferred fish she needs is only available in one area of our world, and that area is also the nesting ground of the Leviathan."

She gasped at this news, but before she could answer, he continued.

"I can see that you weren't. I don't know whether to be relieved to know you weren't ignoring our sacrifice at the Remembrance Day ceremony, or angered that you weren't informed, perhaps both. Among my people, there's no greater honor than to sacrifice your life trying to save someone else, and we willingly took that risk to save Little Flower's people, yet those who died were not honored by the Council, or even compensated, and we don't understand why."

Marsee was shocked to hear that the families weren't being compensated. That was a protected right when a parent or partner died. "You have every reason to be angry and upset. This is the first I've heard of it, and I honestly don't know why your people have been ignored. But I promise you this, I will personally ensure that their names are added to those brave souls who died during the rescue, and that they'll be remembered for eternity for the sacrifice they made to save my sister and her people, and I'll do everything I can to find out why they haven't been honored, or their families compensated for their loss."

He took a deep breath, and his skin radiated the dark colors of mourning, before he managed to control himself.

"I take it someone you cared about was one of those lost?" she asked kindly.

He nodded. "My mother."

"I am so very sorry for your loss," she signed. "She must have been an incredible person to be willing to risk her life for someone she'd never met."

"Thank you. There is more. My father, enraged, and grieving, fought with our district's Councilor, or so I've been told. He was taken by the Sea Patrol, and I haven't seen or heard from him since. All requests to find out where he is, or what happened to him have been ignored. We have several other people missing as well, and I fear for their safety. I don't condone the violence that has occurred, and try very hard to keep our protests peaceful, but so many are grieving and frustrated and just want answers, and we're being provoked and taunted at every turn."

Marsee nodded. "I don't know what happened to your father, or the others, but I intend to find out and, for better or worse, will let you know. Will you send me their names and when and where they were taken or last seen?"

He nodded, but then turned away to bring his emotions under control. When he turned back around, he continued. "Since we took sign as our official language with the Consortium, we've seen an exponential increase in the number of visitors to our planet, as well as people leaving to visit the other worlds."

"I'm aware of this," she signed. "That's partly why I'm here."

He nodded. "For a long time our ability or lack of ability to speak easily with the other species has meant we've been fairly isolated. Now though, new platforms are being built all over our world to support both the construction of more interplanetary ships, and house the influx of travelers, in addition to the Habitat that continues to be expanded upon to support the species of Earth. We recognize that there was little option except for those species to come here, as our ocean was the closest match for their world, and to remain in the quarantine tanks, that they were quickly outgrowing, would have been cruel. But these construction projects are being done in haste, and without regard to the surrounding environment, our culture, or the people who live there. We're not against these changes as some might think, because we know they'll ultimately be good for our people. We just want construction to slow down so we can have enough time to relocate the plants and creatures that already live in those areas, and to be adequately compensated when our homes and businesses are commandeered for these projects."

Marsee nodded. "Those are all reasonable requests, and frankly, ones you shouldn't have had to make in the first place. I'm curious why there's so little regard for the surrounding areas, or your people. Have you been given any indication at all as to why?"

"Outside of the Habitat, no. In that instance, it made sense that we needed to build something as quickly as possible. But I fear it was done too quickly. We proposed several sites as being better locations, but those requests were ignored, and we weren't given any indication as to why."

She nodded. "I was told this morning there've been several violent outbursts, and that two people have died by the hands of your protestors."

He nodded and let out a heavy sigh, his skin tinged with regret. "Sadly yes, at the new shipyard. The construction crew was drilling through the nesting grounds of a rare sea creature. The protesters were trying to stop the construction to save those creatures, but the off-world crews wouldn't stop, or so I've been informed. It's hard to find out what actually happened, as many of the people who were there are also missing. I've not been able to find out why the construction workers wouldn't stop. Our people could have relocated those creatures in a matter of hours, so it's not like the project would have been delayed for long, nor are we allowed anywhere near the platform now to try and investigate."

"Were they able to relocate the nests?" she asked.

"From what I understand, no, and those creatures are now endangered because of it," Deep Current replied.

Marsee was horrified to hear this, and confused as it went against everything they believed in. "Send me whatever information you have around that particular incident, as well as information on the endangered species. The shipyard is a Guild project, and neither Ellie or I were informed of the deaths until this morning, nor were we informed where they occurred, and that concerns me, and I know Ellie will be just as concerned. What of the incident that happened yesterday? What happened there? I was told that your people prevented the Council from leaving."

Deep Current flashed orange and red in outrage. "I've seen the news reports, and I swear we did not do what we were accused of. We were protesting just as we were this morning, when several councilors came out and motioned us forward. We thought they wanted to talk to us, but instead they started insulting us. The moment someone flashed their anger in response, the Sea Patrol came out of nowhere, and started attacking us without warning. Many of my people were injured trying to escape, and those wounded fear going for medical care."

Marsee's look of astonishment clearly surprised him as well.

"I see you didn't know this either," he replied with just the barest hint of frustration.

"No, I did not. Is there more?"

"Yes, but this is minor in comparison to everything else. Some have even called it petty. I hesitate to even mention it," he said, flashing his hesitation.

"Go on. Your other requests have all been valid. Even minor issues can grow into major ones over time. It's better to fix them early on if we can," she encouraged.

He nodded the point and continued. "We're excited that more people want to visit our world, and that we can be full members in the Consortium now. But those visiting are not respecting our ways, and are causing damage to our environment in the process." He pointed to a Flyer off in the distance, who had just picked a flower.

"Even here in this sanctuary, where so many of the plants and creatures are endangered, we have people disrespecting the hard work of the gardeners and caretakers, and picking flowers for their own benefit, and denying their beauty to others. Pilots from the other worlds dive into the seas and disturb the creatures and people who live there, flying where they want, with no regard to the marked paths and currents. Plants and creatures are being taken off-world for private collections, many of them protected or endangered. Even regular interactions with off-worlders are challenging, as our culture and customs are ignored. We've been asked to change so much, but it seems like others have no desire to learn or change as well, and are here just to take, and not share."

She nodded and considered before responding. "I understand how frustrating that must be for you. My mentor spent a good portion of our time on our trip here teaching me your customs. I honestly had no idea our cultures were so different. I'm sure I'll make many mistakes purely out of ignorance. Others wouldn't have the benefit of my mentors decades of experience with your people to learn from. Perhaps training programs would be beneficial? We've had to do the same with Little Flower's people as we've learned each other's culture and customs. For instance, the only time they go around without clothes on are when they bathe in private or mate. We had no idea, and that likely added to my sister's rapist's idea that they were being forced to mate. Perhaps I can help do the same with your people? We can have cultural lessons added to the school programs so that children know more about your world, and we can make those same programs available to anyone who visits."

He flashed his gratitude. "That would be wonderful. Thank you."

"Now as for the ships flying where they shouldn't be, do you know if this is by pilots from the Ship's Guild, or regular citizens visiting?"

"It's usually the smaller shuttles, at least as I've been informed. The pilots in the Ship's Guild are well trained and rarely cause problems. They tend to stick to the platforms anyway," he responded.

She nodded. "That could be a training issue as well. I've only just earned my shuttle license, and I was never taught anything about water currents during my training, or even asked about it during the test I had to take. Granted none of our shuttles are designed to fly underwater, and I live in the desert, so there isn't exactly a lot water for me to fly into."

His skin rippled in amusement at the comment.

"I imagine most off-worlders would have to borrow a shuttle from the Ship's Guild, so that could just be an oversight, and should be easy to fix. Is there anything else?"

"No. Those are our major complaints. Thank you for taking the time to listen."

She nodded, and looked away to take several moments to consider, and then carefully relaxed her control on her instinct, making sure her claws remained sheathed, and took a deep sniff.

***I smelled no deceit. He was telling the truth, as he knows it.***

Trusting her instinct she turned back around. "All of your concerns seem legitimate and worthy of discussion to me, or answers to your questions at the very least. Would you be willing to give me a tour of those places you're the most concerned about, so I can see the destruction with my own eyes?"

Surprised flashed on his skin at her response and he blinked for a second before responding. "Of course, gladly!"

"Good. Send me those locations as well as anything else you can think of, and I'll see how that fits with the Senior Guild Master's plans for our visit. I want to check out at least a few of those locations. Thank you for taking the time to talk with me, and helping me better understand your concerns. Will you meet with me here tomorrow at this same time? That should give me enough time to find out at least some of the answers you're looking for."

He nodded. "Of course. Thank you, Translator."

"You're very welcome, Deep Current. Until tomorrow?" she asked.

"Until tomorrow," he replied with a deep bow of respect.

She bowed back, grabbed her drone, and sped off to find answers.

# CHAPTER 7

# Jer: Venom

An hour after his arrival in the ward with Hope, Myra cleared him from observation. His larger size saved him from experiencing any major complications from the sand spinner venom. It was also clear that he ended up with a smaller dose than the others did. His stomach was upset, but he wasn't sure if that was from the venom or his fear.

The others were awake but still in a great deal of pain that their normal pain management treatments weren't touching. Myra had been pacing, trying to soothe an absolutely inconsolable Hope. The poor cub was crying so loudly that even he could hear it. GrandFather had been moved to another room so he could be monitored as well, but Myra told him she expected them all to recover. It would just take time for the anti-venom to work.

He left the Trauma Center and made his way to the kitchens. He was not looking forward to this conversation. He really liked Jordan, and she was one of the most popular Hue-mans, but she'd claimed the kitchens as her domain, and no one made or delivered anything without her knowledge. He'd assumed the delivery had been from her, as she'd done on numerous occasions over the past six months, as they'd struggled through Little Flower's illness. It had been in the standard delivery box, and he'd figured it had been sent to his office, knowing that Little Flower was recovering from her surgery, and that they were likely not at home. Honestly, he hadn't even questioned it, and had been pleasantly surprised by the gift.

It was approaching time for the noon meal, and the kitchens were packed with people preparing the meals needed to feed thousands of people of all six species. The moment he walked through the door he was assailed by a multitude of scents, and the noise made his ears flip back. He scanned the crowd trying to find Jordan, but she found him first, aware of everything that happened in her kitchen.

"Councilor Chenzira, what brings you here?" Jordan asked.

"I came to talk to you," Jer replied.

"Can it wait until after the noon rush?" she asked with a frown.

"Unfortunately not," he replied. "Have you made a batch of brownies recently?"

"Yes, last night, they're for lunch today. Why? Are you looking for some?"

"No. Have you given any out yet?" he asked.

"Not that I'm aware of, unless someone snuck one when I wasn't looking," she replied.

"Good. I need you to package them all up, and then we need to have a conversation in my office."

"All of them?" she asked, clearly surprised.

He nodded and she raised her eyebrows, but did as he ordered. He followed her through the kitchen to the rack where they'd been stored. On the way she tapped one of the Hue-mans on the shoulder to get her attention.

"Sarah, bring me two of the largest storage containers, please."

"Yes, Chef," came the reply. A minute later, Sarah arrived with two large tubs.

"Help me put all of the brownies in here," she told the young woman, and they quickly transferred the dozen trays of freshly baked brownies into the containers.

When they were done, Jer picked them up. "Sarah, run the empty trays through the cleaners twice before using them again," he ordered, and then motioned for Jordan to follow him.

"Jeffrey, I need to leave for a few. You're in charge," she signed, after tapping one of the males on the shoulder to get his attention.

"Yes, Chef," came the immediate reply.

They left the kitchens into the relative quiet of the halls, and made their way down towards his office. He stopped on the way and dropped off the containers at the Trauma Center, handing them to Brice to test.

"What's going on, Councilor?" Jordan asked.

"Not here," he replied and motioned her back out. When they were safely in his office, he motioned for her to have a seat, which she did. He sat in his own chair and flipped on his privacy shield. "Chef Jordan, did you deliver or send a delivery of brownies to my office?"

"No, Councilor. I did not. Why?"

"Someone left a large basket of brownies outside my office this morning before I arrived. They were all laced with sand spinner venom."

Jordan gasped. "I swear I would never do anything like that! Was anyone hurt?"

"Yes. Little Flower, GrandFather, and Hope all had severe reactions to the brownies I shared with them. They're still recovering, and in a great deal of pain." He watched for her reaction and noticed she appeared very angry at hearing who had been affected.

"No one harms a baby on my watch. Whatever you need from me, Councilor, it's yours."

He nodded. "Good. What I need right now is a statement detailing when you made the brownies, who was with you, and your whereabouts since then."

She nodded and he flipped open his tablet and began recording.

When she was done, he continued. "I'm assuming your work roster is up to date?"

"It is. I have two people out on maternity leave. They're due any day now, and Steven sliced his hand pretty good last night. Last I heard, he didn't leave the Trauma Center until this morning, and is taking the day off, but everyone else was at their regular shift both yesterday and today," she replied.

"Thank you. That's all I need for now. However if you see or hear anything, please let me know."

"Of course," she replied, and stood to leave. She made it halfway to the door before stopping and turning back around. "Councilor, I've watched the entirety of Little Flower's trial, and what she said was true about our people. I've gotten to know most of them over the past several months and well, if anyone has anything against your family from amongst ours, it would be Damon and the few people he hangs out with. They're the most vocal and upset about the lack of representation on the Council, and being stuck here because they aren't considered an adult yet. For most of my people though, we're far better off here than we ever were before, and there really isn't anything for us to complain about, not since we arrived in New Hope anyway. Your people have provided everything we need, and then some. More than we ever got from our own government in the past for sure. The biggest complaint I hear is people missing specific foods or the heat. Even traveling isn't that big of an issue since all of the other species seem to want to come here to visit with us, but I think you should be careful. I don't begin to understand all of the cultural implications, but the other councilors were livid about your promotion to Senior Councilor, and well, as it was left outside your office, it wouldn't surprise me in the least if you weren't the intended target."

He raised his brow at that and she turned and left. He sat there thinking for a while, and then started pulling up duty rosters, and calling people to confirm Jordan's story. Brice called to let him know that the other brownies were clear of venom, and he ordered them returned to the kitchens. He identified several others he wanted to question, with Damon at the top of the list, but decided that could wait. He needed to call Marcus.

Marcus answered right away and glared when he saw Jer's expression "What happened this time?" he asked, without even a hint of the normal teasing when Jer called with bad news.

"Someone tried to kill me this morning," he replied with a growl.

"Explain," he ordered.

Jer filled him in on the details of what he knew so far.

"Dark moons, Jer. Why does everything seem to happen to your family?" Marcus muttered when he was through. "Sand spinner venom? How does someone even get a hold of that without severe risk to themselves in the process?"

"I have no idea, Marcus, but right now I have two possible motives. One, someone is mad at me and my family because of the lack of representation among the males, and the other is a vendetta against me for gaining the senior council position for the Hue-mans."

"Seriously though? An assassination attempt?" Marcus shook his head in disbelief. "I can't even remember the last time that occurred."

"Why else would Sand Spinner venom be in the food? It's not like someone mixed up ingredients, and put something we're allergic to in it by accident."

Marcus nodded the point. "I'm inclined to believe it has more to do with the male's representation, seeing as we ran out of time before bringing their item up for discussion. It's one of the first items we have on the agenda for the next meeting and that's only a few weeks away. It still doesn't make sense. If they killed you, people would be even less inclined to vote in their favor. As for someone in the rest of the Full Council, I've heard nothing from anyone since the last meeting, and our ratings are even going back up. They're far more mad at Ellie these days."

"What other reason could there be? We've personally spoken to everyone directly and indirectly involved in the land transfer. Hold on, I just received an urgent message from Clear Seas," Jer said, as the notification flashed on his tablet.

"I got one too," Marcus replied.

Jer opened the message and started reading. He read it twice to make sure he wasn't misreading it.

"Dark moons..." Marcus whispered.

# CHAPTER 8

# Marsee: Conspiracy

The moment Marsee left the pavilion, two members of the Sea Patrol swam up beside her and escorted her to the entrance of the council building. As she approached, an honor guard swam up to meet her.

"Translator Chenzira?" he signed.

"Yes," she signed back.

"Please follow me. I'll take you to the entrance of your council box where the Senior Guild Master is waiting for you," the guard said. She followed him down several hallways before they paused in front of a doorway. "You'll need to touch your paw to the sensor for it to open. Only you and the Senior Guild Master may enter."

The door swished open at her touch, and she could see Ellie seated at a desk on the other side of the static shield, with the Council already in session beyond. She thanked the guard and hung up her drone next to the Guild Master's before entering. She managed not to stumble this time as gravity returned, and paused to hang up her mask before taking the seat beside her mentor.

Ellie looked over at her as she slid into her seat but didn't say anything, although she noticed that Clear Seas noticed her arrival as well. His skin didn't show any of his emotion, but she could see some of the tension leave his body as he realized she was safe. He gave her the slightest of nods before refocusing his attention on the Councilor speaking.

Ellie picked up her tablet and gave her a slight nod that she should pick up hers.

*How did it go?*

*Good I think. Lots of conflicting information that doesn't match what Clear Seas told us, or what was in the news report, but if what Deep Current said is true, then something fishy is going on.*

*Horrible pun. What did he say?*

*A lot. They're concerned about missing people and the destruction of the nesting grounds of an endangered species in the construction of the platforms and the Habitat. Also, visitors are causing problems, taking things, flying outside of established sea lanes, and disturbing people. They also want compensation and recognition for lives lost fishing for the Hue-mans and homes that have been taken to build the Habitat and platforms.*

*I see what you mean. Those are all legitimate concerns. It doesn't make sense that they're being ignored by the Council.*

> *There's more. Those two deaths Clear Seas mentioned were at the shipyard and Deep Current says that yesterday's altercation was a set-up. He says they were motioned in by several Councilors and insulted to get a response out of them, and as soon as they did the Sea Patrol attacked them.*

Ellie looked up and over at her when she read that, but didn't respond right away. Marsee watched as her mentor's expression went from astonishment to carefully controlled neutrality.

> **Talk to no one about this, even Clear Seas, until we have more information.**

As soon as she nodded, Ellie deleted their conversation, set her tablet down, and appeared to focus her attention back on the Councilor that was still talking, her expression changing to one of bored politeness.

Half an hour later Marsee's tablet buzzed letting her know she had a message. Checking, she saw it was from Deep Current with the information she'd requested. She read through and frowned. There were far more missing people than Deep Current had led her to believe. She sent off a quick reply thanking him for the information, and then taking the cue from her mentor, copied the information over to her personal documents, saved it with the title 'homework', and secured it behind a password before deleting the message.

She set her tablet down and tried to focus on the meeting. It wasn't long before her expression matched that of her mentor. *How does my father do this day in and day out?* she wondered. *If this is what Ellie expects me to do with the rest of my life, no thank you, Nardal is welcome to the position.*

Even her instinct was yawning by the end of the session.

*Knock it off, will you?* she told it. *It's hard enough staying awake as it is.*

**Sorry. Wake me when this is done,** it said, and it was all she could do to keep from yawning in response.

When Clear Seas called a recess, Ellie slapped the button that activated the privacy shield. "We've only got a few minutes before Clear Seas makes his way over here," Ellie said. "When he asks, tell him only that you've been given information that you wish to validate first before discussing."

"How am I going to validate this information? I'm not ranked high enough. Can I use your access?" Marsee asked.

"Technically yes, legally no. We need to do this by the book. Ask Clear Seas for access. If that doesn't work, talk to your father. He would have access, especially around anything to do with the Habitat, but don't tell him just yet. Let's make sure there's actually a problem first."

"What makes you think he doesn't already know?" Marsee asked.

"Because both he and Marcus would have warned me if they knew violence was involved," Ellie replied.

Marsee flicked an ear back in understanding. "I want to tour some of these sites that Deep Current mentioned, as well as the Habitat, if we can arrange it," Marsee told her mentor.

"And I fully intend to go to that shipyard, sooner than we had planned I think. The Master Builder and Guild Master in that district have some explaining to do," Ellie growled just as the door dinged. "That would be Clear Seas." Ellie left the privacy shield up but motioned for her to open the door.

She did and Clear Seas entered into the small water entryway, the door closing behind him. "Senior Councilor," Marsee nodded in greeting.

"Translator, I am relieved to see you unharmed. I take it your conversation went well?"

"It did," she said, without volunteering more.

Clear Seas seemed surprised by her lack of further information. "Would you elaborate on what was discussed?"

"Deep Current provided me with their main concerns, as well as several pieces of information that I would like to verify before bothering to discuss with you or the Council. I wouldn't want to waste your time if he wasn't telling the truth. Would it be possible to gain access to the official reports and any footage from the various incidents with the protesters, so I can see for myself what happened, not just what has been reported to the public?"

"Of course, Translator. I'll make sure you're sent the information within the hour. Is there anything else I can do?" he asked.

"Actually yes. On a more personal note, I was hoping to fit in a tour of the Habitat while we're here. I know you're aware of the health issues my sister has been facing these past few months. She's been really depressed about it lately, and I was hoping to cheer her up with some footage of the creatures from her home."

"It would be my honor to show you around the Habitat, Translator," Clear Seas replied.

She nodded her thanks.

"I was also hoping you and the Senior Guild Master would join my family and I for the evening meal tonight. My youngest son, Stormy, is a huge fan of your books, and has asked me about once an hour, since he learned of your expected arrival, if you were going to come to dinner."

Marsee managed to keep her confusion off of her face. "I wouldn't want to disappoint a fan," she told the Senior Councilor. "We would love to join you for dinner tonight."

"Excellent! I'll let my family know and be over after the afternoon session to show you the way. Until tonight?"

"Until tonight," she told him, and he turned, and swam out.

Marsee turned and glared at her mentor. "*You* have some explaining to do."

"Not here. Let's head back to the room. We can talk over lunch," Ellie replied.

Marsee continued to glare, but nodded. They sent their tablets back to their suite and followed after. When they made it back, Marsee wasted no time. "Talk," she ordered her mentor. "What have you done and why does the Councilor's son know about my books?"

"Well aside from the fact that you had copies of 'The Adventures of Crawly Man' made for the Hallowed Eve festival, in case you'd forgotten, I had the rest of your translations scanned and put online, not just available for print as you've been told. Every one of them is on the top downloads list, while several of your most recent are also on the top print list too," Ellie said, ducking into the kitchen, and opening the refrigeration unit.

"You did what?! And why haven't I seen them?" she asked, following Ellie into the other room. She *had* forgotten about the copies she'd had printed for the celebration, what with everything else that had happened that day.

"I had the techs hide them from you. I didn't want you to get overwhelmed when they became so popular. Your mother agreed," Ellie replied.

"Why would you do that?" Marsee flopping down in a chair, glaring at her Mentor.

Ellie turned to look at her, "Why what? Scan them in, or hide them from you?"

"Both."

Ellie pursed her lips and sighed. "Marsee, there's an enormous demand for anything having to do with the Hue-mans. Besides, we scan in all new books for download, and make sure there are printed copies in the Archives."

"My books are in the Archives?" Marsee asked, honestly more stunned about that than being on the top downloads list. She hadn't seen them when she'd visited, but then the Archives were vast. Even the public section was more than she'd ever be able to read through in hundreds of lifetimes. She didn't really see the books as hers, but as the other authors, but just knowing her name was in the Archives and would exist forever was honestly rather intimidating.

Ellie snorted at her reaction. "Yes. The Hue-man section is small, but it's entirely made up of your translations, and we can barely keep enough copies in stock."

"Why didn't I see it when we visited?" she asked.

Ellie laughed. "Because I distracted you with older books from the ancient archives, which if I remember correctly, you asked to see."

Marsee just grunted, acknowledging the truth.

"Your books alone have essentially funded resource allocation for New Hope for the past several months, since the vast majority of the credit goes to the original author. Plus you're preserving their history, which is invaluable. In a generation or two, most of that history would be lost if it weren't for the work you're doing. We knew how overwhelmed you get when there's a lot of attention paid to you, so we decided it was best to keep that knowledge from you, so you wouldn't panic and overthink the work you were doing."

Marsee rubbed at her face. "So the whole Translator bit isn't just about sign language and the trial?"

"Nope. You're the most popular translator on all five worlds, ever," Ellie said, handing her something to drink. "And in case you haven't noticed, the prints of your artwork are pretty popular too, especially here."

"Just how popular is 'popular'?" Marsee asked.

"Lets just say, we had to add three new servers to support the demand for 'The Adventures of Crawly Man as translated by Marsee Bet Chenzira'. We're actually considering splitting the top downloads list to give the other authors a chance against you," Ellie said, as she pulled a platter of sliced fruit out of the fridge. "I wouldn't be surprised if everyone has read it by now. As for your prints, they're the most requested, here anyway, outside of the ones your sister did of you. Those are pretty popular too although nowhere near as popular as they'd be if I could share those other drawings you've done."

Marsee groaned. "Can I go home and hide in my room now?"

"Nope! Welcome to fame, Translator. You'd better get used to it, because it's not going away any time soon." Ellie set the tray down on the table next to her, and pulled up another chair. "But we have more important things to talk about, namely what happened with your meeting this morning. Tell me everything."

Marsee glared at her mentor, but then spent the next half hour going over everything, and sent Ellie her 'homework'.

Ellie read through it and then replied with a message that read, "Mediocre effort, I expected better than that from you. I want a detailed document on the various stains used with rock wood, and the effects they have if spilled on fur by morning."

Marsee smirked at the response, and replied with a 'Yes, ma'am.'

A few minutes later, a message arrived from Clear Seas with her authorization and links to the archives where the information was stored. They moved over into the main sitting area and Marsee pulled the information up on the large monitor there, starting with the protest from the day before.

"It matches what Clear Seas said," Marsee said, frowning.

"It does and it doesn't," Ellie said. "Go back and watch the beginning again. It's been altered."

Marsee looked at her mentor in surprise and started the video again. She hadn't noticed any editing.

"There," Ellie said.

When Ellie pointed it out, it was obvious, cleverly done, but obvious. They watched the other footage as well, and now that they were looking for it, it was clear that the other footage had been edited too.

"So, what does this mean?" Marsee asked.

"It means that someone is hiding something, and until we find out why, everyone is suspect."

"Do you know who those councilors are?" Marsee asked, returning to a spot where there was a clear shot of them.

"Some of them. Spotted Trout and Crystal Cove," Ellie replied, pointing out two of them.

Once Ellie did, Marsee recognized them from the tour.

"The rest I don't. That doesn't mean they're involved, since we don't have the unedited footage. Do we know who the junior councilor was that was injured the other day?"

Marsee flicked through the reports until she found the information. "Her name is Tall Grass. She's the Junior Councilor for Rip Current from the East Sea district."

"Any relation to Deep Current?" Ellie asked. "The East Sea district is where the Habitat and shipyard are being built."

Marsee put in a search request against the public census, "Oh this is interesting…"

"What is?" Ellie asked.

"Rip is Deep Current's uncle on his father's side. Deep told me that his father was missing after getting into an argument with their councilor, which, based on where it says Deep's father lives, would be Rip. Even if he was distraught from his partner's death, I can't imagine his own brother would arrest him over that, so where is he?" Marsee pulled up a record of Rip Current's public council history and started scanning, seeing if something else had been going on around that time.

Ellie frowned at this information and took the tablet from Marsee before she could read through the first page and typed away at it. Marsee couldn't see what she was doing from this angle. A moment later she frowned.

"What is it?" Marsee asked.

"It says here that Clear Seas submitted the evidence from the protest yesterday *and* modified it a few hours later. I have no idea what was changed though. That's not displayed. I'm going to contact one of my techs and see if she can figure out what was changed, and if possible see if we have the original footage. I can't tell if he just uploaded what was sent to him, or if he edited the video itself."

"Shouldn't that be visible on the video meta data?" Marsee asked. That had been covered in one of her tech classes.

"It should, but it's missing, and *that* shouldn't be possible," Ellie replied, and showed her.

Marsee frowned, "It's not that hard to make those changes, if you have the right software and access."

"Technically yes, but any footage uploaded to the archives requires that information to be included, and the software wouldn't allow it to be edited once it's in the archives, which means someone modified it on the server," Ellie replied with a heavy sigh. "And only a handful of people would have access to do that."

By the time they needed to head back for the afternoon session, they'd only determined that the majority of the missing persons were from the same district, which happened to be Rip Current's district, but since the two violent protests had happened in his district, that made sense. Marsee hadn't been able to find any record of what had happened to the missing people.

"I don't like this at all," Ellie told her before they left. "There should be at least some record of the people taken into custody and 'dealt with' as Clear Seas indicated. There's a significant amount of paperwork needed when an execution is involved. At a minimum, it requires Clear Seas authorization or review if someone should happen to be killed by the guard."

"Do we have enough information to talk to Clear Seas?" Marsee asked.

"Not really. All we really have is evidence that the videos have been edited. Anything else is just conjuncture. There's nothing to indicate motive either, and I don't know if Clear Seas is involved, or if something fishy, as you put it, is going on with Rip Current. Nor do we know if the videos were altered before or after they were entered into the archives."

"Any suggestions on what I should say if he asks? I'm not sure how long I can avoid telling him what Deep Current wanted, and I don't have any information to give Deep Current on his missing people tomorrow."

Ellie thought for a while. "I think it's fair to say that what Deep Current told you doesn't match with the information you've reviewed so far, and ask about the people taken into custody, and why that information isn't available. Don't mention anything about the footage being altered though."

The afternoon session was far more interesting, as part of it covered the needs of the Habitat. Marsee made a point of thanking the Council for their efforts on behalf of her sister's people, which appeared to go over well with everyone, and she managed not to throw up from nerves, so that was a plus.

Ellie discretely pointed out Rip Current, and Marsee recognized him as the councilor that had seemed the most annoyed at being overlooked by the vendors. They paid extra attention when he spoke, but found nothing concerning about his words or the items he voted on, but she did catch him looking at them several times, and her crawly senses, as the Hue-man cubs called her instinct, were tingling.

After the meeting was over, they sent their tablets back to their suite and waited for Clear Seas to arrive, but left the privacy shield up. When he arrived and asked if they'd made any progress on their investigation, Marsee did as Ellie suggested, and asked about the missing information.

Clear Seas frowned. "I honestly don't know why that information would be missing, and I find that very concerning. Please give me a moment so I can put in a request to investigate before we leave."

She nodded and waited as he fired off a few messages.

It took about twenty minutes to make it to his home which was located in a small cluster of homes near the outskirts of the city. The majority of Clear Seas home had been carved into the side of an underground mountain, and as they approached the last dwelling, she could see a small Sprite peering out of a window.

When the Sprite saw them, he disappeared from view and a moment later came barreling out of the door as fast as his little tentacles could take him, wearing of all things a bright red cape. Marsee wondered what that was about since the Water Sprites didn't wear clothing, any more than any of the other species did, except for the Hue-mans, although she had noticed that jewelry like her sister wore at the Trial were being sported by many of the younger Sprites.

The little Sprite was flashing his excitement as he approached. "Translator! You came! I can't believe it!" He came to a stop in front of them, practically quivering with excitement.

"You must be Stormy," Marsee signed, and Stormy nodded emphatically. "I heard you were a big fan of mine."

"The biggest! I love the Adventures of Crawly Man! Could he really spit a web out of his wrist?" Stormy asked, making several of the poses in the drawings.

"So the Hue-man cubs assured me," Marsee replied. Her tail was curling in amusement at his obvious excitement.

"That's so weird!" Stormy said. "Will there be another episode? I have all three!"

"I don't know. Right now, I'm working on a translation of another of their gods. This one is called the Night Flyer," she told him.

"Does the Night Flyer fight the darkness too?" Stormy asked.

"He does, but do you want to know a secret?"

Stormy nodded wide eyed.

"He doesn't have *any* superpowers. He's just a regular Hue-man, but uses his brains and technology to bring the bad guys to justice, and uses his black costume to protect himself and sneak up on them and make the bad guys *think* he has superpowers."

"No way!" Stormy exclaimed. "Do you think I could grow up to be a superhero and fight the darkness someday too?"

"Absolutely, but you don't need to be a superhero to fight the darkness, you just need kindness, compassion, and a whole lot of bravery and courage."

"And a really cool costume!" Stormy added, spinning around to show off his cape.

"That does help," she admitted with a smile. "I haven't seen the capes before. Crawly Man doesn't have one, but some of the other Hue-man gods do, including the Night Flyer. This one looks really nice though," she told Stormy.

"Capes have special meaning for us," Clear Seas explained. "Outside of the occasional protective gear, it's the one form of clothing that we have. Historically it's been reserved as a symbol of great honor, and typically given posthumously, although the Leviathan Cloak hasn't been awarded in a few hundred years, now that we can drive them off. It is fitting that many of the Hue-man gods wear them to fight the darkness. Plus a costume in the form that Crawly Man wears would interfere with our gills."

"That makes sense," Marsee replied.

"The cloaks for the children are very popular," Ellie added. Marsee raised a brow at her mentor, wondering just what else she'd not been aware of.

"All right Stormy, that's enough for now. Why don't we let the Translator meet the rest of the family? You can talk about her books after dinner," Clear Seas said.

Stormy wilted. "Yes, Papa. Can I show her my Crawly Man toy first though?"

Clear Seas nodded and Stormy bolted for the house.

Marsee turned to Ellie. "There are toys too?"

Ellie made a very innocent expression and just shrugged.

Marsee turned back to the Councilor who was still watching his son bolt for the house.

"Forgive my son, for his rudeness," Clear Seas said, when he looked back at her.

"There is nothing to forgive. If you asked my Papa, he'd tell you I was just as precocious at that age. You saw the video of my niece with the laser pointer. Not only does she look like me, but I've been told she acts just like I did too. Besides, unlike when my niece is around, my tail has remained unshredded." Marsee brought her soggy tail around to show him. "In all honesty, if I had the opportunity to meet some of my favorite authors I'd probably be just as excited."

"That can easily be arranged," Ellie said with a smile.

"Really?!" Marsee squeaked.

"Rank has its privileges," Ellie replied with a chuckle.

Clear Seas also made a sound that closely approximated their laughter, and his humor rippled across his skin. "Come then, let me introduce you to the rest of my family."

They followed Clear Seas inside, where everyone was waiting for them in their family room. It was a small gathering. Only Clear Seas, his partner Jewel, and his three children, Temperate, Jade, and Stormy were in attendance. Jewel, she found out, was a historian and ran one of the museums that Clear Seas had pointed out in their tour, and when he informed everyone that this was Marsee's first trip off-world she immediately went into full tour guide mode, and gave Marsee a tour of their home explaining how everything worked. Clear Seas and Jewel had both been off-world before, but the others had not, and they were just as curious about how everything worked on her world.

Their home was absolutely stunning, and if she hadn't gone through a doorway she would have been convinced they were still outside, as nearly every surface was covered in flowering plants, and the floor, rather than being stone like she expected, was covered in some sort of short moss like plant. Jewel was apparently also an avid gardener, like her mother, and helped to maintain the Arboretum.

Unlike the Council Building, which had been designed with the other species in mind, Clear Seas home was uniquely Water Sprite. The home itself had been carved out of the rock following a natural cave system. According to Jewel, this was their preferred type of home as it provided a natural defense against the larger predators like the Leviathan, and didn't require the energy expenditure of a static shield to protect it. Rooms branched out in all directions, not following any sort of flat layout like she was used to.

Stormy insisted on showing off his room, and she'd struggled hard to adjust to the fact that the entrance to his room was through a hole in the hallway ceiling, one that was barely big enough for Ellie to squeeze through. The room itself was smaller than she'd expected too, only a fraction of the size of her tower room. There was a large sleeping net hung from one wall to another that reminded her of the Hue-man's hammocks that they'd added to the pool and garden since arriving.

Stormy demonstrated how it was used in childlike flair, and showed how it rotated to whatever position he wanted. She explained how the Hue-mans had something similar, but that they and most of the Hue-mans preferred to sleep on pillows or beds, and then explained that she'd created a hanging bed that she could swing on, and that raised her up off the ground so she didn't have to worry about crawlies.

He had several hanging nets that were for lounging or sitting in, and a desk that he pinned papers to with clamps to keep them from floating away. A small net hung suspended from one of the sides and allowed him to wrap his tentacles through it and stay in position while he worked. One wall was covered in nets where his objects were haphazardly stored, and on another, he had a display shelf that he just had to show her. On it were every one of her books, from the cubs books to the more adult history books. A clamping system provided pressure to keep the books from drifting off in the slight current she could feel. The rest of his walls were covered in drawings, many of which were characters from her books. She took the time to check them all out and comment on them. For his young age, he was a surprisingly good artist, and even Ellie commented on it, which sent him into a complete rainbow of emotions again. She might be the Translator, but Stormy clearly knew who Ellie was too, and when *the* Senior Guild Master said your drawings were good, it wasn't just the empty praise given to children.

Stormy showed off his Crawly Man toy, complete with fully articulating joints, and when he pushed a button, a tiny web floated out. Afterwards, Stormy asked if Marsee would sign his book. Marsee examined it and the pen with interest, never having seen one of the Water World books or writing utensils before, and they spent several minutes discussing how they were manufactured so that the water wouldn't damage them or fade the ink. The ones at the celebration had been gone long before she'd arrived. Clear Seas informed her that this was the one he'd picked up when he was there. Stormy had an actual first edition copy.

Marsee thought for a while and then on the inside cover wrote:

> *To my biggest fan, Stormy,*
> *When you grow up to be the greatest SuperHero our worlds have ever known, I hope you'll let me be the one to tell your story. - Translator Marsee Bet Chenzira*

When she handed the book back and told him that this was the first book she'd ever signed, his skin positively exploded into a rainbow of uncontrolled excitement that lasted for several minutes.

"Thank you ,Translator! I will treasure this always!" he said, and carried it with him for the rest of the tour.

When they made it back to the family room, Jewel had Stormy put his book away so it wouldn't accidentally get damaged during the meal.

Stormy bolted off, not wanting to be away from Marsee for a second.

"You know, he's not going to sleep for a week now," his mother signed, once he was out of the room, and they all laughed.

The next several hours were spent enjoying what was arguably the best meal she'd ever had, and discussing the many challenges facing the Hue-mans. They wanted to know everything, and they all had dozens of questions about the topics in her various books. Marsee was surprised at how well Stormy understood them for his young age, and it was clear that he'd read them cover to cover many times, because he had several passages memorized.

After the meal, Stormy asked if he could see the new book she was working on.

"I haven't finished translating it yet. It's only in Hue-man and Saber at the moment," she replied. "And I didn't bring my tablet with me as I'm not sure if it's water proof."

"I can read Saber," he replied. "You can borrow my tablet. Please?"

He looked so hopeful, that she relented, and he bolted out of the room to grab his tablet.

She looked over at Ellie who was chuckling quietly. "What?" she asked.

"You are such a softy when it comes to children," Ellie replied.

Marsee raised a brow. "I wouldn't want to disappoint my biggest fan, now would I?"

That caused everyone to burst out laughing.

Moments later Stormy returned with his tablet and Marsee logged into her account and sent him her latest version before logging back out again.

He drifted back over to his seat, nearly missing it as he read. It was quite the experience to watch him read, as his emotions flashed with everything he read.

"I personally think it's Marsee's best work yet," Ellie commented, as they watched Stormy.

"I can't wait to read it then," Clear Seas replied. "Assuming Stormy stops reading long enough to share."

"You?" Marsee asked, surprised.

"I've read all of your translations as well," he replied. "It helps me to understand the Hue-mans better. As a Senior Councilor, they are my responsibility as well, and there's a rather surprising amount of overlap between our own history. We were much like them not so long ago."

"Really?" Marsee asked. "I'll be honest, I've not read much in the way of history from your world. I've found it hard to come by, fiction yes, but not history. I've learned more from Ellie the past few days than anything I've found on my own."

Clear Seas nodded. "That was done on purpose. My grandfather feared that the rest of the Consortium would not trust us if they knew our full history. Our version of your Great Awakening happened not all that long before your people arrived, and we have worked hard to become better people since then. I was considering releasing some of that history, but now I'm not so sure. There's still a great deal of fear of the Hue-mans after what your sister said, and I worry that telling our own history would negatively affect my people if others knew, especially in light of the violence we're seeing with the protests."

Marsee nodded her understanding. "I've had similar conversations with GrandFather regarding the history book he's writing. Much of what he's written so far is very difficult to read, horrifying if I'm being honest. Part of him wants to forget the past and even any mention of the violence that occurred, but he believes that remembering the past means you'll be less likely to repeat those mistakes, and show how far you've come, even if it is painful. It's a challenge though as they don't even agree on much of their own history, as it was often tainted or destroyed by those who won, to make them appear righteous in their use of violence."

"That happened with us as well," Clear Seas replied. "Which is an added challenge. If I did release some of it, would you translate it?"

Marsee blinked in surprise, but nodded, and Ellie grinned at her.

At that point, Stormy had finished reading and looked up. "So what do you think? I've only shared it with Ellie so far," Marsee asked.

"Honestly?" he asked.

"Honesty is usually best," she replied with a grin. "Even if you hate it. I'll be devastated of course, but better I know before it goes to print." She pretended to be crushed, and everyone laughed.

"I don't hate it at all," Stormy replied. "I think it might be my favorite. It's more...real than the others, but also more uncomfortable too, and I'm not sure why. The story has a similar theme to the others."

"That's because the villains are Hue-man too, and could be any one of us. The hero isn't perfect either," Marsee replied. "There's the potential for darkness in all of us, a monster waiting to pounce on its prey, yet even the worst of us aren't all bad, and have the potential for good. It's what we do when faced with that darkness that matters. Far too often there aren't good answers, or even right ones. All you can do is your best, and pray it works out."

Stormy nodded. "Thank you for letting me read this ahead of time."

"No sharing with anyone," Ellie ordered with a glare. "Not until I get my copies. Well, you can share with the others here, as I'm sure they're just as curious, but that's it."

"I promise," Stormy replied. "But please don't take too long. I can't wait to talk about it with my friends."

"I'll see what I can do, but someone's been keeping me very busy lately," she said, with a grin towards Ellie.

Ellie just rolled her eyes.

Stormy shared it with the others, and Marsee waited uncomfortably while they read it too. Ellie's expression had changed to one that Marsee couldn't quite decipher, but she didn't ask, because soon Clear Seas was looking at her with another equally unreadable expression.

She raised a brow but didn't say anything, letting the others finish.

"I really like the artwork. It's very different, but it fits somehow," Temperate said when he finished, and the others agreed.

"Thank you," she replied.

They chatted some more and then Clear Seas escorted them back to their suite. "I don't know what your schedule is but if you're free tomorrow after the noon meal, I would be honored to take you out to the Habitat for a tour," Clear Seas said.

Marsee checked with Ellie, who nodded and replied. "We have a meeting with Guild Master Agate in the morning, but our afternoon is currently free. I expect that Agate will want us to eat our noon meal with her. So perhaps we could meet an hour later, just in case our meeting runs long?"

"Excellent, I'll meet you here tomorrow and we can take my ship." At that point, he turned and faced her. "Marsee, it was a real pleasure getting to know you better tonight. Please do not take offense by my silence around your latest book. I agree with Ellie, I believe it is your best work yet. You've given me a lot to think about today, and I would like to discuss it and your other translations more later, once I've had a chance to gather my thoughts."

"None taken, and the pleasure was all mine," she replied.

He nodded with respect. "Until tomorrow?"

"Until tomorrow," Marsee replied, and waited as he turned and left.

The moment the door closed, Marsee sighed and flopped down in the chair by the fire again.

"I have never been more proud of you," Ellie said, sitting down across from her.

Marsee raised a brow. "For what, not throwing up from nerves fourteen times today?"

Ellie chuckled briefly but then sobered. "No, because you really stepped up today. Every second of today, you've shown yourself to be a leader, and you didn't hesitate when it mattered, from standing up to Clear Seas this morning, to saying exactly the right thing to the protesters. You took an incredible risk in meeting with Deep Current, and handled it flawlessly as far as I can tell. You even managed your role in the Council today as if you'd been doing it for years, and not just thrown into it the night before. Even your counsel to Clear Seas and his son, was thoughtful and insightful. You surprised Clear Seas, which I've rarely seen. For that matter, you surprised me at least half a dozen times today, and I know what you're capable of."

"Thank you," Marsee said.

"And you didn't throw up on the Council," Ellie added, with a curl of her tail.

"Trust me, I came close several times," Marsee replied.

"I know, but you managed not to anyway. Now, we have work to do."

Marsee sighed and crawled out of her chair to grab their tablets from the tube system, and handed Ellie hers afterwards. They spent another several hours preparing for the meeting with Agate the next morning, and researching the altered footage.

"I'm starting to get a bit of a headache from looking at this screen. I think I'm going to take a swim through the gardens. Did you want to join me?" she asked her mentor.

"No, I should probably finish up a few reports I've been putting off, and then head off to bed. There should be a first aid kit in the waste room if you need something for that headache. Don't stay out too late. Morning comes far too early here," Ellie reminded her.

Marsee nodded, and made her way down, after dropping her tablet off in her room, and taking out her hearing aids that she'd put in earlier to listen to some music while she researched. She noticed someone from the Sea Patrol following her as she left the tube, but decided to ignore them.

It was late when she entered the garden, and while the lights had been dimmed, the path was lit up by phosphorescent plants that reminded her of the garden back home at night. There were few people in the garden, and before long she'd found a secluded spot. The solitude was welcome from the crazy day she'd had. She was actually very proud of what she'd accomplished, and how well she'd handled all of it, but she was nearing her limits. She floated and considered everything she'd learned so far.

*So what do you think of Clear Seas?* she asked her instinct.

**He's comfortable in his power and sees no need to flaunt it. He lives modestly and his cubs lead honorable lives. They wanted us to be comfortable and showed genuine interest in the wellbeing of our sister and her people. I sniffed no deceit or ill intentions.**

*So what's going on with the protesters, and why aren't their demands being met?*

**Someone else is trying to claim power.**

That made her eyebrows raise. *Who? Rip Current?*

**Possibly. He did not like being ignored. He is someone who craves the attention that comes with power. That makes him dangerous, but since he already has rank and power, it is possible someone else is trying to discredit him too.**

She'd been alone with her thoughts for maybe half an hour, when the guard that had been following her swam up.

"Excuse me, Translator, I have a message for you," he said, holding out a scroll bound with ribbon.

Marsee swam over to collect the scroll the guard held out. He handed it to her and she slid the ribbon off and started to unroll it. Before she could read it though, she felt something press into her side and pain ripped through her, so intense she couldn't cry out, before the world went dark around her.

~~~~~

Marsee woke with a start, and found herself lying on a rough stone floor, facing a rock wall. The air smelled dank and stale, and she shivered from the cold air and her damp fur, and her side ached. Sitting up with a groan, she spun around to take in her surroundings, and found herself on a steeply sloping shelf on the side of a large cave.
~~~~~

Large stalactites hung from the roof of the cave all the way down into the water. A dim light came from between a pair of them. She couldn't see the far walls or even the top of the cave she was in. Struggling to control her growing panic, she felt her neck and realized her mask had been removed. She was trapped here, wherever here was.

"Who are you and what do you want with me?" she called out to the shape she could just barely see behind the light.

The person merely chuckled, the sound echoing off of the cavern. The light slowly dimmed leaving her in a dark blacker than the blackest black she'd ever experienced in her life. She'd grown up on a world with two suns and three moons, where even on the stormiest of nights, it was never truly dark. It was too much and she screamed in fear, and those screams resonated and bounced off the walls coming back to her, sounding eerie and off-key.

The voice chuckled again, much closer this time.

She froze, flicking on her instinct trying to locate the person.

Her instinct growled low and menacingly and she did nothing to stop it.

"Oh don't stop on my account. You scream oh so beautifully," a raspy voice she didn't recognize oozed.

"Why are you doing this? Let me go! Please!" she cried out.

"I can't have you ruining my plans. You're far too nosy, but I do hope you enjoy your stay in my finest suite, while I deal with your meddling mentor."

"What do you mean?" she asked, terrified now for Ellie.

He just chuckled. "I really do hope you were telling the truth about knowing how to swim. Have a good night, little kitten."

There was a splash and then overpowering silence. Even her instinct couldn't hear anything except for the tiny skitters of small creatures and the drip of water off of the stalactites. She carefully crawled back until she was up against the far wall and shook with fear.

"Please! Whatever you want, I'll do it! Just let me go!" she called out, but there was no answer, not even a chuckle.

When something crawled across her paw she flicked it away in terror and started screaming again. She called for help, pleaded to be released, and eventually descended into her terror, and screamed until her voice was barely a whisper.

It was only then that she realized the danger she was truly in, as water started lapping against her feet, and she understood what he'd meant about being able to swim. The tide was coming in. Scrambling to her feet, she tried to find higher ground and see if she could climb the wall, but it was too steep. Her claws found no purchase in the smooth rock, and there was nothing she could do, but wait.

# CHAPTER 9

# Myra: A Mother's Worst Fear

Myra paced in the hallway, trying to keep herself awake. She'd barely slept for the past several days, and the moment she had, her family had been poisoned. Hope had finally calmed, but the poor cub had screamed for hours until the venom was finally out of her system. They couldn't even scdate her because it interfered with the anti-venom. Yawning again, she gave up and walked into the supply closet and pulled out another stimulant, popping it in her mouth.

"That's the last one, Myra. If you don't go home and get some rest, I'm going to sedate you and drag you into a room," her mentor said behind her.

"I promise I will, just as soon as Little Flower, Hope, and Grand-Father are cleared to return back with me. I'm not leaving them alone if someone is trying to hurt them."

He sighed but nodded. "I thought you should know, Brice cleared the other brownies. The venom was just in the basket delivered to Jer."

Myra growled. *They were trying to kill Jer,* she thought, wondering once again if the others were targeted or just him. *Just him,* she decided, since they were sent to his office not to their home.

Ammond said nothing about her growling, unbecoming of an on-duty healer as it was. She could tell he was just as furious about what had happened to her family, although he was hiding it much better. Then again, he had more than a century of experience on her at hiding his emotions. "As for the others, take them home. I just finished examining Little Flower. I'd rather she stayed here another night, but frankly, I'm more concerned about you right now than I am any of the others. Go home. Get some sleep. That's an order."

Myra nodded and walked back to Little Flower's room. She found her daughter sitting up and snuggling with Hope while she talked with GrandFather. "Ammond says he's cleared you all to return home. Are you ready to get out of here?"

Little Flower nodded, but GrandFather shook his head. "I was wondering if we could make a quick detour to the barn on the way back to the tower. I have a surprise for Little Flower, well two actually as of this morning. I've been wanting to show her for months, but since she's refused to leave the room, I haven't pushed it, and I think it might cheer her up."

Little Flower said something to him in her language, and he nodded.

"Can we?" Little Flower asked her, looking excited about whatever it was.

Myra was exhausted, and didn't really want to walk over to the barn, but it was one of the first times she'd seen her daughter smile in months, so she nodded.

GrandFather took Hope from Little Flower, swinging her up in the air, making the cub giggle.

Myra sighed with relief. *If Hope is feeling good enough to giggle, she must be feeling better.* Hope had finally stopped screaming, and there appeared to be no permanent injuries from the sand spinner venom. They had no experience with what it did when ingested, but a sting was often fatal, long before help and the anti-venom could arrive. It would take a few days before they were sure there were no lasting effects, as many long term issues from the neurotoxin didn't show up right away in her own species.

She grabbed Little Flower's dress and slippers from the storage compartment, quickly changed her daughter out of the robe she'd been in, and scooped her up to follow out after GrandFather. Ammond nodded to them on the way out and gave her a pointed look, which she nodded back to. It took all of her self-control not to roll her eyes at him. The stimulant would be good for another hour or two anyway, so she had time before she would even be able to sleep, and anything to cheer up her daughter would be a welcome relief. She let Brice know on the way out that they were heading to the barn, in case Jer was looking for them.

A few minutes later they were entering the barn. She had only been here a few times, and not since Little Flower's coma. The odd smells made her nose twitch with curiosity. It wasn't just the animal smells, but the strange green plants they ate and used for bedding. *I should find some time to visit the greenhouse again,* Myra thought absently. The plants from Earth were fascinating to her, especially considering how well many of them were doing on her planet, far better than many of their own, which had come from their old world, and didn't do well with the intense sunlight and heat of their new one. That fact was surprising considering the difficulty many of the Earth animals had surviving in the same conditions. She hadn't been there since Hope was born either.

Little Flower breathed deeply as they entered and sighed with happiness. "I missed that smell," she signed.

Mrya sniffed again. *This is a comforting smell to them?* she wondered. *How odd.* However, if her daughter found comfort here, she would make sure to bring her regularly. Anything to get her out of her room. *I should have suggested a visit to the barn a long time ago.*

She followed GrandFather down several of the large aisles before he turned in and brought them over to a stall. Inside was one of the long-legged grazers, although she struggled to remember what the sign was.

"Mama, set me down," Little Flower signed.

Surprised at the request, she complied, and helped Little Flower to stand. Her daughter grabbed tightly to the bars on the sides of the stall and peered in. When Myra looked up again, she realized that there were two creatures, as the first one moved to approach them.

"GrandFather, he looks just like Buster!" Little Flower signed, and then quickly grabbed the stall again.

Myra blinked in shock. For several seconds, Little Flower had stood, completely unassisted, and she hadn't even noticed!

GrandFather handed Hope over to her so he could sign easier. Hope snuggled down in her fur and began sucking her thumb for comfort.

"She, and there's a good reason for that. Come over here." GrandFather waved, walking down several stalls.

Myra watched as her daughter carefully made her way, holding on to the railings that made up the upper portion of the stall. The look on her daughter's face was one she hadn't seen in a very long time, excitement. Myra's tail curled with happiness as her daughter put more effort into those few steps than she'd put in for weeks, and with far more ease than she'd had in the past too. *The nanos are working! Thank the moons!*

GrandFather was grinning. He looked up at her, and she smiled back. He'd noticed too.

She slowly walked alongside Little Flower, tail now curled lightly around her daughter, ready to catch her if she should start to fall. When her daughter made it about half way, one of the other creatures stuck its head out and grabbed GrandFather's hat and started shaking it.

Little Flower let out a high pitched screech of happiness, and actually bounced a little in place. "It can't be!" Little Flower signed. "Is it really him?"

GrandFather's smile lit up even brighter. "It really is! They rescued him too!"

"I can't believe it!" her daughter signed, and Myra noticed that tears were streaming down her face as she looked up at her. "I thought you didn't rescue him?"

"You know this...creature?" she signed, still unable to remember the sign for the long legged grazer.

"He's called a horse," GrandFather signed. "And this is Buster. The horse I asked about the day I arrived. My partner Ben raised him from a foal. He's been in our family since before Little Flower was even born. They grew up together."

GrandFather reached up to try and take the hat back, but Buster lifted it far above GrandFather's head causing Little Flower to screech with laughter.

*What a glorious sound!* Myra thought. She hadn't heard her daughter laugh since the day she woke up.

"But how though?" Little Flower asked.

"Translation error, I guess. Buster was gelded, so he wasn't counted as male."

"I do not know the word 'gelded'," Myra said. Grandfather had used the Hue-man spelling for the word.

"It means we made it so he couldn't reproduce," GrandFather explained. "Anyway, apparently they've fixed that, and Buster is now a proud father, with several more on the way. He's the only adult male we have, for now."

Myra nodded her understanding. "Yes, once the two males were born we were able to repair his injury. I am sorry. I didn't realize you count infertile males as male. We have a separate term for those that cannot produce offspring. This was not the result of an injury? You did this on purpose?"

"Yes. It makes them calmer and easier to handle especially when a mare is in heat. The males will fight to establish dominance, which can be dangerous for everyone, including the horses. We'll need to watch out for that when the colts get bigger."

GrandFather opened the stall door once they'd made it and helped Little Flower inside. Myra stayed outside, afraid to scare the creature. The horse was far bigger than Little Flower and practically knocked her over with a bump of its head.

"Are you sure this creature is safe to be around?" she asked.

"I've trusted him with my life on many occasions," GrandFather signed, which absolutely floored her.

Little Flower leaned up against Buster, giving the big horse a hug, and the horse laid its head over her shoulder and nickered, giving every appearance of returning the hug.

"What do you mean you've trusted him with your life?" Myra asked.

"This old brute of a horse is probably the smartest horse I've ever known. For much of our history we used horses to help with labor, tilling our fields, pulling or carrying loads far greater than we could manage, and for transportation. I've ridden him home in a blizzard where I couldn't see two feet in front of me, but he made it home without issue. He's warned me of bad footing, dangerous creatures, and even saved my life from the sand spinner two months ago, and routinely finds and kills them."

"Ride?" she asked. Surely she misunderstood. He couldn't be implying what she thought he meant, could he?

"Ride, as in sit on top of. We use leg pressure and a special harness to tell them where to go," GrandFather explained.

"A wild animal nearly ten times your size would let you do that?" she asked incredulously. Little Flower hadn't stopped hugging the creature, but Myra noticed that her legs were starting to wobble. "She's going to fall," she signed.

GrandFather spun and scooped her up, and, rather than answering her first question, tossed Little Flower up on the back of the horse, who didn't so much as flick an ear at the motion.

Myra stood there in shock, mouth hanging open. "That's it, I've fallen asleep on my feet and I'm hallucinating," she signed, and then dug a claw into her palm to make sure she was actually awake.

Little Flower leaned over and continued hugging the creature, who turned its big head back and nuzzled her daughter's leg, causing Little Flower to giggle again.

GrandFather laughed. "He's not wild. He's domesticated, and you're not hallucinating. Our people have a very long partnership with horses. Some cultures considered them gifts from the gods and sacred. Little Flower has been absolutely horse crazy since she was nearly as young as Hope. She used to ride Buster every time she came to our home for a visit, and even entered him in a competition once. Riding is a lot harder than it looks. It takes a great deal of balance, strength and trust. You might want to consider it for pickle torture once she gets a little stronger."

Little Flower must have been watching as she gasped, and pushed herself up into a sitting position. "Yes! Can I? Please Mama? Riding is so much more fun than the rubber bands."

"You *want* to do this?" Myra asked, shocked. Little Flower hadn't asked to do anything relating to her physical therapy since she'd woken up. Not once. Usually it was all she could do to get her to leave her bed, and half the time she had to pick her up and physically move her.

"I do!" she signed. "Please?"

"Can this be done safely?" Myra asked. "I'm worried about her falling."

GrandFather nodded but then tilted his head, considering. "Well we should probably craft her up some riding gear first. She'll need special boots, pants and a...a hard hat. I don't have the sign for it, but it's designed to protect her head from an impact."

"I'm not sure we have anything like that. We don't really need it. Our skulls are pretty thick."

This statement caused both GrandFather and Little Flower to burst out laughing.

"What did I say?" she asked, which just caused them both to laugh even harder.

"I'll explain later. You were saying?" GrandFather replied, still chuckling.

"Oh, just that I'm not sure we have anything like that. Maybe in the Ship's Guild for the test pilots. I could call Sampson and find out."

"Please?" Little Flower begged again, so Myra shifted Hope to her other arm, carefully, since the tiny cub had fallen asleep, thumb still tucked in her mouth, and peeled her tablet off her harness and placed the call. She would do anything to keep her daughter engaged and enthusiastic.

"Myra, what a pleasant surprise. What can I do for you?" Sampson asked, answering almost immediately.

"I was hoping you might have a solution for a little problem I have. My daughter apparently has absolutely no sense of self-preservation and, well, it's probably easier just to show you."

She flipped the camera around and watched as Sampson's mouth dropped. She was pretty sure she'd had the exact same expression only moments before.

"Well now, I think I've seen everything," he said.

"I'm sure they'll find something else to surprise us with next week. It seems to be a regular occurrence around here," she replied with a chuckle, flipping the camera back around. "Anyway, my daughter has had some health issues these past few months, and I'd like to find a way to protect her skull from breaking should she fall off, and the only thing I could think of was the specialized gear that the test pilots used when trying out a new ship or shuttle."

"We do have gear that could work, but it would have to be shaped to her head. We also have a crash belt, like the airbags on the shuttle. It expands to protect the person from impact. I could fly over tomorrow or the next day with the equipment," he replied.

Before she could answer though, she heard the sound of Jer yelling from the main door of the barn. "Myra! Are you in here?"

"Over here, Jer," she yelled back. "One second, Sampson," she told him, and turned to see what her partner wanted. The moment she saw his face, she knew something was horribly, horribly wrong.

Jer walked slowly up to her as if afraid of what he had to tell her, blinked at the sight of Little Flower on Buster, and then turned back to face her. It took several tries for him to make the words come out. "I just received a message from Clear Seas..." He paused, closed his eyes and took a deep breath before continuing.

Myra's breath hitched in fear.

"Ellie's been badly beaten and...and Marsee's missing."

Her tablet slid out of her hand and clattered to the floor. A moment later her legs gave out from under her, and she followed it with a soundless cry.

# CHAPTER 10

# Marsee: Darkness

Marsee shivered as cold water continued to rise slowly around her. The only sounds she heard were the sounds of her own breathing, the slow drip of water off of the stalactites, and the skittering of small crawlies. In the absolute darkness they took on terrifying shapes in her imagination. When creatures in the water started to nibble at her feet, she kicked at them and screamed in fear every time.

Hours passed as the water slowly rose above her neck. Eventually she had no choice but to start treading water, thanking every Ancient God in the universe she'd had the courage to take swimming lessons from her sister. The water continued to rise until she could reach up and touch the roof of the cave, and for a time, she worried that the cave would fill entirely, but it didn't.

Hoping to find a way out, she swam around the edge of the large cave. She knew air had to be coming in from somewhere. With her instinct on, she was able to follow the faint scent of fresh air, but only found a small crack. Still, she tried clawing at it, hoping that maybe she could make the hole bigger, but she had no leverage, and the water started to recede before she could make any progress.

She had no idea how long she floated there before the water finally receded and she found her way back to her shelf, but it felt like forever. Shaking the water out of her fur as best she could as it receded, she collapsed exhausted to the stone floor the moment she could safely do so. The water that had once felt warm now seeped the warmth out of her. She shivered from both cold and fear, and curled up tightly to preserve her body heat.

She must have fallen asleep, because she was suddenly jarred awake when something slimy and wet hit her in the face. "What in the moons...?" she muttered in confusion, as she wiped at the slime sticking to her face, momentarily forgetting where she was, and why she couldn't see.

"What a pathetic creature. Are you still cowering in the dark? I expected so much more from the new head of the Guild, but then it's pretty clear to me, you're nothing more than a helpless cub, still suckling on her mama's teat. Why the Senior Guild Master thought *you* were a worthy heir is beyond me." The deep raspy voice oozed contempt from the darkness.

Marsee jumped to her feet and spun to face the direction it came from. "What are you talking about?"

"Oh that's right, Little Kitten. You wouldn't have heard since you were so busy cowering in the dark. Your little mentor is dead, every bone in her weak little body, battered and broken, making *you* the new head of the Guild, not that you deserve it. It's such a waste, really, but like you, she had to go poking around where she didn't belong."

"Liar!" Marsee hissed.

"Now, why would I lie about something like that?" he crooned. "But I suppose you'll need proof. Here."

Marsee felt something hit her in the face and it dropped to the stone below her before she could catch it. She felt around and found the object and tried to figure out what it was. With horror, she realized it was a claw, and she dropped it with a gasp as she recognized Ellie's scent on it..

"Tell me? How does it feel to know that you now control all of the vast resources of the Guild, and yet are completely powerless to use *any* of it to save your furry little hide?"

"Who *are* you? You call me a coward, but you won't even show your face," Marsee growled. Fully awake now but shivering from both cold and fear, she let her instinct roar to life. Her smell and hearing heightened in the pitch black, but she still couldn't make out who or where he was, as the smell of the dank cave and the ocean was overpowering.

"Plausible deniability, Little Kitten. Not that I expect you'll leave my lovely little guest house alive. But, just in case you do, I can't have you able to identify me, now can I?" the voice oozed from a new location.

"What do you want with me?" she asked, trying to keep him talking so she could figure out where he was.

"I would have thought you'd have figured that out by now, but then I guess you aren't as smart as they say you are." The voice came from another direction and Marsee spun again.

"Humor me," Marsee demanded.

"I want to see the terror in your eyes, and to hear more of your beautiful screams. I want you to know what *real* power is before you die. Your family's little coup and rise to power was a stroke of brilliance, I'll give you that. Your parents should have been killed, or at the very least stripped of their rank, along with all of the other councilors from your world. Instead, you somehow managed to trick that idiot Tabor into resigning and lock herself up, got your father and uncle both elected as Senior Councilors, and had all of the resources of five planets redirected to turn your home into a veritable castle and sovereign territory. But that wasn't enough for you was it? You then somehow managed to convince the Senior Guild Master herself to hand over her entire empire to you as well. You've made a lot of enemies across all five worlds with your actions, Little Kitten."

"How is any of that my fault? I just translated Little Flower's words, and I was just as shocked by the Guild Master's announcement as everyone else."

The voice laughed from a new direction. "Oh Kitten, I saw how little it took for the Guild Master to convince you. You might not admit it to yourself, but you want that power. You crave it, just like the predator inside of you wanted to kill that little rodent you call your sister."

*How under the three moons does he know about that?* she wondered. "If anyone is craving power, it's you. I'm not the one going around and kidnapping people."

"Oh no, Little Kitten. I don't crave power. I *have* power. You see, the difference between us is that I'm not afraid to use it, to do what needs to be done to save my planet from being overrun by an invasive species."

"What species?" she asked. "None of the creatures from Earth have been marked as being invasive. For that matter, there are so few of most of the species that keeping them from extinction is the bigger problem."

He laughed. "Oh, I'm not referring to any of the pathetic creatures that were brought from that dying planet. I'm referring to yours. None of those other species would last a day on either of our planets if they were let loose, not even that palm waving rodent you pretend is sentient."

"Of course she's sentient!" Marsee growled. "The Full Council voted on it and it was unanimous."

"Oh please. Half the Council just wanted control over your planet, and your Council had no choice but to vote her as sentient. To do otherwise would have been a death sentence. The rest would have voted the same way if she'd been nothing more than a gelatinous blob, just for the opportunity to strip even a little bit of power away from your Council. You've held control over our worlds for far too long," he said, moving to another position.

"You lie," she hissed.

"Do I, Little Kitten? Tell me. Why do you think the Council was so upset when your father was nominated? It wasn't because your father had just been banned by the Senior Council to run again. Everyone knew he would take the fall. He did publicly claim responsibility for your council's actions after all. No, it was because it gave members of *your* species too much power over the rest of us. I'll admit, even I wasn't expecting *that* little turn of events, convicted criminal to Senior Councilor in less than an hour. Although watching Tabor publicly humiliated in front of all five planets was especially enjoyable to watch. She's been far too insufferable for decades, walking around like she owns the universe. She certainly had no qualms about taking your future cubs from you for your mother's crimes, or planning to blame you when she planned to kill your sister. I wonder just how many children she's killed in her time as Senior Councilor? How many of them were killed simply because they'd grow up strong enough to challenge her? Would they have survived if given the same chance your father and uncle gave you? Tell me, how do you think she managed to kill all of those cubs and stay sane herself?"

Marsee didn't answer right away. She'd had many of the same questions and thoughts about Tabor, although the thought that Tabor had planned to blame her for Little Flower's death was one she hadn't had before. *Was that her plan? How would he know unless he was there? He doesn't sound like Clear Seas. If it's not him, is he lying, or does he have information he shouldn't have?*

"What does it matter what Tabor did? My uncle and father are not her. They're honorable and wouldn't do what she did."

"Is that so, Little Kitten? They're the ones that found and suggested the rape precedent to the Senior Council. I wonder why they did that? Why would your father suggest that your mother be killed and all of her children be sterilized, unless he didn't want you to have cubs?"

"He was trying to keep me from being killed," Marsee hissed. "He was trying to change the precedent."

"If you say so, Little Kitten." She heard the water shift and his voice appeared in another area moments later. "But even Tabor said there wasn't precedent as part of Consortium laws at the trial. There's certainly nothing in the archives. Archives, which you as a citizen could have easily accessed yourself. That last trial happened long before the Consortium existed, and the *only* place it existed was in your uncle's archives, which you helped scan in. If they'd kept their mouths shut, the Senior Council would have just gone with victim's choice. No, your father and uncle wanted you sterilized, you and your little niece, the one who looks just like you. She's a bit old to still be pouncing on tails is she not? I thought psychosis was just something that happened to single cubs, but your niece has litter-mates. Seems to me it might just run in the family. Then again, your father was an only cub too, was he not? I wonder if he had problems too."

He chuckled in response to her silence.

"He has, hasn't he? I wonder who he's killed? Your grandparents perhaps? They died not long after putting a child down to psychosis. Your mother was on the watch list for six months after killing your sister's rapist. Yet your father wasn't. How odd that the Council gets such an exception, or the Guard. How do they stay sane?"

"My grandparents died in a shuttle accident during a storm," she replied.

"Did they? Or was he just hiding their bodies? I'd think your grandparents would have been competent pilots, and would know to land before the storm hit. Why didn't they?"

He shifted again.

Marsee tried to follow the sounds of his movement in the water, and frowned at the conversation. Her father had admitted to her that he'd come close to hurting one of his proteges, and she was sure her father didn't hurt her grandparents, but her instinct wasn't so sure. It still didn't trust him. He did bring up a good point though. Why was it that her father and the Senior Honor Guard weren't on the watch list if they had to be there to witness the execution, if her mother had to be. The Senior Honor Guard had tested her father, but that hadn't been until after she'd overheard him saying that he didn't trust himself.

"He might not be capable of killing you, but he's come close hasn't he? How many times has he had your neck in his mouth? How's your broken shoulder? Has it fully healed?"

*How does he know that?* she wondered.

He must have noticed her confusion. "Oh yes, I know all about that incident. You see, when someone comes into the trauma center with bite and claw wounds, a flag gets put on their medical record. Funny how no one in the guard came to talk to you to find out if your father had been abusing you. What did he do or say to get the Senior Honor Guard to close the case, I wonder. Were you losing control, or was he?"

"Neither," she replied. "It was a misunderstanding. I was upset about my sister's illness and went for a run. He thought I was losing control and tried to stop me."

"By attacking you? I doubt that. No, I think he saw you take off at a run and lost control and attacked you instead," he replied, shifting again.

"He didn't lose control," she replied, but she hesitated as she remembered the moment where she'd thought he was losing control.

*Why hadn't he just tried to get her to stop before pouncing on her?*

"You are a horrible liar," he replied. "But I understand. It's in our nature to want to believe our parents have our best interests at heart, even when they don't. Even when they bite and claw us and break our shoulders. But you'll soon see how little he cares for you, how he cares more about his power than you, assuming you last that long. I wonder, how long will you last before the monster inside you breaks free?"

Her instinct suddenly locked on to him, and it was almost as if she could see him now. Even the ripples his motion made in the water, as they lapped up against the ledge and walls of the cavern she was in, seemed to ripple in her mind. She didn't know if she was imagining it or not, but she didn't care. She prepared to leap, trying to make it appear as if she were cowering in fear, and not readying herself to attack the moment he was within range.

*Not yet!* her instinct warned.

"Of course, even members of your sister's people have seen through the lies your family has weaved to gain power, and want you all gone. In fact, by the time your father gets here, to try and save your furry little hide, assuming he's not dead already, your little rodent of a sister and her vile offspring will be dead by her own people's hands. Can you imagine the horror on your father's face when he arrives to try and save you, only to find out his other daughter is dead too?"

*Now!* her instinct growled, the moment he came close to the ledge.

"Leave my sister alone!" Marsee screamed and leapt for her captor, claws outstretched and teeth bared. For a moment, she thought she'd succeeded in catching him off guard as her claws sank into his skin, but then pain arched through her body and she fell, half submerged into the water, her muscles spasming violently from the electric shock he'd delivered. She'd forgotten about their natural defenses. The agony was so intense she couldn't even cry out, or make herself move her face out of the water to breathe.

Her captor grabbed her by the scruff of her neck, lifting her face out of the water. "Oh, my feisty little kitten, your teeth and claws will do you no good. You're weak and helpless, just like the rodents you've taken in, and no one will ever find you here, so you'd better behave, or I might just decide you're not worth the effort to keep alive."

She tried to swipe at him, but he poured electricity into her. Nothing existed but the pain. It felt like her very body would explode at any moment. She screamed until she couldn't even do that anymore, unable to even breathe.

He paused, let her catch her breath, and the second she tried to fight back, he started again.

"You're a m...monster," she managed to growl out, the next time he paused.

"I may be a monster, Little Kitten." He shocked her again briefly, making her yelp. "But I'm not a complete monster. When your father fails to follow through with my demands, I'll have to send him a little present reminding him I mean business. Out of the kindness of my heart, I'll let you decide which body part I send him first."

Fear made her try to fight back again and get away, but more pain exploded through her. "Wh..a..a.t D...demands," she managed to force out through her shaking body when he finally stopped again.

"Oh, it's nothing all that difficult. All he has to do to get you back in one piece, is to step down and give up his power. What do you think, Little Kitten?" He shocked her again. "Will he do that, or will he honor his oath and protect his people before you? Give up all his power and authority over the entire universe, for you, a diseased creature that should have been put down months ago? If he does find you, will there be anything left of you in there? Will you still be his Little Kitten? Will he even bother to give you another chance, or just have the Guard kill you before you can hurt someone?"

He poured electricity into her until she stopped screaming, and tossed her head back onto the ledge, where she could do nothing but lay there, shake violently, and whimper in pain.

"So tell me? What will it be, Little Kitten? Those pointy ears of yours, or perhaps your, oh so distinctive tail? Maybe I should remove those lying paws yours, one claw at a time, like I did with your mentor? I suppose that might be the kindest. That way when your father finds you, you won't have the claws to kill him with." He emphasized each body part with a gentle caress followed by a brief jolt of additional electricity that made her cry out as her body arched and spasmed with pain.

She couldn't do anything to fight back. Her muscles just didn't work.

"Think on it, Little Kitten." He shocked her again. "And I do so hope you enjoy the meal I brought for you. It's a rare delicacy from your sister's home world, or so I'm told. There are only a handful of them left in existence. It would be a real shame to let it go to waste, my furry little kitten."

He leaned over and grabbed her by both sides and she screamed again for another long eternity before he finally stopped.

"You do scream oh so beautifully. Until later, my Little Kitten," he said, breathing hard as he patted her lightly on her head.

She jumped and screamed even though he didn't shock her that time.

He chuckled. There was a small splash and then absolute silence again.

She lay there and shook long after the worst of the effects of the electricity wore off, her terror more paralyzing than the shock had been. Eventually though, she managed to slowly crawl the rest of the way out of the water and found the slimy creature her captor had thrown at her. When she picked it up, it wiggled limply in her paws and she realized it was still alive. Carefully making her way to the water's edge, she let it go, hoping it could survive on its own. She was hungry and thirsty, but there was no way she was going to eat whatever that slimy thing was, even if it wasn't endangered. She washed the slime off her paws as best she could, and then tried drinking the sea water, but the salt water tasted horrible.

*I've got to find a way out of here,* she thought. *If I don't, I'm as good as dead anyway.*

Even though her body was still screaming and twitching with pain, she crawled carefully into the water. Taking a deep breath she dove down as far as she could, until she couldn't take the pressure in her ears anymore and her body screamed for oxygen, trying to feel for an opening. She gasped as she returned to the surface, caught her breath, and moved several feet over and tried again, and again, and again.

Hours later, she found herself back at her ledge, and with an exhausted and defeated cry, she heaved herself weakly out of the water. Numb and cold from the water that had leached the heat out of her, she shook as much off as she could and tried to rub herself dry.

Still damp, she curled into a tight ball to conserve her heat and sleep. Terrified, freezing cold, homesick, exhausted, and aching with pain, she prayed to the Ancient Gods for someone to find her before it was too late, and prayed that he'd been lying about Ellie and the rest of her family, but deep inside she knew he wasn't.

# CHAPTER 11

# Myra: Hopelessness

"What do you mean she's missing?" Myra finally managed to say, hugging Hope protectively in her arms.

"Clear Seas says they were supposed to meet up to tour the Habitat, but when he arrived at their suite to pick them up, no one answered. Ellie told him that they had a meeting at the Guild in the morning, so he figured they were running late and called to find out how long they would be. When they didn't pick up, he called the Guild, but Agate informed them that she'd received a message from Ellie that morning that there was a change of plans and that they'd be over in the afternoon. Concerned, Clear Seas overrode the entrance to the suite...and found Ellie unconscious and badly beaten in her room. He said it looked like there had been a fight and furniture was destroyed. Ellie's currently in surgery. Marsee was not in the suite."

"Ancient Gods, no," she whimpered.

GrandFather must have helped Little Flower down off of the horse because the next thing she knew, he was setting Little Flower down beside her. "What's wrong?" he asked.

Myra realized that Jer hadn't signed the information, so she answered. "Ellie's been attacked and Marsee's missing."

Little Flower gasped in horror, and then grabbed Hope from her and started hugging her tightly and rocking back and forth.

"Did Marsee lose control of her instinct or did someone take her?" Myra asked.

"I don't know," Jer replied. "I don't know if she would have been able to leave the suite if she did lose control. That would all depend on how far gone she was. But since someone tried to kill me, my guess is that someone took her. It's too much of a coincidence not to be related."

"What are they doing to find her, and how badly is Ellie injured?" GrandFather asked.

"Clear Seas didn't say about Ellie, just that she was in surgery, but he says he's martialed their entire Honor Guard and Sea Patrol to look for her. He's also put out a planetary missing persons report. They'll find her. It's not like there are many of our kind on their planet, and she has a very distinctive coat."

"We need to go look for her," Myra said.

"Myra, we can't. It'll take four days to reach her."

"I can't just stay here and do nothing!" Myra snapped at him.

Before Jer could respond, his tablet went off.

"What is it?" Myra asked as Jer opened his tablet and read, and then swallowed hard as his ears flicked back. "Tell me!" Myra ordered.

Jer didn't answer.

"What is it? I need to know."

He still didn't answer, just kept reading. She was even more scared when his mask suddenly slammed on, hiding his emotions.

"Jeran Frederick Chenzira, answer me this instant! What is it?" she demanded with a growl, tail lashing in frustration.

He took a deep breath before answering. "They found a ransom note. They're demanding removal of all off-world people and creatures from the planet, that the Habitat be fully dismantled immediately, and demanding that I step down as Senior Councilor. It states that if we don't comply, then...pieces of the Translator will be delivered for each day it takes."

"Who would do such a thing to my baby?" Myra wailed. "And what do they have against you? This is the second time you've been targeted."

Jer was silent as he considered. "Assuming Ellie was a target too, and not just beaten trying to protect Marsee, then they're upset because our family has too much power. Between Marcus, Ellie and I, we have significant sway in the Council right now. If Ellie wasn't a target, then it could just be anger over me being promoted in the first place, but according to Clear Seas, Marsee met with the leader of the protests they've been having, yesterday morning, their time, someone by the name of Deep Current. That's their current suspect, since the ransom note fits in with the protesters demands."

"If she was working with the protesters, why would they hurt her?" Little Flower asked.

"That's a good point. I honestly don't know," Jer replied. "It's entirely possible that it's unrelated, or the demands are being used as a distraction."

"When they find whoever did this, I am going to rip the skin from their bodies, one agonizing inch at a time, if they even so much as hurt a single piece of fur on her body," Myra growled. She stood and started to pace, needing to do something but not knowing what to do.

"Myra!" a voice yelled her name.

"Over here!" she yelled back.

Myra and Jer turned to see Brice running towards them, tablet in hand. "I have a message from the Senior Healer treating the Guild Master," she called out and handed her the tablet when she arrived. "I think they were trying to reach you."

Myra took the tablet and read the message aloud that had been sent nearly two hours earlier. "The Guild Master woke briefly before we started operating and insisted we tell you to read Marsee's homework. She wouldn't let us operate until we promised to do so, and to not tell anyone else she'd woken."

She handed the tablet back to back to Brice, and explained what was going on, as Jer logged into Marsee's account. As her parents they'd had access when she was a minor, although as a Senior Counselor he could have overridden it if he needed to, and they clearly needed to. Jer started to scroll through her messages and found a thread marked homework. "Found it."

Myra stopped pacing and peered over his shoulder in time to read the reprimand from the Guild Master. "That reprimand has Ellie all over it, but Marsee hasn't been working on crafting skills at all with Ellie. What's in the attachment Marsee sent?"

Jer clicked on it and a password screen came up. He tried entering his credentials but they didn't work for some reason. He frowned. "That shouldn't be possible. Any idea what the password would be?"

"Little Flower?" Myra suggested. Jer tried with no luck. "What password would Marsee choose that Ellie would think we'd know? Hope?"

He tried that, "Nope."

"Try rocking chair," Myra suggested, when she re-read the reprimand and realized what it was referencing. That worked and they both started reading. Myra looked up at Jer with concern when she was part way through. "This doesn't make sense. These are all valid concerns that the Council *should* be looking into."

"I'm going back to my office and calling Marcus. You should go back to the tower and lock yourself in until I get back. Someone is after our family. I'll send a warning out to the rest of our family too," he told her.

"Councilor Chenzira, wait," Sampson said.

Myra bent over to pick up her tablet from the floor and handed it to Jer. She'd completely forgotten about Sampson.

"What is it, Sampson?" he asked.

"I can get you to the Water World in just under a half a day," Sampson replied.

"How?" Jer demanded.

"We're testing new jump engines for the smaller ships. It has the same emergency jump drive we had on the ships sent to Earth. I'd recommend those other ships but it would take the nearest one another day to get here. We've only tested these new engines a few times so far, and it'll be a very uncomfortable ride, since the ship hasn't been outfitted for passengers yet, but I can get you there, if you're willing to take the risk."

Jer nodded. "I am. Please have the ship prepared."

"Yes, sir," Sampson said, and hung up. Jer handed the tablet back to Myra and bolted back to his office.

Myra watched him leave and turned back to the others. "Come on Little Flower, let's head back. GrandFather, I'd like you to come too.

He nodded, slid the stall door shut and picked up Hope.

She picked up Little Flower and hugged her tightly before setting off for the family room of the tower. When they arrived, she shut and locked the ancient door. The lock was stiff from decades of not being used. Once closed, she helped Little Flower into the waste room before laying her in her bed, at her request.

GrandFather placed Hope in her crib and sprawled out on the couch. As worried as they were about Marsee, they were both asleep in minutes, still recovering from the effects of the venom.

Myra sat in her rocking chair and flipped open her tablet. It had started dinging non-stop on the way back to the tower and was flooded with messages from concerned friends and family who had seen the first of the news reports that had come in from the Water World. She scrolled past them until a name she didn't recognize caught her attention, marked urgent.

> *Hello, Please call me back when you are in a private and secure location. This is important and it's about your daughter.*

Myra placed the call immediately.

"Healer Chenzira?" the person on the end of the call asked.

"I am. Is this Master Tech Lowell?" Myra asked.

She flicked her whiskers forward in a yes. "Forgive me, but I need to be sure you are who you say you are. Can you tell me the color of the Guild Master's favorite stain?"

"Green," she said without hesitation. "Although it works better as fur dye."

Lowell nodded. "Thank you. First off, I want to say I'm very sorry to hear about what happened to your daughter. Secondly, the Guild Master asked me to research some information, and told me that if anything happened to her or your daughter that I was to contact you with my findings, and to use that specific question set to verify you were you. She didn't trust anyone else with this information."

"Go on," Myra said.

"Are you aware that your daughter met with the leader of a group of protesters outside of the Council yesterday morning?"

"I am and I've seen the information he provided her. He's also the primary suspect in her kidnapping."

"I believe that's a set-up. Clear Seas provided Marsee with access to view the archives to corroborate the information Deep Current gave her. When they reviewed footage from an altercation the day before, they noticed that the video had been tampered with, along with other footage. The Guild Master asked me to try and figure out who had done that tampering and see if I could find the missing footage. There are only a few people with clearance and the access to edit evidence, namely members of the Council and the Senior Archivist, and that access and the changes made, are all logged."

"Hold on. Jer should hear this. Let me conference him in."

Lowell nodded.

Jer answered Myra's call immediately. "Hey, I was just talking with Marcus..."

"Is he still on the line with you?" Myra interrupted.

Jer nodded.

"Good, add him to the call, he needs to hear what the Master Tech has to say too." A few moments later Marcus was on the line.

"Are you in a private and secure location, Councilors?" Lowell asked. When they confirmed they were, she shared the same information.

"So you know who made those edits?" Marcus asked.

"Yes and no," Lowell replied. "I know who it *says* made those changes, but the logs have been altered and the prior version deleted, and frankly, no one should have access to do that. There are at least a dozen checks and safeguards that should have not only prevented that from happening, but notified various people, including the Senior Council, Senior Archivist, and even Ellie for that matter."

"So who does it say made those changes?"

Lowell shared her screen so they could see the information for themselves. "Senior Councilor Clear Seas."

They were all silent for several long moments. Myra's tail poofed straight out in fear.

Eventually Marcus spoke. "Notifications aside, could you make those changes?"

Lowell didn't answer right away, but finally she nodded. "It wouldn't be easy but I probably could, same with any level three or four master, but not without notifying someone."

"I want the names of every master tech level three and four, where they're located, and any ties that they might have to Deep Current or any of the Councilors on the water world," Marcus ordered.

Lowell turned and did something on another tablet and moments later their tablets dinged. "I've sent you the roster of every level three and four and where they are located. The rest will take time. I'll send you an update as soon as I have it."

"Start with anyone on the Water World," Jer suggested. "They're more likely to be involved anyway."

"Yes, sir."

"Is there any way you can restore the missing footage?" Marcus asked.

"Remotely no. I've already tried. If I had direct access to the backups and servers, I might still be able to. It depends on if the backups were tampered with as well. To do that though, I would need actual physical access to those rooms, and only the Senior Council, Senior Archivist, and Ellie have access. Anyone else would have to be physically escorted in, like I would need to be."

"Granted. How long do you think it will take to find anything?" Jer asked.

"At least a day, once I'm there."

"You don't have any way to access that remotely?" Marcus asked.

"No, the servers I need access to don't allow for remote communication on purpose, to avoid tampering. I'd have to be on site."

Jer frowned. That was too much time. "Can you vouch for anyone on the Water World to do that research for you?" Jer asked.

Lowell thought for a moment and then shook her head. "Normally I'd say yes, but if Clear Seas or the Archivist didn't do it, someone else did, and this could be giving them a way to get rid of any remaining evidence."

Jer nodded. "Are you in Council City?"

Lowell indicated she was.

"Good. Meet me at the ShipYard in an hour."

Lowell nodded and hung up.

"How are we ever going to find her if Clear Seas is involved?" Myra asked.

"I don't know, Myra. If the logs have been altered then someone could be trying to frame Clear Seas as well," Jer replied.

"If there's even a possibility that Clear Seas is involved, can't the other Senior Councilors take control of the investigation?" Myra asked.

"Well that would assume they aren't involved too," Marcus stated.

"Do you think they are?" Jer asked.

"Honestly no, and I can't believe Clear Seas is either. I've known him as long as you, and knew his father before he died. He's one of the best people I know, but those logs are pretty damning," Marcus replied.

"So do we talk to the other Seniors?" Jer asked.

"I think we need to take that chance," Marcus said. "So far we don't have any evidence that anyone outside of the Water World is involved in tampering with that evidence, and there's enough evidence to implicate Clear Seas."

"That may be, but someone also targeted me directly. That both of these events happened on the same day, can't be a coincidence. Someone else has to be involved," Jer replied.

"Agreed," Marcus said with a heavy sigh.

"Myra, we'll talk later," Jer said, and hung up.

Marcus disconnected a moment later and the call ended.

Myra stared at the blank screen for several minutes trying to figure out something, anything, she could do. She quickly ran through the rest of her messages but there wasn't anything other than concerned friends and family, reaching out to offer their assistance. She watched the news broadcasts but they didn't have any more information than she did. Hopeless, she rocked in her chair, watching her family sleep, and praying to the Ancient Gods to protect her family once more, wondering how she would ever pay the debt she was racking up.

# CHAPTER 12

# Kendra: Failure to Protect

Kendra read the message from Senior Councilor Surellis twice and swallowed hard before moving on to the message that came in from Senior Commander Rynhold. She sat there for several moments considering her options, none of which were good.

Frowning, she placed a call to the North Plains Guard Hall, the district where Chenzira's older children and grandchildren lived.

"Ma'am?" Senior Guard Alyx Taton asked, answering the call.

Kendra gave a rapid fire update of the situation. Taton hung up to enact her orders, without so much as a 'Yes, ma'am.' Normally, she'd have reamed out her subordinates for not responding with respect, but in this situation, every second could mean the difference between life and death for Chenzira's family. The moment the call went dark, she hit the switch on the comms unit attached to her carry harness. "Avery, Quinn, my office now!" she growled.

"Yes, ma'am," came the immediate response.

Moments later they both came bolting through her door at a full run. She flicked her hand motioning for Quinn, who was last in, to shut the door, and activated her privacy screen the moment it was shut.

"We have a situation. Someone just tried to poison Senior Councilor Chenzira with sand spinner venom. Little Flower, GrandFather, and Hope were also affected, but they're all recovering. At approximately the same time on the Water World, Clear Seas found that someone attacked and severely injured the Senior Guild Master, and Marsee is missing."

"Was Marsee taken or did she lose control and attack the Guild Master?" Quinn asked.

"Kidnapped. Clear Seas found a ransom note," Kendra replied. "Additionally they were both under guard at the time, due to violent protests that have been occurring on the Water World, which we were *not* informed of. Those guards are also missing. We don't know if the Guard has been compromised, or if they've been killed."

Both Quinn and Avery frowned at her statement.

"Who's missing?" Quinn asked.

"I don't know yet," Kendra replied.

"What's on the ransom note?" Avery asked.

"That's why I've called you in here." Kendra said, and pulled the ransom note up on the screen so they could read it for themselves.

Quinn, her second, who was normally reserved, let out a slew of swears, which made her raise an eyebrow, but she didn't stop him. She felt the same way.

"Marsee is as good as dead, and they're going after Chenzira's remaining children," he said afterwards. "There's no other reason for that demand, and there's no way they'll be able to meet the other demands, not in time."

"Sadly I agree," Kendra said. "If she's not dead already, there's no way Marsee will survive this without losing control of her instinct, even if she is the first to ever regain control. Chenzira and Surellis are leaving for the Water World in an hour, emergency jump. Oscar says he has room for six guards on the ship."

"I'll go," Avery and Quinn volunteered at the same time.

Kendra raised her brow. "You can fight over it in a minute. At this point we can assume that finding Marsee will be a recovery and containment issue, not a rescue, as much as I wish otherwise. I've got Taton putting eyes on Chenzira's family in North Plains. It's New Hope I'm worried about. As you know, we don't have guards on the ground there. The Hue-mans still won't allow it, and now that they're recognized as an independent planet, I can't do anything about that, even though they've reached town size, until they change their minds. Although, I can't say I blame them after what we did to them. Surellis has given us permission to infiltrate if we can figure out how to get in there without being observed, but any approach to New Hope or the surrounding area will be noticed. They've just shut down the air space."

"Fly in on a trauma ship?" Quinn suggested. "We could pose as healers."

"I thought of that, but it's too obvious. They'd be the only ships allowed to fly," Kendra said, shaking her head. "Assuming they aren't lying on the ransom note and the guard is compromised, not just attacked, they'll be able to track any ship or shuttle coming or going from New Hope and listen in on the air chatter. Posing as healers is not a bad idea though, once you get there. With the new Trauma Center, there are dozens of new healers around New Hope."

"What about taking Chenzira's ship back?" Avery suggested.

She considered and shook her head. "I'd say yes, but only if Chenzira was heading back. If his ship showed up and he didn't exit, they'd get suspicious, and it would be far too easy to watch for someone exiting."

"That just leaves taking a ground crawler as close as we can and going in on foot, possibly after dark," Quinn stated."

Kendra nodded. "Agreed. Sand Dune is the closest Guard Hall, but that's almost two hundred leagues out. If it's compromised too, they may have eyes there as well, so you'll need to be cautious. Avery, I want you to split your squad up. Half will go with you, half with Quinn. Both will be risky. Containing Marsee with half a squad won't be easy, assuming she's still alive when you find her, but I fully expect there will be fighting in New Hope. You pick who goes where."

Avery and Quinn played the Hue-man game of rock paper scissors. It had been taught to them at the Agency by one of the older cubs, and had spread like wildfire through the guard due to its quick game-play. For all its simplicity though, their skills at reading people made it rather challenging to win. It took several rounds before a winner was decided and they each took off to prepare for their separate tasks.

Kendra watched them leave for a moment, sending up a silent prayer to the Ancient Gods, but then jumped slightly as an emergency alert blared the announcement of the closure of the airspace to anyone with a shuttle or ship license.

*Gods I hate that noise,* Kendra thought. *After two hundred years, you'd think I'd get used to it.*

She fired off a message to her senior guards planet wide, to put them on high alert in the event this was a distraction to get both Seniors off planet. She had no idea if any of her people were involved or not, but she trusted her seniors. She'd worked with most of them for decades.

Moments later another message came in, this time from Stinger, the Senior Honor Guard on the Water World. She read it, frowned, trying to decide if she trusted the information, and bolted out of the room to make further plans.

# CHAPTER 13

# Jer: Emergency Jump

Jer ran with everything he had for Marcus's office the moment his ship landed, not caring about the murmurs that followed him as he ran past people on his way. Marcus was pacing in his office. The sight made Jer's heart nearly stop. He'd never seen Marcus upset enough to pace before. Not once. Not ever.

Marcus spun the moment he appeared and shut the door. Slamming the privacy screen on, Marcus walked over to him and stared into his eyes, sighed with relief, and gave him a hug. "If you have *any* problems, you let me know immediately," Marcus said. "How's Myra? Is she under control too?"

"Terrified, but fully in control, same as me," Jer replied, but slumped down into the nearest chair, burying his head in his paws. "Ancient Gods, Marcus. What are we going to do? I don't know how to protect the rest of my family or save Marsee. Even if we find her..." He couldn't finish. *This would surely push Marsee over the edge. It would push anyone over the edge, even if they weren't suffering from psychosis.*

What he hadn't told Myra was that the ransom note had also stated that they were watching the rest of his family, and if there was even a hint of a guard around his other children, they and Marsee would be killed immediately. He had no idea if that was just to keep him off balance, or if they planned to hurt the rest of his children or his people.

With Clear Seas now implicated, they had no idea if the guards were missing, involved, or if any of it was true or not, or for that matter why they were doing this.

The demands did seem to implicate Deep Current and the protesters, but that didn't explain why they'd attacked Ellie, unless she'd been trying to defend Marsee, and after what he'd read of their actual demands, he was even less convinced the protesters were behind this. But if what Lowell found was true, then this wasn't just an attack on his family, it was an act of war.

Before Marcus could answer there was a knock on the door. Marcus turned off the privacy screen and opened the door to let the Senior Honor Guard in. Jer took a deep breath and sat up, pulling his emotions back under control.

"Councilors," Kendra said with a nod.

Once she was in, Marcus shut the door and activated the privacy screen again.

"Jeran, I've just been informed that my guards have visuals on your children in their home in North Plains. They're keeping their distance, per the ransom letter, but can get to them in under a minute."

Jer sighed with relief and nodded. "That's better than nothing. What about my family in New Hope?"

"That's harder as we don't have anyone stationed there, and the nearest guards are currently in Sand Dune," Kendra replied. "I don't know how compromised the guard is, if it even is. I know the mother of one of the two missing guards. Tanner is one of the best there is, so I personally find it hard to believe that her son would be involved. I don't know the other guard though. In any event, we need to consider it a possibility that there are others involved, especially since you were targeted directly. As such, I'm only trusting those people I know personally. Avery will bring half his squad with you. Oscar says the ship you'll be going on won't have room for more than that, but I've already sent several squads via normal transport. I'm sending several more squads to Sand Dune in the event an attack is planned on New Hope. Included will be the other half of Avery's squad, under the command of my second, Quinn

Bluestone. From there, he's going to sneak out of Sand Dune, take a ground crawler to about ten leagues out from New Hope, and go in on foot to sneak in under the cover of darkness. Once they're inside, they intend to pose as some of the new healers for the Trauma Center, and we'll have your family move back to the Trauma Center under the excuse that there's something wrong with your daughter. We should be able to protect them there."

Jer nodded. "Should we have them move now?"

Kendra pursed her lips. "No. I don't want to move them until the guards are there. If they do anything out of the ordinary, whoever is behind this might get suspicious. Right now they're reasonably safe in the tower, unless someone has a weapon we don't know about, but you'll need to be very cautious about what you say to her. Someone could be listening."

His and Marcus's tablets dinged and Marcus checked. "Wind Rider has issued a vote of no confidence in Clear Seas."

Kendra pursed her lips. "Clear Seas? What don't I know?"

Jer looked at Marcus trying to decide if they could trust Kendra. Marcus knew her much better than he did. Marcus nodded.

"We've uncovered evidence that showed Clear Seas altered video of the most recent protests," Jer explained. "Which matches what Deep Current apparently told Marsee. Plus the demands the protesters told my daughter are all valid and worthy of investigation. It doesn't make sense that they'd be behind this, not if she was working with them."

Kendra leaned back in her chair, stunned, and then frowned. Jer could see her eyes following thoughts as she connected pieces and then took a deep breath. "Councilors, there's something I need to tell you."

Both Jer and Marcus looked at each other and then back at Kendra.

"Go on," Marcus commanded.

"Are you aware that I have clearance to access all security footage and camera's on the planet?" she asked.

They both flicked their ears back in surprise. "I did not, but I suppose that makes sense," Jer replied. "Why? Would you have access to be able to see who took Marsee?"

"No, just for Saber. Stinger does and he said they've found nothing on the nearest cameras, and the one in the suite had been disabled. They're checking other footage to see if they can find something, but if the Guard is involved, that could be a lie." She paused, opened her mouth to speak, and then closed it again, and was silent for several moments before continuing. "Jeran, after you and I spoke that day in the courtyard, I too was concerned that the Seniors would attempt to commit genocide after your daughter's testimony. I put guards on Little Flower and GrandFather."

"I am aware of that," Jer replied. "And that your guards protected Little Flower, going so far as to raise a stunner at Tabor. That fact is the only reason I'm trusting you right now."

She nodded. "That's fair, and I figured you would know. In addition to that, I sent several squads of guards to the Agency as a precaution, with orders to bring the seniors back for trial, if they tried something, and I accessed the security camera in the Senior's conference room, and watched all of their deliberations. I wanted to have advanced warning, so I could stop it before anything happened."

Jer raised a brow, as Kendra was admitting to treason, even if it had been to save the lives of his people, but he didn't interrupt.

"That access was logged and Tabor was informed, although I didn't realize it until later. The morning your daughter was called to the conference room, they fully intended to kill her and Marsee. I didn't know until later. Tabor ordered me to her office under the guise of discussing security when they announced your partner's verdict. Only moments after I arrived, Tabor got a message and left. As soon as she did, she locked me in and deactivated my account, so I couldn't warn anyone. It took me a while, but I eventually found footage of the Senior's conversation and plan, in Clear Seas suite. They'd intended for Clear Seas to zap them both and then use Marsee's psychosis as an excuse for their deaths, and then head to the Agency and take out the threat there, even knowing full well they might be executed later for doing so. Only Quinn's presence and the fact that Little Flower called them out on it, stopped it. Out of all the councilors, Clear Seas was the most vocal against you, your partner, and Little Flower's people, and he was the one to suggest editing the security footage."

Jer closed his eyes and took a deep breath to try and control the crushing pain of betrayal he felt, but it was Marcus that spoke first.

"We all figured that was what was happening when Little Flower was called back the second day, without Marsee," Marcus replied. "We just didn't know what to do to save any of them. That doesn't necessarily mean Clear Seas is behind this, but the comment on altering the footage is pretty damning in conjunction with the other evidence, even if it is circumstantial. Any chance you saved that footage?"

Kendra nodded. "Yes, sir."

"Good. Send that to us," Marcus replied.

"Why didn't you mention this before?" Jer asked.

Kendra frowned. "Councilor, I was prepared to commit treason. I figured that wouldn't go over well if you knew, even if it was to protect your people."

"I'm honestly surprised Tabor didn't have you arrested or at least demoted," Marcus replied.

"Honestly, so am I. Tabor showed up after they were done questioning your daughter and told me she knew what I had seen, and what I had planned in response, and informed me that they had changed their minds and voted in favor of Little Flower and her people. Once I confirmed that both Little Flower and the rest of her people were safe, we both agreed to drop it, and after that, Tabor stepped down and locked herself up, so I saw no reason to bring it up. I fully understand you may not trust me anymore and will step down if that's what you'd like."

Before either of them could answer though, their tablets dinged again. "Sammie's agreed on a vote of no confidence as well," Marcus stated after reading it.

"Good. Let's get going then," Jer said. "We're running out of time. Kendra, you were willing to risk everything to protect my daughter and people. That's good enough for me."

Marcus nodded his agreement and they left at a full run to Marcus's ship, so they could hop over to the ShipYard. Several guards were waiting for them by their ships, but the moment Marcus hit the switch, Kendra stopped them from entering and the guards swarmed the ship, checking it over. The moment they cleared it, Jer bolted for a seat and clipped into his harness. Marcus ordered the pilots to take off and Jer called Myra.

"Myra, we're on our way. Stay in the tower until you hear from me. I love you," he told her.

"I love you too, Jer. Be careful," she replied, and he hung up.

They landed a minute later and Jer bolted out of the ship before they even had clearance from the pilots.

Oscar was waiting for them. "This way, Councilors. The ship's not quite ready, but we're working on it."

"What's the delay?" Jer growled.

"It's an experimental ship, as we were just starting to test the smaller engines," Oscar replied. "There are only jump seats for the three pilots. We're fitting emergency harnesses now. We should be ready to take off in half an hour, but it's going to be a bumpy ride."

Jer growled at the delay, but there was little they could do without jump seats or harnesses for the takeoff. They were led over to a tiny ship, not much bigger than his old shuttle had been. People were swarming everywhere to prepare it for take-off. "We're waiting for Master Tech Lowell as well. Is she here yet?"

"I don't know," Oscar replied, and one of the guards bolted back towards the terminal to find out, before anyone could even order it.

A guard exited the ship carrying several items, and Kendra waved him over. "Councilors, I'm not sure if you're aware or not, but Avery is both my nephew and my protege. On my honor and my life, you can trust him and his squad."

Avery raised a brow at Kendra at those words, but nodded to her and them. "On my honor and life as well," Avery replied, and proceeded to strap some sort of tube device to Jer's harness. "This is a crash shield, just in case. This switch will activate it. Keep it on the entire flight. And this is a tracking beacon. If there's a problem, hit this switch and the guard will be able to find you anywhere on the planet. Normally I'd just clip it to your harness, but any of the guards would know what it is. Put it in your pouch."

Jer took the tiny device wishing Marsee had one on her right now, and stowed it, while Avery did the same with Marcus. A few minutes later, the guard returned with Lowell helping to carry a large case. He watched as Avery examined the case and contents, revealing a large jumble of tech and wires. Jer had no idea what any of it was, but apparently, Avery did, for most of it. What he didn't, he questioned Lowell. When the guard was satisfied, he loaded it onto the ship himself, and said something to the other guard, who disappeared again.

"I wasn't informed of the Tech's presence on the ship. I've had Aris head back for another crash shield and harness," Avery explained at Jer's questioning look. A few minutes later Aris returned again and outfitted Lowell, while Avery took the harness and disappeared onto the ship. It was all Jer could do not to pace while he waited, although he checked his tablet several times for updates, of which there were none.

Finally, the people installing the safety harnesses exited the ship, followed by Sampson. "We're ready to go, Councilors," Sampson replied, but like before, the guards swarmed the ship, checking it over before letting them on.

Jer climbed into the tiny ship and peered dubiously at the seats bolted to the outside wall of the ship.

"Have a seat, sir," Sampson motioned to the seat closest to the front. He sat on what was basically nothing more than a barely padded fold-out metal bar. Sampson clipped him in and made sure the harness was tight and secure, before doing the same with Marcus. The guards all seemed to know what to do. Avery was helping Lowell. Once everyone was situated, Sampson walked around handing everyone multiple bags to throw up into, and anti-nausea tablets.

"I don't get jump sick," Jer said, lifting a paw to stop Sampson.

"You will," Sampson replied. "Emergency jump is nothing like a regular jump."

Jer raised a brow but took the proffered items. He took one of the anti-nausea tablets and stowed the rest, tucking the bags under the straps of the harness as the guards were doing. Moments later, they were in the air. He'd never taken off while sitting sideways before though.

Avery instructed them how to hold onto the harness, and tuck their head, so that their arms protected their head and neck from the strain of the g-forces as they exited the planet. As soon as Avery indicated they were ready, Sampson punched them out of the atmosphere.

It was louder than Jer had ever experienced before and the harness dug deep into his skin. It lasted for far longer than he was used to too, and he realized that there weren't the normal anti-gravity systems in place to compensate, as they were suddenly floating in zero-g.

"Hold on to your stomach's people. We're jumping in three...two...one," Sampson said.

Jer had experienced jump at least a hundred times in his career, but this was completely different. The normal implosion of the universe and back was there, but rather than feeling like he was being compressed into nothing, it felt like he was being stretched apart and half of him left behind on Saber.

When his vision returned it took him a while to remember how to breathe. He looked down, half expecting that half of him would be missing. The normal rainbow of the universe was now sickly brown and green, and moments later he was fumbling for a bag as part of his stomach finally caught up with the rest of him. He wasn't the only one. Marcus and Lowell were already throwing up and the guards looked as green as the universe and were swallowing hard.

"Cursed eclipse, Jer. Remind me to never travel with you again," Marcus muttered at him, when he finally stopped throwing up. "I'm pretty sure half of me was left behind on Saber."

"No worries," Sampson called back from his seat. "It'll catch up when we get to the Water World."

"Oh, joy," Marcus muttered.

# CHAPTER 14

# Marsee: Declawed

Hours later Marsee was woken as something hit her in the face again.

"So tell me Little Kitten, have you decided what gift I should send your father to convince him I mean business?" her captor asked.

She turned her head and glared at him as she flicked her instinct on.

"What's the matter? You're shivering. Are you too afraid to answer me?" he taunted.

"I'm n not af fraid of you. I'm c c cold," she growled at him.

"Ahhh, well then. We can't have that. Let me help warm you up."

She heard a splash and tried to move away, but her shaking limbs wouldn't obey her fast enough. Suddenly pain exploded along her body again, and she screamed.

*Fight Back! He's on land and weak!*

She forced herself to try and move past the pain, but barely managed a weak swipe at the hand that held her, which he easily avoided.

*Give me control!* her instinct demanded and she did. She managed far better that time, but he caught her arm.

"Now, now, Little Kitten," he crooned.

Pain increased and her muscles locked. Even with her instincts help she was unable to move. Eventually the pain stopped as he dropped her. She lay there panting, unable to even lift her head or whimper.

"That wasn't very nice of you, Little Kitten." He shocked her again. "I'm only trying to help, unlike your father who hasn't even responded to my demands. I guess he doesn't love you as much as you thought he did."

Her tormentor began pulling her towards the edge of the shelf by her tail. She tried digging her claws into the rock to stop him, but he just yanked harder, making her yelp, and then shocked her again.

"It's quite the dilemma he's facing. Step down from the Senior Council and give up all his power and authority, or save you. So far he's choosing power over you. I wonder what he'll do when he realizes I follow through with my threats? Which does he love more, do you think? Power or his little kitten?"

He shocked her again. Eventually, he let go and she heard him splash back into the water.

She swore at him in three different languages, and pulled herself back up into a crouch the moment she could make her muscles move again.

"You're a feisty one, I'll give you that," he said a moment later.

She leapt but he easily moved out the way, and she landed in the water with a cold splash. She tried swiping at him anyway, but he easily avoided her.

"Now, look what you've gone and done. You've wasted all my hard effort to warm you up. What a naughty little kitten." He snuck up behind her, grabbed her by the scruff, zapped her, and threw her back on the ledge as if she weighed nothing. She hit hard and felt something give in her previously injured shoulder and it throbbed. She pulled herself slowly up and tested her shoulder.

"Oh, I'm sorry. Was that a little too hard? I thought for sure you'd land on your feet."

She swiped at him again, but she missed and he grabbed her arm again, jolted her again with enough electricity to make her legs buckle out from under her. "Ahh I see. So, that's your answer then, Little Kitten?"

He pulled her forward, continuing to jolt her with electricity. She tried pulling away and swiping at him again with her other paw but her body wouldn't respond. Suddenly something slammed down on her outstretched paw and she screamed with pain as she felt several bones snap and break, unable to do anything about it. But nothing compared to the agony she felt as one of her claws was ripped from her body with a twisting, sickening pop.

"I do so love the way you scream. It has such an intoxicating melody," he purred, grabbed her by her scruff and pulled her closer, and then shifted his grip to grab both of her sides again.

She heard an odd rhythmic thumping, and for what felt like forever, he continued to jolt her with bursts of electricity along her sides that made her writhe and scream in agony, unable to move or do anything to make him stop.

He continued to taunt her, saying Little Kitten every time he shocked her, and eventually, she couldn't even tell if he was shocking her or not when he said that phrase.

She cried for hours, long after he'd left. Limping away from the waters edge as far as she could go, she shook what water she could off of her fur, curled back into her protective ball, and licked at her throbbing paw, trying to make it stop hurting and bleeding. Eventually it stopped bleeding, but the pain never receded. She lay there shivering, wondering whether her father or anyone was ever going to find her, and if he was even looking for her? Was her tormentor right? Had her father chosen power over her, or was he just trying to scare her more? Her father had always chosen the people over her in the past.

*Maybe I should just jump in the water and get it over with,* she thought.

**If you give up, he wins,** her instinct replied.

She looked up because the voice hadn't come from within her head, it was in front of her, and she blinked. There standing in front of her was the mental image she'd always had of her instinct, glowing in the absolute darkness around her. "I'm losing my mind," she muttered.

**Maybe,** it replied. **Or maybe you're finally finding it. He was weaker this time. We were able to fight back. Next time we'll have him.**

"How? My paw is broken, and quite likely my shoulder too. I'm missing a claw, and even if I do somehow manage to beat him, how am I ever going to get out of here?" she asked, wallowing in her pain and misery, not even remotely caring that she was speaking to a hallucination. It was better than being alone in the dark.

*Honestly, we'll probably die here, but if we're going to save our family, he needs to die here too. Now stand up and start moving. If you lay there, you're going to freeze to death before he returns. And while you're at it, find whatever it was he threw at you and eat it. You need the calories. It will help us stay warm.*

Her instinct had a point, so she heaved herself on to three feet, too exhausted to pull herself up to a full standing position and started slowly limping along the ledge, following the wall. When she felt water, she turned and walked back, this time a body length away. Eventually she found the slimy creature her captor had thrown at her, and collapsed to the ground beside it and started eating. It was the most revolting thing she'd ever eaten, but she ate every last bit of it, bones and all, and hobbled over to the water to rinse the horrible taste out of her mouth.

*Drink, our body can process the salt,* her instinct told her, so she shrugged and drank deeply. It was vile but she was thirsty, and it was better than whatever it was she'd just eaten.

*Good, now keep walking.* She walked for what felt like hours, her instinct telling her everything it had noticed about their enemy, until she collapsed from exhaustion, asleep before her body hit the ground.

She didn't wake again until the water lapped against her injured paw. *Dark moons, not again!* she whimpered. *I'll never make it.*

Still, she moved to the highest spot on the ledge, waiting for the water to rise, and dozed for as long as she could. Eventually she had to start swimming again, but this time was far worse. The creatures appeared to be attracted to her injured paw, as there were far more swimming around her, so she had to keep that one out of the water, but holding on to the wall caused her to whimper in agony.

Still, on the off chance they could make progress with the air hole, she swam over and the moment she could reach, started digging. A small piece of rock broke free and for a moment she cheered as tiny shaft of light came in, but as her eyes adjusted, she could see that there was no way she could dig her way out. The tiny tunnel was too long and far too narrow.

Still, she floated there, gazing up at that tiny pinprick of light for as long as she could. She was so exhausted, it was all she could do to stay awake. Every time she started to drift off, she sank below the water and woke with a start, coughing and gasping from the water she'd inhaled.

*Give me full control,* her instinct demanded, and she did, not even hesitating. The pain receded to a dull ache, and she half dozed while her instinct kept her afloat. Eventually the water receded again and her instinct brought her back to the ledge and forced her to walk until she was dried off.

She tried to make it let go and let her sleep before then, but she was too weak to fight back.

*Sleep now, I will guard you,* it said when she was finally dry.

She was asleep before her body hit the stone.

<div style="text-align:center">~~~~~</div>

She had no idea how long she slept, but when she woke, she woke to darkness again, her instinct off and the tiny beacon of light gone. She limped over to the water and drank, and noticed that her mental image improved as she walked or lapped up the water. *This must be what Little Flower meant by echo location, and what the night flyer used. How odd.*

She started walking again to loosen her stiff muscles and wait for her tormentor to return, but she was exhausted and weak, and eventually curled up to conserve her energy and lay there, tapping regularly with a claw, wondering if she was really seeing things or just imagining it, and wondering how she was seeing with her instinct off. She flicked it on to confirm it had really been off, and the cave around her brightened even more, lit up with each tap and the faint colors of scent from the crawlies on the walls and ceiling. She sighed with relief. Even if it was imagined light, it was better than nothing.

When he returned, she was ready.

*Don't give away that you can see him and go for his throat. You'll only have one chance, so make it work.*

"Hello, Little Kitten. I trust you slept well?" he purred.

She flinched but didn't answer, instead she gave herself over to her instinct and kept tapping.

"What? Not even a hello for an old friend? And here I brought you something to eat."

He flung something at them, and they deliberately let it hit them.

"While you dine, I thought you might like to know that your father still hasn't responded. I guess he didn't care for you all that much after all. Pity. I might just have to change my plans. I was looking forward to watching you kill him."

*Distract him.*

"You lie. My father is probably already on his way here, and when he gets here he'll tear you to shreds, if I don't get to you first," she growled. She kept tapping and watched as the bright blob her instinct saw shifted and started climbing onto the ledge.

*Wait until he's fully out of the water.*

"Who knows, maybe he is, but it'll take, what, seven of our days for him to arrive. Do you think you can live that long? Do you honestly think your father expects to find you alive? No, he'll keep his power and bury you. Sad really, but I imagine the funeral for the beloved Translator and the Senior Guild Master will be one for the history books."

*Now!* her instinct roared. She exploded forward, claws and teeth outstretched, but the moment she leapt her vision vanished, and she didn't see him roll away. Pain spasmed throughout her body and she screamed as he grabbed her and threw her to the ground again. She tried to fight back but he grabbed her injured paw and squeezed, pinning her in place by applying pressure. She felt something else snap in her paw, and she screamed even louder.

"So what will it be, Little Kitten? Another claw or perhaps something more distinctive like these beautiful ears?" He lightly touched her ear and she screamed even louder. It felt like he was burning her ear off. "Ahhh...No? Well then, I guess we'll just go with another claw and save that ear for tomorrow. He held her, jolting her with electricity for what felt like another eternity, before finally stopping.

"Are you still you in there?" he asked, tapping on her head.

"Even if I do succumb to psychosis, I'll still be far less of a psychopath than you," she growled at him through clenched teeth, when she recovered enough to speak. The rest of her body was still spasming from the electricity.

He snorted with laughter. "You might be right, but I do so love a challenge. I wonder what the Consortium will think when their beloved Translator turns into nothing but a wild animal, and they all find out about your disease. Not only will your family be destroyed, but if all goes well, your entire species too."

The moment she started breathing normally again, he resumed shocking her. With each shock he told her another new and horrifying idea of what he planned to do with her once she lost herself to her psychosis, mixed in with all the ways her father was and had chosen power over her.

There was nothing she could do to fight back. She tried giving herself over entirely to her instinct, but even then they couldn't do more than a feeble swipe. If she dared to fight back, the intensity of the shock increased to where she couldn't even breathe. Eventually, she just hid in the corner of her mind, doing her best to endure the pain, until she finally passed out.

She didn't even wake as he pulled out another of her claws.

"Sleep well, Little Kitten," he said, as he patted her on her head, and gave her one final jolt before sliding off the ledge and into the sea.

# CHAPTER 15

# Myra: Prayers

Myra set her tablet down, praying that Jer would be safe and that they would find Marsee before it was too late, wishing there was something she could do to help. As exhausted as she was, she forced herself to stay awake to protect her family. She sent a message to her other children, asking them to check in regularly, and then stood to pace, unable to sit still any longer. Every noise outside of the tower made her ears twitch.

"Myra, you need to get some sleep," GrandFather said, after getting her attention.

She was practically asleep on her feet, but she didn't dare go to sleep. She shook her head. "I'm sorry. I didn't mean to wake you, but I'm not leaving you unprotected," she signed back.

"How are you going to protect us, if you can't even stay awake?" he asked. "Go to bed. At least for a few hours. I'll watch them."

*He has a point,* she realized. "Do not leave the tower," she ordered and left, waiting until she could hear the sound of the lock close behind her. She didn't return to her room right away though. Instead, she climbed the tower to Marsee's room. She hadn't been up here in months, not since before Hope was born. She walked over to Marsee's hanging bed and grabbed the stuffy she'd had since she was a small cub and sniffed deeply. It smelled of Marsee, and she shook with barely controlled fear. Her instinct wanted to act, but even her instinct didn't know what to do to save Marsee. With a heavy sigh, she turned to walk out of the room, but stopped as she saw the painting on the wall.

With a gasp, she walked over and examined it closer. Light flickered on, causing the creatures in the frame to dance and sparkle in a rainbow of colors. The painting was Little Flowers. That was obvious by her signature, but she wondered who made the frame.

*Did Marsee do this?* Marsee had done some carving in the past, and was talented, but she'd never done anything like this before. She'd never had the patience to complete more than small pieces prior to gaining control of her instinct. Myra ran her paw over the frame. *She must have. There's no way she could have afforded a masterpiece like this. The wood alone would have cost her a year's credits, if not more.*

Everyone knew rainbow wood was ridiculously expensive. It was difficult to work with as it came all the way from the Ice Planet, where they had few natural resources to ship off the planet. To even have access to rainbow wood as a journeyman was surprising. *I wonder if she asked Ellie for it.*

She wandered around the room, stopping to look at some of the other pictures Little Flower had done, most of which centered heavily on Marsee, and a number of other sculptures and crafts that Marsee had done throughout her childhood. When she made it to her daughter's desk, she found a sketchbook lying out on the desk. Thinking it was for one of the translations she was working on, Myra flipped it open, curious, and gasped at what she found.

*These are beautiful, vibrant,* Myra thought as she flipped through the pages, but then frowned as she realized what she was seeing. *Marsee's painting with her instinct on?* She frowned with worry and confusion as she wondered what that would mean for Marsee. To keep her instinct on and in control long enough to paint these said her control was solid, but the more you used your instinct, the greater the risk of loosing control later.

The drawings were stunning, far better than anything Marsee had ever drawn before, and she saw no hint of Marsee seeing anything as a predator. The last page was one of Hope, curled up next to Little Flower sleeping. The love Marsee felt for the two radiated off of the page. There was little sign of Little Flower's illness in the drawing either, and judging by the length of Little Flower's hair and Hope's size, Marsee had drawn it right before leaving for the water world.

Worried someone might find the book and unsure of what this meant for her daughter, she knew she needed to talk to Jer about it, assuming Marsee was found alive. She returned to her own room, sketchbook and stuffy in hand, but as exhausted as she was, she couldn't fall asleep. She eventually gave up, deciding she needed a sedative. Her fear was far too strong to allow her to sleep. She climbed the ramp again and knocked, but no one answered, so she peered in the window and found GrandFather had fallen back to sleep. She watched them sleep for a while, worn out from their ordeal earlier, and made her way back down to her room.

She called Ammond, asking him to bring something over and they spent a long time talking about everything that had happened. He agreed to check on them and bring them their evening meal, and left after giving her a long hug. She sent GrandFather a message, telling him which sedative she'd used, knowing he'd know what to do to wake her if he needed her, and considered locking her door, but decided that he'd need a way to get in to wake her if he did need her.

*Whoever is behind this is after Jer anyway, not me,* she thought, and gave one final prayer to the Ancient Gods to protect her family, as she administered the sedative. The hypo clattered to the floor, unnoticed, as she fell instantly asleep.

# CHAPTER 16

# Quinn: Desert Hike

Quinn sat at the controls of the ground crawler, as the last hint of dusk vanished, wishing the crawler could go faster. They still had several hours to go before they were supposed to ditch it and go out on foot. *You'd think after a century of being a guard, I'd be used to waiting,* he thought. But he had a bad feeling, and his gut was rarely wrong. Something was going to happen in New Hope, he just knew it. That Marsee was missing was bad, really bad, and not just because of her psychosis, or the fact that she was the daughter and niece of two Senior councilors, and the protege of the Senior Guild Master.

"Quinn...Do you think this is..." Hallie started. "I mean...Marsee...the prophecy. Is this the start of the war?"

Quinn didn't answer right away. He'd always been skeptical about the prophecy, told around campfires and at night during training missions, right up until the day Kendra had shared the information she had, handed down from one Senior Honor Guard to the next, since long before the Great Awakening. He'd been watching Marsee since she was a tiny cub staying in the council nursery, and it certainly seemed like it. But if it was, they were in for a world of hurt, and six guards didn't stand a chance against what was coming, especially if Marsee died.

"I don't know," he said finally. "But we should treat this like it is. What I do know is that the people of New Hope are in danger, not just Chenzira's family. The Hue-mans are far too vulnerable, and it wouldn't take much to wipe out the entire species, especially if there are guards involved. The Water Sprite ships are all equipped with stunners to defend against the Leviathans. They'd be more than strong enough to kill the Hue-mans, and it wouldn't take much to take out New Hope entirely."

Hallie was silent again, but Quinn's thoughts now focused on the prophecy, which very clearly called out the Ice Giants, not the Water Sprites, but ten thousand years left a lot of time for things to get muddied. He was just about to pull the shuttle over for a pee break when it suddenly pitched forward and came to a complete stop. He was thrown hard against his harness as alarms started blaring.

"What's going on Quinn?" Hallie asked.

"I don't know yet," Quinn replied. He shut down the crawler and unclipped from his harness. "Is anyone hurt?"

"No sir," everyone replied.

Quinn unclipped his flashlight and hit the switch to the door. Jumping down, he turned and looked at the front of the crawler and swore.

"We're stuck," Quinn called back. "Everyone out and start digging," As the rest of his squad piled out, he walked over to examine the crawler closer. The front right track had sunk into the sand, right up to the floor of the crawler. He walked around to the other side to see if he could peer under, dropped down onto all fours, and swore again. "Never mind. The axel's broken. We're going to have to go on foot from here," Quinn replied.

"We're not even halfway there yet," Hallie replied. "It'll take all day to get there, at least."

"Yup," Quinn replied. "That it will." He unclipped his tablet, but as expected there was no signal. He considered hitting his emergency beacon, but decided against it, knowing that could give away their position and put Marsee and the others at further risk. "Get ready. We're moving out in five," he ordered, and moved away from the crawler, dug a hole, peed, and covered it back up, before jumping back in the crawler and grabbing his gear. The others were doing the same.

He was ready before the rest, and took a few minutes to examine the maps. They could cover terrain on foot that the crawler couldn't, but much of this area was unexplored and uninhabited. They might be able to cut several hours off of their journey by taking a different route, but that was riskier as it cut straight through the uncharted wilds and not the normal paths the locals used. His gut was screaming that time was of the essence, so he decided to risk it, and plugged in the course he wanted to take and picked out the first landmark in the distance.

Clipping his tablet to his harness, he adjusted his pack for travel on all fours. That done, he turned and looked back to the rest to make sure they were ready. The moment the others indicated they were, he took off in a ground covering lope, praying they would make it in time, and hoping that the thin slivers of the new moons was not the bad omen it portended.

# CHAPTER 17

# GrandFather: Skin Deep

James's tablet ran with an incoming call and he jerked awake. Fumbling to answer it, he saw it was from Henry, and he grinned.

"I just heard the news. How y'all doing?" Henry asked.

James sighed. "Let's just say I'd rather be stung than ingest sand spinner venom. My stomach feels like it's been eaten from the inside out, but I'm better. Thanks for checking in."

Henry frowned. "So, no idea who's behind this?"

"I have my suspicions, but no evidence," James replied. "I know I should be off investigating as Acting Senior, but Myra's still sleeping. She's been awake for days, and I'm not leaving Jessica alone."

"Why didn't Chenzira call in the Guard?" Henry asked.

James frowned, as that thought hadn't crossed his mind before. Granted, he'd been half out of it all day. "I'm not sure, but I'm guessing because there are guards missing too. They don't know if they're involved or not. He doesn't know who to trust. He didn't say anything before he took off, but then I've never seen him so out of sorts."

"Well if I've learned anything about their history, they've never had to deal with anything like this before," Henry replied.

"True," James said, and looked at the time. Jer would still be on his way to the Water World. "Are you still planning on going out tomorrow morning?"

"The weather looks like it's going to hold, but I don't really want to go out while everything's a mess," Henry replied.

"You should still go. It would do Buster some good, and I'm probably going to miss my shift and lesson tomorrow anyway."

"You sure?" Henry asked, his face lighting up.

"Henry, I know that look. You're just as horse crazy as my granddaughter. Thank you for at least asking about me first. That's better than Jessica ever did. I always rated third on hugs when Jessica visited our home. Buster first, then Ben, and then me. Enjoy your ride. Let me know when you're back though. If you wouldn't mind."

"Of course and thank you. Do you need anything?"

"Nah, Ammond came by a few hours ago, and I expect Myra will bring something when she wakes up, but thanks for asking," James replied.

Henry nodded and hung up.

James smiled wistfully at Henry's enthusiasm, wishing it was directed towards him instead, and then flipped open the news, scanning for any new information about Marsee or Ellie, but nothing new had come in since the last time he checked. Sighing, he checked on Hope, changed her diaper, and watched her and Jessica sleep for a while, before laying back down again. He hadn't been lying, whatever was in that venom had done a number on him and he felt miserable. He was asleep again, almost immediately.

~~~~~

The next morning, something woke James well before dawn. Thankfully feeling significantly better than the day before, he peered outside but didn't see anything. He briefly checked his messages for something from Jer, but didn't see anything there either, and set his tablet down again, not wanting to wake Hope or Little Flower with the light.

He stood at the window looking out for a while. He didn't like sitting around just waiting and hiding. He was a man of action, and he had his suspicions about who had poisoned them. He just had no idea how they were involved in what was going on with Marsee and the Senior Guild Master though, or how to prove it, and he didn't have
~~~~~

the authority to lock anyone up without any proof, like Jer did, and he doubted bringing them in for questioning would do any good either.

He'd seen how angry the other councilors had been when Jer was nominated, and both Jer and Ellie had a significant amount of power, as would Marsee in the future. *If this had been on Earth, my money would be betting this was a coup. The real question is who's behind it.* He'd spent much of his time with all of the Senior Councilors at the last Full Council Meeting, and his gut had said they were all people who could be trusted. His gut was rarely wrong. Being in two minority groups meant he had a lifetime of training at learning who he could and couldn't trust. His life depended on getting that right. His bet was that one of the other high ranking councilors from the Water World was behind this. He didn't know the others nearly as well, but there had been a few that had made him uncomfortable. At the time, he'd chalked it up to unfamiliarity with the species, and their still limited knowledge of sign language.

His stomach rumbled in hunger and he frowned. It was too early yet for the cafeteria to be open, and they'd eaten everything Ammond had brought over the night before. He thought about calling the healer for another meal, but Ammond had been awake almost as long as Myra had been, caring for his granddaughter. Myra had sent him a text stating that she was going to take a sedative to help her sleep, but he'd expected her to be up here hours ago, and he was starting to worry, although as exhausted as she'd been, he wouldn't be surprised if she was still sleeping. He looked at the ancient door to the tower room and frowned. It could only be locked from the inside and if he left to find something to eat or check on Myra, it would mean the door would have to remain unlocked. His granddaughter wouldn't be able to climb the chair he'd had to drag over to lock it after Myra left, or have the strength to turn the ancient wheel. It had taken everything he had to lock it himself.

Someone had already tried to kill them once, although whether they were the target, or if it had just been Jer they were trying to kill, he didn't know. Did he dare leave Little Flower and Hope unprotected for the few minutes it would take? He looked outside again. It was still very early. If he hurried, he could check on Myra, grab something from the kitchen, and be back in under ten minutes.

Deciding, he walked over and gently woke Little Flower up. "Hey, sweetheart. I'm going to go check on your mother, and find us something for breakfast. Will you be okay here by yourself for a few minutes?" She nodded and asked him to lower the bed, which he did, and then quickly unlocked the door, shut it, and made his way down to the room below. He found Myra's door unlocked, which he'd expected, and quietly entered and walked over to the bed where she was sleeping. He tried shaking her awake.

"Myra, wake up," he called out, but she didn't respond. He checked the hypo that was sitting on the table beside the bed and frowned. It looked like she'd taken another dose in the middle of the night according to the dosage and timestamp on the hypo. If so, it'd be another hour or two before she'd wake up without an anti-sedative. He considered going back upstairs and grabbing one out of the supply cabinet, but decided she probably needed her sleep more, and an hour or two wouldn't make much difference. He didn't have anything to tell her anyway, and she'd just worry. *She needs the sleep,* he decided. He quickly left, shutting her door behind him, and jogged down to the kitchen.

Jordan was already there along with several of the early crew prepping for breakfast. She saw him and stopped what she was doing to come over and greet him. "GrandFather, how are you feeling?"

"Much better, thanks. I need to pick up a meal for Myra, Little Flower, Hope, and I," he stated.

"We're still preparing the hot dishes, but grab a tray and take whatever you want out of the cooler," she stated, and so he did, grabbing a large thermos of juice, several pre-made bowls of fruit, and a small dish of butter. On his way out he grabbed a loaf of freshly baked bread off of one of the trays. They had utensils back in the room so he didn't bother grabbing any. Thanking Jordan on the way back out, he walked quickly to the room and shoved the heavy door open, walked over, and set it down on the table next to Little Flower's bed.

"Hope you're hungry," he told her. "They had your favorites this morning."

"Why, yes, I am," came a male voice behind him.

He spun around to find Damon Minor leaning up against the doorway. James frowned and placed himself between Damon and his daughter. "What are you doing here, Damon?" There was only one reason Damon would be here this early, and it wasn't for breakfast.

"Is that any way to treat a friend? And here I thought you were inviting me to breakfast," Damon said as he pushed off the doorway and walked into the room, heading for Hope's crib.

James ran over to block him, hands up. "You need to leave, Damon. Now."

"Oh I don't think so. Your furry little guardians are away, although it certainly did take you an awfully long time to leave the room. I've been waiting for hours," Damon said, and before James knew what was happening, Damon had grabbed his shirt and placed a knife against his neck. James lifted his hands in surrender, waiting for an opportunity to strike back. This wasn't the first time someone had threatened him with a weapon.

"Why are you doing this, Damon?" James asked.

"Why? Isn't it obvious? To try and stop you and your little harem of cats from destroying my life," Damon replied.

Before James could answer, Hope woke and started crying. Damon looked over and James struck, simultaneously aiming to punch Damon in the throat while trying to block and gain control of the knife. Damon saw the motion and shifted out of the way of his punch, but James managed to block the knife arm enough to get away and not have his neck sliced open.

Damon followed with a swipe to James's midsection and he tried to move out of the way again, but he wasn't quite fast enough and he felt the knife cut him. It stung but he didn't stop to see how bad, and tried to rush Damon and grab the knife before it could return.

Damon shifted and redirected James's energy, and he found himself being tossed through the air into Hope's playpen. The wood shattered painfully around him. Before he could regain his feet, Damon kicked him hard in the side, and James curled up into a ball to protect his head and sides from the next kick, but it didn't come.

"No! Leave her alone!" Little Flower yelled.

James struggled to his feet to find Damon holding a screaming Hope with the knife held tight to her neck. His granddaughter was struggling to her feet to try and save her daughter.

"If either one of you moves, she dies," Damon hissed. They both froze.

"Please Damon, let her go. She's done nothing to you," James begged.

"No, I don't think so. No, what's going to happen is you're going to slowly walk over to your granddaughter and carry her down the ramp and outside, where you'll find a crawler waiting, and if you see anyone you're going to pretend like nothing's wrong."

"Damon, please. Leave Little Flower and Hope out of this. I'll go with you," James said.

"The only way they're staying here is if they're dead. It's your choice," Damon sneered.

James swallowed hard, nodded, and slowly walked over to Little Flower and picked her up.

"Whatever happens, save Hope first," she whispered in his ear.

He nodded ever so slightly, and proceeded to walk out the door and down the ramp, praying that Myra had woken with the sound of the crash, but her door never opened. He continued on outside without seeing another person. The crawler Damon had mentioned was some distance off, and he shifted Little Flower in his arms and kept walking. His stomach stung with the weight of her against his wound but he ignored it, trying desperately to figure out what to do.

Damon jumped up and slapped the door switch on the crawler. "Put her in the seat in the back and strap her in, then do the same for yourself," he ordered.

James did as he was ordered and watched as Damon shut the door and placed Hope in the front seat and picked up a rope.

"Hands behind the seat. If you try anything, I'll kill you."

"Damon, please don't do this," James said, as Damon tied the ropes so tightly that he was worried he'd lose circulation in his hands.

"Shut up," Damon said.

"When they catch you, this won't end well for you."

"I said, shut up!" Damon replied, and hit him multiple times in the face, breaking his nose, with a loud, painful crunch.

"Stop, please!" Little Flower called out.

"Shut up or I'll do the same to you," he signed back, and then slapped her hard against the side of her face.

"Please, leave her alone," James begged. "She just had surgery!"

Damon turned and hit him again so hard he was knocked unconscious.

~~~~~

Little Flower cried out again as her Grandfather slumped in his seat. Damon turned towards her and raised his hand again. She ducked and cowered as best she could, and to her relief, he didn't hit her.

"Hands behind the seat," he growled.

She did as ordered and once she was tied up, he buckled Hope into one of the front seats, and then climbed into the driver's seat and buckled himself in. He quickly plotted a course and the crawler took off. Silent tears started streaming down her face as she looked out her window and watched as they drove away, unseen and unfollowed, wondering if she'd ever see her home again.

For a few brief minutes after she'd woken from surgery, she'd begun to live again, after the past two months of depression, the loss of that brief euphoria was nearly as crushing as her fear over her family's safety. While better than she had been, she was still useless and unable to do anything to protect her family or herself.

Damon drove for several hours, only stopping once to open the door and pee.

"I need to go too," she said.

"Pee in the seat," he muttered.

"I can but then you'll have to smell it," she replied. "And what will your friends say if you damage their crawler?"
~~~~~

He grunted but apparently that was enough to convince him. He walked over and looked at her. "Try anything and I'll kill you. They don't care if you're dead or alive."

She just snorted at him. "Damon, I couldn't walk out of this shuttle on my own if I tried. I just woke from brain surgery yesterday and I really don't feel good."

He grunted again, but untied her and carried her out. She didn't try anything. Realistically there wasn't anything she could do. If he left her here, she'd be as good as dead anyway. Plus, she hadn't been lying. Her head had started to throb and her vision was blurry, telling her there was something very wrong with her. She fell the moment he set her down, and he roughly picked her back up. She was thankfully wearing a dress so she just spread her legs and let the pee go, hoping it would splash on him. She glared at him the entire time, and he at least had the decency to look embarrassed.

When she was done, he lifted her back up and threw her roughly over his shoulder. She nearly panicked, and it was all she could do to keep from screaming as the motion triggered another flashback of her rape. He set her roughly back in her chair, and it jarred her head making her wince, but he didn't seem to notice or care, and simply tied her back up again.

GrandFather hadn't woken the entire time and the front of his shirt was soaked with blood. He was still breathing, so she knew he was still alive, but she was very worried about him. They eventually stopped and Damon hopped out for a while. She tried wiggling loose but he'd tied her too securely, and he returned before she'd made any progress. Hope had woken and cried multiple times throughout the journey, and Damon had picked her up and tried to calm her. She could smell that her daughter needed changing, and he clearly knew it too, but there weren't any supplies in the ground crawler to change her with.

They waited there for several hours before Damon stood up, kicked one of the seats, and stormed outside.

*Whoever they were waiting for was late,* she thought as dizziness and fatigue threatened to pull her under.

# CHAPTER 18

# Marsee: Lost Hope

Marsee woke slowly and in so much pain she couldn't think. Her paw throbbed and she could smell fresh blood on it. Carefully licking the blood away, she whimpered when she realized she was missing another claw. *I can't do this anymore,* she thought and picked herself unsteadily to her feet, and started walking towards the water, to end it.

***If we don't fight, our cub dies,*** her instinct said beside her, its glowing illusion the only comfort she had.

She was honestly surprised it wasn't physically stopping her. Suicide was rare for her people because the moment they tried, their instinct would stop them, and prevent them from moving.

Her instinct looked at her with love. ***I would not make us suffer but if we're going to die anyway, we should kill him first.***

"I don't have anything left to fight with," she said, but stopped at the edge of the water and flopped down to drink, as her thoughts turned to Hope, knowing she would never see her cub again. She shook her head. *Little Flower's cub,* she reminded herself. Her thoughts were slow and muddled, and it was getting harder to separate her own thoughts from her instincts, but she didn't try shutting it off, unwilling to face her captivity alone.

***Little Flower may have given birth to her, but you've cared for her the most. She's your cub. Protect her. Protect your sister. He***

*needs to die. It's the only way. We can do this. We're still alive, and as long as we're alive there's still a chance we can kill him.*

"For how long? I'm so cold, and I hurt so much." Her voice sounded weak and tired even to her.

Her instinct merged with her again and took control without asking. She didn't even try to fight it. The pain lessened instantly and they began to hop on three feet, trying to warm up, but even her instinct was having a hard time making their body move. Their body was shutting down and they knew it. They walked for hours, while she hid in the corner of her mind, curled up in a tiny ball until her instinct could no longer make them move and they collapsed exhausted to the stone.

"This is it, isn't it?" she asked her instinct, which was once again beside her.

*No, we just need rest,* it replied and curled protectively around her, offering the illusion of warmth and comfort. But they both knew it was lying. *Sleep,* it whispered. *I will protect us.*

Marsee sighed and closed her eyes, knowing she would never wake again. With a sense of relief, she allowed herself to go and gave up her body entirely to her instinct, even that last little bit that was her. She no longer had the will to fight, neither him or her instinct, and felt herself slide down into a deep abyss, where the pain and fear couldn't reach. She had once feared this darkness, but now welcomed it.

Her last hope was that her instinct might be able to do what she couldn't and prayed that he would return next, and not someone she cared about, because she knew her instinct would do everything in its power to kill whoever they were, or die trying.

# CHAPTER 19

# Change of Plans

He floated off in the distance watching his feisty little kitten sleep, curled up in a tiny ball on the ledge. His plans were going well. Word had just come in that the Little Rodent was caught in his trap, and would soon be dead. His spies had informed him that King Pussy Cat and his little brother had jumped, which gave him several days to play with their little princess, and put a few more plans into action. By the time the week was over, the entire Senior Council would be his, but for now, he had time to play.

"Hello, Little Kitten," he called out.

Marsee didn't move, so he threw the breakfast he'd brought for her, hitting her square in the face. She still didn't move, didn't even flinch.

Frowning, he swam closer and confirmed that she was still breathing, not that it really mattered, but he was having so much fun playing with his latest toy, and was hoping to get a few more days at least. She lasted much longer than his other toys before passing out, and he just loved how she screamed. It had such a beautiful pitch and cadence to it. He grinned at the memory.

Cautiously, fully expecting another attack, he climbed out of the water and started to crawl over. As expected, she exploded the moment he was on the ledge. He rolled out of the way and zapped her, sending her flying into the water with a yip.

He dropped back in the water, swam over, and grabbed her by the scruff, pouring electricity into her before she could recover and attack him again. He had to give her credit though, she was at least trying to fight through the pain, which no one else had ever managed before, but he frowned as she didn't scream. He changed the output slightly, not enough to kill her, but close, but she still didn't scream, and still managed to fight, actually managing to scratch him. He threw her back up on the ledge with disgust, before she could get a better grip on him.

"Is that any way to greet your old friend, little kitten?" he asked as he checked his scratch to make sure it wasn't deep or obvious what had happened. *Not even deep enough to bleed,* he thought, dismissing it.

She didn't respond, but eventually climbed back to her feet and turned to face him with a growl, and began pacing on the small ledge.

*Her growl is almost as lovely as her screams,* he thought, and sighed with pleasure as he watched, wondering just how far gone she was. *That little tidbit about her species certainly was informative. Once the rest of the Consortium finds out the pussycats are one bad day away from turning feral, they'll be kicked out immediately. The question is, when and where do I unleash her? I don't think she's going to make it until her father arrives. I suppose I could move her, but that would be risky.*

He'd been trying to decide for hours. Several thoughts raced through his head before he settled on one. *Yes, that will do nicely and get rid of another target at the same time.*

"I thought you might like to know, I've received word that the rodent you call your sister should be dead in an hour or two," he called out.

Marsee growled and hissed in response.

"What? Nothing to say?" he asked. "I could pass a message on to her before she dies if you'd like. I'm not a complete monster after all. Just say the word."

Marsee said nothing, just continued to growl and pace.

"Is that a no then? So be it. Your father still hasn't responded to my demands. I guess we know the answer to that question too."

More growling. She paced for a minute but then tripped over the fish he'd brought, leaned down to sniff at it, picked it up in her mouth, and carried it as far away from the edge of the water as possible, growling and protecting it just like any wild animal with their prey, and began eating, intermingled with growls in his direction.

When she was done eating, he grinned. "Did you enjoy your meal?" he asked.

She hissed at him.

He remained quiet and after a few minutes she seemed to forget him and began licking at her mangled paw. He remained silent, curious what she would do and watched as she continued grooming herself with her tongue, something he knew the pussycats didn't do because they felt it was uncivilized.

*That didn't take very long,* he thought. *I was hoping you'd stick around a few more days at least. Oh well, it was fun while it lasted.*

"Rest well, Little Kitten, I've got another errand to run, but I'll be back shortly, and when I do, you and I are going to have a very educational field trip to the Council Platform Primary School."

She pinned her ears and hissed in his direction before resuming her grooming.

He chuckled and swam off.

# CHAPTER 20

# Quinn: Unexpected Prey

Quinn's squad had been traveling for hours and had just skirted a small section of forest. While this part of the world was nothing but sandy desert most of the year, there were other trees that had adapted to the intense summer heat besides the giant bandalas. The ghost trees were one such adaptation. Rather than sending roots down into underground aquifers, they hibernated for half of their year, losing all of their leaves until the rains came each spring. Long spiky thorns kept most of the larger predators away, but provided coverage from the sun for the smaller creatures. They were transitioning from summer into high summer, and it had been a rainy enough spring that the trees still had most of the leaves that gave the ghost woods their name, a translucent lavender that was nearly grey matched the bark and made the trees look like all color had been leached out of them. While it would have provided cover from the sun, going through the woods and avoiding the thorns would have been far too slow, so he'd chosen to go around. It added to the leagues they needed to travel, but would ultimately get them there quicker.

Thankfully the morning had been cool and overcast allowing them to travel quickly, but they weren't even halfway to New Hope. Even with all his training, he was exhausted, but neither he or the rest of his squad complained. Lives depended on them. Deciding they needed a break, he led them over to the nearest bandala.

"One hour," he told everyone and proceeded to break off one of the roots to refill his canteen. After a long drink, he shrugged off his pack and flopped down to begin stretching and cool down exercises, as did the others.

When that was done, he set an alarm, on the off chance he actually fell asleep, and closed his eyes. Over a century of training allowed him to half doze while still remaining alert for sounds. This far out in the middle of nowhere, crawlies and other predators were a major risk, so he kept his ears focused on every sound, but tuned out the sounds of his squad settling down to nap. As he did, he slowed his breathing and allowed his body to relax.

Half an hour into their rest, he heard a sound he wasn't expecting to hear. Opening his eyes and sitting up, as he noticed the others were doing, he watched as a small interplanetary ship appeared over the horizon, flying far too low, heading deeper into the Wilds, but then it stopped, hovered for a bit, and landed just over a distant hill, between them and the ghost woods they'd just passed.

"I thought all shuttle and ship traffic was grounded," Hallie said.

"It is," Quinn replied and considered. The ship was in the opposite direction of where they were heading and it would probably take them an hour to get back there, but if the markings on the ship were any indication, it was an Ice Giant ship. That species couldn't handle the heat of this part of the world for very long, even on a cool day like today. "There's absolutely no reason for them to be out here either. Come on. We're going to investigate. If there's a problem, they'll need help, and if not, then they're up to no good." His gut, however, was screaming no good. All incoming ship traffic should have been rerouted to the nearest major city hours ago. *If they're involved in this mess too...* He didn't want to think about the implications of that.

He grabbed his pack, clipped it on, and started running, not even bothering to see if his team was ready. He knew they'd catch up. His estimate was fairly accurate. Forty-five minutes later, they crested the top of a hill and found the ship parked below. He flattened himself to the ground immediately. The rest of his squad did the same, crawling up next to him.

"Ancient Gods, Ice Giants? This has to be…" Hallie whispered.

"Enough," he growled and Hallie shut up. "Focus on the problem at hand, not some ten-thousand year old prophecy." To be fair to her though, he'd been thinking the exact same thing.

He shifted to grab his long distance viewers and unclipped them from his harness. The ship itself was old and of Ice Giant design, however it was unmarked, which was unusual for an interplanetary ship. Most ships were owned and maintained by the Ship's Guild and loaned out to the various Guilds, and they usually had them painted with official guild markings. Very few people had the resources for a ship of their own, and those were almost always marked too, at a minimum with a designation number that should be easily visible on both sides of the ship, which meant they were either hiding something, or they were up to no good. *Both,* he decided.

Based on the age though, it was possible that someone had bought an old ship that had been decommissioned and fixed it up, or it had been handed down over the years. The Ice Giants had few natural resources, as most of their world was buried under glaciers, but once uncovered, was minerally the richest planet in the Consortium. Most of the interplanetary ships were built on the Ice Planet, as it was far cheaper to build where the resources were located than transport them to another planet. Decommissioned ships were highly valued and often purchased or restored by private citizens, rather than recycled, as travel anywhere on the Ice Planet, without a ship or shuttle was pretty much impossible. The Ship's Guild turned a blind eye to the practice as long as they were regularly inspected.

He focused on the cockpit trying to get a good look inside but there was too much glare from the sun. Examining the terrain, he clipped the viewers back on his harness and slunk back a distance before angling further down the hill and creeping up to try again. The others followed wordlessly.

"Definitely Ice Giant," he whispered. "Two in front, and at least one in the back, maybe two. I can't get a clear view of the passenger windows. The pilots are just sitting there, waiting. If there was a problem with the ship, I'd expect them to be working on it."

"Maybe they're waiting for someone to come get them," Lark suggested. "They've been here for almost an hour. It's possible they couldn't fix whatever was..."

Lark stopped speaking instantly when the main door to the ship slid open, and a pair of male Ice Giants stepped out. Unlike his own species, the males were significantly larger than the females, primarily bi-pedal, and stood a good twenty-five feet tall, nearly ten feet taller than Quinn. Their large bodies were covered in a thick layer of fat and long white fur that insulated them from the harsh cold of their world. Long fangs and claws, were their primary natural defenses. Quinn knew he would be hard pressed to defeat an adult male in claw to claw combat, as his own fangs and claws weren't long enough, but these giants were also sporting stunners. He frowned at that, as only members of the Guard and Council should have access to stunners.

"Gah. This planet is awful," one Ice Giant said.

"I don't know how they stand this heat," the other replied, and started walking in their direction.

Quinn looked around quickly, found a small stand of scrub trees, and took off at a full run. It wasn't much, but it would have to do. The others followed and they ducked behind and flattened themselves to the ground only moments before the giants appeared over the ridge.

"Still nothing. Where is he?" the first one muttered. "He should have been here an hour ago."

"There's nothing worse than having to wait for your prey," the second muttered. "It's far more fun to track them down."

The first snorted. "They won't be much of a challenge either way. From what I understand, the little rodent can't even walk anymore. Shame really. She was a feisty one. I wonder how much of a challenge the male will be? Well, come on. It's far too hot to wait out here. You might want to track them down, but I don't. Not in this heat."

They waited for several minutes before talking. Quinn didn't give the all clear until he heard the faint sounds of the ship's door open and close. "They must mean Little Flower," Hallie whispered.

"Agreed," Quinn replied. "We'll need to take them out before we can call in reinforcements. That ship would pick up our tracking beacon if we activated it. The question is how. They'd see us coming and take off long before we could get to the ship, and they're just as armed as we are. We'll need to take them alive for questioning if we can too."

"Whoever has Little Flower would be arriving by ground crawler. Perhaps we can stop them first," Keeta suggested.

"We don't even know if they're actually on their way," Quinn stated. "They're late, which means something's happened."

"I suppose we could just wait for them to come out again," Hallie suggested.

"We might get two of them, but that won't stop the pilots," Quinn replied, tilting his head as he considered. "Although, it's possible the pilots don't even know what's going on. No, I think we need to lure them away. They're bored, and they're looking for a hunt. I say we give them one."

"What are you suggesting?" Hallie asked.

"They'd run, if they saw all of us, but if they think we're just some hapless citizen that happened to come across their path, they'll want to get rid of the evidence." Quinn pulled up the maps and satellite footage on his tablet again and examined the nearby terrain. He pointed to the ghost woods. "Here. There's enough ground cover for us to hide and we'll have a much easier time of moving around than they will. It looks like there's a trail here. That's where I'll enter. Hallie, I want you and Keeta to keep heading for New Hope. When you get an hour out, hit your tracking beacon. That'll be far enough away not to cause suspicion, but if for some reason we aren't successful, they may come to investigate, thinking it's their missing crawler. Lark, I want you to circle around and see if you can find any registration numbers on that ship. Follow if it takes off, but keep your distance. You three, head here. I'll give you a twenty minute head start."

Quinn divvied up his pack into the others, keeping only the stuff on his carry harness. As tired as he was, he'd have to be light to be fast enough to stay ahead of the giants and their stunners, at least until he made it to cover in the trees. That done, he nodded and everyone took off on their assignments.

Exactly twenty minutes later, he took a deep breath and started walking forward, staying low to the ground until he neared the top of the hill, and then crawled up to peer down at the ship again. It hadn't moved. Backing up, he stood up on two feet and started walking forward again, stopped, just long enough for the two giants to open the ship's door and peer up at him. He turned and ran with everything he had.

"Wait! Come back!" he heard one of the giants call out, but of course he didn't.

Risking a glance back, he saw them in hot pursuit as he'd expected. Moments later, the blue orb of a stunner flew past him, just barely missing him. He veered and refocused on his run, ears back, listening for the sounds of pursuit. Another orb missed him again and he dug deeper. If he made the tree line, he'd have cover and be significantly safer. Nearly a minute passed without signs of another shot, so he risked another glance back and found they were still following, but they'd fallen back out of stunner range.

Pretending to look frantically around for an escape, he then turned and angled towards the direction of the path he was looking for and slowed his pace just a tad. He didn't want to get too far ahead, or they might give up and return to the ship. He did sigh with relief when he made it to the tree line and cover.

*There!* Locating the path he ran down it for a length, staying as low as he could to avoid the worst of the thorns, but they still grabbed and tore at his fur, and he was sure he'd have dozens of small cuts by the time this was over. Seeing a good hiding spot, he ducked off the trail, diving behind a small collection of boulders.

"Here, kitty kitty," taunted one of the giants, close enough that Quinn knew he could hit them with his own stunner, but he hadn't made it to the others yet, and was still in view of the ship. If he returned fire, they'd know he was a guard and the ship would likely take off, especially if he missed and the two had a chance to call back. He was ranked the best fighter in his guard, and hadn't lost a match to his own species in close to fifty years, but his stunner skills were barely adequate. They were just too new, and he died far more often than he liked when training with the Ice Giants. The only species he couldn't beat in a physical fight were the Water Sprites, and that was because their natural defenses and speed in the water rarely let him score a win before they knocked him out.

Still, he had no desire to face the giants in a physical fight, if they'd even let him get that close. He peered around the boulder and then took off in the other direction, purposely making noise.

"He's over there!" the other one called out, and a moment later the tree beside him crackled with the bolt of electricity that hit it.

*Too close!* he thought, and dug deep, weaving around trees and boulders until he made it to the trail again, trying to gain some distance. *A few more minutes and they're going to start overheating,* Quinn thought, as another bolt of lightning just missed his back, making his fur stand up on edge.

He glanced back and saw that one of the giants was already tiring and falling behind, but that glance cost him, as he tripped over a root and went flying. He tucked into a roll, but ended up sliding down the embankment on the side of the trail, and twisted his leg hard. He picked himself up, pushing the pain away. Limping away as fast as he could, he took the first opportunity he found to hide.

"He's injured! We've got him now, Brack" the first giant called out.

"Eenowk, wait," the second called back, short of breath. "I'm too hot."

"You really need to do more warm weather training, brother," Eenowk replied.

"Warm weather? This is an inferno. The gods wouldn't even come here," Brack muttered. "I'm calling the ship. We can track him from the air. Injured, he won't get far, and we can't risk him getting away."

"Fine," Eenowk muttered, and then yelled out in Quinn's direction. "You can run and hide, kitty cat, but we'll find you."

Quinn swore as the two brothers started making their way down out of the tree line. If they made it to the ship, he'd never be able to stop them. In the distance, he heard the sounds of the ship taking off and cautiously peered out. *I'm too far away,* he thought and started to limp forward, following, but they made it out of the woods before he could get within distance of his stunner again, and he watched as the ship landed and they boarded. Moments later it took off again. It wasn't long before they located him, and came to a hover above him.

The door opened and they started firing. Swearing, he took off, looking for better cover, but hadn't gotten far when his ears picked up the sounds of another ship approaching. Ducking behind a tree, he turned and looked back and saw three ships heading towards them, all painted the distinctive red of the Ship's Guild. Looking back up at the Ice Giant ship he swore, figuring they'd take off, but instead, they hovered.

Quinn frowned, trying to decide if the Ship's Guild was involved, or if something else was going on. They should have been able to take control of the ship remotely, but the ship still didn't move or land. The three ships took up position around the Ice Giant's ship and began closing in, trying to pressure them to land, which told Quinn they were on his side, but moments later, the Ice Giant's ship exploded.

The Ships Guild's ships veered off, pushed back by the shockwave, but undamaged thanks to the shields they'd had enabled, which visibly rippled with the impact. Quinn bolted as fast as he could away from the ship, as shrapnel began to fall around him. He hadn't gotten more than a few steps when something struck him in the back of the head, and he fell, unconscious before he even hit the ground.

# CHAPTER 21

# Henry: Tracker

Henry woke to the blare of his alarm, long before the sun was up, checked the weather report, and grinned with excitement. The forecast hadn't changed overnight. It looked like it was going to be one of the rare cool and overcast days on this inferno of a planet, and the forecast claimed the expected rain should hold off until after he got back. It would be a perfect morning for a trail ride before his lesson with Nazari.

He was honestly surprised that James was letting him take the horse out, especially with everything going on. That thought made him frown with worry, so he quickly checked the news to see if there were any updates. He frowned again at what he saw, but there was little he could do to help there, and it was far too early to call James to offer his condolences.

*He might not even know yet. I'll call when I get back.*

Sighing, he tossed his tablet on the bed before climbing out, and walked buck-naked over to the chair where he'd tossed his work clothes the night before. He picked them up, sniffed, and decided there was no point in showering and putting on clean clothes if he was going out riding. He'd shower and do laundry when he got back.

Clothed, he walked over to grab the breakfast he'd brought back the night before, and scowled at it, no longer particularly interested in it.

Jordan was doing wonders with food in the kitchen, but she was still limited to what they had to work with, and he was getting sick and tired of the same old fish and fruit. By the time he'd made his way to the cafeteria the night before, all the good stuff had been taken. Sighing, he grabbed a couple of the large purple fruits, deciding to eat on the way over to the barn, and grab something better afterwards once the kitchens were open for breakfast.

*Maybe I'll bring breakfast over to James,* he thought. *Of course, that's assuming he would trust what I brought him after what happened to them yesterday.*

He left his apartment, his mind lost in thought as he considered his relationship with James. They worked and trained together daily now, and had even started hanging out in the evening, playing games and reminiscing about before. James was quickly becoming one of his best friends, but he was beginning to wonder if James was interested in more than that, not that anything could happen until he earned his adulthood again.

He'd been surprised when James had passed along his interest in becoming an animal healer to Nazari, and that Nazari had taken him on as an apprentice. James and Nazari both had a wicked sense of humor that made learning the difficult material fun. He'd never been particularly good in school and hadn't even graduated from high school, but Nazari was patient and a very skilled instructor. She went at his speed, never moving on until he fully understood the material. If his teachers back on Earth had been as patient and understanding, he probably would have done far better in school. Either way, the work was easier than anything he'd ever had to do before, and he considered himself very lucky to have survived the Cataclysm and ended up in such a good situation, even if the first few years of isolation had been pure torture and hell was several degrees colder by comparisons most days.

What he hadn't expected was for James to suggest that he take Buster out for a trail ride. It was one thing to work the horse in the safety of the arena, but going outside came with added risks. He knew that the horse belonged to James's former partner, and how much the horse meant to him because of it. It made him wonder if it was James's way of flirting with him, or if he was just being a good friend.

James had asked him once if he'd had any family before, but he'd stated he didn't want to talk about it, and to his surprise James hadn't brought it up again. He'd grown up in a very religious family that saw his preferences as a sin, and when he'd come out of the closet as a teenager, his step father had kicked him out of the house, and his mother had gone along with it. The man had been physically abusive, so it had actually been a blessing in disguise.

He'd had a number of relationships over the years, none of which had worked out, for a variety of reasons, and his last one had turned sour very quickly. He wasn't sure he was ready to try again, but he was lonely, and the evenings spent with James and his family were quickly becoming the highlight of his day. He had to be careful though. He didn't want James to think he was only interested in order to earn his adulthood, nor did he want to make things awkward if he was misreading the situation.

The lights flickered on as he entered the barn, and the animals inside made a loud racket. He heard Buster's deep voice over the din, and chuckled as the insistent neigh turned into a knicker the moment he came around the corner. He and Buster had become good friends after hunting the sand spinners, although he was sure Buster just liked him for the star fruit. He handed over the cores of the fruit he'd eaten on the way over, to Buster's evident delight. "Sorry old boy, you're going to have to earn the rest of your breakfast this morning. I thought we'd go explore a little first."

Buster tossed his head, but didn't seem to be all that upset as he led the massive draft horse out into the aisle to groom and saddle him.

It had been years since he'd ridden a horse for any length of time, even before, and he'd only worked Buster a few times since that first day with James. After being kicked out of his home, he'd ended up on a cattle ranch, where the owner had taken a chance on him, and he'd spent almost two decades there before the owner had ended up selling. He'd spent far too many days entirely on horseback, and he honestly thought he'd never ride a horse again after he moved to the northeast with his boyfriend at the time. Buster was far taller and wider than he was used to riding, but almost as responsive once he'd dusted off the English commands that Buster had been trained with, rather than the western ones he was far more comfortable with.

Since he'd only worked with Buster in the Arena, he figured he'd start by riding around the compound first, to see how the old boy handled outside. If that went well, he'd head out and explore the area a little. He didn't want to go too far due to the risk of predators, which were far too big for his own liking, but he was feeling a little trapped in New Hope, even as nice as it was. He wanted to see more of this strange new world and the four other planets in the Consortium, but that likely wouldn't happen for a long time. Until then, he'd be stuck here. If everything went well, he hoped to be able to convince Nazari or one of the other cats to go out for a longer ride with him. They'd be big enough to keep the predators away.

The sun hadn't even broken the horizon when he led the giant horse outside and leapt on. Buster was full of energy, snorting, and tossing his head, but responded well to every command he gave in the yard, and stepped out without hesitation. Buster seemed to be just as excited to explore as Henry was, ears forward, checking everything out, and pushing the pace to see what was around the next corner. He snorted once and pinned his ears as they passed the goose pen, when one of the temperamental birds made a hissing charge at them, but other than that, didn't seem fazed by anything. Considering how different everything was here, Henry was shocked. He'd expected at least one major spook, or at least some hesitation.

After nearly a full circuit without incident, and Buster still enthusiastic to be out, he turned the horse away from the compound, and nudged Buster into a trot up the hill. Buster wasted no time in moving forward, and indicated he wanted to go faster, so Henry let him shift into a canter. Buster tossed his head and leapt forward at almost but not quite a buck in his enthusiasm. Henry applied leg pressure and the reins and Buster shifted over. He tested in the other direction and when

Buster was clearly still paying attention, he let the horse have his head. Buster stretched out and surged forward. He wasn't the fastest horse Henry had ever ridden, but pretty close, and far more powerful. For all his size, he was remarkably smooth to ride at the canter and gallop, especially when compared to his bone jarring trot.

His massive hooves beat the ground in a rhythmic pattern that filled an empty spot in his soul that he hadn't realized was missing. He whooped with excitement and adrenalin, and leaned in as the hill steepened, urging the horse faster. Buster snorted at him and stretched out even more. The horse kept up his ground eating pace until they made it to the top of the hill. When Henry sat up, Buster slowed his pace and snorted back down to a trot and then a walk, but there was still a bounce in the horses step and plenty of energy left.

He was trying to decide where to go next when Buster snorted, flicked his ears back, and turned his head to look behind him. Henry spun the horse around to see what was bothering him, prepared for the horse to take off, but Buster just stood there, head up and ears forward looking back at the compound.

On the far side of the compound, over by the Tower, he saw someone walking across the field to one of the many ground crawlers parked haphazardly around the place. When he realized who it was, he swore. James was carrying what looked like Little Flower. And Damon, of all people, was following closely behind carrying the baby.

Henry's hackles rose. He'd done his best to stay clear of Damon, once word of his tattoos had made their way around to him. Once a white supremacist, always a white supremacist, and he'd seen nothing of Damon's behavior to indicate otherwise, especially not the last couple of months. Every day the man seemed to get angrier and more belligerent.

GrandFather's hesitation as he carried his granddaughter into the shuttle told Henry everything he needed to know. If he didn't do something quickly, his best friend was as good as dead, and likely the others too. He had no doubt of it. He reached in his pocket for his tablet and swore, realizing he'd left it in his room. *Of all the days!* he grumbled to himself. As the ground crawler took off heading away from him, and disappeared over a hill, he realized it would take far too long to make his way back to the compound to try and find someone this early in the morning, so Henry turned Buster in the direction the shuttle had taken, and asked for a canter. Buster snorted once and dug in without hesitation. He pulled up when they cleared the next hill. Henry could still see the shuttle off in the distance and smiled. That idiot was traveling in a straight line and leaving a trail as clear a day behind him in the tall grass.

The ground crawler, for all its technological advancements, was a slow vehicle, only traveling about thirty miles per hour at top speed. But Damon wouldn't be able to go that fast. The auto-pilot and sensors needed time to scan the roadless terrain and pick a safe path through the shifting desert sands, scree, and thin layer of grass on top. Henry turned to look back in the direction of the compound, and swore as dozens of the other crawlers took off, heading in different directions on auto pilot. He turned back towards the crawler Damon was driving and watched it dip below another hill and made up his mind. He clucked Buster back into motion, keeping an easy but ground covering pace.

Buster didn't hesitate or give him any grief about leaving the safety of the compound behind, and seemed focused on the shuttle ahead.

"You're a good horse, Buster, but your owner is going to need everything you've got to bring him home."

Buster pinned his ears and snorted loudly in response, which made him chuckle. Henry was sure he was the one who was going to be struggling before the day was over, and he was pretty sure Buster knew it too. If the horse could roll his eyes, he was sure he would have done that too.

Henry paced the eager horse, trying not to burn him out, knowing that Buster had very little in the way of training or formal exercise over the past couple of years, and frankly he had no idea how far Damon planned to go with the crawler. He hoped that someone would notice that Buster was gone and follow the trail. With hundreds of crawler tracks around the compound picking one set out would be impossible, especially with the others that had taken off moments later, but Buster's big hooves should be noticeable. Still, he stopped several times and carved his name into rock outcroppings and smaller trees along the way, along with an arrow pointing in the direction he was going. If nothing else, it would help him find his way back, he hoped.

When he came close to one of the giant bandala trees, he veered off course to find water for them. Most of the streams from the spring rains had already dried up, and the few puddles he found were too stagnant to risk drinking from, or allow Buster to drink from either. In one of the survival courses the Sabers had given, he'd learned that the great trees always formed over underground aquifers, and that the roots could be broken off and would drip water. It was how animals of the desert found water during the long months of the dry season, and where the Chenzira's had gotten their water from originally, although now they had a proper well and rain collection systems, as the needs of the compound were far more than one tree could provide, no matter how massive they were.

Cautious and on the lookout for predators, he approached. Buster gave no indication that he smelled anything, and he didn't see anything but a few smaller creatures about the tree, none of which he identified as being particularly dangerous as long as he didn't get too close. Sliding off of Buster, he stretched and rubbed at his sore backside. They'd been riding for hours at this point, and he was already starting to feel it. Walking over to the tree, he found one of the smaller roots and kicked hard, snapping it off. Sure enough water started dripping out, not fast, but fast enough. After grabbing several handfuls for himself, he broke off several more roots so that a small pool formed and led Buster over to drink. After another long drink for himself, he clamored back on, far less gracefully than before, and took off again. It wasn't long before he was back on the trail.

Henry didn't have a compass or much in the way of supplies, but he never went anywhere without the pocket knife he'd commissioned from the Guild, and his pockets had a way of collecting small objects. At one stop for water he took assessment of what he had with him. In addition to his knife, he had Buster's hoof pick, the Saber's equivalent to a book of matches, a wad of bailing twine, a pencil, and surprisingly half of a chocolate chip cookie. He'd forgotten he hadn't finished it the night before.

They'd been traveling for some time when Buster turned suddenly. Henry corrected him but Buster refused. This surprised him greatly, since Buster hadn't refused a single command all morning. They were on rocky terrain and the trail wasn't immediately visible but Damon hadn't changed his path in over an hour. Henry tried again. Buster refused to move forward, tossing his head and pawing at the ground. He examined the area around them, and didn't see anything immediately concerning and Buster wasn't spooking like he had with the Sand Spinner. He tried a third time but Buster planted his feet and snorted. Henry tapped his fingers and made note of a rock formation ahead and gave Buster his lead. Buster immediately turned in the direction he'd wanted to go all along, and picked up his pace. Henry let him trot it out for a few minutes, and then stopped amazed when he saw very clear marks from the ground crawler.

"Good Boy!" Henry said, patting the horse, and then turned Buster around to back track to where the trail had changed. Buster didn't hesitate, which surprised him again. Side stepping Buster next to a small rock formation, he scratched his name and an arrow into the rock, put his knife away, and then turned Buster back to the trail.

From that point on Henry let Buster have his say. Twice Buster refused to go down embankments and he let Buster pick his own way across, both times Buster found a safer way down, and multiple times Buster snorted at something, backed up and found another way around. He'd seen just how good the horse was at picking out Sand Spinner nests, so he didn't even bother to correct the horse if he spooked at something.

At one point he saw a flock of the larger four winged vulture birds, but they didn't come close, seemingly interested in something far off in the distance, and Henry never saw anything larger, although Buster likely did. Once when he was starting to get thirsty again, he'd decided to veer off course towards one of the bandala trees, but Buster snorted and refused to approach. Henry didn't push it, and at the next one Buster walked up without issue.

Sometime in the late afternoon they approached another one of the massive trees, and he decided it was time for another break. He'd been riding in two-point for the past half hour to take the pressure off of his sore backside. Buster surprised Henry once again by not waiting for him to break off one of the roots, and instead kicked out several on his own. Clearly the horse had been watching.

"You are one smart horse, Buster. Glad they saved your fuzzy behind." Kicking off another root for himself, Henry took a long drink and considered what to do next.

He loosely tied Buster near a thick section of wild grasses, so the horse could rest and graze, and started climbing. It took him nearly fifteen minutes to climb the massive tree to the top, and he was breathing hard by the time he arrived, but it had been worth it. Off in the distance he could see the crawler just sitting there. Damon had stopped. It would still take Henry several hours to get there, but he was far closer than Henry had expected him to be, and he wondered why Damon had stopped.

Henry carefully worked his way back down the tree and picked out Buster's feet, checking for signs of injury or damage while the horse continued to graze. So far the massive, plate-sized hooves were holding up with only a few minor chips, but the terrain was getting rockier and Buster didn't have shoes. None of the horses did. The Sabers had been horrified at the very idea, and had flat out refused to allow it. Instead they had created a variant of the nano cream, which had significantly improved the strength and health of the hooves. Henry didn't care either way as long as the horses were healthy, and it certainly seemed to do the trick.

He'd have to slow his pace and check far more regularly, just to be sure, but if Damon didn't move off again, he should be able to catch up before the suns started to set. He really didn't want to be out at night when the larger predators started hunting, but at this point, it looked like that was going to be a real possibility.

He gave Buster a quick check to make sure the saddle wasn't rubbing, and walked over to one of the massive roots to use as a mounting block to climb on. His legs were tired and swinging up into the saddle used far more energy than he had left. He wanted to save what he could in case it came to a fight with Damon.

"Just a few more hours old boy and we'll either catch up to James or start looking for someplace to hole up for the night," he told the horse.

Buster snorted in reply and started walking at Henry's nudging. He stopped several times to check on Buster's feet and gather a few edible plants to munch on along the way. It wasn't much, but he could manage for a day or two without ill effects. The half cookie was already long gone.

As dusk approached, he cleared the top of a hill and saw the ground crawler sitting in the valley ahead next to a medium sized tree with the mountains rising sharply behind it. Damon hadn't moved. *What is he waiting for*, Henry wondered. *That crawler could easily travel through the night.* Then he realized it wasn't what, it was who. Damon was waiting for someone. He quickly scanned the area in the dimming light and found a small stand of rocks and trees off to the side, close enough to scout the crawler, but far enough away to hopefully keep from being noticed by the internal sensors if Damon fired up the crawler again.

He was just about to dismount when Buster snorted and looked behind them, head up, ears forward, and nose flaring. "What is it, boy?" he asked. He signaled to Buster that he could turn around. The horse spun and took a step forward, stopped, and snorted again. Henry didn't see anything at first, but then what he thought was a rock formation in the dimming light, shifted. Buster saw it too and snorted loudly, the short staccato noise echoing off the canyon.

"Easy boy," Henry crooned, preparing for Buster to take off in the other direction at any moment, and he watched as whatever it was crept slowly closer. Henry swore. Something very large was stalking them, and they didn't stand a chance.

# CHAPTER 22

# Petra: Confession

Petra drifted in and out of consciousness for some time before her tormentor returned.

"Ahh, you're still alive. I'm impressed. I thought for sure you'd be dead by now. If you confess to your crimes, I might just be kind and put you out of your misery," he said.

She didn't even bother replying as he entered the cell carrying a large bag. She braced herself for more abuse, but he ignored her, and after dropping the bag, swam over to the male who had spoken to her before and checked his pulse.

"Dead," he muttered. "Oh well."

He proceeded to unhook the dead body, and then opened the bag, revealing someone else. He quickly restrained them in the place where the other person had been and floated away, checking the others. She watched, unable to do anything as he shocked several of the others, making them scream. He pulled down one other body, and shoved both roughly into the bag he'd brought the other person in, and left again.

Several minutes later there was a groan, and the newest captive lit up his skin to look around. She watched as he went from confused to horrified. "Bottomless depths..." he swore.

"Pretty much," Petra snorted. "Who are you?"

"Honor Guard Red Fin," he replied and frowned. "I know you. You're Petra, Wind Rider's daughter, right?"

"Someone's been doing their homework," she said.

"Apparently not well enough," he muttered, and examined his bindings, trying to figure out how to get out of them. As he did, she explained what had happened to her.

Half an hour later, by her internal clock, her tormentor returned. "Ah, you're awake. Perfect," he said to the guard, and swam back in the cell, but rather than tormenting the guard, he swam over to her instead, and twisted her broken wing hard. "Ready to confess to killing the Senior Guild Master yet?" he asked.

"If you think I'm going to help you get out of your own crimes, you're sadly mistaken," she hissed at him.

"Oh, not my crimes. I had nothing to do with that. You and your sketchy friends did, at your mother's orders. You didn't think I wouldn't find those messages did you? We know it was you. We did find one of your scales in the Senior Guild Master's suite after all," he replied with a sneer.

"Evidence you ripped from my side and planted," she growled back, wondering if he was telling the truth about Ellie. She had no doubt he was trying to blame her mother for it though, if Ellie was dead.

"Now, would I do that?" he asked. "But that's okay. I figured you wouldn't confess to save your life, so we'll see just how many lives you're willing to kill, starting with this one." He swam over and began shocking Red Fin, making him scream. Sickening colors raced across his skin, that matched exactly what she was feeling. She didn't know what to do to help him. She knew she was dead anyway, but if she confessed, like he wanted, then her mother would be killed.

He stopped after a while and turned back to her. "So what's your answer? Shall we see just how long I can drag out his death?"

"Say nothing," Red Fin ordered. "He'll kill us both the moment you give in to his demands. I don't care if he kills me."

"You keep your mouth shut," he growled, and backhanded Red Fin hard across the face.

That told her Red Fin was right. He shocked Red Fin again and the screams went on for what seemed like forever before Red Fin slumped. He checked the guard's pulse and turned back to face her. "Well, if you won't confess to save him, I'll just have to find someone better." He proceeded to swim around the cage considering everyone there, but eventually disappeared around a bend in the cave wall, returning several minutes later dragging a small female Water Sprite. She couldn't have been more than ten years old, Petra realized, and she was horribly malnourished.

Petra swallowed hard as he dangled the child in front of her. "Tell me, Nest Mother, just how strong are your maternal instincts? Are you so callous as to ignore the screams of a child?"

"You wouldn't," she growled.

Ripples of sickening humor raced across his skin. "I think you know me better than that by now," he said, and the child began screaming and writhing in his grip. She flinched involuntarily, and he grinned wickedly at her, but surprisingly stopped shocking the child. "I think we may have found a winner," he said. "Ready to confess?" When she just hissed at him, he began shocking the child again.

"Stop," Petra growled, unable to bear the screams of the child. "I'll do what you want."

"Excellent," he purred, and tossed the child aside who swam away quickly. He unclipped his tablet and positioned it such that her injuries and the chains didn't show. "Read exactly what I have here. Change anything and she dies, slowly."

Petra swallowed hard as she read what was there, terrified for her mother, and horrified by what he planned or had already done with Marsee, she wasn't sure which, but nodded. He hit record and she began reading. When he was done he clipped his tablet back to his harness and turned to look at her. "Now, was that so hard?" he asked.

"I suppose you're going to kill me now," she said.

"Oh, no. Why would I do that, when I can have the pleasure of your screams?" he purred.

An eternity later, she passed out.

# CHAPTER 23

# Myra: Hunter

Myra slowly woke as the sedative wore off and rolled over, blinking in confusion to see the sun shining through her window. Either she hadn't slept very long or she'd overslept. The sedative should have worn off late that evening with plenty of time to take a watch so that GrandFather could sleep. She went to grab her tablet to check the time, but it wasn't where she'd left it.

*That's odd,* she thought, and looked around trying to see if it had fallen on the floor, but she couldn't find it anywhere. *Did I leave it upstairs?* She tried to remember, but her thoughts were slow, still groggy from the sedative. *No, I texted Ammond and GrandFather.*

She looked over at the hypo on her bedside table and frowned. The timestamp was wrong. She'd taken the sedative late afternoon, not in the middle of the night. *Did I wake and take another dose?* She couldn't remember. Confused and groggy, she stumbled around the suite looking for her tablet, thinking maybe she'd been sleepwalking and dropped it somewhere, but she couldn't find it.

*Where is it?* she wondered, and then made her way over to the waste room. Yawning, she splashed some cold water on her face to try and wake up. *Maybe I went upstairs to check on everyone.* She needed to check on them anyway, so she made her way out of the room and climbed the ramp to the next floor, but froze with instant fear when she saw the door was open. Instantly wide awake, she listened but didn't hear anything, and then sniffed deeply.

***Blood!***

She bolted into the room and stopped. No one was there. Hope's playpen was destroyed and her nose picked up the smell of blood on the broken pieces.

*What happened?* she wondered as she looked around the room, noticing that GrandFather and Little Flower's tablets were still there, and a tray of uneaten food was on the table beside her daughter's bed.

Hoping that Little Flower had simply fallen into the play pen and been hurt, and not something far worse, she bolted out of the room and leapt off of the second floor balcony, not even bothering with the ramp. Landing on all fours, she ran for the Trauma Center. People ducked out of the way, as she ran past. As she slammed through the Trauma Center doors, she saw Ammond talking with one of the other healers, and her heart nearly stopped when she saw their expressions.

"Ammond! What happened? Where are they?" she called out.

He turned to look at her with confusion. "Where are who?"

Myra skidded to a stop, horror on her face as she realized what his answer meant. "The door to Little Flower's room was open when I woke up. Everyone was gone. Hope's playpen was destroyed and there were drops of Hue-man blood on it. I figured something happened and they came here."

"I haven't seen Little Flower since I checked on them around midnight," Ammond said.

"Dark moons. Ammond, someone has taken them!" Myra cried, and started pacing trying to figure out what to do. She bolted into her office and dug through her desk to grab her spare work tablet, and logged into her account checking for messages from Jer or Marcus, but there wasn't anything from them yet. She fired off a quick message to them, and copied Sampson just in case.

Ammond followed her into her office, walked around her desk, and sat down next to her. He reached out and took her paw. "Myra, there's something you should know…"

She looked up from her table and made eye contact with him. Seeing grief in his eyes, she started shaking, terrified of what he had to say.

"Myra, Ellie's dead."

Myra shoved back in her chair away from him, shaking her head. "No. No, she can't be! I don't believe you."

"It's all over the news. I'm so sorry, Myra, but there's more."

"Ancient Gods! Please, no. Not Marsee too!" she whispered.

"As far as we know, she's still alive...but a package was delivered to Clear Seas office containing one of Marsee's claws."

Myra's ears flicked back in horror and then switched to fury as her instinct roared to life, demanding blood.

***We will find them, and we will kill them slowly, and painfully, for daring to hurt our family!***

"Myra! Switch it off!" Ammond signed.

"I am going to kill whoever is behind this," she hissed at Ammond, but brought her growling instinct back under control. "Dark moons, Ammond! Ellie's dead and someone's declawed Marsee? How could they do that? She's just a *baby!*"

Ammond wrapped his arms around her in a hug, and she collapsed against him crying for several minutes, before a thought broke through her grief and she sat up.

"When did you find out? Why didn't you wake me?" Myra asked.

"Last night. I'm sorry. I came by as soon as I found out, and I saw that you'd taken another dose of the sedative, so I figured you already knew and were trying to sleep through the grief. I checked on the others too and they were all sleeping. That was just before one. I was just about to head over to be there with you, but you woke up sooner than I expected."

"So they could have been missing for hours by now? Moons, they could be anywhere!"

"Are you sure they're missing?" he asked.

"My personal tablet is also missing, and someone obviously gave me another round of the sedative, maybe two. I had a really hard time waking up. I suppose it could have been GrandFather, but if he was sleeping when you checked on him, maybe not. Both of their tablets were still in their room, and there was a tray of untouched food. GrandFather wouldn't have left the safety of the locked room with everything going on without his tablet."

She buried her head in her paws trying to figure out what to do next. Panic, grief, and the lingering effects of the sedative muddled her brain. Jer and Marcus were both gone. *Who do I call? One of the other councilors? Can I trust them? What if they're behind this too?*

"Alright," Ammond said calmly, "We'll start by putting out a compound wide alert, to see if anyone has seen them, or knows if anyone else is missing too. You do that and start searching the compound. Start anywhere GrandFather or Little Flower would likely to go, the kitchens, garden, barn. I'll put out a missing persons alert for the three on the emergency system, and contact Councilor Parner. Marcus would have put him in charge when they left for the Water World. Also, find Jordan and have her start organizing a search of the compound."

She nodded and sent out the message and then bolted for the cafeteria. It was the closest, and Ammond was right, she needed to talk with Jordan anyway. With GrandFather missing, Jordan was next in line.

She slammed through the door, but the room was mostly empty. She turned to leave but stopped when she saw Jordan waving her arms, running from the back of the kitchen and trying to get her attention.

"Myra, I saw GrandFather early this morning, maybe about 4:30. He picked up breakfast for everyone. I haven't seen him or any of the others since. I'll coordinate identifying if anyone else is missing, and get back to you."

She sent that info off to Ammond, which cut down the time they'd been missing significantly. "There was blood in Little Flower's room. Hope's play pen was destroyed. I'm pretty sure they've been taken," Myra told Jordan after the message was sent.

Jordan's face hardened with the same rage Myra was feeling. "We'll find them and make sure they pay for it. No one kidnaps a child on my watch and gets away with it. I promise."

Myra nodded and ran to check the garden next. She was halfway across the courtyard when Brice ran out. "I just saw your message. They aren't in the garden. I just checked it, and I've been in there for the last hour."

She didn't even stop to reply, just veered and made for the barn. *Maybe there had been an emergency with one of the animals, and GrandFather left in a hurry to care for them. Or maybe Little Flower wanted to see Buster again.*

She prayed as she ran, not even remotely expecting to find them there. When she arrived, she skidded into the barn, her claws slipping on the stone floor with a loud screech as she nearly collided with Nazari.

"I was just coming to find you when I saw your message. Neither GrandFather or Henry Curtis showed up for their lessons. GrandFather texted me last night that he might not be able to make it with everything going on, but Henry has never been late or missed a shift or lesson. I checked and he had the morning off from chores. I did find something though. Buster, GrandFather's horse, is also missing, and so is the gear they use to ride him. I know Henry has been working with him lately, so it could be completely unrelated, but I'm worried Henry could be hurt. Both Henry and Buster would be easy targets for predators."

"Henry wouldn't have hurt GrandFather or the others. I'm sure of it. Unless GrandFather went out with Little Flower on Buster and Henry went out to find them, but that wouldn't make sense. GrandFather wouldn't have left the tower without letting me know, and we haven't made the protective equipment for her yet, and it doesn't explain the blood or damage I found in the tower. It's probably unrelated, but we should probably search the area for Henry anyway."

Myra's tablet blared with the missing person's alert as it was pushed to every device within two hundred leagues of here. It was all she could do not to whimper at the sound. She paced instead, trying to figure out what to do next, but stopped when her tablet dinged again. She swore when she saw the contents of the message. "Ancient Gods please protect my family!" she cried out and grabbed her tail, squeezing hard.

"What is it?" Nazari asked.

"Damon Minor never showed up for his work detail this morning either, and they just checked his suite. It's been cleaned out. I knew we should have done more about him. Both GrandFather and Little Flower warned us about him. We should have arrested him the moment we were poisoned. I'm a moons' forsaken idiot. Henry could be in just as much danger if he's involved in this." She fired off a message to Ammond and Jer letting them know about Henry, Buster, and Damon's missing status, and that Damon was their current suspect.

"All of the shuttles are grounded right now while they look for Marsee, so maybe Damon made them ride out on Buster," Nazari suggested. "I'll circle the compound and see if I can find any sign of the horse. Why don't you go back to the tower and see if you can find a trail from there, and if not, meet me back here."

Myra nodded. It was better than doing nothing, and she was completely out of other ideas. She bolted back to the tower and slid into her room, clipped on her carry harness, and ran up the ramp to the other room. She grabbed emergency supplies, in the event they did find Henry injured, affixing them to her harness, before quickly scanning the blood on the play pen and confirmed it was from GrandFather.

Then, after taking several calming breaths, knowing she was breaking all the rules, and would likely find herself back on the watch list for another six months, she flicked on her instinct. It roared to life, having been growling and pacing in the background, just waiting for her to act.

She breathed hard, taking in the familiar scent of her family, the sweet tang of GrandFather's blood, and a scent she didn't recognize. She slowly walked down the ramp and considered which way to go. She breathed deeply again, and scents from people swirled in her brain, so strong they were almost visible.

*There!* her instinct called out, focusing in on a tiny drop of blood on the floor and then another, and finally a larger patch on the door leading outside the compound. The scent followed straight out for some distance before it completely vanished. She growled as she circled, trying to figure out where it went. She could smell the scent of ground crawlers, but there were crawlers everywhere and the tracks all criss-crossed making any trail impossible to follow.

"Myra!" Nazari yelled, getting her attention and then signed. "Did you find anything?"

Nazari was far off in the distance, just coming around the other side of the compound. "They were here but the scent is gone. They must have left in a crawler, she signed back. "What about you!"

"Yes, I've found Buster's tracks!" she replied. Myra bolted to catch up with her. "It looks like he was moving fast up this hill." Nazari pointed out Buster's hoof prints.

The trail was clear and easy to see once you knew what you were looking for. They ran up to the top and found that Buster had milled about for a bit, turning to look back at something, before changing directions completely and heading off at an angle in the direction of the Wilds. They could see for several leagues but she couldn't see any sign of them.

She turned to look back to see what Buster had been looking at, and saw the Tower off in the distance, easily visible from here. "If Damon took the others and Henry was out riding, maybe he saw it happen, and followed after. The direction Buster is heading would meet up with anyone heading straight out into the Wilds."

"You could be right," Nazari agreed.

"I'm going after him. It's the only lead we have," Myra said, pulling out her tablet to fire off a message to Ammond, telling him what she planned.

"I'm coming with you," Nazari said, and Myra smiled her gratitude.

Message sent, they took off easily following Buster's trail. It was almost an hour though, before Nazari pulled up.

"Myra, look. This looks like a crawler track."

Myra checked it out and sniffed. "Henry's been here too. He must have gotten off of Buster. I can smell him now."

Nazari sniffed and nodded her agreement.

"Nazari, look! It's Hue-man writing! And an arrow! He's leaving us a trail!" She pulled out her tablet and swore. "Moons, we're already too far out in the Wilds for a signal. Do we turn back and risk losing the trail or keep going?"

"We keep going. There's rain in the forecast. If it rains we'll lose any chance of following them," Nazari replied.

Myra nodded, and they took off again. Her instinct had locked onto Buster's scent, and between that and the large divots the horse left in the ground he was fairly easy to follow. She only lost it briefly a few times over rocky terrain, but with Henry's arrows they were able to find it again, and when the crawler's tracks and Buster's veered, they followed the horse. Usually that was to stop for water or to pick out better footing for the horse, but several times they sniffed out predators ahead. One spot had them particularly confused as Buster's trail stopped and then backtracked. It wasn't until they spotted Henry's marker that they realized Henry must have lost the trail too, and backtracked to let them know where he was going.

"He's heading for the mountain," Myra said.

"That doesn't make sense. The crawler wouldn't be able to go up that terrain. It's too steep," Nazari replied.

"Nothing about any of this makes sense, Nazari. Maybe he's looking for somewhere safe to spend the night. Either way that's where Henry's going, so that's where I'm going."

Before long they came across the crawler tracks again. *How did Henry know?* Myra wondered. This was in a completely different direction than the crawler had been going before, and they'd seen no indication that the crawler had changed directions. Even her instinct hadn't picked up on the crawler's scent.

Twenty minutes later though, she stopped hard as her instinct locked on to Little Flower's scent, and the sharp tang of urine.

"Nazari, wait up!" she called out to the healer that was currently in the lead. "I smell Little Flower." Myra stopped and brought her instinct further to the foreground, and examined it and the other nearby scents. "I can only smell Little Flower, the crawler, and what must be Damon. I'm pretty sure they just exited the crawler, walked over here, so she could pee, and returned to the crawler afterwards. He has to be carrying her, because her scent is only here."

Relieved to know her daughter was still alive, she was worried about GrandFather and Hope. *Why didn't GrandFather get off to pee too? How badly is he injured?* They took off again, pushing themselves harder over the rocky terrain, but stopped at a bandala tree for water, and to discuss what to do next. It was nearing sunset and tracking them in the dark would be dangerous and difficult.

She had never run this long before, or even attempted to track prey, nor had she'd ever been out this far in the Wilds. She wasn't sure anyone had, not even the surveyors. This had been protected land for thousands of years. She guessed they'd traveled close to forty or fifty leagues by now, and they were now deep in the foothills of the mountain. The footing was becoming far more challenging, and they'd recently had to slow their pace to keep from slicing their paws on the sharp rocks.

Her instinct was growling with impatience at the delay, and anger at Damon for harming her family. She wanted to keep going until she found them, or dropped from exhaustion, but Nazari was thinking they should find somewhere safe to spend the night.

"Henry stopped here too," Nazari said, as they broke off roots for water. "And I think he might have climbed the tree."

Myra sniffed and then her nose crinkled with the smell of scat. She followed it around the tree to a large patch of grass that had been cut short by the grazing horse.

"Nazari, they aren't that far ahead. Buster's droppings are still fresh," she called out. "Let's see if we can catch up with him for the evening. It won't be safe for him out here at night, and even if we haven't found the others, I'd feel a lot better if Henry had protection from predators."

Nazari snorted. "He's already got two of the biggest predators on this planet stalking him, and I'm absolutely astounded they've made it this far as it is."

"Henry's not the one that needs to be worried about being stalked," she growled, and took off.

# CHAPTER 24

# Jer: Arrest

"Hold on to your tails people, we're about to exit," Sampson announced, and without further warning the universe imploded and exploded around them again. The rest of Jer's stomach finally caught up with him and threatened to go on without him, but he managed to keep his stomach contents where they belonged. Then again, he didn't have much left to throw up. He'd been sick the entire trip. From the sounds and smell of things, the others had not been so lucky. Poor Lowell had been fairing the worst, never having been off-world before. *I bet she'll never want to travel off world again*, he thought absently.

Jer could see several ships approaching them at speed. "Unidentified ship. This air space has been closed to all traffic. Turn around and head back to your home planet. If you don't leave within thirty seconds, you'll be forced to land and your ship impounded," came a stern warning over the communications system. Jer's ship was so new that it hadn't been assigned a designation yet, so it wasn't surprising that they were being challenged.

"Sea Patrol, this is Commander Nichola Sampson, designation 723A65B. I have Senior Councilors Chenzira and Surellis onboard. We are requesting permission to land at Council Platform immediately. I'm sending you their authorization now."

"I'm sorry Commander, Councilors, I've been given direct orders not to allow anyone to land at Council Platform."

Jer's anger flared and it was all he could do to keep from growling. He tapped Sampson on the shoulder to let him know he wanted to speak. "This is Senior Councilor Chenzira. A member of my species was brutally attacked and my *daughter* kidnapped on *your* world. If you do not personally escort us to Council Platform, I will have you placed under arrest by the full authority of the Council, and stripped of your rank permanently for interfering in an investigation. *Do I make myself clear?*"

"Yes, sir! Perfectly, sir! If you'll follow me," came the immediate and very nervous reply. The lead ship flipped around in a maneuver that made Jer's stomach groan, and sped down to the surface. Sampson followed close behind. The moment Jer connected to the planetary network he started scanning for messages and pulled up the latest from Clear Seas.

"Gods..." Jer whispered.

"What is it?" Marcus asked, worry etched on his face.

He couldn't speak for several moments, and just read the message over and over, not wanting to believe it. He looked up at his mentor, swallowed hard, and it took him three tries to get the words out. "Ellie's dead."

Marcus's ears flicked back in his own horror and grief. Gasps followed his announcement, and Lowell started growling.

"Is there any news about Marsee?" Marcus asked quietly.

Jer went back to scanning through his messages. "Nothing recent. That was the last message I had from Clear Seas, and it was sent just after we jumped. If he sent something else, we've missed it while we were in jump, and it hasn't caught up with us yet."

"Check for a press release," Marcus suggested.

Jer pulled up the news and started scanning as they began their descent into Council Platform. He was still looking for information when they pulled up next to what looked like Ellie's ship. He put his tablet away and shook his head. All the news reporters were discussing currently, was Ellie's death, and what that meant for the Guild if the Translator wasn't found. Jer raised an eyebrow at the title they'd given Marsee, wondering again why they were using that instead of her guild rank, as it had been in the ransom note too, and they appeared to be using it with far more respect than normally given to a translator, almost as if she were the only one.

He didn't wait for the official permission to disembark either. The moment the ship stopped, he unclipped his harness, stood, and walked to the door, waiting for the moment the display indicated they were secured, and it was safe to exit the craft without flooding it. A few moments after he felt the gangway bump the ship, the light turned from yellow to blue. He slammed open the door and stormed out, the others following behind. They'd already discussed their plan on the long and uncomfortable journey. Marcus would take Lowell and one of the honor guards directly to the archives, while he and the rest would take Clear Seas into custody.

When he arrived at the main terminal no one was there to greet him, which wasn't surprising since no one had expected his arrival. They'd purposely not let Clear Seas know they were coming, so he kept walking. Only the gate attendant was there, not that he paid her any real attention. To her credit though, she remained calm in the face of his anger and the half squad of guards following behind him on full alert.

Before he made it to the exit however, several Water Sprites approached at a fast swim. He recognized several of the councilors in the group, but frowned when he didn't see Clear Seas.

"Senior Councilors, we were not expecting your arrival for several more days. May I ask how you arrived so quickly?" Councilor Current signed. That was surprising as he knew Rip could speak his language, but he dismissed it. It was their official language now after all.

"Obviously. Have you found my daughter and those responsible?" he growled, not bothering to say how he arrived.

"I'm afraid we haven't," Current replied, flashing his deep regret and apology.

"And what of the ultimatum?" he asked, his tail lashing in both fury and fear that his daughter was still missing. He didn't care if that was unbecoming of a Councilor. He wanted people to know he was angry, and would use every ounce of his authority to get his daughter back. If Clear Seas was behind this, then it was a declaration of war, and he was more than prepared to fight.

With the delays needed to prepare the ship for departure, and the shorter days on this planet, he only had a few hours left to find his daughter before the ultimatum was up. They'd already passed a full day on the Water World, and he prayed that Marsee's kidnapper was using the standard interplanetary day, rather than the local one, in his ransom note.

"We've redirected every passenger and cargo ship to the various platforms for loading passengers. We'll be holding them in orbit until this passes. Cargo ships are currently loading the sea creatures. As for dismantling the Habitat, the only possible way would be to use mining explosives, but we've identified a fault near the habitat, which could cause an earthquake to be triggered. We have demolition experts laying the charges, but we're not sure if we can get all of the creatures cleared in time," Rip answered.

"We're also evacuating the nearby community but several people are refusing to leave, as are many of the off-worlders," another councilor replied, his skin flashing colors of worry and apology.

Jer pulled on his fur and growled in frustration. He knew it was a lot to ask of complete strangers to upend their lives for his daughter, but if they didn't, they would be complicit in her death. Plus, if he gave the order to blow up the Habitat, he could be putting others at risk to find his daughter, and he knew she wouldn't want that. Knowing her, she wouldn't want the Habitat destroyed either.

"If they won't leave voluntarily, arrest them, but hold off on destroying the Habitat until you have a direct order from myself or Marcus. I want everyone out and safe before those explosives go off. Where's Clear Seas?" He didn't wait for an answer, and started walking for the exit again.

"Clear Seas had to leave to attend to a family emergency a few minutes before word of your imminent arrival came in. I believe he should be at his home right now. Would you like us to take you to him?" Current asked as he swam hard to keep up with Jer's pace.

"I know where he lives," Jer growled. He'd been to Clear Sea's home so many times he'd lost count, both as a child when he'd begged to travel with his father, and usually with every Full Council meeting held on the planet since he'd been elected a councilor.

As he entered the main part of the platform used for off-world housing, he could see that people were lined up waiting for the lifts on dozens of the floors, with everyone heading up to the public transport terminal, and they all clearly recognized them, as the building quieted as people realized what was going on. He ignored them, grabbed a mask off the wall, and slapped it on. The moment it was fully activated, he stepped through the sonic shield, yanked one of the drones off the wall and took off, not waiting or caring if the others were ready and following.

He pushed his drone as fast as it would go, and dove for Clear Seas home. His ears popped with the rapid change in pressure as the mask struggled to keep up. Ten minutes later he pulled up in front of the home of what he'd once thought was a close friend. Shoving down the anger and betrayal he felt, he took a few deep breaths before swimming up to knock on the door. The others arrived just as he knocked.

Clear Seas opened the door, and a brief flash of astonishment crossed his skin as he saw him there, and then worry when he saw the group behind him.

"Jer, I didn't expect to see you for days, how..." he began speaking in Saber, but Jer cut him off.

"Senior Councilor Clear Seas, I am here as an official representative of the Senior Council. We have evidence showing that you altered information in the archives relating to the protests that my daughter was investigating. We believe that Ellie was attacked and my daughter abducted in order to keep them from discovering this information. A vote of no confidence has been taken, and you are being stripped of your rank and placed under arrest until such time as we can prove otherwise."

"Jer, please! I would never hurt your daughter or the Guild Master," Clear Seas replied, flashing astonishment. "Ellie was a good friend of mine, has been for decades."

"That is not for me to decide at this time. Will you come willingly or will we have to restrain you?" Jer asked.

"I...of course I'll come willingly, but I promise you Jer, I did *not* do what you are accusing me of," Clear Seas insisted.

"Papa, what's going on? Why is Councilor Chenzira saying you took the Translator? You wouldn't do that! You're trying to save her!" Stormy swam around in front of his father through the open door to stand between them, as if guarding his father from Jer, a book clutched tightly in one of his arms.

Jer struggled to keep his mask in place as he recognized the cover. It was one Marsee had translated.

Clear Seas looked at Jer for a moment, and then floated down to face his son, and made him turn around. "Stormy, it's alright. This is just a misunderstanding. I need to go with the Senior Councilor now, and I need you to be brave and be a good boy and stay here until your mother returns. Can you do that for me?"

"Yes, Papa," Stormy replied, clearly very scared as his skin was tinged in white.

"That's a good boy," Clear Seas said, and gave his son a quick hug before motioning him back inside, and shutting the door. Stormy floated up to look out the window.

Clear Seas looked at his son through the window for a moment, his body tense.

Jer frowned, wondering if Clear Seas intended to attack, or if he was just worried about his son's safety. "Honor Guard Aris, please remain here with Stormy until his mother returns." He was not going to leave Clear Seas son unprotected, regardless of whether or not Clear Seas was involved. If he wasn't, his son was in danger too.

Clear Seas sagged with relief, turned, and flashed his gratitude before swimming over towards the other guards, who took up position around him. Avery held up a shock collar. It would prevent Clear Seas from using his natural defenses and shocking the guards. Clear Seas sighed, but took it and put it on while Aris swam over and entered the house behind Stormy.

Jer turned to face Rip Current, "Councilor, please inform the rest of the Council that there will be an emergency session in an hour."

With that, Jer took off towards the council building and holding cells to begin the interrogation of an old and trusted friend. It was a somber procession as they swam back to the platform. Water Sprites stopped to watch in silence as they passed. Jer wished he'd been able to do this in private, but he was running out of time. Every second that ticked by carved a deep wound on his soul. They entered the lower levels of the council building where the rarely used holding cells were located, and found Marcus waiting for him by an open door. Clear Seas swam in. Jer followed behind, while the rest of the guard took up position on either side of the door, and at either end of the hall.

"Where's my daughter," he growled the moment the door was shut.

"I honestly don't know," Clear Seas replied, flashing his grief and sorrow. "I've had every room, home, and shuttle in this district searched twice, and we've found no sign of her. I have teams searching the surrounding wilds and every known cave in the area, and the other councilors are doing the same in their districts. The Sea Patrol is investigating any heat signature even remotely matching hers, and I've offered a reward for any information leading to her location. If it's mine to give, I will do so, gladly. Jer I promise you, I would never hurt your daughter. If you don't believe me, believe my son. He's Marsee's biggest fan, and if I hurt her, it would devastate him. But Jer, there's something you.."

"And what of the rest of my family?" Jer growled, cutting him off.

"I don't understand, Jer. What are you talking about?" Clear Seas asked. "I've not heard of anything else happening."

"Someone dropped off a basket of brownies, laced with Sand Spinner venom. Little Flower, GrandFather, Hope, and I were all poisoned, mere hours before your message came in. It nearly killed the others. I doubt I will ever forget the sound of Hope's screams."

Clear Seas flashed his horror at the news. "I swear, Jer. I had nothing to do with that either. I don't even know what a brownie is. But listen, Jer..."

Jer glared at him. "How do you explain the tampered evidence and logs regarding the incidents with the protesters and Deep Current? Only you and the Senior Archivist have access to modify evidence like that."

Clear Seas frowned at him in confusion. "It's been tampered with too? I knew there was missing evidence, but I didn't know anything was tampered with. As soon as your daughter informed me that evidence was missing, I contacted the Archivist to investigate. I'm still waiting on that report. I haven't made an edit in over five years. The last time I only made a change to correct the spelling of a name. I don't even have a clue how to change the logs. Ask anyone, tech was never my strong suit."

"So you're saying you didn't edit the uploaded security footage from the latest protest?" Marcus asked.

Clear Seas shook his head. "Edit it? No. I haven't even had a chance to watch it yet, what with everything else going on."

Jer raised a brow. "So you just uploaded evidence without watching it?"

Clear Seas shook his head again. "No. I didn't upload it, the guards did. As no one was hurt, they were processed and released. I didn't even know about the incident until about an hour afterwards, as I was meeting with Rip Current to go over numbers for the Habitat, in preparation for the resource allocation meeting."

He frowned, trying to decide if he believed Clear Seas. "If you aren't tampering with the evidence, why then did you suggest tampering with the video when you intended to kill my ward, and blame my daughter's psychosis for it?"

He had watched the video Kendra had shared with them on the long flight to the Water World, and he honestly wished he hadn't. To see someone he considered a friend calmly discussing killing his daughter, and blaming her for what they planned sickened him.

Clears Seas was silent and then slumped. "So you know about that?"

Jer growled at Clear Seas. "I fully understand discussing the threat that the Hue-man's posed after Little Flower's statement, but killing my daughter too, and blaming her for it? I thought you were my friend."

"I'm sorry Jer. About all of it. In a hundred years, it's probably the first time I've truly regretted a decision. I hated the very idea of hurting you and your family, but I saw no other way. We knew Kendra was watching our deliberation, and if we'd summoned Little Flower without her translator it would have raised suspicion with her and the rest of the guard. Tabor was adamant that Marsee was a dangerous threat, due to her illness, and would lose control and turn into a wild animal the moment we did anything, and that none of your species, including you, would have doubted it. I didn't believe it, not after how calm she remained after Little Flower sniffed out what we planned, but I'll be honest, when I saw how badly Ellie was injured, I thought Marsee had done it, until we found the ransom note and realized the guards were missing too."

Jer was silent for a while, chewing over that. It matched what he'd seen in the video, and to be fair, that had been his first thought too when the message had come in, even though he'd just been poisoned.

Before either he or Marcus could reply, Clear Seas continued. "Jer, your people haven't faced down the threat of war in ten thousand years, but it hasn't been all that long for my people. My grandfather fought in the last one. It took place about twenty years before your people showed up, and a lot of people died. Even the hint of a weapon was outlawed afterwards, ruthlessly. Only the stunners on the ships were allowed as a long range version of what we can do naturally, and only because it was the least violent method of controlling the Leviathan. I didn't even want to authorize the hand stunners for the trip to Earth. I was terrified that we'd bring that kind of violence back with the Hue-mans. I would do anything to protect my people as I know you would, but I promise you, I did not hurt Ellie or kidnap your daughter, and I no longer consider your people a threat. I saw that for myself at the Hallowed Eve festival. You've done good work with them."

Jer flicked both ears back in surprise. "War? I watched your people's sentience trial, and there was no mention of that kind of violence in your immediate history."

"My grandfather lied," Clear Seas replied. "He had everything moved from the Archives as well. He figured if you knew, we'd never be allowed in. My people weren't any better than the Hue-mans, although we've made significant progress, or at least I thought we had. Crime has decreased significantly since my grandfather's time, and until the recent violent protests, I haven't had to execute anyone in years."

Jer wasn't even sure what to say in response to that. "You've had to execute people over the protests? Why didn't you say something before Marsee came to visit?"

"Because that was months ago, back when I had to leave our conference on Digger, and I honestly thought no one would hurt them. They've both done more for this planet than any off-worlder. I tried to take precautions, and had locks added to their suite, and guards posted on them at all times, just to be safe. Plus, since that incident, the protests have mostly been peaceful, up until the one that happened the morning before your daughter arrived, and at that point it was too late to stop them from coming."

Jer raised a brow. "So why did you let Marsee speak to the protesters?"

Clear Seas snorted. "You're children can be very persuasive when they want to be, and honestly, what I was doing wasn't working. Her ideas before did more to help stop the protests than anything else we were doing, and I'd hoped that her popularity would help to calm the current situation, and it certainly seemed to. Jer, you would have been so proud of her. She handled the situation like she'd been doing it for decades."

"Councilor Current says you had a family emergency, what happened?" Marcus asked, changing the subject.

"Temperate was in a shuttle accident. I'm still not sure exactly what happened or his condition, but I was told his squadron was chasing off a Leviathan at the time. Jewel went straight to the trauma center when we found out, while I pulled Stormy out of school, just in case this wasn't an accident. We stopped at the house so Stormy could pick up a few items. I was just about to bring him back to my office when you showed up."

There was ding on his tablet with Myra's tone. He'd silenced everything else as had Marcus. Before he could look though, there was a knock on the door. "Come in," Jer yelled, expecting it to be Current coming to find him to prepare for the meeting, but was surprised when the door opened to reveal someone he only vaguely recognized, carrying a small box. "Who are you?" he growled, and the person flinched.

"Jer, go easy please. That's my Senior Staffer. What is it, Jelly?" Clear Seas asked.

"Sir, another package arrived…" Jelly couldn't continue, just handed the box over to Marcus, who was closest to the door, and flashed deep sorrow before leaving the room in a hurry, the door swishing closed behind her.

"Another?" Jer growled at Clear Seas. "Why didn't you mention it?"

Clear Seas opened his mouth to answer and swallowed hard. "I'm sorry. I figured you already knew. My message must have passed you while you were in jump. We received one of Marsee's claws yesterday afternoon almost exactly a day after we found Ellie."

Jer's heart cried out for his daughter. He hadn't been fast enough. If they were hurting her, he knew there was probably nothing left to his daughter, even if they did find her. They all looked at the box in Marcus's hands. Swallowing hard, Jer held his paw out and Marcus handed it over. Jer slowly took the cover off of the box with a shaking paw, and then cried out in horror at the sight of one of Marsee's mangled claws tied neatly with ribbon to a small pillow. Under it was a piece of paper. He reached in and slid out the paper.

> *I can do this for days. The question is, can she?*

He read the note aloud and then handed both to Marcus. Jer's paws shook with barely controlled rage, and he turned and glared at Clear Seas, but paused. Clear Seas looked positively sick. That wasn't the reaction he was expecting. Before he could get his brain to even form words, there was another knock on the door.

"Enter," he growled. The door swished open to reveal Sampson. "What are you doing here?" he asked, surprised.

Sampson held up his tablet. "I just received a message from Myra. GrandFather, Hope, and Little Flower are missing."

Jer growled, spun, and slammed Clear Seas up against the wall. "What have you done with them?" he yelled.

"I swear, Jer, on my oath, and all my ancestors and the lives of my family, before the Gods of the Bottomless Depths, I had nothing to do with this," Clear Seas signed, unable to speak with the grip Jer had him.

"Jer, let him go," Marcus ordered, pulling him back.

Jer growled at Clear Seas a moment longer before releasing him, yanked the box with the claw out of Marcus's hands, and started swimming out of the room with Marcus behind him.

"Jer, stop!" Clear Seas demanded.

Jer turned and growled at him. "What?"

"There's something I need to tell you and Marcus," he said. Pointedly looking at Sampson and the open door. Jer glared at Clear Seas a moment longer and motioned Sampson out and shut the door.

"Talk," Jer commanded.

"Ellie's not dead, at least she wasn't the last time I had an update from the Senior Healer. I put out a fake death announcement to protect her until she was recovered enough to give a statement. Only she and a select group of her healers know. I don't know who I can trust, and I was too afraid that someone would try to sneak in and finish her off if they knew she was still alive. She's the only lead we've got. Whoever attacked her wanted her dead, and they came very close. I couldn't put an honor guard on her because I had several stationed outside of Ellie's suite, and they're still missing. I don't know if they're involved, or if someone killed or took them too."

Jer sighed in relief hearing that Ellie was still alive, and prayed that Clear Seas was telling the truth, but the reminder about someone in the Guard being involved was flat out terrifying. They were the ones out looking for Marsee.

"Who sent you the footage from the protest," Marcus asked before Jer could wrangle his fear back down.

"Senior Honor Guard Stinger," Clear Seas said.

Jer swallowed hard at the implication. "I'm never going to find her, am I?" he whispered.

"Everyone on my planet is looking for her, Jer, not just the Sea Patrol and Guard. Once Ellie wakes up and we know who did this to her, we'll find her," Clear Seas replied.

"For your sake, we'd better," he growled, and spun to swim out of the room. He hit the switch hard to open the door and swam out.

"Jer, wait up!" Marcus called.

Jer slowed allowing Marcus to catch up, but didn't stop.

"Where are you going?" Marcus asked, when he left the council building instead of turning to swim to the higher level.

"To the Trauma Center. I need to confirm that this belongs to Marsee and to confirm Clear Sea's story," he replied.

"Good idea," Marcus replied and checked the time. "We still have a little time before the meeting. I'm going to talk to Stinger, and if there's still time, take a quick look at the suite. I'll meet you back at the conference room."

Jer nodded but didn't stop. A few minutes later he was at the Trauma Center and Jer demanded to see the Senior Healer in charge.

"I'm sorry, sir. She's in surgery right now," a very young healer signed.

He growled and the healer flinched. "If I have to talk to her while she's in surgery, I will. This is important."

"I'll...I'll see if she's available," she said, and swam through the door. A minute later she returned. "Follow me please." He followed her down several halls before she stopped him. "Wait here," she signed, and swam through the door.

Peering through the window he gasped. Ellie was the one being operated on. He couldn't see any of what was going on. There were too many healers blocking the view, but he recognized her face as it was turned towards him, a mask over her nose and mouth. *She's still in surgery?* he thought, horrified at the extent of the injuries she must have sustained, and watched as the triage nurse swam over to the Senior Healer. She handed off her tools to another healer and swam out the door.

"You have two minutes, Councilor. What is it?" she asked.

"We found this. I need to know if it belongs to my daughter, and how is she?" he asked, nodding towards the surgery.

"She's still alive, which frankly, with her injuries should have killed her long before we found her, but she didn't sustain any injuries that can't be repaired with time. This is her third surgery, and it'll be at least another hour before we're done with this one. She'll need at least two more once she's recovered some." The Healer took the box and opened it but didn't show any surprise at what she saw. "This is too small to belong to the...her," The Senior Healer nodded in Ellie's direction, "so it's probably your daughter's. I'll need my scanner. One moment." He watched her swim through the doorway again, pick up a scanner and return, as the implications of what she'd said hit him.

"Did she have a claw removed too?" he asked once she returned.

"Councilor, they were all removed, and I've lost count of the number of fractures we've repaired. I've seen victims of Leviathan attacks in better condition." He blanched. If they'd been capable of doing that to Ellie, what was happening to the rest of his family, to Marsee?

"Your daughter's name day?" the Healer asked.

He gave her that information and she pulled up Marsee's medical history and began scanning the claw.

"It's a match, and from the cellular decay, I would say it was removed about six to eight of our hours ago, which is consistent with the scan of her other claw. It's been too long to reattach, but we can use it to re-grow a replacement when you find her. And before you ask, I'm not finding any evidence of any other genetic material. If there was, it's been washed clean." He nodded and she called back to one of the other healers to fetch a stasis unit. "Do you need anything else?" she asked.

"No. Thank you."

She nodded and returned to surgery. He watched for a few moments before swimming back to the Council Building, his thoughts in a whirl. From what the healer had mentioned, he now had an approximate time to aim for before his daughter was harmed again, and when he'd have to relinquish his seat on the Council to protect her from further harm. Until then he needed his authority to help find her, although neither he or Marcus believed her kidnapper would release her, even if the demands were met. *A claw can be replaced,* he told himself, *and at least you know she was still alive as of six hours ago.*

He was halfway back to the Council Building before he remembered Temperate's accident. He turned and swam back to the Trauma Center and stopped at the triage desk.

"Was Temperate Seas brought in from a shuttle accident, and if so, how is he?"

"Yes, sir," the young healer replied. "But I don't know how he is. Would you like me to find out?"

He nodded, and she bolted out of the room again. A few minutes later, she returned.

"He's still being triaged, but he's awake and his condition is currently listed as stable."

"If that changes, have someone inform me," he ordered, and swam out without waiting for a reply.

# CHAPTER 25

# Wind Rider: Framed

Wind Rider paced in the hatchery, riddled with indecision. She was already overdue to lay her latest clutch, as one problem after another had prevented her from making her way to the hatchery, but every fiber of her being said she needed to get to the Water World as quickly as possible, only the ships couldn't support a clutch, and there weren't any hatcheries on the Water World. If she left, she'd lose her clutch.

She'd never be able to make it there and back before the need to lay became unbearable. It was already uncomfortable, and it would take at least a day before she was done laying, but she was positive something had happened to her daughter too. The last message she'd had from her was nearly a day before word about Ellie and Marsee had come in, and it would take almost six days to reach the Water World. Six days she couldn't afford to be out of communication.

"Ma'am, you need to calm down. It's not good for the eggs," one of the attendants said.

She glared at the attendant, but winced as her body demanded she lay. *Lay the eggs first. That'll give Jer and Marcus time to investigate,* she decided again, although she nearly turned around and walked back out.

Wobbling over to the nest, she forced her body to relax and begin the laying process. Once somewhat comfortably settled on the nest, she unclipped her tablet again, and scanned for a message, praying there would be one from her daughter, even though there hadn't been a notification since the last time she'd looked. There wasn't. Hissing in worry, she nearly threw the tablet across the room.

*Where is she?* she asked for the hundredth time.

She pulled up the last message she'd received from Petra and stared at it, wondering again why Petra had been so angry with her. She'd done everything she could to allow Petra the freedom to explore her passions, and had even sided with her daughter's preference for nesting location, even though it was so far away. She'd thought Petra would have been happy, but the response she'd received instead had shocked her. Then when news of Ellie's attack and Marsee's kidnapping had occurred, and Petra hadn't responded, she'd been terrified, but at first thought that Petra had been called in to help with the search and evacuation, and had perhaps been too busy to respond, but it had been far too long since that last message.

*Petra should have had a few minutes to respond by now. Is she just mad at me for some reason, or did something happen to her too? If so, why haven't they had a ransom note for her yet?*

Finally, unable to stand her worry anymore, Wind Rider logged into her daughter's account and began reading through her daughter's messages, most of which were from other people looking for her. With every message, her worry increased. About ten minutes later she came to a group thread between her and the other two pilots on Ellie's ship, and her heart froze at what she read.

*No. I don't believe it!* Wind Rider thought. *She can't be behind this.*

Moments later she received a message from someone she didn't know.

***I know what you did. I have your daughter and her recorded confession of what you made her do. If you want her to live and that evidence to disappear, all you have to do is publicly admit what you did. You'd better hurry though, she could really use some medical attention.***

A picture appeared of Petra locked in chains with her beautiful purple wings hanging broken and tattered. Wind Rider gasped in horror causing her senior attendant to ask if there was a problem. She hissed at him.

*Of course if you don't care about her, then perhaps you care about your eggs. I expect you to be here and turn yourself in, in two days time. If you're not, every hatchery on your planet will be destroyed. Tell anyone about these messages and I'll know, and your daughter will die, slowly.*

*Two days?!* She'd never make it to the Water World in two days. As she stared at the message, at a complete loss for what to do, the messages suddenly vanished.

Moments later she had contraction. From the pain caused by the size of the egg, she knew it was a rare female embryo before it had even been scanned. She turned to look and gasped as the light purple color of the shell matched Petra's egg. When the attendants came to claim and transfer the egg, she snapped and furled her wings protectively over her daughter, hissing at them to back off. *No one was touching her children! No one!*

Her senior attendant motioned the others to back off and grinned at Wind Rider. A female egg was cause for celebration. "Shall we move your daughter to your personal incubator, Nest Mother? It's safer for her there. You'll want her to stay warm and protected."

Wind Rider hissed at him again. He wasn't the least bit phased. While she rarely reacted as strongly, it wasn't unusual for nest mothers to react instinctively and become protective over their eggs, especially in their first few clutches, or if there was a female egg in the clutch.

She hovered protectively over her egg, trying to decide if she could inform her senior guard about the threat, or if that would just get Petra killed.

*Remember your oath, Wind Rider,* she chided herself.

It nearly tore her heart out, but she called the head of her guard and ordered extra patrols on the hatcheries, hoping that if she didn't explicitly call out the threat she'd received, that it would be enough to protect her daughter, assuming she wasn't already dead. When he asked if there was a problem he should be aware of, she just stated that she was probably being overprotective, having just laid a female egg, with everything else going on. He seemed to accept that as just cause, and she waited, curious if another response would come in.

When nothing did, she breathed a sigh of relief, and finally relaxed enough to allow her attendant to transfer the egg to her personal incubator, but she followed him the entire way, and then locked it, marking the egg as hers.

She stared through the window for several long moments, before waddling back to her nest to lay another egg.

"Two!" her attendant exclaimed before Wind Rider could turn and look.

She just stared at the second female egg in almost as much shock as the attendant. No clutch ever had two female eggs, not in thousands of years.

*Well, at least my people won't suffer from our loss if Petra and I are executed,* she thought morosely, as she followed the second egg over to the incubators. She stared at the second egg, this one more blue than purple, wondering if she'd live long enough to meet her daughters. She would gladly admit to anything to protect her children, but she'd never make it in time.

She paced as she tried to figure out what to do. *Should I just admit to it now or do I tell Marcus and Jer? If I do, and they start looking for her, will they just kill her, and release the confession anyway? But what if I'm wrong and she is behind this? If I don't tell them, Marsee could die too. How did he know I'd read her messages though? Only the Senior Council should know I accessed her account without logging a ticket. Was this Clear Sea's doing? I wonder if Jer and Marcus have arrested Clear Seas yet?* She stopped and froze. *Whoever sent this has to be on this planet. It arrived too soon after I saw Petra's messages to be from the water world, unless it was just a coincidence.*

She stopped pacing, and tried to figure out who the person was that had messaged her. All she had was the name. Everything else had disappeared. She opened the census registry looking for the name, but groaned when the results came back. There were hundreds of people with the name of Snapper Fish on the Water World, and none on Flyer.

Growling again, she made her way back to the nest and called the local commander of the Ship's Guild.

"Ma'am?" the Commander asked when she answered.

"I need to leave here in a day, give or take, and get to the Water World as fast as possible," she said. "Is there any way I can get there in a day?"

The Commander nodded. "I figured as much, ma'am, what with everything going on. We can have the transport ship we originally sent to Earth here by then for you to use. With the emergency jump we should be able to get you there in just over eighteen hours. It'll be an uncomfortable trip. Emergency jump is...unsettling."

"I don't care. I'll take it. Thank you," she said, and hung up. She curled up on the nest again to wait for her next egg, but the only thing she could see was the sight of her daughter, battered and broken, floating in chains, and there was absolutely nothing she could do to help her.

# CHAPTER 26

# Marcus: Stinger

Marcus watched Jer swim off across the square towards the Trauma Center and sighed with worry for his younger brother and family. He was relieved to hear that Ellie was still alive, and prayed that Clear Seas was telling the truth, but if he was, then who was behind all of this, and what was their real goal?

Shoving his worry behind his mask, he turned and swam up to the next floor, where Stinger's office was located, and found the outer office empty, save for a single guard.

That guard snapped to attention the moment she saw him. "Sir, if you're looking for the Senior Honor Guard, he's in Command."

Marcus nodded and turned, making his way down to Command, where he found dozens of Sprites flashing far quicker than he could follow in communication with others. The monitors on the wall showed various maps with thousands of points lit up.

He watched unobserved for several moments before swimming in, but eventually, the room stilled and communication paused as he was noticed. One Sprite, that Marcus had only met a few times, turned to face him, and stiffened when he realized who was there.

Stinger flashed a wave of regret and apology. "I'm sorry, sir. We've not found her yet. I assume you're here to arrest me?"

Marcus raised a brow. "Should I be arresting you?"

"No. I had nothing to do with this," Stinger replied. "I give you my word, but I recognize you have no reason to trust me, or any of us for that matter. My guards are missing, and if they're behind this, then I'm ultimately responsible for their actions. I've failed you, and failed to protect them, and I'll take whatever punishment you deem fit."

Surprise rippled through the room at his words. Marcus tilted his head in acknowledgement, but then motioned towards the door, keeping his own surprise firmly locked down. Stinger swam out without further word, and Marcus followed him back to Stinger's office. He shut the door behind him, and set up his tablet to record the conversation, even though he knew everything in this room was automatically recorded.

"Tell me what you know," Marcus demanded.

"We have record of Marsee entering the suite at 8:04 pm, which matches when Clear Seas says he dropped them off, and again at 11:30 pm. Ellie entered the suite at 2:24 am. Guild Master Agate received a message at 5:15 am from Ellie indicating a change of plans. Clear Seas entered the suite at 2:03 pm, when he found Ellie and called for help three minutes later. We had the expected check-in from the morning guard at 6:58 am, but no updates afterwards."

"You didn't find that suspicious?" Marcus asked.

"No." Stinger replied. "They were on a dark watch. Their beacons are monitored, but communication is limited to avoid giving away their position. We've found their beacons, but haven't found them."

"Have you found any evidence of them on the security cameras?" Marcus asked next.

"No. The one in the suite and just outside was tampered with. Somehow, whoever did this managed to loop footage of the empty suite and entrance, and we found nothing on any of the nearby cameras. They don't appear to be altered, which would indicate that the people involved had knowledge of where they were located."

Marcus frowned but nodded. "And of your search?"

"We've searched every home and building in Council Platform, twice, with different guards checking each time. The same has happened in each of the major cities, and has shifted to the smaller communities and surrounding wilds. We've had no leads either. A few people have mentioned seeing Marsee in the Arboretum the night before, which would be consistent with when she re-entered the suite, but that's it. We did find the ransom note in the Arboretum, but we have no idea when it was left, and no footage of the area where it was found."

"How well do you know the guards that were watching her?"

"They are, or were, some of my best guards," Stinger replied. "I honestly find it hard to believe they were behind this, and fully believe they're dead."

"The protest the other day, where the Sea Patrol was called in. What happened?"

"Several members of the Council were leaving the building when the protesters rushed them and prevented them from leaving. Thankfully no one was hurt."

"That's not what the protesters claim," Marcus replied. "According to the information Marsee left us, they said they were called in and then insulted, and several of their members were hurt in the process."

Stinger flashed confusion. "I'll admit I wasn't here when it happened, but I watched the footage and I wasn't told that anyone was hurt, on either side. Several people were arrested, but most fled the moment the Sea Patrol arrived."

"Where were you?" Marcus asked.

"The Willow District, visiting family. My sister just gave birth," Stinger replied.

"Send me their contact information. Did you retrieve the footage or did someone else?"

"Clear Seas uploaded it, as far as I know. Rumor has it you arrested him for altering the footage?"

Marcus raised a brow at just how quickly that information had been spread. Only a few people would have been with Jer at the time and known why Clear Seas was arrested. "He states your guards up-loaded it."

Stinger flashed surprise. "That wasn't what I saw when I viewed it. It very clearly showed Clear Seas uploaded it."

"Who told you about the reason for Clear Sea's arrest?"

"I received notification from Rip Current about an emergency Council meeting being scheduled, and the reason."

Marcus had him show him the message to confirm. "Are the protesters you arrested the other day still being held?" Marcus asked.

Stinger shook his head. "No, they were all processed and released, pending review by the Council."

"Released? Deep Current indicated they were all missing, along with close to fifty other people over the past year."

Stinger blinked at him and flashed his shock. "Missing?! I'm not aware of anyone else missing. I swear."

Marcus shrugged. "We have no way of knowing if any of that is true or not, but we did find evidence that the footage from the other day was altered."

Stinger sighed and leaned back in his seat. "I'll send you a list of everyone that was on duty that day, assuming it hasn't been altered either. You'll want to talk with Tanner, she's my second, and her son is one of the missing guards. She was in charge that day."

"How soon after the incident did you watch the footage?"

"Not until the next morning," Stinger replied. "I saw it on the news first."

Marcus pulled up the recording. "Can you identify the councilors involved?" He was pretty sure who they were, but he wanted confirmation.

Stinger didn't even look at the video. "Spotted Trout, Whispering Fronds, and Crystal Cove."

Marcus nodded. "Thank you. Has anyone investigated the suite yet?"

"No. Just Clear Seas. None of my guards can enter the suite without difficulty. We do have statements from the off-world Healers and Clear Seas, which should already be uploaded for evidence."

"I'll confirm with the Healers. What suite were they in?" he asked next. That hadn't been on his report.

"The one typically reserved for you," Stinger replied.

Marcus raised a brow at that. "Why my suite?"

Stinger shrugged. "I have no idea. That order came from Clear Seas."

Marcus nodded. He'd run out of questions and considered what he'd learned. "I don't have any evidence to say you're involved at this point, but I don't have anything that says you're not either. For now, I'm not relieving you of duty. Stay in Council Platform. If you do need to leave, I want to know why and where you're going first."

"Yes, sir," Stinger replied. He honestly seemed surprised that Marcus wasn't relieving him of duty.

"You're surprised, why?" Marcus asked.

"Because you have no reason to trust me," Stinger replied.

"True, but I have no reason to trust anyone else either. I am putting Avery in charge of the search following the council meeting," Marcus said.

"Yes, sir."

"Where's Tanner now?"

"Out on search," Stinger replied. "I can get her here in fifteen."

Marcus checked the time again and frowned. He wouldn't have enough time before the meeting.

"Call her in. I'll question her in front of the Council," Marcus ordered, and left to examine the suite. He had just enough time to get a quick look if he hurried.

When he arrived he used his authorization to open the door, not sure what he was going to see, but everything looked normal at first. He glanced in the nearest bedroom, not seeing anything, and then made his way to the interior suite and swallowed hard at what he saw.

"Ancient Gods," he whispered.

The room was a disaster, and there was far more blood than he'd ever had the horror to witness in his career.

Deep inside he felt his own slumbering instinct stir, reacting to his horror at what Ellie must have gone through, and fear for his missing family. He squashed it down hard, turned and left. It would take far more time than he had to examine the suite, and he needed time to prepare for the meeting.

But the beast inside him, woken by the harm done to his family and friends, refused to settle back down to slumber, and paced in the back Marcus's mind. They both knew that if Clear Seas and the protesters weren't behind this, then someone else on the Council or Guard likely was, and if this was a coup, then he could very well be swimming to his death.

By the time he approached the council building again, Honor Guards were stationed outside the entrance, as was standard procedure before a council meeting. He glared at both guards, praying they wouldn't try anything as he swam past.

The both looked away unable to meet his eye, flashing regret and shame.

He said nothing as he swam past but breathed a sigh of relief once he made it safely inside.

Two more guards were stationed outside of the senior's conference room as he approached. They reacted the same way, and even swam off some to give him distance to pass through.

"Sir, we recognized that you have no reason to trust us, but on our honor and lives, I swear we had nothing to do with this," one of the guards stated. "Two of your guards have been stationed inside the council chamber."

He nodded at them for recognizing his lack of trust in them, and quickly made his way inside. Jer was already there and pacing. He spun when Marcus entered.

"Has something else happened?" Marcus asked.

"No, I just can't sit still," Jer replied.

Marcus swam over to his brother and pulled him in for a hug, grabbing him by the scruff. "We'll find them and we'll make those who did this pay for it dearly."

Jer shook in his arms, but eventually calmed and pulled away with a nod. "Clear Seas was telling the truth about Ellie and Temperate.

The Senior Healer confirmed the claw was Marsee's and likely removed about six hours ago."

Marcus frowned. "Six hours? Well, at least we knew she was alive then."

Jer nodded and gave a full rundown of he learned.

Marcus did the same. He looked up at the clock and frowned. "It's time. Are you ready for this?"

Jer snorted at him. "I believe the phrase GrandFather used was 'I'd rather have my arm stuck up a chenzie's butt. It's far less painful."

Marcus burst out laughing in surprise. "I won't disagree there, even though I've never had that distinct pleasure. I'll take GrandFather's word for it," but then he sobered. "If the deadline has already been passed, when do you want to step down? Now or wait until the end of the day?"

Jer frowned. "I'll step down after the Habitat is destroyed. I'm hoping that if we at least show we're trying to do as requested, they'll let Marsee go."

"You know they won't," Marcus warned.

"I know, but I can still hope. Come on. Let's get this over with." Jer swam over to the entrance to the council chamber and waited for Marcus to fill in behind him, took several calming breaths, and hit the switch to the door.

While never particularly religious, Marcus sent up a prayer to the Ancient Gods as he entered anyway.

Jer as the highest ranking member of the Senior Council in attendance, by a whopping day, started the meeting and swam forward. "Following word that my daughter had been taken hostage, I logged into her account, and found notes and information provided by Deep Current regarding the protest that occurred the morning my daughter and the Senior Guild Master arrived on this planet. His claims of what happened that day did not match official evidence, and it was determined that the recording of the altercation that occurred has been tampered with. According to the information, the last person to edit that record was Clear Seas. We do not know if he did in fact make those changes, or if someone else has figured out how to tamper with official evidence in order to make it look that way. Until we are able to confirm who edited that footage, the Senior Council has taken a vote of no confidence in Clear Seas, and temporarily arrested and removed him from office. Until such time as my daughter is returned safely, and Clear Seas guilt or innocence is determined, no Senior Councilor will be elected in his place."

Murmurs and flashes of light followed this announcement, which Marcus wasn't surprised about. Preventing a vote was unprecedented but they weren't going to hand over a council to someone who might be staging a coup. He scanned the chamber, looking for anyone who looked either pleased or angry by Jer's announcement, and found several, which was concerning.

"Councilor Spotted Trout, please stand." When the councilor in question had floated up from their seat, Jer continued. "Please tell the Council what happened at the protest the morning before my daughter arrived?"

Marcus listen and watched closely as Spotted Trout gave the same story as shown on the altered evidence. Whispering Fronds, and Crystal Cove gave the same testimony. He didn't expect them to say differently, but if they did find out that the footage had been altered, they now had the councilors lying under oath.

"Honor Guard Tanner," please come forward.

A large female Sprite swam forward out of the visitors booth, her body stiff with tension, but her face the calm mask of a guard.

"Honor Guard, it is my understanding that you were in charge the morning of the protest," Jer said.

"Yes, sir," she replied.

"Did Honor Guard Stinger inform you of why you were placed in charge?"

"Yes, sir. His sister just gave birth and he was taking leave to visit them," she replied.

"Please inform me of what happened at the protest, from the moment you were informed."

"I was in the Guard office when the call came in. Command dispatched the Sea Patrol as their ship was closest. When I arrived on scene a minute or so later, both Honor Guards stationed at the entrance had been knocked unconscious, along with several other people, and the councilors pinned against a wall, surrounded by the crowd. I stunned several people, attempting to make my way to the councilors, before backup from the Sea Patrol and Honor Guard arrived. When they arrived, the crowd dispersed. Those stunned were restrained and woken, along with the guards. As no one was seriously injured, they were processed and released pending further review by the council."

"Who uploaded the footage from the altercation?" Jer asked.

"I don't know, sir." Tanner flashed her apology. "Before I could sign off on it, Clear Seas called indicating that he wanted a hidden watch on your daughter and the Senior Guild Master. In light of the recent events, I chose to do that myself, until they were safely in their suite. As it was late when I returned, and as Stinger was expected back in the morning, I left the case for him to close out."

"Call in the guards that were at the entrance," Jer ordered.

"I can't sir. They're missing, along with my son, who was guarding your daughter when they were taken, and three others," Tanner replied, flashing her worry and apology. "On my life and honor, I swear my son would not do this. He would give his life to save your daughter, and I fully believe that's what happened." Her skin rippled with grief, and she had to take several calming breaths before bringing her emotions back under control.

Marcus saw the slightest shiver from Jer's tail. He was honestly surprised Jer was maintaining his calm as well as he was. Jer nodded and dismissed the guard before turning to swim back to his seat. His face was the calm mask expected of a Senior Councilor, but Marcus knew his little brother too well. Jer was terrified.

*If the guards wouldn't protect his family, how did Marsee stand a chance?*

# CHAPTER 27

# Super Stormy

Stormy watched as Councilor Chenzira turned and swam off, with the guards surrounding his father. The other councilors remained behind watching the procession as well. Stormy shifted his attention from his father to the councilors and frowned, not liking what he saw. They looked at each other briefly with expressions that he didn't quite understand. They didn't show their emotions on their skin, but he was sure they were happy about his father being dragged off. All but one of the Councilors swam off to catch up with the group, but the one Chenzira had spoken to turned and swam off in the opposite direction.

Stormy hugged his precious book, trying to decide what to do. His tentacles were twitching. He just knew that the councilor knew something, but he wasn't sure what to do. He doubted the guard would believe him after his father had just been arrested. *You don't need to have super powers to fight the darkness, just bravery and courage,* he told himself, and turned to head in the direction of his room.

"Where are you going?" the guard asked, looking at him with a frown.

"My room," Stormy signed and swam off. The guard followed behind and proceeded to check out his room before letting him inside. Stormy waited patiently, practicing the calm mask his father had been teaching him, to do his best not to give away what he planned, and then swam in, locking the door behind him after the guard exited. After setting his precious book on his desk, he swam over and hit the hidden switch behind his bookshelf and a small panel opened, just big enough for him to squeeze through. He lit up his skin and swam through the small tunnel that led through the mountain side to the emergency exit, and sighed with relief when he saw the councilor still swimming off in the distance.

*I'll find you, Translator. I promise!* he thought, and swam hard to keep the councilor in sight, hoping that if he saved his hero, then she would be able to save his Papa. He just prayed he was right.

Stormy swam harder than he'd ever swum before, ducking behind buildings and hiding in the seaweed as he tried to keep up with the councilor that had shown such glee at his father's arrest. *Being a superhero is hard work,* he thought, as he peered through a tall clump of sea grass to watch as the councilor ducked inside a building. A few minutes later he reappeared with something rolled up and tucked under his arm, and took off again.

Stormy waited until the evil villain was just barely out of sight, before swimming as fast as he could from one hiding place to another. After another ten minutes of this, the councilor left the confines of the city and well established travel lane, and swam out into the wilds. *Where is he going?* Stormy wondered, but still followed out after, well aware that this was far beyond where he was allowed to swim, and completely off the normal and guarded swim lanes. That fact made him even more convinced this councilor was behind the Translator's disappearance. He just hoped he'd be able to find his way back, assuming he wasn't eaten by a predator first.

Nearly an hour later, he was hiding behind a rock formation when his nemesis stopped, looked around to see if anyone was watching, and then ducked through some tall grasses against the side of a cliff, and disappeared.

*Woah! A secret lair!* Stormy thought, and waited for the councilor to reappear.

...

...

And waited.

...

...

He was debating with himself if he should check it out, afraid that the councilor had snuck out another exit, when he suddenly reappeared, this time carrying something big and bulky over his shoulder.

Stormy wasn't sure what to do as there wasn't anywhere good to hide up ahead. They were at the Ridge, the remains of an ancient mountain that had been worn down to nothing but small islands, that marked the edge of the Trench. After that there would be nothing but open seas for nearly a hundred leagues. He'd been out this way once on a school trip, to see the islands, but they never went down into the Trench, or further out to sea. That's where the Leviathan lived. He decided to wait to see if the councilor would return. If he didn't after a while, then he'd go check it out. Stormy's patience was rewarded when the councilor returned only a few minutes later without whatever he'd been carrying and swam quickly past, on his way back the way they'd come.

Stormy counted slowly to a hundred, to make sure the Councilor was truly gone, and then swam as fast as he could through the canyon, up to the edge of the Trench, and peered down. He couldn't see anything in the darkness, so swallowing hard against the fear rising in throat, he dove down, looking frantically for whatever it was the councilor must have thrown over the edge.

He swam down for a good fifteen or twenty minutes, far deeper than he'd ever gone before. He was shivering from the colder water, and starting to feel uncomfortable from the deeper sea pressure. It was getting darker the deeper he went, and he decided to risk lighting up his skin to see better. If he didn't see something he'd have to turn around and head back soon anyway. As soon as he did, he saw a small ledge below him, in front of what looked like a cave entrance. On the ledge was the large object, now teetering precariously on the edge.

Diving hard, he made it to the object just before it went over, and pulled with everything he was worth to drag it back onto the ledge.

Whatever it was, it was heavy. Once it was no longer at risk from falling further, he examined the object. It looked like a large bag, but he couldn't see any way to open it. Realizing it must be upside down, he shoved it hard, digging his tentacles into a crack in the ledge for leverage. Eventually he was able to roll the heavy object over and found the seam.

With trembling hands, he carefully opened it and then swam back in horror as a large webbed hand flopped out. *Someone's in the bag!* If he hadn't already had his skin lit up to see, he'd have been pure white with terror. *Come on Stormy, be brave like the Night Flyer. You need to find out who it is.* He was just relieved it wasn't the furry arm of the Translator, like he'd feared.

He slowly opened the bag all the way, but it was too dark for him to make out who it was, so he lit his skin up brighter so he could get a better look, and then gasped! It was the man they were all looking for! *Is he dead? How do you even tell?*

Stormy shook Deep Current hard and the man's eyes fluttered open briefly before closing again. *He's alive! Now what do I do? He's too big to swim back with.* Before he could figure out what to do, there was a screech that made his blood freeze.

Everyone knew that sound. *Leviathan!*

Stormy cautiously peered over the ledge and saw the massive shape of the Leviathan below, heading straight towards him. Scrambling quickly back, he grabbed the edge of the bag and pulled with all he was worth towards the cave behind him.

*Come on Stormy, You're a superhero, use your super strength! Pull!*

Suddenly, whatever the bag was catching on must have given way as he practically flew towards the cave with Deep Current in tow. He made it to the cave just as the great head of the Leviathan started appearing above the ledge.

He fought hard to lock down his emotions and keep his skin from lighting up with fear. *Stay dark, stay dark, stay dark!* he told himself. *Superheroes are brave. They aren't afraid of a silly old Leviathan. You're a creature of the dark, just like the Night Flyer, and the Leviathan is too big to get into this tiny cave.* He hoped. He practically stopped breathing as the giant eye of the Leviathan appeared, nearly as big as his Papa, and not ten feet from him, and then sighed with relief as it slowly continued on, ignoring him.

It was another twenty minutes before Stormy dared to move and when he did, he dragged Deep Current further into the cave, away from the Leviathan that continued to hover just outside. When he was far enough in that he was sure the creature couldn't get him, he let off a little bit of light to get a better look around. He was in a long tunnel. *Probably an ancient lava tube.*

Turning his attention back to Deep Current, he hovered and thought. *If the councilor was trying to get rid of Deep Current, then Deep Current must not be the one who took the Translator. Does that mean the councilor did?* He thought so. *So, where is she? Another cave or maybe the one he ducked into earlier? Did he throw her over the Trench too? Oh I hope not!*

He gave Deep Current another hard shake, and this time he woke up.

"Who are you?" Deep Current flashed, groggily.

Stormy didn't say. He knew everyone would recognize his name. He was surprised Deep Current didn't recognize him, but it was dark in the cave. "Are you Deep Current?" he flashed.

"I am. Where am I?" Deep Current sat up, rubbing the side of his head.

"In a cave in the Trench. Don't go out. There's a Leviathan just outside," Stormy warned.

"How did we get here? For that matter, what are you doing here? You're far too young to be in the Trench by yourself."

"I followed one of the councilors who came to arrest my father, and watched him throw you over the edge. Before I could figure out how to get you out, the Leviathan showed up."

As if to accentuate his story, the Leviathan let out another loud screech, making them both jump.

"Well then, I guess I have you to thank for saving my life. Who's your father?" Deep Current asked.

Stormy didn't reply, instead asked another question of his own. "Did you kill the Senior Guild Master and kidnap the Translator?"

"What?! The Guild Master is dead? Bottomless Depths! No, of course not!" Deep Current said. "Why would I kidnap the Translator? She was trying to help me. Who would do such a thing? Tell me, which councilor dumped me over the edge?"

"I don't know. I've seen him before, but I don't remember his name. He came with Senior Councilor Chenzira and several others. The Senior Councilor didn't say his name." He was pretty sure that the councilor had been at his house before, but his father brought dozens of people by on a regular occurrence, and he was horrible at remembering people's names. There were just so many people that his father expected him to know. *I need to work on that more,* he thought absently.

"Who's your father? I need to know. He's in a lot of danger from this other councilor," Deep Current said.

Stormy thought for a while before deciding to trust Deep Current. "My father is Senior Councilor Clear Seas, or he was anyway. Councilor Chenzira said he's been stripped of his rank for..." Stormy thought for a moment. "...for tampering with evidence in the archives related to the murder of the Guild Master and kidnapping of his daughter. I don't know why they think that though. Everyone is looking for you."

"I swear, I did no such thing. The last I remember, I was waiting for the Translator in the Arboretum. She was supposed to meet up with me to give me information on what happened to *my* father. She was late and I was about to leave when someone from the Sea Patrol approached saying they had a message for me from her stating a change of location. I arrived but someone shocked me and I don't remember anything else until I woke up here, just now."

"So someone is trying to hurt both you and my father?" Stormy asked, frowning at the expression on Deep Current's face. Although Deep Current kept his skin dark, Stormy had a feeling that it was a mix of anger and betrayal.

"It sure looks that way. I need to warn the Senior Council," Deep Current said. "But first we need to find a way out of here. Come on, let's see where this tunnel leads. Maybe there's another way out."

The lava tube continued down at a gradual slope for a long way. It was almost too deep for him and he struggled to breath, but it was safer than going back out with the Leviathan. They saw a few smaller fish, but nothing dangerous, not with Deep Current there anyway. Just as he was debating telling Deep Current he needed to go back, they found a branch that went back up. They followed it back up and found several more branching tunnels. They followed several that all ended in dead ends before one where they suddenly found themselves floating above water. Deep Current flared his skin to light up the area around them and Stormy gasped. The Translator lay curled up in a ball on a small ledge.

"Translator! Wake up!" Deep Current yelled out in her language, but she didn't respond.

"What's wrong with her?" Stormy asked.

"I don't know," Deep Current replied, and heaved himself up on the ledge and started to crawl his way over to her. The moment Current was out of the water, Marsee exploded with a snarl in Current's direction. Deep Current rolled away and back into the water a mere fraction of a second before Marsee's attack landed. Stormy swam back in a hurry to get away from her swiping claws.

"Marsee. I'm not going to hurt you. We're here to rescue you," Deep Current both flashed and spoke in her language, once he came back above the water.

Marsee continued to growl and pace along the ledge.

"Marsee, I promise. I didn't do this to you," he tried again.

Stormy's skin lit up in a mix of fear and worry too. She looked so fierce and wild, not even seeming to notice her mangled paw. "Translator, it's me, Stormy Seas. Your biggest fan, remember? I would never hurt you," Stormy signed. "We're here to help."

Marsee stopped and tilted her head at him, looking at him in confusion, almost as if she didn't remember him, but then moments later, she suddenly collapsed, her body shaking hard for a few moments, and then stilled.

"Marsee?" Deep Current called out in her language, but she didn't respond. He cautiously swam up again and slowly reached out to shake her shoulder. She didn't move. He felt her ears and carefully examined her paw. It was swollen twice the size of the others and covered in blood. Deep Current checked her for other signs of injuries but didn't find anything. Unable to wake her, he turned to talk to Stormy. "She's alive, but she's been injured and she's really cold. We need to get her help and quickly, but there is no way we can take her down the lava tube without a mask."

"So how do we get her out of here?" Stormy asked.

Deep Current swam back and forth, trying to figure out what to do, and then stopped to stare at the Translator for a moment before turning back to Stormy. "You need to go for help. I'll stay here and guard her in case her kidnapper comes back, and try to warm her up. But this is very important, you can't tell anyone but her father what you know or how you know it. If the councilor who did this finds out before her father does, all of our lives are at risk. Do you understand?"

Stormy gulped but nodded.

"If you can't find her father, find a mask and bring it back and we'll drag her out." He paused as if making a difficult decision, and then made an expression of pain and sorrow before adding. "Tell Chenzira that I was sent to my uncle's house in Council Platform. Now go."

Stormy dove and swam for all he was worth. He took two wrong turns before finding his way back to the ledge. Creeping slowly to the edge of the cave, keeping his skin firmly blacked out, even though he was shaking in terror, he looked out. The Leviathan was still there, but looking away from the small ledge.

Very slowly, he creeped out of the cave and drifted up, trying to move as little as possible. It felt like it took forever to make it up and over the ledge but as soon as he did, he took off again, trying to figure out where to go to find the Translator's father. Then he remembered that he said there would be an emergency council meeting. *It's been hours, but maybe it's still going,* he thought. *Either way, he'd most likely be at the council building.*

Stormy dug deep and swam even faster. His little tentacles ached with the effort, but finally he could see the entrance to the council building and hovered. The honor guard was at the entrance, indicating the Council was still in session, and he breathed a sigh of relief, but then frowned. *How am I going to get inside without telling the Guards what I know? They'd never believe me anyway,* he thought, and then smiled. *No one would expect a young fry like me would break into the council chamber while it was in session either. I just hope they don't recognize me.*

Calming his breathing, he slowly swam up to a group of other small fry playing in the park and then made his way over to the council building but down from the entrance. As expected, the guards completely ignored him as he swam past and floated nearby. He pretending not to pay any attention to them, and started acting like he was waiting or looking for someone. He waited until they stopped someone else. When he was sure they weren't watching him, he ducked inside, and bolted for the council chamber.

"Stop! Get back here!" The guard called out, but he didn't stop. Instead, he swam faster. There were two more guards by the entrance to the chamber, and they tried to stop him too, but he ducked and swerved around them, and swam as fast as he could into the chamber with the guards right behind him.

He found the Translator's father sitting at the Senior Councilor's podium and frantically signed and flashed "I know where she is!" a moment before he was tackled hard from behind by the guards.

"Stop!" came the command from the Senior Councilor. "Let him speak!"

The guards let him go, but didn't back off. Stormy frantically looked around the chamber at the other councilors, until he found the one he was looking for.

"I found Deep Current *and* the Translator. Deep Current didn't do it. He did!" Stormy said, pointing to the councilor that had thrown Deep Current over the ledge. The Council erupted with the accusation.

"Guards, arrest Rip Current!" the Senior Councilor roared. The guards left his side, swarmed Rip Current, and quickly collared him to prevent him from using his electric defenses on anyone.

"I did no such thing! Let go of me this instant!" the councilor flashed, as the guards dragged him down in front of the Senior Councilors. "He's lying to protect his father."

"I am not!" Stormy signed back. "I promise!"

"Stormy, this is a very serious accusation you've made. Tell me what you know and how you know it," the Translator's father signed.

"When you left with my father, I saw *this* councilor show his anger at you for telling him what to do, and then happiness as my father was escorted away. I didn't like it, so I snuck out of our house and followed him, first to a house where he picked up something, and then to a hidden cave by the Trench. When he came out of the cave he was carrying something really big and heavy and swam towards the Trench. He returned a few minutes later without it. After he left, I swam down into the Trench and found it lying on a ledge in front of a cave. When I looked at it, I saw it was a bag and opened it and found Deep Current asleep inside."

"Are you really going to believe the lies a child?" the councilor flashed, his arms now cuffed and restrained, preventing him from signing.

"Enough!" the Senior Councilor growled at Current. "Interrupt again, and I'll have you executed now." Stormy jumped at both the volume and venom coming from the Senior Councilor. Current glared at the Senior Councilor, who just glared right back, tail lashing, before calming himself and turning back to him.

"Please continue, Stormy."

"Before I could wake him up, there was a screech from a Leviathan, so I dragged him into the cave only moments before the beast floated past. When it was safe to move again, I dragged him further into the cave and woke him up. He said he didn't do it. We couldn't leave by the cave entrance, so we explored the cave, which turned out to be a series of lava tubes. We swam for a long time before we ended up surfacing in a large cavern. It's there we found your daughter. She was awake at first and attacked Deep Current when he tried to climb on the ledge to check on her. She stopped when she recognized me, but she seemed confused. Moments later she collapsed and started shaking really hard, and now won't wake up. Deep Current says she's really cold. He stayed behind to guard her and told me to come find you and a mask so we could get her out. I had to sneak past the Leviathan to get out, which took forever, and then came here as quickly as I could."

"Guards lock Rip Current in a holding cell. I'll deal with him later. Someone find me a spare mask, notify the healers, and get several Sea Patrol shuttles here immediately. We'll need to scare off that Leviathan."

Several 'Yes, sir's' answered and various people scattered to do as he ordered.

"Come on then, Stormy. Show me where my daughter is." The Senior Councilor motioned him back out.

They turned and swam out of the council building to find several Sea Patrol shuttles already descending to meet them in the courtyard, while the people in the park hurriedly swam off to make way. Once onboard, Stormy gave instructions and the pilot took off, the other shuttles following behind. Along the way, he pointed out the house where the councilor had stopped. Councilor Chenzira had the shuttle stop and ordered one of the two honor guards on the shuttle with them to remain and to not let anyone but himself or Councilor Surellis to enter.

"You swam all the way out here by yourself, Stormy?" the Senior Councilor asked as they approached the Trench.

"I did. The cave where Deep Current was in, is behind that clump of seaweed. I had to swim for a good fifteen or twenty minutes down into the Trench before I found the other cave," he said pointing in the general direction.

"I have confirmation of a Leviathan ahead," their pilot called out. "Ships two and three, you're the bait. Four and five, be prepared to fire."

"Yes, ma'am!" came the reply and two of the ships dove over the edge. "We have visual confirmation. She's a behemoth alright, Old Bessie, if I'm not mistaken. Shots fired. She's in pursuit." The scream of the

Leviathan echoed through their ship, moments before the other ships reappeared and sped off out to sea, the Leviathan close behind. As soon as the monster was fully out of the Trench and chasing after the lead ships, the other two came up behind and opened fire. The Leviathan screamed again and switched to chase after the second set of ships. The first two used the distraction to flip around and join the others, opening fire again. The Leviathan screamed and then changed her mind about attacking and swam off to get away from the annoying creatures stinging it. The four ships chased after.

Once the Leviathan was far enough away, their pilot dropped down, lights scanning the cliff face, until they found the tunnel. It was too small for the craft to enter, so they exited the shuttle, the Senior Councilor using a drone to keep up with Stormy, and carrying a face mask for Marsee, with the pilot and remaining guard following behind. Stormy led them down the tunnels, only making one wrong turn before arriving at the cavern.

Deep Current had apparently climbed back onto the ledge and pulled her away from the water that had risen and was nearly up to them. He was wrapped tightly around her.

The Councilor leapt out of the water and shook his daughter. "Marsee! Marsee, wake up!" Neither she or Deep Current stirred. Her father slapped the mask on her and picked her up, but stopped as something fell out of Current's hand. The Councilor bent down and picked up the object and growled at what he saw before putting it in a pouch on his carry harness.

Stormy couldn't make out what it was before the Senior Councilor jumped back into the water with his daughter. The guard climbed up and dragged Deep Current into the water, and they all raced back to the shuttle.

When they exited the cavern, a trauma ship was waiting for them. They took custody of the two patients, and flew back to Council Platform with the honor guard ordered to go with them, and to not leave Marsee's side at any time.

Stormy entered his ship with the pilot and waited while the Councilor swam back into the cave and quickly returned with the bag that Deep Current had been in, and they piled in their shuttle and quickly rose out of the Trench.

"Squadron, we've secured the Translator. You're free to return to base."

"Yes, ma'am" came the reply.

Stormy was shocked when the Councilor didn't immediately head for the Trauma Center, but made the pilot stop outside of the other cave entrance. He ordered Stormy to remain in the ship with the pilot and left to examine the cave. He returned a few minutes later and then moved on to the house Stormy had pointed out. Once again he was ordered to remain on the ship, while the Councilor went inside. Twenty minutes later he returned. The Councilor's tail was lashing as he left the building.

Stormy wondered what he found that made him so angry.

Finally the Councilor directed the pilot to take them to the Trauma Center, but when they arrived, the healers flat out refused to let them in to see the Translator and Deep Current, even with the Senior Councilor demanding he be let in, and indicating that he'd strip her of her rank, if they didn't. Surprisingly though, he didn't follow through with that threat when the healer refused to back down. They stared at each other for several long moments, before the Senior Councilor growled, and instead told them that no one was to be allowed in their rooms unless they were a healer, and turned to Stormy. Stormy had never seen anyone stand up to a Senior Councilor like that, well except for Little Flower.

Stormy flinched from the anger still on Councilor Chenzira's face.

Jer immediately calmed himself when he saw Stormy's expression. "I'm sorry Stormy, I didn't mean to scare you. I'm just very worried about my daughter. I owe you everything for finding her. If it's within my power to grant you, it's yours."

"I just want my Papa back," Stormy said. "He didn't do this. I swear."

Jer took a deep breath and nodded, "Come on then."

A few minutes later, they were in front of his father's cell. Honor Guards were everywhere in the hallway. Councilor Chenzira put his paw on the lock and the door opened, revealing his father. Stormy raced in and tackled his father in a hug.

"Stormy! What are you doing here?" his father asked, and looked up at Councilor Chenzira in confusion.

"It looks like you owe your son that reward," Councilor Chenzira said. "He found Marsee and Deep Current. You're still a suspect but you're free to go home. Consider yourself under house arrest."

Councilor Chenzira motioned to one of his guards. "Escort Clear Seas and his son back home, and if he needs to leave his house for some reason, go with him."

"Yes, sir," the guard replied.

Turning back to his father, the Councilor continued. "I'll let Stormy explain what happened. I need to return to the Trauma Center."

"Sir, before you go, there's something else I need to tell you," Stormy said.

"What is it?"

"Can you shut the door, please?" Stormy asked instead.

The Senior Councilor raised an eyebrow, but did as requested.

"Before I left to find you, Deep Current made me promise not to tell anyone but you, because he was afraid if anyone else found out, more people would get hurt. What I didn't say earlier is that Deep Current *was* waiting for your daughter in the Arboretum, but not to hurt her. He was there because she was supposed to be bringing him information about his missing father, but she didn't show up. Instead someone from the Sea Patrol did, saying they had a message from her. That message stated there was a change of location, and that she would meet him there. When he arrived someone knocked him out. That's all he remembered until I woke him up."

The Senior Councilor and his father shared a look that he didn't understand.

"Did he say where he was redirected?" his father asked.

"Yes, sir. He said it was his uncle's home. Here in Council Platform," Stormy said.

"You did the right thing. Thank you for telling me and keeping it secret until we were alone," Councilor Chenzira said. "Is there anything else?"

Stormy thought hard to see if he forgot anything else, and shook his head. "I don't think so," he finally said.

"How did you sneak past the honor guard?" Chenzira asked.

Stormy looked over at his father. He'd been instructed to never tell anyone about the secret passage, but his father nodded. "There's an emergency escape from my room," he replied. "I locked the door, but once inside the tunnel, there's no way the guard would have been able to follow. She's too big."

Chenzira looked over at Clear Seas with a raised brow.

"Assassination attempts were common in the past. This has been my family home for many generations," Clear Seas replied. "Even without that, it's protection from natural predators too. A Leviathan could easily break through the front wall of our home."

The Councilor tilted his head in acceptance of that fact, nodded his thanks to Stormy again, and left.

"Well, Stormy, sounds like you have quite the story to tell me," his father said.

He waited while the guard removed the shock collar from around his father's neck, and then told his father everything as they swam home, unable to keep the happiness off his skin to have his father free and the Translator located.

"I'm very impressed," his father said as they approached the market. "What would you like for a reward?"

Stormy shook his head. "I don't need or want anything. I've already got it. Councilor Chenzira asked me the same, and I told him I just wanted you back."

His father flashed surprise, and then pride, but said nothing as they swam through the silent market, and the rest of the way home.

When they swam inside, the look on Honor Guard Aris's face even made his father chuckle.

"How...How did you get out of your room?" Aris stammered, not even remembering to sign.

"Well obviously, I'm a super hero. I can swim through walls," Stormy signed back, and swam off to get his treasured book from his room with the colors of his father's laughter lighting up the room behind him.

# CHAPTER 28

# Avery: Instinct

Avery followed the healers off the ship and into the trauma ward. He was astounded Marsee was still alive, but very worried. He had enough medical training that he could have easily qualified for a journeyman's rank if he'd bothered to test for it. His senses told him as much, if not more than the medical scanners did, as there were things he could sense that the scanners could not.

One such thing that all senior ranked guards in his species' guard could do was see a person's soul boundary. It was how they were able to see when someone was struggling with control of their instinct and not just upset, or worse, fully lost to their instinct. That information was a closely guarded secret in the Guard, and he was almost positive that even if they healed her, there was next to no chance that Marsee was still in there, especially after the expanded account Stormy had given on the way to the cave, and all the injuries he'd been able to sniff out.

He kept out of the way as Healers swarmed the room, including one he recognized as the Senior Guild Healer. The monitors sprang to life the moment Marsee was transferred from the ship's stasis chamber to the static tube, the Sprites equivalent to a trauma bed, and his nose flared with the smell of blood.

"Bottomless depths. How is she still alive?" one of the other healers flashed.

Avery thought much the same as the scanners confirmed what he'd already sniffed out.

"If she's anything like her mentor, pure stubbornness," the Senior Healer replied, and went to work trying to save Marsee's life.

Avery snorted at that comment. The Senior Guild Master's reputation preceded her. She had to be stubborn to stand up to the demands of the Council. Nearly an hour passed before they stopped treating her when Marsee's head shifted.

The Senior Healer reexamined the scans. "I think she's starting to wake up."

Avery frowned and swam over. "Put the shield around her. She may react with violence if she sees you." He was pretty sure she would. He saw no signs of her soul boundary, which meant it was most likely that she was fully lost to her instinct.

The healer nodded and did as requested. "I wouldn't blame her if she did. It's pretty clear from the electrical burns, one of our kind did this. Between that and the hypothermia, she'll likely be very confused as well."

Marsee's eyes slowly fluttered open. At first there was no response as she shifted her head to look around the room, but the moment she made eye contact with the Senior Healer, Marsee practically exploded with feral rage, hissing and spitting as she tried to attack, but the shield blocked her, and she began growling and clawing at it instead, trying to find a way to get out.

"Marsee you're safe," Avery called out, trying to get her attention.

She turned to him with a growl, ears flattened to her skull.

"You're safe," he signed. "You're in the trauma center. You're okay. No one is going to hurt you," he signed over and over again, and sighed with relief and more than a little astonishment when he saw a flicker of Marsee's soul boundary return, and she paused briefly in her frantic clawing at the shield. "That's it, deep breaths. You're safe. No one is going to hurt you. I will protect you with my life. I promise."

He was shocked there was even anything left of *her* to fight back with after what had been done to her.

Her eyes darted between him and the healers, and returned to clawing at the shield, still trying to find a way out, but it wasn't as frantic as before, more methodical now, testing the shield. Still, if any of the Water Sprites approached, she growled, hissed, and spat at them.

He motioned them back and they followed his lead. "It's okay, Marsee. They're healers, like your mother. They just want to help you," Avery signed. "I promise, they're not going to hurt you. Come on back to me. Shut your instinct down. You don't need it anymore. You're safe. I will protect you instead."

The Senior Healer looked at him in confusion over that comment but turned to Marsee. "Marsee, can you understand me?" the Senior Healer said in Saber, "I promise, little kitten, you're safe."

The healer's expression was one a mother used to try and calm a scared cub, but instead of calming, Marsee yipped and flinched as if she'd been struck, and immediately started spitting and growling again, and resumed her frantic clawing at the shield trying to find a way out. She didn't even seem to notice her injured and broken paw.

"Use sign language," Avery ordered. "That cuts through our instinct better, and avoid using that term of endearment. She reacted like she was hit. We don't know what else was done to her."

Turning back to Marsee he called out her name again to get her attention, and continued in sign. "Marsee, you're safe. The shield you're in is designed to treat your injuries. It's the Sprites equivalent to a trauma bed. No one is going to hurt you."

Marsee looked at him, and calmed slightly as he repeated the information.

"That's it, come back to me. No one is going to hurt you. They're only trying to help heal your injuries. She stopped clawing at the shield to watch him, but fear radiated off of her any time she glanced at the other healers in the room.

"Marsee, can you understand me?" the Senior Healer asked again, this time in sign language.

Marsee blinked, tilted her head slightly, and slowly nodded.

Avery sighed with relief again. She wasn't speaking, but she was responding, which was an improvement.

"Good. I want to give you something for your pain. I promise I'm not going to hurt you. May I come forward?" the Senior Healer asked.

Marsee considered and nodded again.

The Senior Healer slowly moved forward and adjusted the shield slightly, just enough to access the upper portion of Marsee's arm. Marsee tensed but didn't pull away as the healer injected the pain medication.

Avery watched as Marsee visibly relaxed as soon as it took effect.

"There. That's better, isn't it?" Hyacinth asked.

Marsee nodded again.

"Now, we're not trying to restrain you. The tube you're in is treating your injuries. It's a special kind of nano wash. Do you understand?"

Marsee nodded again.

"Good. Now, I need to finish repairing your paw. We have new claws being printed, and we'll replace them later after you've had a chance to recover some. Can I do that now?"

Marsee pulled her paw up to look at it, as if now only just remembering it was injured. She winced as she tried to move it and growled again, pulling it in close to protect it, and began licking at it.

Avery frowned. The urge to lick an injury was instinctive, and one they worked hard to stop cubs from doing by making the nano cream taste horrible.

"I am not going to hurt you. I promise. Please let me treat you," Hyacinth signed, adjusted the shield slightly, and then held her paw out waiting patiently for Marsee to decide.

Marsee growled and pinned her ears back at the healer in warning, but hesitantly extended her paw over, and flinched as it made contact with Hyacinth, but relaxed again when nothing happened.

"That's it. Thank you for trusting me," the Senior Healer flashed slowly, keeping the light of her skin dim.

It took almost another hour for the healers to repair Marsee's paw as much as they could. Marsee didn't take her eyes off the Senior Healer the entire time. When the healer was done, Marsee took her paw back and cradled it protectively, and only then looked around the rest of the room, and made eye contact with him again.

"Do you know who did this to you?" Avery asked.

Marsee shook her head and opened her mouth to try to speak but the words wouldn't come out.

He frowned in concern, and her eyes expanded in fear.

"Please don't hurt me," she signed awkwardly, as one hand was now in a cast. "I don't know why I can't speak, but I'm me."

"That's not surprising with the types of injuries and trauma you've had. Try not to worry. Things will start working again when you warm up," the healer said, but looked at Avery with a frown, obviously wondering why Avery would hurt Marsee.

Avery nodded his understanding, and Marsee took a deep breath, sighing with relief.

Her instinct was still on, but she was mostly in control, and most importantly not hurting anyone. *She's just terrified,* he decided. *And she has every right to be, after what was done to her.* He'd seen more than a few people mute with terror in his life, and he knew that didn't always mean psychosis. He knew enough from the medical scans to know she'd been tortured, but he was astounded she was recovering as quickly as she was, much less at all. He'd seen people lost to far less than what had been done to her. He decided he would wait until she'd had a chance to fully recover before passing judgment on her. He wouldn't be able to do anything anyway while the healers were watching, and as she wasn't actively hurting anyone, he didn't have grounds to pass judgment without a member of the Senior Council present.

The Senior Healer turned back to help the others clean up from the surgery and Avery took that momentary distraction to see if he could get Marsee to turn her instinct off.

"Marsee, I promise you're safe. Can you try turning your instinct off now?"

Marsee's eyes flicked to the Water Sprites again, and he could smell her fear even through the static shield.

"No one is going to hurt you. I promise. Your instinct protected you and kept you alive, but now you need to turn it off. Let me protect you instead," he signed.

Avery watched her closely. There was no sign of a struggle anymore. She just didn't want to turn it off.

"I don't want to. I'm scared," she signed finally, confirming his suspicions.

"I know. What was done to you was horrible, but no one is going to hurt you again. I won't let them," he promised. "I can tell you're in control, but I need to see that you can still turn it off."

She swallowed hard, the scent of her fear blooming again, but she nodded, and he watched as she turned it off without difficulty, and then yawned as the effects of her ordeal instantly caught up with her, no longer held at bay by her instinct.

He sighed with relief. "Thank you. Rest now. I will guard you," Avery said. "I promise. You're safe."

Marsee nodded and closed her eyes, instantly asleep.

"Do you want to explain what that was all about?" the Senior Healer asked.

"All what was?" Avery asked, being purposely obtuse.

"About her instinct and why she would think you would hurt her because she couldn't speak," the Senior Healer replied.

Avery frowned and purposely looked at the other healers in the room. He knew Hyacinth was the Senior Healer for the Water Sprites, not just for the Trauma Center, so she had enough rank to keep this secret, although he would have thought she'd already know. The Senior Healer motioned the other healers out and waited.

"Marsee had psychosis," he signed, once everyone was out of the room.

"Had?" the Healer stated, flashing both concern and surprise, and looked back at Marsee. "I thought that was fatal for your species."

"It is. She's survived two episodes that we're aware of. Three if you count her behavior when she woke up. Although I wouldn't put it past anyone to attack the first person they saw, especially after what was done to her. We've recently learned that those with psychosis can sometimes understand sign language where they can't understand speech. Her father and uncle came close to having to put her down with the last episode before she snapped out of it. Going non-verbal is a really bad sign, and she knows it."

"Well between the electrocution she's endured and her hypothermia I'm impressed she can even speak or understand sign," the Healer replied. "She may have trouble speaking afterwards from her injuries. The electrocution alone can cause neurological issues, although I'm surprisingly not seeing much sign of that. We won't know for sure the extent of her injuries for a while, certainly not until she's warmed up. Half her systems are still shut down from the hypothermia."

"I am aware of that, but what she went through would be enough to put any of our species over the edge, whether we had issues with our instinct before or not," Avery said.

"Seriously?" Hyacinth asked.

Avery nodded.

"Huh, well I'm certainly going to have a conversation with Nerissa for leaving that bit of information out." She sighed and turned back to look at Marsee. "Whoever did this to her was trying to kill her. I honestly can't believe she's still alive. Based on the extensive burn marks, she took enough of a charge to kill a juvenile Leviathan."

"Neither can I," Avery replied and winced in sympathy. He'd experienced the Water Sprites charge in training many times, so he knew just how painful it was. "I've seen people lost to far less. Approach slowly and make sure she's fully awake and aware of her surroundings before treating her."

"That's standard procedure in a trauma situation like this," Hyacinth signed, "but I'll remind my healers to be cautious. Do you think there's concern for further issues?"

Avery turned and looked at Marsee's sleeping form. "I honestly don't know. Everything about Marsee is unique. She's responding and cooperating, even though she's terrified. That's far better than I was expecting, certainly not as scared as she is. As long as she's not startled, I think she'll be safe."

The Senior Healer nodded and left.

Avery watched Marsee for several minutes, lost in his own thoughts, before taking up station next to her tube so he could see anyone who entered, and then fired off a message to Kendra to get her thoughts.

# CHAPTER 29

# Jer: Trauma Ward

Jer paced in the empty waiting room outside of the Trauma Unit. He'd been there for hours. Marcus joined him and brought him his tablet, which he'd left behind in his haste to find Marsee. He sent Myra a message telling her they'd found Marsee and promised to send her an update as soon as he knew more. Afterwards, he read through the unread messages she'd sent and frowned.

"What is it, Jer?" Marcus asked. "Have they found the others?"

"No. Myra says Damon, Henry, and Buster are also missing."

"Who are they?" Marcus asked.

"Henry Curtis is apprenticing with Animal Healer Nazari along with GrandFather. He's a good friend of GrandFathers. Buster is GrandFather's horse. Apparently they were rescued together. It's Damon Minor that concerns me. GrandFather told me months ago that he didn't trust him because of some of the skin drawings he used to have. Apparently they represented a group of people that severely disliked people with dark skin. Damon has been one of the most vocal about the lack of male representation at our Local Council meetings. That GrandFather and Henry are both missing is very concerning. Henry's skin is several shades darker than GrandFathers."

"Why would he take a horse or Little Flower and her cub though?" Marcus asked.

"I have no idea. Apparently though, Hue-mans used to ride horses for transportation. When I found Myra in the barn, Little Flower was actually sitting on top of the horse. It's possible that Henry and Buster's absence is unrelated. Myra said she and Nazari are following his trail. It's possible they were attacked or hurt. As for Little Flower and Hope, leverage maybe, or it's a further attack against me? Anyway, Myra said GrandFather was watching Little Flower and Hope while she slept for the first time in about four days. Little Flower just had another brain surgery and had some pretty severe complications. Myra spent the entire time in Little Flowers room only napping occasionally. I honestly don't know how she was even still awake. She said Ammond had to give her a sedative to fall asleep. Someone apparently gave her another dose, maybe two as she had a hard time waking up. When she finally woke, she found Little Flower's room a disaster and some of GrandFather's blood on the broken pieces of Hope's playpen. She never heard a thing."

"They couldn't have gotten far. All of the shuttles are grounded, which means they would have had to take a crawler or gone out on foot. Could that be why the horse is missing?" Marcus replied.

"I suppose that's possible, although I have no idea how much weight the horse can carry. Did you order the stop to the demolition of the Habitat?" he asked, changing the subject.

"I did and spoke to both the Senior Healer as well as the demolitions expert there. I didn't want there to be any chance of missed communications," Marcus replied.

"Good thinking," Jer said, and resumed pacing.

"Have you had any update on Ellie's condition?" Marcus asked after a while.

He nodded. "She's still in surgery."

"Still?" Marcus asked, horrified.

Jer nodded. "Oh, that reminds me, I found this when we rescued Marsee." Jer showed him the claw he'd found.

"Moons. Another claw?" Marcus whispered.

Jer sighed and continued to pace.

An eternity later, a healer floated through the doors of the Trauma Unit. "Councilor Chenzira?"

"Yes? How is she?" Jer replied.

"She's alive. If you'll follow me I'll take you back to Senior Healer Hyacinth to discuss the extent of her injuries."

Jer motioned for Marcus to wait and followed the healer back to an office where the Senior Healer was waiting for him.

Once he was in, Hyacinth swam over and shut the door. "Your daughter is still alive, but we still have her condition listed as critical. Our biggest concern right now is a severe case of hypothermia. Her temperature is dangerously low but improving. Her right hand was badly broken and shows every sign of being crushed by a blunt object. Two claws were removed, as you already knew. We've repaired the broken bones, and are currently printing replacement claws, which will require another surgery once she's warmed up and out of danger. Surprisingly though, she only had a minor infection, which appears to be responding to treatment. She had a hairline fracture on her right shoulder and water inhalation. The scans also indicate she's been electrocuted, quite likely many times. She has extensive burn marks throughout most of her body, causing second and third degree burns. From the severity, it's my medical opinion that whoever shocked her was attempting to kill her. The burn marks are consistent with a full charge and duration of an adult of our species, along with dozens of smaller charges."

Jer was unable to keep from growling at that announcement. The Healer flinched and he immediately stopped. "Sorry," he said. I'm not growling at you, but at what was done to her."

She nodded, "I fully understand your anger. Please forgive my reaction. It uh...surprised me."

He nodded at her words, allowing the misdirection, knowing that sounds had very different meanings for her species, and wondered briefly how she'd interpreted it, but those thoughts stopped cold as the Senior Healer continued.

"It is also my belief that she would not have made it another fifteen minutes, and the only reason she made it as long as she did is because Deep Current used his own body heat to keep her warm."

"How is Deep Current?" Jer asked, swallowing hard at just how close he'd come to losing his daughter.

She pursed her lips and sighed before continuing. "He was dead on arrival, and we were not able to resuscitate him. He suffered massive burns to his lungs from being out of the water for too long. It would have been a long and agonizing death."

Jer nodded his understanding. Not only had they completely misjudged Deep Current, but he'd given his life trying to save his daughter. It was a price Jer knew he would never be able to repay. "Can I see her?" he asked.

"Of course. She's awake, but before I take you back, be warned that she was confused and was unable to speak when she woke. It's quite likely she won't be able to for a while. That's a common side effect of the injuries she's sustained. Once she does regain her voice it may be slurred or she may stutter. I'm not seeing any major neurological issues in the scans, but that doesn't mean they aren't there. Until she's recovered from the hypothermia we won't know if there are any other issues we have to deal with. She's not out of the deep yet, not by many leagues."

Jer frowned, hearing she was having trouble speaking. "Did she act violently when she woke?" he asked, afraid to even ask it.

The healer nodded her head. "Some, but we were prepared for that, after everything she's been through. We had her confined behind the static shield of the trauma tube when she started to wake. She was confused and lashed out at first, and tried to escape. It took her a while to calm and trust us, but I don't blame her there. She did eventually though. She was able to sign but hasn't spoken yet, although she does seem to understand it and Water Sprite. Per the guards instructions, though, I've instructed all of my healers to speak in sign with her."

Jer frowned to hear she was non-verbal, although he was relieved to hear she was signing. That was far better than he'd been expecting.

"I did speak to the guard and he informed me of your daughter's…prior illness. I don't believe she's reacting any differently than anyone else would in her situation. He believes she's not a risk as long as we're cautious around waking her up, and try not startle her. Either way, she's in a static tube for treatment so she can't hurt anyone."

Jer sighed with relief. If Avery hadn't killed her outright, then she must be still in control. How that was possible, he had no idea, but he sent up a prayer of thanks to the Ancient Gods for the miracle. He nodded his understanding, and followed the Healer back to a room where Marsee lay suspended in a tank of water. Avery floated at attention next to her. Jer took a deep breath seeing the guard next to her, but he only nodded to Jer and swam out, giving them the appearance of privacy. Sighing with relief again, Jer swam up next to the tank and placed his hand on it, wishing he could hold her. It felt cold to the touch, and he looked questioningly back to the Senior Healer.

"We need to raise her temperature slowly, so that her organs have the best chance of coming back online. Too fast and her body won't recover without damaging itself further. It will take another hour or two for her body temperature to come back up to normal," Hyacinth explained.

He nodded his understanding and turned back to his daughter. "Hey kitten," he said quietly.

Marsee yipped, growled, and twitched in her sleep.

At the growl Avery swam back in the room.

"She's still asleep," Jer said, raising a paw to Avery to stop him, as Marsee continued to growl and twitch in her sleep.

"Sir, that's the second time she's reacted badly to that phrase. We don't know what kind of emotional trauma she's experienced. You should use caution and avoid that term of endearment."

Jer frowned, struggling to contain his rage at what had been done to his daughter. "Marsee, sweetheart, I'm here," he said a little louder, trying to wake her from her night terror without startling her.

Marsee opened her eyes and smiled weakly at him. "Papa!" she whispered.

"Hey there. How's my little kitten?" Jer asked, ecstatic to hear her speak, but deciding to test out Avery's comment. He needed to know for himself.

Marsee yelped with an involuntary flinch, growled, and looked away, clenching and unclenching her unbroken paw. "Please don't call me that anymore," Marsee's voice was slow and slurred, almost as if her tongue was three times too big.

Jer frowned and shifted to the side so he could look into his daughter's eyes, relieved to find her instinct off, but horrified at the look of pain and fear on her face. "Why not? What happened to you?" he asked softly.

Marsee's eyes flashed to the Healer and Avery, and then back to him with a frown.

"I'll give you some privacy," the Healer said, and left. Jer indicated Avery should leave as well, with a nod in the direction of the door. Avery immediately swam out and took up guard outside.

"Marsee, I know this will be hard, but you need to tell me what happened, and who did this to you."

Marsee swallowed hard. "Papa, is Ellie dead?"

Jer looked back at the guard floating outside and frowned before turning back. "No," he signed. "She's in surgery right now. She was badly beaten, but the last I heard, she was still alive. But you can't tell anyone. We're telling everyone she's dead to protect her until she's awake and can give a statement."

Marsee closed her eyes for so long, Jer thought she'd fallen asleep. "What about Little Flower and Hope?" she finally asked, without opening her eyes, her uninjured fist clenched tightly.

Jer didn't answer right away, and she opened her eyes and looked at him with worry and grief on her face. He sighed. "I don't know. Little Flower, GrandFather, Hope, Henry, Damon, and a horse are all missing."

"Oh Papa! H...he said he was going to k...k...kill them," Marsee wailed, her voice stuttering as she began to shiver.

"Who did?" Jer asked. Rip was right about one thing. He couldn't take Stormy's word of what happened, even though it matched what he found.

"I'm n...not sure. He k...kept me in the d...dark. Oh Papa, it was so very d...dark. I just heard his v...voice. It was rough and gravely."

Jer considered. Clear Sea's voice, like every Water Sprite he knew that could speak his language, was melodic. *I suppose they could have been masking it somehow.*

"Do you think it was Deep Current or any of the protesters?"

"No. He had no m...motive. His people are m...missing too. I was trying to find out what ha...ha...happened and I was t...taken by someone in the Sea p...p...p...Patrol," she finally managed to spit out.

"Are you sure?" Jer asked, frowning at how hard it was for her to speak, and hearing that the patrol was mentioned again.

"They were wearing the p...p...patch. They approached me in the garden the second n...night we were here. I was t...trying to relax b...before bed. They handed me a note and I w...w...woke in the cave."

"Who do you think did it?" Jer asked again.

Marsee closed her eyes and started shaking violently. "Marsee! What's wrong?"

Marsee opened her eyes again and tried replying, but couldn't get the words out, just a stutter. "C...C...C...Co...Co"

"Healer! Somethings wrong! Healer! Help!" he yelled. The Healer was there in moments, examining the monitors and Marsee's shaking body.

"She's okay. Her body is finally starting to try to warm itself up. She's just shivering. Marsee dear, you're okay. Try to relax and let it happen. This is a good thing," the healer instructed.

"O k...k...k...kay," Marsee managed to struggle out through her violently shaking body.

"This is going to take a while, try to distract her," the Healer said, and left again.

Jer turned back to his daughter. While he needed to question her, as hard as she was shaking, it was unlikely he was going to get much in the way of an answer. "So, You'll never guess what I saw the other day."

When he finished telling her about seeing Little Flower sitting on top of one of the horses, and how he belonged to GrandFather before, and that apparently the Hue-mans could ride them, she stared at him in shock.

"They f...f...f...found B...b...bust...t...ter!" Marsee finally managed to force out.

"It would appear that way," Jer replied. Before he could say anything further, the Senior Healer returned. He was surprised that she'd returned so quickly.

"How are you feeling, Marsee. Are you in any pain?" she asked.

"N...n...no. I'm c...c...cold, so v...very c...cold."

The healer smiled. "Oh good. That means your nervous system is finally back online. It's really bad when you can't tell you're cold. You're doing really good. Councilor, a moment of your time?" The Healer nodded towards the door.

Jer followed the healer out of the room and across the hall into an empty one. "Is Marsee okay?" he signed, not wanting to risk Marsee overhearing.

"Marsee is progressing nicely. I wanted to let you know that the Guild Master is finally out of surgery," the Senior Healer signed back.

"What's her long term prognosis?"

"Thankfully, she didn't suffer any major trauma to her brain or spine, just a minor concussion, but with as many broken bones as she had, I expect she's going to be walking with a limp for a long time, and she's going to need at least one more surgery to finish repairing her paws. It's going to be a while before she's going to be able to craft anything, much less hold a pen without pain, but with time she should make a full recovery."

"That reminds me," Jer said, pulling the claw out of his carry pouch. "I found this with Marsee. Could you confirm it belongs to the Guild Master?"

She pulled the scanner off of her harness and examined it. "It is," she said, handing it back. "And before you ask, no, there's nothing on there to identify anyone else."

He frowned. "Do you need this to repair the Guild Masters paw?"

"No, we didn't need them. We had a full scan of the Guild Master on file to reference," she replied.

"You did? Why?" he asked.

"That information is unlikely to be pertinent to your investigation, so I can't give that out without her consent, even to you," the Senior Healer replied.

Jer nodded and placed the claw back in his pouch. "How soon before we can wake her?"

"Not until tomorrow at least. Her condition is still too unstable to risk it. She needs time to heal."

"If that changes let me know. I want to be there when you wake her, and I don't want anyone in that room with her or Marsee that you don't personally know and trust with your own life. We have one person, but we still don't know who else is involved, and I don't want to release Ellie's condition until after we've had a statement from her. Under no circumstances is anyone from the local Sea Patrol or Honor Guard allowed access."

Hyacinth nodded and he turned and swam back into the room with Marsee. Marsee had fallen asleep in his absence, although her body still shook with her shivers. He was starting to loathe medical monitors and trauma centers. He sent Myra a message and a picture of Marsee's sleeping form, with the monitors behind her, knowing that would calm her fears more than anything. With one final look at his daughter's sleeping face, he left to find out what that monster had done with the rest of his family. Charter or not, if he needed to, he was prepared to rip the information from Current's body, one bone at a time if that's what it took to save his family.

Before he left though, he called in another of the honor guards he'd brought with him, and ordered them placed outside of Ellie's room, with a very short list of authorized healers allowed to enter, and gave the same instructions to Avery.

He met Marcus in the waiting room and filled him in on Marsee's injuries, but Marcus refused to let him leave the Trauma Center. "Stay with her, Jer. She needs you. I'll go knock some sense into Rip and finish examining the suite. I'll meet up with you here first thing in the morning."

"Marcus, I can't just sit here while Little Flower and the others are still missing!"

"Yes, you can. Right now, you need to be a father more than a Senior Councilor, and if you need to do something, do some research. We need to figure out what else Rip Current was up to, but do it from Marsee's room. She's been alone in the dark and tortured for days. She needs you to be there when she wakes and scare off her nightmares."

"Marcus..." Jer grabbed the back of his scruff, frustrated, worried, and not knowing how to choose between his daughters.

"Would you rather she wake up to you, or the guards? Now go." Marcus physically turned him around and shoved him back towards the doors.

Jer sighed and swam back to Marsee's room. She was still asleep so he crawled into one of the hanging nets, and pulled out his tablet to begin his research. To his surprise and frustration, he found he couldn't access Rip Current's account, which shouldn't be possible. He fired off a message to Marcus asking him if he could, and switched over to start digging through the official logs and tickets in Rip's district queue, although he had no expectation that any of it was accurate at this point.

Marcus texted him later informing him that Rip refused to speak, and it was all Jer could do to keep from growling and waking his daughter. Additionally, Marcus couldn't access Rip's account either, but said he would follow up with Lowell to see if she could figure out what was wrong.

Marcus had been right. Marsee woke several times during the night screaming and growling from her nightmares, instinct on and panicking at finding herself underwater, and not being able to leave the warming tube. After the second time, he kept the light on, which seemed to help calm her quicker. He wished he could hold her but being there seemed to be enough, and once fully awake, she quickly brought her instinct back under control and fell back to sleep almost immediately, exhausted from her ordeal and the effects of her treatment.

He dozed fitfully through the night, checking his tablet often for an update from Myra, which never came, and he wondered what in the world she was up to. It wasn't like her, but there was little he could do from here.

The healer's swam in and checked on Marsee hourly, but it wasn't until early the next morning that the Senior Healer informed him that she was downgrading Marsee from critical to serious, and would likely have the surgery to finish repairing her paw later that morning if she continued to improve.

Marcus arrived shortly after, but Marsee was still sleeping.

"How is she?" Marcus whispered.

"They've upgraded her condition to stable, but she had a rough night. She woke several times from night terrors with her instinct on, but was able to shut it off once she realized where she was."

Marcus frowned. "I suppose that's far better than we had any right to hope, and if the worst we have to deal with are night terrors, then I think we're very lucky."

Jer didn't reply.

Marcus spun to face him. "What happened?"

"That's the question, isn't it? What did that monster do to my baby? If you'd heard her screams..." Jer swallowed hard to keep from crying from the anger and pain he felt for his daughter.

"She hasn't told you anything else?" Marcus asked, his face softening with sympathy.

"No. Once her instinct was off, she fell back to sleep almost immediately."

Marcus nodded. "Well come on then. We have work to do."

Jer sighed, took one last look at his daughter, and swam out.

# CHAPTER 30

# GrandFather: Out of Time

James woke hours later with a throbbing headache, a very full bladder, and a broken and swollen nose twice its normal size. The swelling made it difficult to open his eyes. His stomach stung, but from what he could tell, it had been a shallow cut. His hands felt stiff and achy, but he was still able to move them which was good. Damon hadn't completely cut off the circulation in his hands, although it was close. His shoulders, which had been wrenched back behind him, screamed from the unnatural position they were held in, and the wide seats made it impossible for him to reach the knots.

They'd stopped somewhere, and from what little he could see, they were near the mountains in a small valley as rocky scree surrounded them on all sides. It was after sunset but not completely dark out, which told him he'd been unconscious all day. Damon was in the front seat, which he'd reclined, and was snoring, loudly. He couldn't see Hope with the seat turned away. He looked over and saw Little Flower, head nodding as she tried to stay awake. He wiggled his feet trying to get her attention and it worked.

She looked over at him slowly and he frowned. She looked horrible.

"Are you okay?" he mouthed.

She shook her head slightly. "No, sick, head hurts, thirsty," she mouthed back. "You?"

"Head hurts too, but I'll live. How's Hope?"

"Sleeping, I think," she replied, swallowed hard, and closed her eyes.

James swore. His granddaughter needed medical attention, and quickly. She should have been home and resting after her surgery. He needed to do something, but he couldn't if he was tied to the seat. He wondered how long they'd been stopped and, for that matter, why. *The crawler's auto-pilot would have been able to travel for days so there's no reason for Damon to stop unless he's waiting for someone. The same people who kidnapped Marsee, perhaps?*

He waited for Little Flower to open her eyes again. "How long have we been stopped?"

She shrugged. "Two, maybe three hours," she replied.

*That's a long time to sit and wait,* he thought, guessing that Myra would have had half the planet looking for them by now. *So was this planned, or did something go wrong, and whoever he's working with didn't show up?* "One of us needs to get untied. Can you act sicker? I'll try to get him outside. Do you think you could make it to the door to lock it?"

"Don't know. I could try, but I don't need to act," she said, and proceeded to throw up and then slump in her seat.

"Hey, Dung face! Wake up!" James yelled.

Damon snorted awake and glared at him. "Oh, great. You're awake," Damon muttered. "What do you want?"

"My granddaughter is sick. She just had major brain surgery and needs medical attention. Please let us go, or at least untie me so I can check on her," James said, with more than a little panic on his face.

Damon slid out of his seat and walked over, gaging slightly at the stench. He shook her hard. "Wake up little brat," he said. She didn't respond.

"Don't do that! You'll just make things worse!" James pleaded, fairly worried now. Either she was really good at acting, or she really was sick. Damon shrugged, and walked back to his seat. "Damon, please! I know why you hate me, but she doesn't deserve this."

"It makes no difference to me. They didn't care if she was dead or alive as long as they got her."

"They might not care, but you're better than that. Besides, if the others find us first and she's dead, it'll be a death sentence for you."

Damon seemed to consider it for a moment.

"Please just let me examine her," James begged.

Damon growled, but reached in his pocket and pulled out his knife, and slowly walked back over to him. "Try anything and you're both dead."

"I promise I won't."

Damon snorted his disbelief, but started untying him anyway. The moment his hands were untied from the ropes, they started screaming in pain, and he clenched and unclenched his fists trying to get the circulation going. Once they were working somewhat, he unhooked his harness, slowly slid out of his seat, and shuffled over to her. He put a hand on her forehead. It was hot to the touch.

"She's burning up, Damon. Do we have any water?"

"Just examine her," Damon growled.

James carefully lifted her head up and opened each eye and swore. One eye was dilated. She was actually in serious trouble. He checked her pulse. *That's strong at least,* he thought.

"Damon, this is no trick. I promise you. She's in very serious trouble right now. She needs medical attention or she'll die. She should be laying down too and these ropes are pointless. She can't walk. She's been in a coma for months and can barely use the bathroom by herself. Please, let me untie her and treat her. There should be a first aid kit on the crawler. They're standard equipment."

Damon motioned for him to proceed, and James let out a sigh of relief. He quickly untied her and reclined the chair and then slowly shuffled over to the compartment where the first aid kit should be. Damon hadn't untied his legs so he could only move a few inches at a time. James let out another sigh of relief when he saw the kit and carried it back over, setting it on his seat, and opening it. It was full stocked.

James did his best to hide his glee as he saw what was included. They had a chance now. He rifled through the supplies in the kit, trying to hide his actions. He activated the emergency beacon as he shoved it aside, hoping that Damon wouldn't know what it was. No matter where he was on the planet, this should be picked up by one of the satellites in orbit. He just needed to keep them both alive and Damon distracted until help could arrive.

He pulled out the scanner and it confirmed what his physical exam had shown, although it did also show that she was still awake. There was swelling on her brain and she was fighting a raging infection. He pulled out the hypo and checked to see what was included in the kit. Finding an antibiotic that was safe for their species, he put it in the hypo and dosed her. *That should kill the infection anyway,* he thought.

But there wasn't anything in the kit to treat the swelling. She would need surgery for that. There was a small tube of the ubiquitous nano cream. It probably wouldn't do much, but he applied what little there was to her head anyway. If nothing else it might help with the pain. Then considering what else was in the kit, he dug out an anti-nausea tablet and stuck it in her mouth. He checked the scanner and saw that the antibiotic was already helping, but it wasn't doing much for the swelling in her brain.

"Well," Damon asked.

"She has a high fever and a serious infection, but she's also having complications from her surgery and her brain is swelling. I've treated the fever and infection but I can't do anything about the swelling here. I tried the nanos but they're not having any effect. She needs surgery immediately, or it will kill her." He turned the scanner around so Damon could see but Damon didn't even bother looking.

"You've done what you can. If she lives or dies, so be it. Back in your seat," Damon said.

"Please Damon, I'm not trying to trick you. Please let her go. Send her back in the crawler. I'll do whatever you want, but please, give her a chance. I'm begging you."

"I said, back in your seat," Damon growled.

"Can I at least pee first?" James asked, setting the scanner back in the kit and closing it up.

Damon growled but nodded. "Turn around. You're not going outside without being tied up."

James held his hands up in front instead.

"Turn around," Damon growled.

"What? Are you going to unzip my pants and hold me while I go?" James asked. "I didn't know you felt that way about me."

"You try anything and I'll kill you," Damon said, glaring at him, but tied his hands in front, holding the knife in his teeth. James didn't try anything. He wanted Damon off guard, and right now he was focusing on every motion. James shuffled over to the door.

Damon hit the switch and shoved him hard.

Thankfully James managed to land on his feet, and started shuffling away from the crawler as quickly as he could, hoping to put as much distance as possible between him and the crawler.

"That's far enough," Damon said. So James undid his pants and went.

"So what did they promise you?" James asked, honestly curious. He needed to know who else was involved, and if they had anything to do with Marsee's kidnapping as well.

"A way out of this hippie hell hole, and the right to vote for one, and a chance to save what's left of the human race before the cats ruin it, for another."

It was the opening he was waiting for. "Do you honestly think your skin color is better than mine? You can't even go outside during the day without burning,"

He tried to block, but Damon hit him so hard he collapsed to the ground.

"They're not coming for you. You're just a stupid pawn," James said, as the world spun around him, trying to give Little Flower time to make it to the door and lock it. If she could get away it would be worth it.

Damon kicked him in the ribs again, knocking the wind out of him. He lay there wheezing, trying to find enough breath to taunt Damon again. He wanted Damon focusing on him. He expected another kick but instead flinched as a gob of spit landed on his face. As he wiped the spit off his face he heard Damon walking back towards the shuttle. He shuddered as he heard the door open again. It hadn't worked.

He heard a thud and then the sound of something dragging. He lay there trying to stop his head from spinning, and breathe enough to try something. When he opened his eyes he saw Damon dragging Little Flower over next to him. James swore under his breath, desperately trying to figure out what to do, when Damon left and returned to the shuttle.

Little Flower opened her eyes and lifted her head slightly. "Are you okay?" she asked.

He gave a tiny nod and she quickly laid back down. He heard Damon jump out of the shuttle again and walk over.

"I saw you, you little faker," Damon growled and kicked Little Flower hard in the side. She cried out in pain.

James struggled to sit up, but the moment he moved the world spun on him again. Damon's next words made his blood freeze in terror.

"No worries though. Now you get to say goodbye to your dear old grandfather."

Damon walked over and grabbed the ropes on his hands and started dragging him across the ground. He tried to resist but Damon kicked him again, his boot landing squarely on his broken nose causing pain to explode in his face. It was all he could do to fight to stay conscious as his granddaughter's screams tore through his heart.

"No! Please don't do this, Damon! Please!" she begged.

# CHAPTER 31

# Quinn: Harbinger

"I see how it is. We leave you alone for five minutes, and you're already sleeping on the job."

Quinn groaned as he slowly rolled over, and found Lark and his other guards sitting around him, including Hallie and Keeta. He frowned at the two, who should have been several leagues away by now. "What are you two doing back here?"

"We saw the explosion and came back in case you needed help," Hallie said.

Quinn grunted in acknowledgment as he rubbed the back of his head checking for blood. Surprisingly, even though his head throbbed, he found none, and pushed himself up into a siting position.

"The good news is, you have a hard head." Lark handed him the tube of nano's from her first aid kit. "The bad news is Little Flower, GrandFather, and Hope are all missing, and everyone on the ship is...in bits and pieces."

Quinn let out a string of curses that made the others chuckle, and then winced as he rubbed the nano cream in. "They've got to be somewhere between here and New Hope then. They were expected hours ago, which means they're lost. What about the rest of Chenzira's family?"

"I don't know," Lark replied.

Head treated, he carefully stood up and checked his leg, which ached, but didn't appear to be badly injured. He rubbed some of the pain cream into it anyway.

He had just stored what little was left in the tube when he heard the sounds of another ship approaching. "Looks like we're getting reinforcements," he said, when he recognized Kendra's ship. He made his way out of the woods and into a clearing where most of what was left of the ship had landed in small burning piles of shrapnel. Members of the Ship's Guild were trying to put out the fires before it could spread. Thankfully, most of the ship landed on the rockier terrain. Kendra's ship set down on the other side of the clearing, and he waited as she exited, followed by several squads of guards.

"Report," she ordered.

He gave a rapid fire rundown of everything he knew, while the rest of the guards fanned out to help put out the fire.

Kendra's expression was calm, but she was tapping a claw absently against her leg, which he knew from years of experience meant she was very upset. "Henry Curtis, a friend of GrandFather's, and Grand-Father's horse are also missing. Apparently the Hue-mans can ride them. We don't know if Henry Curtis went out riding, and something happened, or if he was taken too. There are at least a dozen crawlers missing from New Hope, and apparently their tracking beacons have all been disabled, as we can't find any of them. Our primary suspect is a Hue-man by the names of Damon Minor, and two of his friends who have also turned up missing, Paul Markson and Danny Shuto."

"Damon? Well, that doesn't surprise me," Quinn said.

Kendra frowned. "Explain."

"That's the Hue-man I placed a watch on while I was watching Marsee," Quinn explained. "We never did find anything, but he was angry and fairly isolated, never a good combination."

Kendra pursed her lips. She didn't comment, but he had a guess about what she was thinking. If they'd been allowed in New Hope, they might have prevented this a long time ago.

"I didn't know the tracking beacons could be disabled," Quinn said.

"Neither did I," she replied. "That's a flaw we'll have to fix."

"And what of Chenzira's family?"

"They found Marsee. She's badly injured but alive, and surprisingly still in control according to Avery, but she was tortured and struggled hard when she first woke up. Chenzira's older children are currently unharmed, but the Senior Guild Master died from her injuries."

Quinn raised a brow in surprise to hear that Marsee was even remotely still in control, but frowned to hear about Ellie. "Did they catch who did it?"

"They've arrested Rip Current on the word of Clear Sea's son, who apparently found Marsee," Kendra replied.

"Current? Huh. Well, that's far more reasonable than Clear Seas. I never liked him."

Kendra snorted. "I don't think anyone liked him. The question is, who else is involved."

"The Ice Giants anyway, and they were expecting Little Flower hours ago. Something must have happened."

"Agreed. We'll head out on foot. It's possible that Damon dropped them off somewhere and ran. We haven't found any signs of a crawler from the air between here and New Hope, but that doesn't mean anything. There are plenty of places to hide one from view and they could have taken an indirect route."

Quinn nodded. Once the fires were out and what little could be recovered from the wreckage sent back to Council City for analysis, they spread out in a wide search pattern and took off. Two hours later, he stopped briefly to rub some more nano cream into his leg, which was starting to bother him again, and took a drink from his canteen, but before he could move off again there was a whistle down the line, indicating that someone had found something. Quinn whistled, to pass along the notice and took off in the direction the whistle had come from. He pulled up on the top of a hill, where the others were grouping. In the valley below, there was a shuttle under a massive bandala tree, surrounded by dozens of the large four-winged harbingers.

Kendra appeared at his side moments later and pulled out her distance viewer. "I'm not seeing signs of movement in the shuttle, but they've definitely got something," she replied, clipping the viewer back to her harness. She motioned, and they followed her down into the valley. The harbingers took flight at their approach. Several carrying objects in their claws. It didn't take the distance viewers to tell it was Hue-man, as the tattered remains of their clothing flapped in the breeze as the harbingers flew away.

Quinn stopped and unclipped his stunner, as did the others, but they were too far away and their shots missed. Kendra motioned for one of the squads to follow in pursuit, while they continued their approach to the shuttle. There was blood everywhere, but not much else. The crawler itself was empty.

They were too late.

# CHAPTER 32

# Jer: The Plot Thickens

Jer left the Trauma Ward with Marcus in tow, giving him a quick rundown of Marsee and Ellie's latest status and what he'd learned so far. "Did you found anything in their suite?"

"Maybe. I want to show you something, and see what you think about it," Marcus replied. They started making their way across the park in front of the Trauma Center when their tablets dinged with an urgent message.

They both stopped to read and he swallowed hard as Kendra's message came in.

"Ice Giants," Marcus muttered.

Jer didn't reply as he was continuing to read. He was shaking in both fury and fear by the time he finished.

"It might not be them, Jer," Marcus replied.

"Regardless of who it is, at least one of my people is now dead, and I've made an effort to get to know all of them," he replied. "I honestly didn't think any of them would be involved in something like this, even Damon, as vocal as he is."

Marcus nodded, and they made their way to the suite in silence. Marcus put in his clearance to enter the room. Jer held his breath as they entered, not sure what he would see, but the room they entered looked perfectly normal, if far nicer than any room he'd ever been given.

"*This* is their suite? Being the Guild Master certainly has some perks," he said to Marcus.

Marcus looked at him, head tilted in confusion. "Jer, this isn't normally Ellie's suite. It's mine. You should have been given one equally as nice since the Trial."

"Nope, the last time I was here they gave me your old room. I might have to put in a complaint though. The fireplace is a nice touch."

Marcus chuckled, but then stopped where he was and frowned.

"What is it?" Jer asked.

"It's your comment. Ellie is high ranking, but she normally only ranks the same suites as the rest of the Council, same as any of the guild seniors, and usually gets bumped down if the Council is in session. It doesn't make sense why she would have been put here. We never hand out the Senior Council suites to anyone but the Senior Council, because we never know when we're going to need them, and Ellie intended to stay through the council meeting, which meant I would have been bumped down."

"Jealous?" Jer teased.

Marcus glared at him. "Like I care where I sleep. No, it's just that I wouldn't have expected anyone to be in my suite, even if Marsee is family. If they bumped her up, I would expect her to be in yours, not mine, since she still lives with you. I suppose if you weren't bumped up to a Senior Councilors suite then it's possible the suites are still being renovated. It's on my list to look into. Stinger said it was Clear Sea's order. I haven't had a chance to confirm yet."

"Or Marsee and Ellie weren't the intended target," Jer suggested. "Someone tried to kill me. They could be after you too. Maybe they were just showing up to booby-trap the suite and found it occupied."

Marcus frowned but nodded, and motioned for him to follow. They started with what Marcus believed was Marsee's room and pointed out the balcony. Surprising in and of itself, he didn't see anything unusual about it, outside of its existence.

Her hearing aids were still on the table beside the bed. Jer walked over, flipped open the case to confirm they were still there, and looked around the rest of the room. The only other thing he found was Marsee's carry harness. The room otherwise looked untouched.

Jer stepped out onto the balcony and looked around. "Are you thinking this is how they accessed the suite?" Jer asked, as Marcus pointed out a smear of blood on the railing. "Marsee said she was in the Arboretum, I figured they just used Marsee's paw print to access it after they took her."

"That would make far more sense. I checked on the static shield around the balcony the first time I stayed in this room. I couldn't find any controls to turn it on or off in the suite, and wanted to know what would happen in a storm or at high tide. Turns out it's tied to the Platform's systems. The only way the shield would ever go down would be if there was a catastrophic failure to the entire platform."

Marcus activated his mask and leaned out placing his hand on the shield, causing it to ripple. "It's a solid shield too. Even with the masks on we wouldn't be able to pass through like we can with the doors. I've already checked with Platform Operations. They've had no indication of any issues with the shields, and the generators are checked daily and have multiple backup systems."

"So maybe they tried to leave this way and found out they couldn't, or they wanted us to think they left this way," Jer suggested.

"I suppose that's possible," Marcus replied. "I found a few drops of blood in the carpet, but didn't find anything around the entrance, which is honestly surprising."

"Is there a dry entrance to the suite?" Jer asked.

"No just the water entrance." Marcus motioned for him to follow, and pointed out the trail of blood through the kitchen and dining area that led towards Ellie's suite.

Marcus stopped him before they entered. "How's your control? There's a lot of blood."

"I'm good," Jer replied, but took several deep breaths to calm and bring everything behind his mask.

Marcus nodded and kept going.

As they approached the suite there were far more visible signs of blood including paw prints and smears. Jer wondered if those were from the healers who had rescued Ellie or her attacker, but even with Marcus's warning, he was completely unprepared for the scene that awaited him.

He nearly lost his stomach. In the spot where Ellie had been found, there was a massive pool of dried blood that had soaked through the carpeted floor, along with something else. Jer carefully walked over, trying to avoid stepping in the blood, and bent down to take a closer look. It was another one of Ellie's claws. He blanched and swallowed hard several times.

"What is it you wanted me to see?" he asked Marcus.

"This. It doesn't make sense. It's too over the top, even for the injuries you told me about," Marcus replied.

"How so? She clearly fought with someone. That would explain all the broken furniture and blood splattered everywhere."

"*That's* what bothers me. Our only suspects are Water Sprites. If it had only been Rip Current and our mystery guard, then they would have had to sneak up on Ellie and shock her. She could have easily avoided them unless she was sleeping, so there would be no need for all this damage."

Jer shook his head. "We know the Ice Giants are involved, at least on Saber. They could be involved here too." He carefully walked around and examined the damage and then taking a chance, flicked on his instinct, letting it have a look. The smell of blood was nearly overpowering at first, and he staggered a bit under the assault.

"Watch your instinct, Jer!" Marcus warned, looking at him in concern, and started to bolt over to him.

"I'm good. I'm doing it on purpose. It was just more than I expected and it...it stinks," he explained, raising a paw to stop Marcus. "My instinct finds it distasteful. Too old."

Marcus frowned at him, but surprisingly didn't order him to stop.

Jer let his senses dig through the layers and filter out the myriad of overwhelming scents, Ellies's scent was on everything in the room. He stripped that off and focused on the blood. There was nearly a wall where the pool of her blood was, and several medium sized whirls of scent outside of the splatter of smaller scents that covered everything. He examined the whirls and found broken pieces of furniture covered in blood, far exceeding the rest of the blood around it. He pointed to one of them. "I think this may have been used to beat Ellie. It's covered in her blood and fur, and there's another piece over there," he said, pointing.

He tried to filter out the smell of Ellie's blood and examined the scents left on the broken furniture, but he couldn't pick anything else up on the weapon. Ellie's blood was too strong, and covered anything else that might be there, so he examined the other scents in the room. Marsee hadn't been in here, or at least not past the doorway. Marcus's scent was here, both old and new, and he even picked up the slightest hint of Tabor, but it was very old. He filtered those out.

"Clear Seas has been here..." He picked up the scent, whirling around the pool of blood, but nowhere else in the room, and followed it back to the door, and then into Marsee's room, but only part way. He squatted down to look at the room from Clear Seas perspective. From here he could clearly see onto the balcony and in Marsee's waste room. "He didn't go any further than here," he told Marcus who was following him. "It fits with what Clear Seas put in his report. I'm not smelling him anywhere else in the Suite."

He filtered that scent out and was left with two unknown scents in Marsee's room that were recent and several others that were older. The older ones went everywhere. "There were two other people in the room recently, but I don't recognize their scent. I'm pretty sure it's Water Sprite though. It has the same salty tang to it that Clear Sea's has, and both scents are smeared, rather than footprints. The first one came in as far as the bed. There are several older scents, but I'm thinking they might be the cleaning crew as they're everywhere."

He followed the more recent scents back out into the entryway and it muddled there for a while. "They didn't go anywhere else in the suite," he said, and filtered that one out. From here, there were maybe still half a dozen fresh scents left and they all went in the same direction, so he followed them back to Ellie's suite. All but one of them went straight for the pool of blood. *Those must have been the trauma ship healers,* he thought.

The last one went everywhere in the room. He filtered everything down to just that scent and tried to make sense of what he was 'seeing'. When he realized that the fainter scent meant it was older as well as smaller, everything popped into focus, and he overlaid that image with Ellie's scent. His head ached from the effort of holding it all in his mind.

"There's only one assailant, Water Sprite, and the scent is familiar. I think it's Rip's, but I'll need to sniff him to be sure. He crawled in, up to the foot of the bed, paused there for a while, and then shifted over here before leaving. Sometime later, he came back. Ellie's scent bounces all over the room. I'm pretty sure he just threw her into the furniture and that's where all the damage came from. She's never dragged off the bed or anywhere, just eventually lands in each of the spots. He left and came back three times at least, maybe four. The trail gets muddled. The last time he spent the entire time over by the pool of blood."

Jer followed the trail out back to the door and then followed it into Marsee's room. "He also went over to the balcony and back out."

*We kill him now,* his instinct demanded with a low growl.

Jer froze, breathing hard, shocked by actually hearing a voice. He clamped down on his instinct, but it wouldn't shut off.

*He maimed our daughter and friend. He needs to die, violently. Tear him to shreds, slowly, and make him suffer for what he did.*

Jer didn't know what was going on, and he tried hard to shut down his instinct again, but it refused. He knew it was because that was exactly what he *wanted* to do.

*So do it!*

His instinct shoved hard, trying to make him leave the room. Unwillingly, he walked out of the room but managed to wrest enough control back to sit down in one of the chairs instead. Breathing hard he dug his claws into the furniture, shaking and trying to fight the urge to tear Rip Current to shreds.

Marcus followed and sat down in front of him, worry etched on his face. "How are you doing, Jer?" he asked, lifting Jer's head to look into his eyes.

"Not good, Marcus," Jer admitted, honestly amazed he could still speak.

"Fight it, Jer. You can do it. I believe in you," Marcus signed, and then grabbed him by the back of the scruff, and pulled hard.

Jer instantly sagged, and his instinct receded, muttering, back into the background where it belonged, although it paced with fury at the harm done to Marsee and Ellie.

"I'm good," Jer said when he felt like he was back in control, and Marcus let go. He leaned back into the chair for several minutes before opening his eyes to see that his mentor hadn't moved, and was still looking at him with concern.

After a few moments, Marcus shook his head. "That was an incredibly stupid thing to do, Jer. Informative, but stupid, and completely inadmissible as evidence. Don't do it again. That was far too close."

Jer nodded in agreement. "So now we just need to find a way to prove it."

"Easier said than done," Marcus muttered, not taking his eyes off of him.

"I'm good, Marcus," he repeated.

"I'll be the judge of that," Marcus growled. They sat there for a good twenty minutes, discussing ideas, before Marcus tested him to confirm he was fully back in control. He had no problems. Marcus sighed with relief and finally backed off. "I should report it to Kendra, but I'm not going to. This is far outside of what any parent should ever have to deal with, but I will be testing you again later, once this is all over. Consider yourself on an informal watch."

Jer nodded, not the least bit surprised. "I fully intended to have you test me anyway, long before this was over with. My abilities to maintain the calm expected of a Senior Councilor are severely lacking right now."

Marcus snorted. "Well, little brother, *that* I can't blame you for at all. Honestly, if you weren't growling at everyone, I would be far more concerned. It's one thing to stay calm when councilors are arguing over budgets and projects, and another when someone hurts the people you care about. Just try to keep your claws in. Ellie and Marsee get the first swipe."

He rolled his eyes at his big brother and walked back into Ellie's room with Marcus close behind. He carefully made his way back over to the pool of blood to examine Ellie's claw again, careful not to touch it, and then pulled out the one he had in his carry sack, and compared them.

"The Senior Healer confirmed this one came from Ellie," he said and then looked at his own claws. Surprising Marcus, Jer took his hand and swiped it along the broken frame of the bed, leaving five deep claw marks in the wood, and then looked at his claws again.

"What was that all about?" Marcus demanded to know. "Getting some of your anger out, or are you having issues again?"

"Neither," Jer replied. He placed his paw, claws extended next to Ellie's bloody claw. His claws showed signs of shredding from the impact with the wood. Ellies were both pristine. "I don't think Ellie ever had a chance to fight back through this whole thing. Neither of these claws are damaged. I think all of this is a ruse to make us think she was attacked by another species, although why he'd bother to remove her claws is still a mystery, outside of being a psychopath. I'll see if the Senior Healer can come over and determine if there is any genetic material on this other claw. The others we have are all washed clean. Maybe she'll be able to tell who else has been in here, and give us something we can use for actual proof. I trust her more than the guards at this point."

"Agreed. Did Hyacinth say if Ellie was electrocuted?" Marcus asked.

"No, but I'll ask the next time I'm over there. Right now, from what I can tell there are only two people involved. Whoever approached both Marsee and Deep Current, in the Sea Patrol, and Rip. At least that's all that came into the suite, outside of the half a dozen or so trauma healers. Everything else is old." Jer stood and left the room. Marcus followed. "Have we heard anything from Lowell yet?"

"No, but she did say it could be a while," Marcus replied. "I'll follow up with her."

Jer nodded. "I'll see if we can wake Ellie up for a brief statement. I hate to do it, but we need confirmation on what happened, for her own safety if nothing else, and I'll see if I can get more information out of Marsee, assuming she's not already in surgery." He walked back into Marsee's room and grabbed her hearing aids and carry harness, and then stopped as a thought occurred. "Marcus, where are their tablets?"

"I haven't seen them. Did Clear Seas pick them up when he was here before?" Marcus asked.

"I don't think so." Jer pulled up the report. "He doesn't mention anything about it. Marsee wasn't sure her tablet was waterproof. She was concerned about that before she left. Maybe it's in the tube system."

Marcus used his authority to try and retrieve them, but found nothing. "I'll check with Platform Operations to see if they were sent anywhere. Why would they take her tablet though?"

Jer shook his head, baffled.

Marcus frowned at him, his claw tapping on the side of his leg as he considered, and then without warning, spun and walked back into Ellie's room.

Jer followed and watched as Marcus started looking under the damaged furniture. He joined in and carefully lifted the remains of a broken table, and gasped at what he saw.

Marcus was there instantly. Underneath the table was a single purple scale. "Flyers too? All that's left is the Diggers. This is getting worse by the minute, Jer."

He shook his head. "This doesn't make sense, Marcus. There isn't another drop of Flyer scent anywhere else in the suite. Saber and Water Sprite, but that's it. This has been planted to look like Ellie was fighting a Flyer. I'm sure of it."

"So who's this from then? None of the missing people Deep Current was looking for are Flyers," Marcus asked.

Jer swallowed hard when he realized who it was. "Petra."

"Petra? Wind Rider's daughter? What would she be doing here?" Marcus asked.

"She's Ellie's pilot, or was, the last time I knew. I met her when we flew to the Trial on Ellie's ship," Jer said. "You were off saying goodbye to your books."

Marcus immediately flipped out his tablet and called Petra but there was no answer. He left a message and then sent one to Wind Rider asking if she'd heard from Petra recently, but that would take a good hour to get a response.

"Marcus, something's happened to her too. I just know it. Ellie's ship should have been commandeered for the evacuation order, but it was still parked."

Without a word, they both bolted for the entrance and made their way to Ellie's ship as fast as they could. Marcus arrived first and entered his authorization. Lights flickered on. "I'll look up front, you check the back," Marcus said, so Jer made his way through the various rooms, but found nothing.

"Nothing," Jer said, when he found Marcus.

"Nothing up front either. No sign of a fight, and all of the pilots belongings are still in their rooms. Who are the other two pilots?"

"I don't remember, but that information should be logged," Jer replied. "I'll look that up, you check Petra's account, see if there's anything there that might tell us where they are."

Jer pulled up Ellie's flight log and found the other two names, and tried calling both of them.

He'd just finished leaving a message on the second one when Marcus gasped. "Oh gods."

"What did you find?" Jer asked.

Marcus just handed him the tablet.

"How well do you know Wind Rider? I can't imagine she or her daughter would be involved in this," Jer said, shaking his head in disbelief.

"Petra would have no problems accessing the suite. Ellie would easily let them in if they showed up," Marcus stated.

"But they weren't in the suite. I swear. I don't need my instinct to tell me that. Flyers smell...spicy, and it lingers. Your nose should be good enough to sniff that out."

Marcus frowned. "If that scale is from Petra, and these texts are altered like the footage, then at this point all of the Senior's children have been targeted except for Sammianna. Apakana doesn't have children. My credit says Temperate's shuttle accident was no accident. He's one of the highest rated pilots in the Sea Patrol."

"Sammianna doesn't have any children," Jer replied, looking at Marcus with confusion.

"No, but she has nephlings," Marcus stated, "and the last I knew, they lived with her."

"If she hasn't been targeted, does that make her a suspect?" Jer asked.

"Sammianna?" Marcus snorted. "That's even less likely than Wind Rider and Clear Seas being behind this. No, this is looking more and more like a coup, than just a random attack by protestors, or even Clear Seas trying to hide illegal activity."

"Agreed. I'll head back down to the Trauma Center, and see what I can find out there, and I'll check on Temperate too. See if you can track down an accident report. I think we should keep Petra's involvement hidden for now until we confirm who that scale belongs to. After that, I think we should head back over to Rip's home, and see if we can find anything there. If you have time, check his office. I'm also thinking we should fly to his district and check out his home and office there. We might have better luck than here."

Marcus nodded and they both made their way down to the exit and sped off in different directions. He returned to the Trauma Center, but was directed to a different room than before. While he'd been out, Marsee had been removed from the warming tank and placed in a dry room. Her immediate care had been transferred to one of the off-world healers who could enter the room. Avery floated just outside and nodded as he passed. He found his daughter curled up in a chair wrapped in several large blankets reading a book someone had found for her. That more than anything told him she would be alright. When he stepped through the static shield, the heat in the room blasted him in comforting warmth.

"Oh that's nice!" he said as he entered. "When we get home, I'm going to spend a week sunbathing on your balcony."

"You and me, both. I don't think I'm ever going to warm up," she said, sitting up, and then shivered, pulling the blanket in tighter. Her voice was much clearer than before. While still raw and raspy, it was free from the slurring and stutter. He walked over and sat down next to her, wrapping his arms around her in a fierce hug. She leaned into his side and he could feel her shiver. Whether they were just from the cold or her fear, he didn't know.

"How are you feeling?" he asked.

"Starving, but they won't let me have anything to eat since I'm going back in for surgery soon. I'm cold and my paw really hurts, but overall, a lot better than before." She showed him her bandaged paw. The fur around her hand had been shaved off, and bandage putty covered the stubby ends of her fingers where her claws should have been. A mesh cast kept her paw flat while the bones healed.

"Oh, Marsee..." Jer said, and hugged her again. They sat there for several minutes, just leaning against each other for mutual comfort. He didn't move until she sat up, and then he turned to face her, his expression serious and his emotions locked tightly behind his mask. "I know this is going to be hard, but I'm going to need an official statement from you on what happened, and I'm going to need as much detail as you can provide."

"How did you find me?" she asked.

"I'll tell you after I take your statement. I don't want to influence what you remember," he said.

Marsee nodded, so he pulled out his tablet and began recording. "Let's start from when you were abducted. Take as much time as you need, and try to provide as much detail as you can."

Marsee swallowed hard, pulled her blankets in closer with another hard shiver, and began.

It was all he could do to keep his tail from lashing and his claws sheathed as she detailed what had happened to her. The beast inside him growled and paced, but he kept it firmly locked down with the promise of vengeance later, once he knew for sure who had done it. When she was finished, Jer paused the recording, and hugged her again, thanking every Ancient God in the universe that she'd survived.

"Oh, Marsee, I'm so sorry. I promise, the person who did this to you will pay dearly for it."

Marsee didn't respond, just leaned against him shivering.

He tilted her head up to look in her eyes, and saw that her instinct was firmly off, but the look of fear in her expression made his heart break. He continued to hug her, purring with everything he had to comfort her, until she pulled away again. When she nodded, he started the recording again. "Do you have any idea who was behind this?" he asked.

"Some, but no real proof," Marsee replied. "Like I said, I never saw him, but it had to be one of the councilors that met us that first day because he made the comment 'I really hope you were telling the truth about being able to swim'"

"Who met with you?" he asked.

"Clear Seas, Rip Current, Spotted Trout, Snapping Turtle, and...Crystal Cove. I think. I didn't recognize them at first. Ellie told me that's who they were."

Jer raised a brow at that. They were all the highest ranking members of the Water Sprite Council, and not who he'd expected to meet Ellie or Marsee. Clear Seas maybe, since he was a friend of the family. His brain was racing with the implications of what her attacker had said about why he'd kidnapped her, but he needed to find out what other information she'd uncovered. "And out of those, who do you think it was and why?"

"The voice I heard wasn't Clear Seas. It wasn't melodic at all. It was very rough and gravely, almost like he had a chest cold. I've never heard the others speak. They signed the entire time, so I don't know what their voices sound like. But I'm pretty sure it wasn't Clear Seas. I thought it was him at first because of some of the comments he made, but..." Marsee shook her head.

"But what?" Jer prompted.

Marsee shrugged. "I don't know how to explain it, but I trust him. Nothing I saw spoke of a desire for power or revenge against our people. If anything he was far more interested in finding ways to help. I think it's someone else on the Council. The morning after we arrived, we found out that there'd been a protest before we'd arrived. Clear Seas came to escort us to the council meeting, along with several members of the Sea Patrol. I insisted on talking with the protesters, against Clear Seas recommendation, and spent about an hour talking with Deep Current about their complaints. They didn't match with what Clear Seas had told us or what had been reported, so I asked for access to the archives so I could see for myself. Ellie noticed that the video had been tampered with and we found evidence of other tampering. Also, there was no indication of what had happened to those who had been arrested. I asked Clear Seas later and he said he'd look into it. About the only thing we've been able to determine is that most of the missing people and protests are coming from Rip Current's district, which makes me lean heavily towards him. He was the most annoyed during the tour. He didn't like that the vendors didn't address him, as did several of the others. At least that was my impression. But Deep Current told me that he'd been told that his father, who is one of the missing people, had fought with their councilor in his grief, and been arrested. That councilor would have been Rip. But that doesn't make sense, Rip is Deep Current's uncle. Rip and his father were brothers. Even if Deep's father had attacked Rip in his grief over his mate's death, I couldn't imagine that Rip would have had his brother arrested."

Jer raised a brow at that statement, but didn't interrupt.

"The only other person I could think of was Deep Current, but I was trying to help him find answers, so I just can't see why he'd want to harm me, unless everything he told me was a lie, and I don't know how to explain it, but I trust him too. I believe he was telling me the truth at least as far as he understands it."

"Deep Current is dead," Jer replied.

"What?!" Marsee exclaimed. "How?"

He explained to her how Stormy had found and rescued both her and Deep. "When we found you, Deep was already dead. He used his own body heat to try and keep you alive until we rescued you. The Senior Healer told me that if we'd been even a few minutes later, it would have been too late for you too."

Marsee put her uninjured paw over her mouth. "Oh Papa! How horrible!"

He nodded his agreement and put his paw against the side of her face to comfort her. She leaned into it and it was all he could do to not show his own horror as a large patch of her fur came away when he removed his paw. He did his best to hide the fur, not wanting to scare her.

"Deep Current told me that his mother had been killed hunting for the food Little Flower and the Hue-mans needed, and that it was a great honor to give their lives to save someone else. It was one of the reasons why he was protesting. His mother hadn't been recognized by the Council, or by Little Flower's people, and no reparations have been made to care for her family. We need to do something for both of them and whatever family they have left. I told him I'd have his mother's name added to the list of people we formally remember on Remembrance Day."

"I'll make sure it happens as soon as we get home," he promised. An hour later, they'd exhausted all of the questions Jer could think of to ask her, so he turned off the recording and attached the tablet back to his harness. "I need to check on Ellie. Have they said when they're going to bring you back in for surgery?"

"They said after I stop shivering, maybe in another hour or so," she replied, but looked away and he could tell something was bothering her.

"What is it, sweetheart?" he asked.

She looked towards the door and switched to sign language. It was awkward, with her paw in a cast, but she managed. "Papa, I promised I'd tell you if I was having issues with my control. I don't know if I am, but I can't remember Deep Current or Stormy being there. We, my instinct and I, knew that we were dying, and I gave up full control to it in order to try and stay alive for one more attempt to kill him if he showed up again, because I knew I couldn't. I could have hurt them. I think he wanted me to lose control to hurt you. He knew about what happened with Little Flower and my illness. I didn't say it earlier because I didn't want that on record. I had a really hard time coming back when I woke up here, but it wasn't like before. I wasn't being pushed out this time. I didn't want to come back, but it recognized there was a guard there, and knew we'd be killed if I didn't. A really big part of me wanted him to, just to stop the pain, and it was actually my instinct that shoved me forward, to save our lives."

His ears drooped as he watched his daughter speak. There was so much pain and fear in her expression, and only a handful of people should have known about her psychosis. Clear Seas being one of them. Her story of her instinct's behavior was curious though. He'd never heard of an instance where their instinct shoved someone back, but he supposed it made sense. The whole purpose of their instinct was to save their lives after all.

"It's okay. You did what you had to do in order to stay alive, and no one was hurt. What's important is that you were able to come back, and I completely understand why you wouldn't want to. I was sure I'd already lost you when Stormy said how you were acting. Give yourself time to recover. If you have issues going forward, let me know, but I am certainly not going to blame you for using your instinct to save your life. That's the whole reason for it."

She nodded and they sat there leaning against each other for a long time before a thought occurred to him. "You said he said things to you that made you believe it was Clear Seas, was it just his reference to your illness?"

Marsee shook her head. "No. He knew what happened during deliberation. I don't know if it's true or not, but he said Tabor was going to kill Little Flower and blame it on me." Marsee looked at him questioningly.

Jer sighed, not wanting to add to Marsee's trauma but nodded. "I just found out about that yesterday. That was the plan the first day you and Little Flower were called to the Senior Conference room. After they killed you, they were going to alter the footage in the Conference room and then head to the Agency and kill the rest of the Hue-mans. Thankfully Kendra's efforts along with your sister's were successful in changing their minds."

Marsee looked away and let out a heavy sigh. "Papa, am I ever going to be free of this? Of people looking at me like I'm going to turn into a monster?"

He was silent, unsure of what to even say. "I don't know. What I do know is that you survived. I know I wouldn't have. Give it time. The more we learn about how sign language helps, the more likely the stigma around this will disappear."

She nodded but didn't reply.

"Was there anything else?" he asked.

She shook her head, but her eyes were haunted, and Jer had a suspicion something else had been said or done to her. He didn't push it though, knowing she would tell him, if and when she was ready.

He hugged her again before he swam out to find the Senior Healer. His own instinct growled deep inside him, wanting to destroy the person who had harmed her, and he fully agreed, but kept it in control. He still had work to do to prove who had done it, and he was beginning to wonder if Wind Rider or someone on the Senior Council might be involved after all.

"How can I help you, Councilor?" the Healer asked when he found her.

"I have a few questions. First, a large clump of Marsee's fur came away earlier. Is that to be expected or is something wrong?"

Hyacinth pursed her lips and then flashed her regret. "It's sadly expected. She might lose most if not all of her fur. It's a side effect of the electric shock she took. With a small shock, she might have just lost fur around the contact points. The fur should grow back, eventually, but it might not."

It took everything he had not to growl at the Healer. "Just how badly was she electrocuted?"

She frowned. "As I mentioned before, whoever did this was likely trying to kill her. They would have used up most, if not all of their defensive charge, and I'm honestly surprised it didn't kill her. Based on her size, it should have."

Jer did growl this time. "Do you have any idea why it didn't?"

"It could be that her fur insulated her. We don't exactly have a lot of experience treating electrical burns on other species. Most of the time it happens by accident, usually by young children who don't always have control over it, but it also could have been that whoever did this wasn't at full charge when they did. It can take a couple of days to fully recover," she replied, and then frowned as a thought occurred to her.

"What is it?" he asked.

"The only other explanation would be if this person knew exactly how much damage they could do to a person without killing them, and the only way to learn that would be with practice."

Jer growled at those implications and wondered if that had anything to do with the other missing people. "Were the Guild Master and Deep Current shocked as well? Stormy said Deep Current was unconscious when he found him."

"I honestly don't know. Deep Current was placed in the morgue as soon as he arrived, as we determined that there was no point in even trying to resuscitate him. As for the Guild Master, we didn't look for signs of it because of the extensive nature of the rest of her injuries, and because she was found in a dry room. Come with me. I'll check now."

He followed her down several floors and into a room that smelled strongly of death. His instinct recoiled at the smell.

She floated over to a tablet and looked something up before opening a small square cabinet and pulled out a long tube with Deep Current's body floating inside. "We've placed his body in stasis until his family can come and collect it. So far no one has come forward." She ran her scanner over the body for a long time before closing the cabinet and turning to face him. "I didn't find any evidence to suggest he was electrocuted, or any evidence of why he was unconscious. It's possible a sedative was used but nothing shows on my scanner. The most common sedatives would have been fully out of his system within a few minutes of waking anyway."

They left the morgue and he followed her back up to the trauma floor and down several halls until he rounded a corner, and saw one of the other guards he'd brought with him floating in front of a door. They swam through and Jer gasped when he saw Ellie's condition.

"Dark moons!" he exclaimed.

The Healer turned to face him and saw where he was looking. "She's actually doing much better than she looks."

"I was going to ask if she'd improved enough to wake her up so I could question her, but now..."

Ellie floated in a tank like the one Marsee had been in. Most of her fur had been shaved off to treat her injuries and she was covered nearly head to toe in the same mesh cast that was on Marsee's paw. Even her tail was in a cast. Only her head and the tip of her tail had any fur left. Her paws looked stumpy and raw where her claws had been ripped out, but what was even more disturbing was the sheer number of angry red scars that were still healing, and the massive purple and blue bruises that stood in contrast to her light gray skin. They covered just about every inch of her.

"The nano solution she's floating in is doing a wonderful job in repairing her injuries. I can give her something for the pain and wake her for a few minutes if you need it. She might panic though, because she won't be able to move with the casts. With her injuries, I don't expect the pain block to last very long, and I'd rather she be sedated rather than have a longer lasting block administered. It's safer with the injuries she sustained."

"The longer we wait, the more time the people who did this have a chance to get away and cover their tracks, or find a way to hurt her again. I want her medical records sent to me as well. I need to know everything that was done to her, in detail, but before you wake her, was she electrocuted?"

She nodded at his requests, and brought up the scans on the display next to her tube. He'd learned quite a bit over the past several months caring for Little Flower, and what he saw made him flinch. The Healer spent a good twenty minutes examining the scans before zooming in on her tail. Small jagged lines were visible from the tip of her tail and radiated down about a paws length. She then swam over to Ellie, did something to the tube surrounding her, and it retracted some. The shimmer of a static shield remained. She picked up Ellie's tail and ran her hand along it. The remaining bit of fur came away in clumps. She turned to him, held the fur up as evidence, and nodded.

"Based on the burn marks on the scan, it was a light shock, just enough to immobilize her, possibly knocking her out. If whoever did this, also did the same to Marsee, with the timing of when everything occurred, it could have been enough of a drain in charge to account for why Marsee wasn't killed. I do know that Marsee was shocked multiple times, on both ears, tail, both sides, back of her neck, and both of her front paws. Her right paw, neck, and sides had the worst burns. Spread out over time that could have accounted for it too."

"That is consistent with what she told me. She said she managed to sink her claws into him once, before he shocked her in the cave. Would you be able to tell if someone had used their charge recently?"

"Yes. A significant usage anyway. I've had all my healers looking for anyone with anything remotely looking like claw marks, and checking every Sprite that comes in for that as well. No one has come in with signs of either. The closest we had was with a small fry, but that was a training issue in school. That was under supervision of healers at the time due to the risk to others, and they wouldn't have been big enough to inflict the kind of burns your daughter had. If someone did get injured, they treated it themselves, or had someone else treat them." She restored the tube before disposing of the fur. "Are you ready to wake her now?"

"One more question first. How long would one of your species be able to survive out of water before they suffered injury or died?"

"It would start to sting almost immediately, but we can easily tolerate fifteen to twenty minutes. After that the lungs start to dry out too much and would start showing signs of damage. After an hour, much of that damage would be irreparable and the person would likely be unconscious or delirious from lack of oxygen, and after two hours, death. Deep Current likely waited too long to return to the water and passed out."

"If someone was out of the water for fifteen to twenty minutes how long would it take to recover, and would you be able to tell if they had been?"

"It would probably take a month for everything to heal if left untreated. Treated, a day or two. You'd know if they spoke. Their voice would be very raspy and rough for several days, even if treated."

"I would like you to examine both Rip Current and Clear Seas for signs they've been out of the water for any significant length of time or used their charge. Also, let me know if any Flyers come in for treatments for any kind of physical injury."

"Flyers?" she asked.

"We found a scale in the suite," he said. "That information is classified, and does not leave this room."

She nodded and considered. "I'm not aware of any Flyers coming in for treatment in the past few days, but I wouldn't have been informed if the injury was minor. I'll look that information up and send you a report.

"Thank you," he said, and flipped open his tablet to start recording. When ready, he indicated she could wake Ellie.

She shifted the tube down around Ellie's head, and applied something to the back of her neck. Then, after a minute, she injected something into Ellie's arm and motioned him over. "It's better if she sees your face first."

He swam over and waited as Ellie's eyes fluttered open and focused on him. "Jer," she whispered. "Is Marsee safe?"

"She is, don't try to move, you're in a cast. The Healers have a pain block on you, which is why you can't feel anything. I asked them to wake you up so I could question you. When I'm done they're going to sedate you again, so you can heal without pain."

She closed her eyes and took a deep breath before opening them again. "Thank the moons," she whispered. "How bad am I?"

"You look far worse than the healers say you are, but you should make a full recovery with time. Who did this to you?"

She frowned. "I don't know. It was late, after ten. Marsee left for a swim in the garden and I finished up a report and went to bed. I heard the door open and assumed it was Marsee returning. A few minutes later, I'd almost fallen asleep when I felt something touch my tail. After that, I can't remember much of anything. I think I might have woken briefly in my room, but I don't remember seeing anyone, not until I woke up here with the healers saying they were taking me in for surgery. It's all kind of fuzzy. I just remember the pain. I think I tried to get them to send Myra a message. Did you get it?"

"We did and Lowell contacted us too. I'm glad you weren't awake for what happened to you. Do you have any idea of who it could have been?" he asked.

She looked up at the Senior Healer and then back to him.

"Come find me when you're done, but don't take too long. That block will only last another five minutes at most," the Senior Healer said, and swam out.

"Someone's tampering with evidence and there are only a few people with clearance or the technical ability to do so. Clear Seas and the Senior Archivist have the security clearance to make the changes, but I can't believe either of them would do this. I've known both of them for years. I don't have any concrete proof, but my whiskers tell me Rip Current has something to do with this. All of the missing people were from his district, including his brother, who was last seen with him. Additionally Rip got his Council seat by default as a Junior Councilor when his father was killed in a shuttle accident. He's also on far too many committees for his rank."

Jer lifted his brow at that, and nodded, honestly not surprised. That fit with everything else he was learning.

"What?" Ellie asked.

"Marsee was abducted, but Stormy followed Rip Current after I arrested his father for tampering with the evidence, and watched as Rip tossed Deep Current in the Trench. He rescued Deep and they ended up finding Marsee in a cave. Deep gave his life trying to keep Marsee warm until we could arrive. Both Deep and Marsee indicate they were approached by someone in the Sea Patrol, and the guards assigned to watch your suite are missing. Additionally someone tried to poison my family right around the time you were found, and several of the Hue-mans are now missing including Little Flower, GrandFather and Hope, and I don't know if it's related but Clear Seas' older son Temperate Seas was also injured in a shuttle accident. On top of that, at least one Hue-man is dead. Three others, that we believe may have been involved in kidnapping my family, are also missing, and an Ice Giant ship was waiting for them in the Wilds. Some of Kendra's guards happened upon them as they were trying to sneak into New Hope. We also found a purple scale in your room about an hour ago. Do you know where Petra is? We haven't been able to reach her or the other pilots, and what we found in their accounts is...pretty damning of both them and Wind Rider."

"Petra? Wind Rider? No. They're not behind this. I'm sure of it. I've had far too many conversations with Petra. She doesn't want to be in the Council, and is honestly frustrated with her mother's attempts to make her join, even though publicly she's said otherwise. She doesn't want her mother to know, and she honestly doesn't want to be a nest mother either, but she doesn't have much choice there. They've had a fraction of the normal female births in the last century or two, but haven't been public about it as they don't want to scare their population. They didn't even want to let Petra off world because of it. They're hoping Petra will be as prolific as Wind Rider. The only reason they allowed it was because I agreed to take her as my pilot, and I had to go before them to vow to keep her safe, even though she's legally an adult. No one has come forward with a ransom note for her? All of Flyer would be panicking if they knew she was missing."

Jer shook his head, stunned by the information Ellie shared about the Flyer's birth rate. "No, we haven't received a ransom note yet. Do you know where she might be?" he asked again.

"They were going on vacation to explore some gem mine or something like that," Ellie replied. "Apparently Petra won't fit once she's fully grown. If they're underground, that could explain why they're not responding, but all of this sounds like someone's staging a coup." Ellie winced. "Jer, I think that block is wearing off."

"I'll get the Healer. Is there anything else I should know?" he asked.

She shook her head. "No, between what I just told you and what I've shared with Lowell, that's everything I know. Moons, why do my paws hurt so much?"

"Every bone in your paws were broken and your claws were all removed," he told her. "But don't worry. They're growing new ones to replace them. You'll recover."

She swallowed hard. The look of horror and pain on her face made him turn and swim fast for the door. He saw the Healer at the end of the hall waiting for him, and motioned her down. She swam quickly to the room and applied something to Ellie's arm.

"I promise you Ellie, I will find who did this to you and make them pay for it."

She nodded slightly before closing her eyes and drifting off to sleep.

He turned to the Healer. "I have a few more questions for you. First, we also found another claw in Ellie's suite. I'd like you to come examine that as soon as you're able, to determine if you can find any other genetic markers on the claw, and the scale we found, and if you can, tell us who has been in their suite. I know it will be painful for you, but it will be greatly appreciated, as I don't really know who else I can trust with this."

She nodded. "Of course, Councilor."

"Thank you. Next, my understanding is that Clear Seas' son was in a shuttle accident. What is his status?"

"Thankfully mostly minor injuries, outside of a badly broken arm. His mother just left to take him home, maybe...half an hour ago," she replied.

"Are you free to come with me now to examine Clear Seas, Rip Current, and the suite?"

"I'll be bringing Marsee in for surgery to repair her paw as soon as she's ready. It would be better if they could be brought here, or if I could wait until after. Depending on how much time it will take to examine the suite, I'll need treatment, and time to recover afterwards."

Jer nodded. "Then I'll meet you here after." He thanked her for her time and she swam out. He fired off a message to Marcus asking him to meet him here too, along with what he'd found out, and let him know he was going to Clear Seas' home to talk with his son, then frowning at Ellie's battered body, swam out.

Fifteen minutes later, Jer arrived at Clear Seas' home and paused before swimming up. So much had happened since the last time he'd been here. He hoped his friend understood why he'd done what he'd had to do, and he prayed that neither he or his son were involved in this mess, but he was still very conflicted about Clear Seas actions at the Trial. He might not have been involved in Marsee's kidnapping, but he had planned to kill Marsee before, and he wasn't sure he could forgive him for that betrayal.

The Honor Guard looked away at Jer's frown, which hadn't been directed at her. "I'm sorry, sir. I should have watched Stormy better," Aris said.

"Sorry, that look was not directed at you. I'm not mad at you. I'm honestly grateful you weren't successful. If you had been, my daughter would be dead. Stormy told me how he got out of the house. You'd have never been able to follow him anyway. If Kendra reprimands you in any way about that, let me know. I won't allow it."

Aris raised a brow in surprise, nodded once, and returned to her on-duty position.

With a deep breath, he refocused on the door, swam up, and knocked.

Clear Seas opened the door but said nothing for a moment, his mask fully in place, then motioned him inside. "Is this an official visit or social?" he finally asked.

His voice was just as clear and melodic as he was used to hearing, and that more than anything convinced him that Clear Seas wasn't the person who harmed Marsee or Ellie.

*What? Our nose isn't good enough? Geesh!*

Jer struggled to keep from laughing at his own thoughts, but a bit of a snort snuck out anyway. "Official. Is there somewhere private we could talk?"

Before Clear Seas could answer Stormy swam up. "Are the Translator and Deep Current okay?" the boy asked in sign.

"Marsee's recovering just fine. She was very impressed at your courage in rescuing her, and told me to thank you. Deep Current though, sadly didn't make it. He gave his life trying to keep Marsee warm," Jer told the boy who had gone from happy to depressed in a moment.

"Oh. So I wasn't fast enough then?" he signed.

"On the contrary, the Senior Healer said that if we'd been another fifteen minutes we would have lost them both. If you hadn't followed Rip Current, and then braved the Leviathan to come find me, she would have died too. There wasn't any way that you would have been able to make it to the council chamber from the Trench and back before Deep Current died. He made the mistake of staying out of the water too long. Even with a drone, I don't think I could have done it."

Stormy nodded and swam off, still radiating his grief. They watched him go before Clear Seas motioned for Jer to follow him to his office.

"How's Ellie?" Clear Seas asked once the door was shut.

"She's out of surgery for now and recovering, but she doesn't know who did this. From the information she provided, Ellie was shocked around ten the night before. She'd gone to bed and heard the door open but assumed it was Marsee returning from a trip to the garden."

"Ten? No, that can't be right. The logs showed her entering the suite around two in the morning," Clear Sea's stated with a frown.

Jer raised a brow. "If the archives can be modified, so can those logs," he said pointedly.

Clear Sea's flashed a range of emotions, from confusion, to understanding, to horror. "Bottomless depths. How did she possibly survive those injuries for that long?" Clear Seas asked.

"Knowing her, pure stubbornness," Jer replied.

Clear Seas briefly flashed humor at that statement before sobering. "So am I correct in assuming that since my access hasn't been restored that I'm still a suspect?"

"Officially yes. It's Stormy's word against Rip's right now. The problem is I just don't have proof admissible in a trial that Rip did either, outside of your son's claims, and you and I both know that's not good enough. You and the Archivist are the only two with clearance to modify evidence, and whoever did this both knew of Marsee's psychosis, that she could swim, and what was planned by the Seniors at the Trial, which narrows it down to the Senior Council, and people that were with you when you met her, and out of all of them, you're the only one that should know about her illness and the Trial."

Clear Seas was silent for a while, considering that information. "So Marsee doesn't know who did this either?"

"No. She was kept in the dark the entire time," Jer said, watching closely for a reaction.

Clear flashed his frustration at that answer, and swore. "Have you spoken to the Archivist yet?"

"Marcus did, and we've revoked his access as well," he replied.

"What about the rest of your family? Have they been found yet?" Clear Seas asked, flashing his concern.

"No," Jer stated with frustration of his own, "and that's turning into a very complicated situation too. GrandFather's friend Henry is also missing, along with GrandFather's horse, and there are three other Hue-mans missing. We believe those three are behind the kidnapping, and quite likely the poison. At least one of my people is dead, although I don't know who yet."

"I'll help any way I can, but I don't know anything about what happened to them. I promise," Clear Seas said, and then frowned at him in confusion, "What's a horse?"

"The long legged grazers, and good. I figured you would. I found one of Ellie's claws with Marsee, which links their attackers together, and since both Ellie and Marsee were electrocuted, it means a Water Sprite was involved. Marsee indicated her attacker had a raspy voice which would also indicate they were out of the water for a significant amount of time. While I can tell your voice is not raspy, I would like you to be examined by the Senior Healer for official confirmation."

"Of course. I'll head up with you right now if you'd like, but be honest with me, Jer. How are Ellie and Marsee really doing?" Clear Seas asked. "I know you were trying to protect Stormy earlier."

Jer sighed. "Marsee's paw was crushed along with the two claws removed, which you already knew about. She suffered from a severe case of hypothermia and the Healer says she was electrocuted multiple times and enough that it should have killed her. Marsee will be going in for surgery to repair her paw shortly. She also had a broken shoulder and suffered from water inhalation." Jer watched as horror and anger briefly passed through Clear Seas' skin before he was able to bring himself under control. "Ellie is still in considerable pain and they're keeping her sedated while she heals. The Healer said she should make a full recovery, although she'll also need another surgery to repair her paws when she's stronger."

Clear Seas paced in his office, anger and regret seeping through his control. "I'm the one that found her, Jer. That's a long crawl for one of my kind. I was exhausted and in a lot of pain in just the few minutes it took to find her, confirm she was still alive, call for help, and get back to water. The amount of damage done to her, even if she was unconscious at the time would have taken too long. Someone else has to be involved, and there wouldn't have been time for whoever took Marsee to make it back to your world and take the others. I'm honestly not sure how you made it here so quickly."

"Emergency jump, and let's just say I don't recommend it. My stomach still hasn't settled. As for there being someone else involved, I agree, which is partly why I'm here actually. How's your son?"

"He's good. A broken arm that will take a few days to fully heal, but other than that he's fine."

"What happened?" Jer asked.

"A run-in with a Leviathan. Why do you want to know? Temperate is a good kid. He wouldn't have done anything to hurt Marsee or Ellie. I'm sure of it. It's not in his nature."

"Do you remember how Rip got his Council position?" Jer asked instead.

Clear Seas thought for a moment and then anger flashed through his skin as he made the connection.

Jer raised his paw. "I don't know if this is anything more than a coincidence, but I need to talk to your son."

Clear Seas swam away and looked out his office window. "Jer, there hasn't been an attempted coup in hundreds of years. Certainly not since my people joined the Consortium. Do you really think that's what's going on?"

Jer didn't reply right away and Clear Seas spun to face him.

"You do. Why? What do you know that you haven't told me?"

Jer just looked at Clear Seas trying to decide what to tell him.

"Jer, if someone is targeting my family, I need to know. Please tell me," Clear Seas begged.

"Let me talk to your son first, and then come with me to see the Senior Healer. If she clears you, I'll tell you what else I know," Jer finally said.

Clear Seas calmed his emotions and nodded. "That's fair. Temperate is staying here for a few days until his arm heals. I'll take you to his room." Clear Seas started swimming towards the door and then stopped and turned. "Can I ask a favor of you though?"

Jer tilted his head and indicated Clear Seas should continue with his request. "If it's within my power to give."

"Will you place a guard on the home of my daughter as well? Right now, I don't trust anyone but the people you brought with you. You know how our society works. As my eldest Temperate should be my heir, but he's never wanted to be anything but a pilot in the Sea Patrol. He hasn't publicly declared his intention not to be a councilor though, and I haven't asked or named him. I think we're both hoping Stormy will want to take up that mantle when he's older. Jade has told me she doesn't want anything to do with it, but would if necessary, at least until Stormy was old enough. If something happened to both of my older children, no one would elect Stormy, since he's not even close to being an adult.

Jer nodded. "That I can do, and gladly." He pulled out his tablet and called Avery, asking him to send one of the honor guards to meet him here. Clear Seas indicated his gratitude and then they swam out and down the hall to the room where his son was. Clear knocked and his partner, Jewel, opened the door.

"Councilor, I didn't know you were here. Forgive my rudeness in not welcoming you," she said.

"There is nothing to forgive, Jewel. I knew you were busy. I came to talk to Temperate. I have a few questions about his accident I need to ask him," Jer replied.

Jewel frowned but let him in.

"What would you like to know, sir?" Temperate asked with difficulty. His arm was in a mesh cast and supported by a sling that had it firmly held in place in such a way as to block his normal visual communication and make sign language difficult. He was lounging in one of the hanging chairs, so he spoke Saber instead. Temperate was still learning to speak their words, as they were slow and halting as he struggled to form the sounds, but for his young age, he must have been practicing hard.

"Tell me what happened with your shuttle accident," Jer replied, motioning for him to remain seated.

"There is not mmm...uch to tell. We were called off the search for your daughter to chase off a Leviathan that was p...pestering the travel lanes near the east side of the city. I didn't react fast enough and the

Leviathan rammed my ship. Before I could recover, the ship spun into the side of a rock wall. The others from my squadron chased it off and I esided...ex...ited the craft. The fuel cell mmmust have been dam...maged because shortly after I ex...ited the craft it es...exploded. That is how I broke my armmm. I was flung into the rocks from the shock wave. My squadron came back, picked me up and brought me to the Trauma Center for treatment."

Jer nodded. "Do you share shuttles or is that your craft exclusively?"

"It's mine. We never know when we're going to be called out, so it's better to have the craft with us at all times, rrrather than have to go all the way back to the base."

"Did you notice anything unusual about the way it handled before the accident, or any indication that there was something wrong with it?"

"No. In fact, I brought it in for regular mmmaintenance earlier this week and had a clean report," Temperate replied.

Jer nodded and made a note to find out who had worked on the craft, and get a copy of that report, and then frowned. "Marcus says you're a highly rated pilot. How did the Leviathan get you?"

Temperate looked away. While his skin didn't reveal anything, Jer could tell he was hiding something.

Jer narrowed his eyes. "Answer me, Pilot," he said with authority.

Temperate sighed. "I was exhausted and didn't report it, like I'm supposed to. I didn't get much sleep the night before Ellie was found. I was here until after ten, following Ellie and Marsee's visit, and then stopped and visited with a friend on the way home. The next day, after I exhausted my emergency flight hours, I joined the guards with the ground search until my next shift. By the time the call for the Leviathan came in, I was having a hard time staying awake, even with the stimulants they were handing out."

Jer raised a brow when Temperate mentioned the time, as it matched when Ellie said she was attacked.

"I can confirm he was here until after ten," Jewel said. "It was closer to eleven before he left."

"Do you have any proof of that?" Jer asked.

Jewel shook her head. "No, but I give you my word."

"Who did you visit with?" Jer asked.

Temperate flashed embarrassment and didn't answer right away.

Jer raised a brow and waited.

"Her name is Melody."

"Her?" Both Clear Seas and Jewel flashed in surprise.

"Is this serious?" Clear Seas asked.

"Not yet," Temperate said, flashing a color Jer had never seen on Sprite before.

"But you want it to be, don't you?" Jewel asked. "I want to meet her."

"*Mother...*" Temperate groaned with exasperation. "I'm not ready for that. That's why I didn't tell you."

"I want to talk to her too," Jer said. "Send me her contact information."

Temperate sighed. "Yes, sir." Moments later Jer had the information and placed a call.

"Senior Councilor, how can I help?" a young female Sprite asked with a look of concern.

"Melody?" he asked.

"Yes, sir," she signed back.

"Have you met with Temperate Seas recently?"

Melody flashed the same embarrassment Temperate had moments before. "Yes, sir."

"When, date and time, as specific as you can," Jer asked.

"Three nights ago?" Melody said hesitantly as she considered. "It was the same night the Translator came to visit with his family. We talked about it afterwards. He arrived around eleven."

"How long did he stay?" Jer asked.

Melody's skin rippled with embarrassment, and the same odd color Temperate had. Temperate began squirming in his net. "He left right before his shift the next morning," she said eventually, although Jer had already guessed that based on her reaction, and Temperate's.

Clear Seas and Jewel were both having a hard time keeping their humor under control, as was he.

"Thank you, Melody. That's all I needed to know," Jer said and hung up. He decided to take pressure off of the young pilot and redirect the conversation. "Have you noticed anything unusual among your peers at the Sea Patrol? Anyone acting odd or complaining more than usual?"

Temperate calmed and thought for a while. "Not really. The only odd thing I've seen is that we had a couple of new transfers a few weeks back, and they're already on council duty. That's not one to be given to new p...people even if they were higher ranked from their district, unless someone requested it."

Jer and Clear Seas looked at each other. "What's your impression of them?" Jer asked.

"Honestly, I haven't interacted with them mmmuch. From what I understand, they haven't mmmade mmmany friends yet, and tend to keep to themmmselves. They've been polite enough the few times I've run into them."

"Can you give me their names and who would have assigned them those duties?" Jer asked. Temperate did. Jer recorded the information, and sent it off to Marcus. There was a knock at the door and Stormy peered in.

"Councilor Chenzira, there's a guard at the door looking for you," Stormy signed.

"Thank you Stormy," he signed back. "Please let the guard know I'll be out in just a minute."

Stormy swam off.

"Is there anything else you can think of?" Jer asked Temperate.

Temperate was quiet for a moment, thinking, and eventually shook his head. "No sir."

"Thank you for your time, Temperate. I hope you recover quickly," Jer said.

"Thank you. If you need anything else, I'll be here for a few days at least," Temperate responded.

Jer nodded, and then he and Clear Seas left. He gave Aris instructions to stay and guard Clear Seas' family rather than following them, and then Clear Seas led them to his daughter's home, which was on the way back towards the Trauma Center. Clear Seas explained what was going on to his daughter, and why they were stationing a guard to watch her. She wasn't happy about it, but she agreed.

When they returned to the Trauma Center and found the Senior Healer, she scanned Clear Seas briefly and indicated he was clear of any lung damage and also fully charged. He could not have been the one to shock Marsee.

Jer thanked the Healer and then asked if there was a private room he could use. She showed them back to her office and left. Jer turned on her privacy shield and then pulled up Marsee's testimony and handed it over to Clear Seas to watch.

Jer watched Clear Sea's reaction closely, and he showed both fear and revulsion at what had been done to Marsee, and what she'd said was the reason behind it. "Bottomless depths, Jer!" Clear Seas exclaimed when he was done and handed the tablet back. "Have the other Seniors been targeted or just us?"

Jer hesitated. "I'm not sure if they're being targeted or involved," he finally said, but decided to give a little bit of information to see how Clear Seas would react. "We can't get ahold of Petra, but we found a purple scale in the suite."

Clear Seas flashed his surprise and concern. "Petra? What would she be doing here? Wind Rider didn't say she was coming for a visit."

Jer snorted and then frowned at Clear. "She's Ellie's pilot. You didn't know?"

"No, I didn't. If I had I would have checked on her immediately," he replied. "Ellie's only been here once or twice in the last few years. Just for Council meetings. She never mentioned anything about Petra. What's being done to locate her? I haven't seen anything go out, or on the news."

"Nothing yet. We're still waiting on confirmation on who the scale belongs to. We've found other evidence which I'm not going to go into detail about, yet, but it implicates all three pilots and Wind Rider in Ellie's attack, and Marsee's kidnapping."

"She would never!" Clear Seas stated. "And I can't imagine Petra would either."

Jer just raised a brow. "I would have thought the same about you, until I saw the video of the deliberation at the trial."

Clear Seas flashed shame and sighed. "Fair, but if you've seen that recording then you know Wind Rider was against it."

"She still agreed to go along with it in the end," Jer replied. "There's more."

"More?" Clear Seas asked with concern.

"Kendra sent guards via crawler and on foot to New Hope, to try and get around the ransom note. Their crawler got stuck and they ended up traveling quite a bit further on foot than planned. In the process, they happened upon a ship of Ice Giants waiting for Little Flower. Unfortunately, when the Ship's Guild noticed their ship in the air and approached, they blew themselves up. We don't know anything but their names and that they were brothers based on conversations that one of the guards overheard. They're common names though, but according to Kendra, there wasn't enough left of their bodies to positively identify them, and their ship was unmarked."

"This is getting out of control, Jer. I just thought Marsee and Ellie were attacked for uncovering the missing archives, but I never expected anything like this. I still have no idea why the archives were altered, unless it was to frame me. However, if what Marsee says is true, then the Council, Sea Patrol, and Guild are all involved, and quite likely the Honor Guard."

At that moment, there was a knock on the door and the Senior Healer entered.

"Forgive my interruption, but I wanted to let you know that Councilor Surellis is waiting for you in the lobby, and your daughter is being prepped for surgery now."

"Thank you," Jer said, and she left, shutting the door behind her.

"What are we going to do, Jer?" Clear Seas asked.

"For now, you're going to go home and take care of your family. Until I have proof that says you didn't alter those archives, you're still officially a suspect, even if you didn't hurt my daughter. I can't change that. I'll swing by when I know more."

Clear Seas nodded and swam towards the door but then stopped and faced him. "Jer, I am so very sorry about what happened to Marsee. I know the pain she went through. As children, we practice our control by shocking each other, so we know just how bad it hurts."

Jer nodded. "The Senior Healer said as much. Apparently there was a training accident recently."

"Jer, I've never been able to withstand more than a few seconds with the charge we could do as children. What Marsee went through must have been absolute agony."

"Show me," Jer said. Clear Seas looked at him in horror. "A brief shock, like you did as a child, not what was done to Marsee. I need to understand," he clarified.

"You would trust me with this? I am still a suspect after all," Clear Seas replied.

"I do. For one, Marcus and the Senior Healer know I'm here with you, and for another, you've been a close friend for most of my life. I never wanted to believe you were behind this, although you and I are going to have a *very* long talk when this is all over."

Clear Seas frowned, opened the door, peered down the hall, and flagged the Senior Healer. She swam over immediately.

"Jer wishes to understand the pain that Marsee experienced. I would feel better if there was a witness and a healer present, just in case. It has been a very long time since I've done this...for practice."

The Senior Healer radiated her surprise, but nodded and flipped open her scanner to monitor. "Close your mouth tightly so you don't accidentally bite yourself."

Clear Seas lifted his hand and held it out to him. Jer took a deep breath and grasped it. Pain like he had never experienced before exploded within him. He wanted to scream but he couldn't. His entire body was one giant spasm of pain, but as soon as it started, it was over. If he'd been on land he would have collapsed. As it was he whimpered and panted with the lingering pain and curled up into a protective ball for several minutes.

"Dark moons! Marsee experienced that?" he said, when he could finally speak again.

"No," the Healer said blandly. "What you experienced only lasted for a second, and was a fraction of the charge Clear Seas could deliver. Based on the burns, she would have suffered far worse pain than that, and it would have lasted minutes not seconds. I'm still completely astounded that she survived. It should have stopped her heart. Then again, the females of most species do tend to have a much higher pain tolerance in order to give birth."

"This is what giving birth feels like?" he asked, astounded.

"So I've been told. I don't have any children yet."

"I think I need to apologize to my mate," he said, and both Clear Seas and the Healer chuckled. Clear Seas left and he told the Healer he would meet her back at the lobby after Marsee's surgery.

Jer waited for Marsee with Marcus, but the lobby was crowded so they didn't talk about their investigation. Several hours later the Senior Healer returned and motioned him through the doors. "Your daughter's surgery was successful and she's ready to be discharged. She'll need to return in two days to have the cast and bandage removed. If she starts to feel pain or you notice any slurring of her words, bring her back immediately, and keep her in the warmer water for at least the rest of the day, preferably someplace both warm and dry."

Jer nodded and made his way back to Marsee's room. He found her curled up in her blanket in a tiny ball on the bed. "Hey, sweetheart. The Senior Healer says you're free to go," Jer said, bending down to pat her.

"I'll stay here, thanks," she mumbled from under the blanket.

"Why? What's wrong?"

She sat up and uncovered her head, fur falling away in large tufts as she did. Nearly half her fur was already missing.

"Oh, Marsee," he said, and pulled her in for a hug as she began crying.

"The Healer said it was from the shock I was given. That my fur 'should' grow back. *Should!* What if it doesn't!" she wailed, and then dove under the blanket again to hide.

"Oh, Marsee, it'll be okay. We'll just have the crafters fashion you some clothing to match your sister's. Just wait, it'll be all the rage and people will start shaving their fur to look just like you."

"No they won't. I look hideous," she wailed from under the blanket.

"No worse than Ellie does. They had to shave most of her fur off too, to treat her injuries."

"They did?" she asked, peeking out from under the blanket.

"They did, and she looks far worse than you," he said. "Now, let me see how bad the rest of it is."

Marsee sighed, but unwound from her ball on the bed and stood up, letting the blanket fall away. Large tufts of fur drifted everywhere. Most of her fur was missing, and she crossed her arms in front of her. "I know why the Hue-mans wear clothing now. I feel so exposed without my fur."

"You know, I've never seen anyone without their fur, before you and Ellie. I didn't realize that our skin matched the color of our fur too. It's actually very pretty on you. Different, but pretty, kind of like your sister's swirls in a way," he said, as he examined her. Thin jagged scars covered her skin in the same pattern that had been on the scanner with Ellie. He frowned and ran his paw along one. "Does this hurt?"

"No," she replied. "Not anymore."

"It's almost like you're wearing a lighting bolt," he said as he finished checking the rest of her out. "Or one of Hue-man's skin art."

Marsee let out a heavy sigh. "I guess."

He gave her another hug. "I'm sure your fur will grow back, but until then, I bet if we asked, the healers would let you keep the blanket, if you want," he said, trying to comfort her.

"Do you really think it looks pretty? Or are you just saying that because you're my father?" she asked, squinting at him in disbelief.

"Both, but I also think it shows just how strong you are. I think you should wear it like a badge of honor. Not only did you survive multiple shocks that should have killed you, with nothing more than lost fur and some thin and intricate scars to show for it, but you stayed alive down there for days, until help could come for you. I've experienced total darkness before, once, for about five minutes, when I was about your age. One of the festivals had a dark room and my friends dared me to try it out. It was absolutely terrifying, and not something I ever want to experience again. I can't imagine the strength of will it took for you to spend all that time down there and not come out a complete blubbering mess, like I would have, or worse. Plus, I had Clear Seas shock me a few minutes ago, so I could feel what you went through. It took me several minutes to stop whimpering from the pain, and that was only after a second. The Senior Healer says you experienced several minutes of that, and I don't know how you managed to even try to fight through it. I couldn't make my body move at all."

"It wasn't minutes, Papa. It was hours. It went on forever. He only stopped when I passed out or stopped screaming, and as soon as I recovered or tried to fight back, he'd start again."

Jer's heart broke at the pain his daughter had endured. "I am so sorry you had to go through that, but I am so very proud of you for having the strength of will to endure."

"Thanks, Papa. Can we stop for something to eat? I'm starving. What they gave me to eat here is…well, let's just say, revolting isn't strong enough of a word. I'd rather eat whatever it was Rip gave me, and that was downright disgusting. One of the creatures was covered in slime."

He laughed, surprised by the change in topic, and the expression on Marsee's face as her nose wrinkled. "Absolutely. But we need to do something first. I need to bring the Senior Healer up to examine Rip Current, and then I'd like for you to listen to his voice. You don't have to go in the cell, but I need you to tell me if it was him or not."

She swallowed hard, but nodded. "I can do that."

"That's my brave girl," he said. "So, do you want the blanket?"

"No, you're right. He tried to kill me, but failed, and I'm done cowering before him, or whoever it was that hurt me," she said, and walked over, grabbed the mask that was sitting next to the mostly uneaten tray of food, slapped it on, and stepped through the shield, leaving a large pile of fur behind.

"Ugh, the water feels so weird on my skin," she muttered with a full body shiver after she stepped through, moving her bare arms up and down in the water, but then shrugged. Jer helped her out to the main desk as she was having a hard time swimming with her hand in a cast. Avery followed behind them. They found Marcus and the Senior Healer both waiting for them in the now empty waiting room.

Marcus looked shocked at her appearance, and gave her a long hug. "I was so worried about you. Are you feeling okay? What happened to your fur?"

"I'm fine, angry, but I'll live," she replied, and ignored the question about her fur.

"The loss of fur is from the electrocution," the Senior Healer explained before Jer could. "It should grow back."

"*Should*," Marsee muttered under her breath.

Marcus examined her injuries closely. "I need to take a recording for evidence," Marcus stated.

Marsee sighed, but nodded, and waited for Marcus to finish. When he was done, Marcus handed her the spare drone he'd brought with him, but she struggled to figure out how to operate it. Her paw was casted such that she couldn't grip with her thumb.

The Senior Healer saw her struggling and made several adjustments to the drone, so that Marsee could control it using her arms rather than her paws, like the Diggers and the Flyers did.

After thanking the Healer, they made their way over to the holding cells. Jer saw several people turn and watch as they swam past, and he saw several discussing her lack of fur. If Marsee noticed, she didn't show it. Thankfully, most people seemed relieved to see her alive. He did see several members of the press, but they backed off at his warning glare and didn't approach.

They entered the hallway with the holding cells and swam towards the door with the two guards on it. Jer floated up, unlocked the door and entered. The Healer and Marcus swam in behind while Marsee and her guard stayed outside. He kept the door open so she could hear.

"It's about time you showed up," Rip signed when they entered. Jer said nothing in response, just motioned for the Senior Healer to begin her scans. "What's this all about?" Rip asked, but again, he waited and said nothing.

"He shows signs of untreated burns on his lungs, and he's only at about a half charge right now," she said.

"Thank you, Senior Healer. That's all I needed to know." Jer's voice was low and threatening with barely controlled fury.

She nodded and left.

Marcus took one look at him, snorted, and followed out after the Senior Healer to examine the claw found in the suite.

He was honestly surprised Marcus left him alone.

"Say something in my language," Jer ordered.

"Why should I?" Rip signed back.

"Because if you don't, I will take that as obstructing an official investigation, and an admission of guilt in the abduction of my children, the beating and torture of my daughter, the murder of the Senior Guild Master, and the attempted murder of your nephew Deep Current," Jer growled.

"What would you like me to say, *Senior* Councilor?" Rip sneered back at him, his voice rough and full of venom.

"It's him," Marsee said, swimming into the room. Rip turned to face her. "It's him alright. I'll never forget that sneer."

"Why hello, Little Kitten. It's so nice to see you alive and well again, although I must say, you looked so much better with your fur." Rip's voice purred, his tone laced with fake sincerity.

Jer saw Marsee flinch as if struck by those words, and he growled and backhanded Rip so hard that Rip flew into the wall behind him. "Marsee please wait outside."

"Save something for me," she growled, and swam out.

Jer put his palm on the door switch to lock the door, and turned back to face Rip, who was rubbing the back of his head where it had hit the wall.

"Now is that any way to treat a friend?" Rip signed.

"You are not my friend, and if you want to save your life, start talking. Who else have you roped into your little scheme?" Jer growled.

"I don't know what you're talking about. I'm not the one who managed to scheme his way out of a Council ban, only to end up *on* the Senior Council."

"This isn't about me, Rip. This is about who you conned into helping you abduct Marsee, your nephew Deep, and the other members of my family. We know there's at least one person in the Sea Patrol or pretending to be, and at least three Hue-mans and four Ice Giants. So who else is involved?"

Rip, just crossed his arms and glared back at him, refusing to speak any further.

Jer took a deep breath confirming Rip's scent. "I know you were in the suite and that you were the one who beat and electrocuted the Guild Master, and that there was one other person with you. Who was it?"

"You know nothing," Rip replied, matching his glare.

"So be it. You had your chance. I will enjoy watching Marsee tear you to shreds, inch by slow inch," Jer growled, and stormed out.

# CHAPTER 33

# Henry: Hunted

Henry froze as a second motion caught his eye. "Saints preserve us," he whispered as another massive shadow slunk slowly towards him. Frozen in indecision, he frantically tried to decide whether to slide off and fight with his knife or turn Buster and risk running in the uneven and rocky terrain.

Suddenly Buster relaxed, nickered, and started walking forward.

"What are you doing, you stupid horse?" Henry said, pulling on the reins to stop Buster, and then realized what, or rather, who was stalking them.

"Nazari?" he signed.

The big cat stopped, sat, and signed back. "Myra's here too."

Henry slid off Buster, wincing at his sore muscles. "The crawler is just ahead. I haven't seen anyone yet though. I just got here, and you two just scared ten years off me."

The moment he was off of Buster, Myra quickly padded up. "Sorry, we were trying not to approach too quickly for fear we'd spook the horse," Myra said. "How did you find them?"

"I was out riding when Buster heard them leave by the tower door. GrandFather was carrying Little Flower, and Damon had Hope. I forgot my tablet in my room so I followed. You should know,

Damon's dangerous. His tattoos represent groups that hated people like GrandFather and I."

"GrandFather told us a while ago. He's been on the watch list," Myra signed.

Henry nodded, not sure if he was happy about there being a watch list or not. *Fat lot of good it did us,* he thought, but then dismissed it as being unimportant right now. "I'm thinking he's waiting for someone. That crawler should have been able to travel for days without stopping, but he's been here for almost three hours now. I spotted the shuttle from one of the bandala trees and he hasn't moved since."

"We noticed you'd climbed it. Do you think he's waiting for whoever took Marsee?" Nazari asked.

"Possibly. I wouldn't put it past Damon to have been behind the poisoning either, but I'm guessing someone else is involved too. I thought it took several days to get between here and the Water World, although I suppose that could be why they're stopped. They could be waiting for them to get here. It would take days though, right?"

"Normally yes," Myra replied with a growl that Henry could feel in his gut, and he winced in both sympathy for Myra and what he was sure was going to happen to Damon once Myra got her paws on him. "However, the air space is closed, so if that was their plan, I doubt anyone is coming for him. The question is, what do we do now?"

"Can you call for assistance now that you know where the shuttle is?" Henry asked.

"No, we lost signal before we saw your first marker. We're too far out in the Wilds right now. There's not enough ground water year round here to support a dwelling or communications infrastructure. That's why the trees are so much smaller and this was designated a wildlife habitat thousands of years ago."

Henry nodded. "So we're on our own," he signed, and turned back towards the shuttle, crawling down low to avoid being seen.

Nazari and Myra slunk up next to him, nearly as low as he was, which was impressive considering just how big they were. He shifted slightly to allow himself to sign better.

"There's a rock formation and a stand of trees over there. I can make my way down walking next to Buster. If the crawler systems are online I'm thinking it will mistake us for one of those six legged creatures. Then if the two of you circle from either direction, I can approach the shuttle and try to distract Damon while you sneak up behind him. We'll need to get him out of the shuttle though. If he thinks he's at risk, I wouldn't put it past him to hold the others hostage or even kill or wound them in an attempt to get away, knowing you'd focus on saving the others rather than tracking him down."

Myra and Nazari both nodded and started slinking away. Within moments he lost sight of them. For all their distinctive coats, they completely blended with the surroundings in the low light. He crawled back, grabbed Buster's reins, and started making his careful way down the rocky scree. He was finding it harder to see his footing with every minute that passed as he descended into the shadow of the valley. He gave Buster some slack, letting the horse pick his way down as he'd be able to see better than Henry at this point. Buster pulled him over to the side and somehow managed to find a rough animal trail down.

When he finally made his way down to the rocky outcrop, he loosely tied Buster to one of the small scrub trees and crept his way closer. Freezing when he heard the shuttle door open, he watched as GrandFather was roughly shoved outside, his hands and feet tied, lit up by the light from within the crawler.

*Well at least he's still alive. That's something,* Henry thought.

He watched as GrandFather relieved himself. He was still too far away to do anything yet. If the sensors had picked him up, then Damon hadn't been paying attention. *More likely though, the idiot shut down the ground crawler entirely as he waited.* Henry was counting on that.

James said something which Henry couldn't fully make out, and suddenly Damon hit him so hard James fell to the ground, and then kicked him where he lay. James didn't move.

Henry swore to himself, hoping his friend wasn't too badly hurt. Damon spat on James and then turned and made his way back into the shuttle. He waited a few moments before continuing to make his way forward.

He'd just made his way up to the side of the crawler, when he heard the door slide open and close again, and listened as something heavy was dragged out. Henry carefully peered around the side.

Damon was dragging Little Flower over next to James. She wasn't moving either. Damon muttered something and turned to head back into the crawler.

Henry quickly ducked back until he felt the crawler shift with Damon's weight inside and peered around the corner again and watched as Little Flower lifted her head. He breathed a sigh of relief. *She must have been faking,* he thought as she quickly laid her head back down.

Rocks scuffled as Damon jumped out of the crawler again and stormed back over to kick Little Flower hard, making her cry out. "I saw you, you little faker," Damon said, as he roughly pulled Little Flower into a sitting position. "No worries though. Now you get to say good-bye to your dear old grandfather."

Henry swore as Damon started dragging James towards the tree, a long coil of rope slung over his shoulder.

Little Flower started screaming.

He peered around and tried to find Myra and Nazari to see if they were in position yet, but he couldn't see much past the light coming from the open crawler door. He heard the sound of another kick and winced as Little Flower's screams increased. Letting out a silent prayer that Myra and Nazari were ready, he stepped out from around the vehicle.

"Let him go, Damon!" he called out.

Damon spun around. "You? How the hell did you find me all the way out here?"

"You left a trail as clear as day. Let him go before the cats eat you."

Buster chose that moment to nicker and Damon smiled wickedly. "Oh I don't think they're here. I think you're all alone. Rode out on one of the horses did you? You know there's no signal out here. So no one is coming to rescue you."

"Believe what you want. Let them go, and you might live," Henry replied.

Damon snorted but dropped James.

Henry frowned when James didn't so much as move.

Damon started walking towards him but then stopped and picked up Little Flower and put a knife to her neck.

Henry swore under his breath.

"No, what you're going to do is toss that knife you're holding over to me and then slowly lay down and put your hands behind your head," Damon ordered. "If you don't, she dies."

"You don't want to do that, Damon. If she dies, you're dead too," Henry said. "Let her go."

"I'm as good as dead now anyway," Damon hissed. "Now move!" Damon raised the knife more and nicked Little Flower's throat.

Henry swore but threw the knife over and knelt down.

"On your stomach," Damon growled.

Henry laid down, and put his hands behind his head, praying that the other two were in place as Damon dropped Little Flower hard and started walking over.

# CHAPTER 34

# Myra: Hunter

Myra slunk quietly around to the other side of the shuttle doing everything she could to keep the raging, snarling beast inside her under control. She'd killed once to protect her daughter, and she would do so again, but not tonight.

*We need him alive to find Marsee,* she told herself. *When she's safe, then we kill him.*

The beast inside her agreed, and she relaxed her control, letting her hunting instinct rise back to the front. The dim light of the new moons, that were just starting to peak over the ridge, bloomed in her vision lighting up the valley below. Scents heightened, she caught a whiff of the horse as the breeze from the distant sea blew inland. She could easily make out the sound of his hooves making their way down the scree, and she hoped that Damon was one of the Hue-mans with damaged hearing. She couldn't remember.

When she'd made it about a third of the way around, she started carefully making her way down the embankment herself. To her other side she heard the sounds of a rock being jarred loose by Nazari's descent. She kept her eyes fixed on the crawler and saw motion inside as someone walked past one of the windows.

*Yes! Their prey was still in there!* both she and her instinct purred.

She'd made it about halfway down the shifting scree when the shuttle door opened and GrandFather was pushed out, bound by his hands and feet. The smell of his blood stung her nose. It was all she could do to keep from growling.

*Can we maim him at least?* her instinct asked.

*Maiming is fine, but we need him alive and capable of answering questions,* she replied.

Her instinct purred its pleasure, and showed her a path free of the loose rocks. She slowly and carefully moved forward, trying to make as little noise as possible.

In the shuttle she could now see Little Flower struggling to sit up, and Myra frowned. She'd been able to stand just the day before, but now she couldn't even sit up. Myra sniffed deeply and caught the smell of sickness, and the mint of nano cream. *Something's wrong with her,* she decided. When GrandFather fell under Damon's blows and wheezed from the kick to his ribs, it was all she could do to not run forward and kill her prey.

*Not yet. We're not close enough,* her instinct warned. *If we go now, he could easily kill GrandFather before we could stop him.*

She kept inching closer. As Damon turned and walked into the shuttle, she risked moving faster, and then slowed again as he pulled Little Flower off of the seat and onto the floor of the shuttle, and then dragged her out and over to GrandFather. He had not been kind to her, and she would remember that when it was time. Damon walked back into the shuttle.

*Move now!* her instinct demanded, and she made it most of the way down before Damon turned and jumped out of the shuttle again.

*Freeze!* Her body froze mid step of its own volition. *We're too close, if we move, he'll see us,* her instinct warned, and then gave back control.

She nearly bolted anyway when Damon kicked her daughter and she screamed from the pain.

*Don't move! If he kicks her in the head, she's dead.*

Her muscles shook as Damon roughly sat Little Flower up and shook her hard, wanting to bolt forward, but her instinct held her firmly in place.

*Not yet!*

Her hackles rose when Damon grabbed GrandFather and started dragging him away, and he was barely able to put up any resistance. *He must be badly hurt,* she decided. Little Flower was screaming and she watched as GrandFather went limp as Damon kicked him in the face. Fear made her hackles rise even more.

*Not yet!*

Henry's voice rang out. She wasn't sure was saying, as she wasn't even close to fluent in Hue-man, but it made Damon stop and look up. Damon dropped GrandFather and started walking towards Henry, who had stepped out from behind the shuttle, a knife grasped in his paw, saying something back. She started creeping forward again, watching as Damon approached.

*Get ready...*

She shifted her weight under her, reading herself to explode forward. He was beside Little Flower now, and she swore as he picked her up, bringing a knife up to her neck. Henry froze and said something. Damon said something else and Henry threw his knife away and slowly laid down on the ground, putting his hands over his head. Damon sneered something and tossed her daughter roughly to the ground, and to her relief he started walking slowly towards Henry.

*A little further...*

When Damon was halfway to Henry, her instinct screamed.

*NOW!*

She exploded forward. Three bounds later, she leapt over Little Flower and pounced on Damon pinning him to the ground with a ferocious snarl.

Damon screamed, and struggled to get away and attempted to cut her with the knife.

She ever so gently extended her claws into Damon's backside, and growled again in warning, and he froze. She was honestly sad he did. She wanted an excuse to dig her claws in deeper. Henry scrambled to his feet and ran over. She heard Nazari behind her but didn't turn to look.

*Why are you stopping? Maim him!* her instinct growled, but she held on tightly not letting it have the revenge they both so desperately wanted. She knew if she gave in, she wouldn't be able to stop, and they needed Damon alive for questioning. With one paw still pinning Damon down, she pinned the paw holding the knife , so that he couldn't attack Henry.

Henry peeled the knife out of Damon's paw and then grabbed the rope that had been coiled around Damon's shoulder and used it to tie Damon up faster than she'd expected. *How did he know how to do that?* she wondered.

"I've got him, Myra," Henry signed. "He's not going anywhere. Go take care of the others."

She didn't waste a moment and turned to find Nazari already treating GrandFather, so she bolted to Little Flower who was laying unmoving on the ground. She ripped the scanner off her harness and quickly triaged her daughter, and swore when she saw the scans. Her daughter needed to get to a Trauma Center quickly, but the ground crawler would take hours to make it back to the compound, and Myra didn't think she had that much time. "Little Flower is in critical condition. How's GrandFather?" she asked Nazari.

"He's not much better," Nazari said. "He needs surgery, and quickly."

"Let's get them on the crawler and start moving. We can treat them on the way," Myra said, gently picking up Little Flower, who groaned at the motion, but didn't open her eyes. Myra made her way onto the crawler and carefully set Little Flower down on the reclined seat, and made her way to the front where she found Hope. She checked the cub quickly, and let out a huge sigh of relief to see that she was only sleeping, and appeared unharmed, if dehydrated, and in desperate need of a new poop sack.

*So does Damon,* her instinct chuckled. That thought made her tail curl.

"Do you hear something?" Nazari asked as she entered the ship.

Myra stopped and listened. "It sounds like a ship, several of them in fact," Myra said.

"That's what I thought. Friend or foe do you think?" Nazari asked.

"I really hope it's a friend. Little Flower won't make it back in the crawler if it's not," Myra replied. She quickly flicked on the shuttles systems and checked the proximity sensors. "It looks like we have five ships coming in from the east," she said, and flicked on the emergency communication channel.

"This is Ship Master Tabor of New Hope Trauma Ship One. We've picked up your emergency beacon. If you can hear me, please respond. I repeat, this is Ship Master Tabor..."

Myra thanked the Ancient Gods and activated the comms. "Tabor! This is Myra, we have two casualties in critical condition, please respond!"

"Myra! Thank the moons! We were hoping it was you. We'll be there in a minute," Tabor replied immediately.

"We'll be ready!" Myra ran back and picked up Little Flower again. Nazari was already making her way back out the door and they watched as two trauma ships arrived flanked by three guard ships. One of which looked to be Kendra's based on the markings on the side. One of the trauma ships landed next to her, while Kendra's ship landed at the top of the valley where they'd first found Henry. There wasn't room in the steep valley for more than one ship to land safely at a time. As soon as the ship was down and the doors opened, Myra ran on. The stasis bays were already open and waiting and she placed Little Flower down, slammed the stasis tube shut, and moved out of the way so Nazari could place GrandFather in his.

"Myra, go with them, I'll stay and follow with the others after Kendra ruffs up Damon a bit."

Myra nodded and Nazari jumped off the ship. The moment she was clear, the ship took off, and Myra made her way up front where Tabor was piloting.

"Where do you want to go, Myra? New Hope or the Trauma Center in Sand Dune?" Tabor asked.

"New Hope. We'll be able to better treat them there," Myra replied.

"That's what I thought. We'll be there in ten minutes. By the way, in case you haven't heard. They found Marsee. She was injured, but she's still alive."

"Ancient Gods, thank you!" she cried out in relief, as she collapsed into the empty seat and buckled in. "Do you know any more than that?" Myra asked. "Is she…" Myra couldn't bring herself to ask.

"Sorry, I don't know what was done to her or if she's…had issues. They aren't saying anything other than that on the news, and showing a brief shot of her being unloaded at the trauma center in a stasis tube. If the guard that was with her hasn't killed her yet, then there's a chance she survived intact, although it's possible she's not awake yet to tell. It looked like Avery, Kendra's nephew, but there wasn't a clear shot of him. They've arrested Rip Current. Rumor has it that Clear Seas son Stormy found her, and broke into the council meeting, swimming past several honor guards in the process. I can't confirm that though as the recording for the council meeting has been restricted, and I don't have access to that anymore."

Myra frowned with concern, but appreciated Tabor's frankness.

"What happened to the others?" Tabor asked.

"They were kidnapped by the Hue-man Damon Minor," Myra said.

"How under the three moons did you find them all the way out here though? This isn't even close to where we've been looking for you," Tabor asked.

"One of the other Hue-mans, Henry Curtis, was out riding and saw it happen and followed, leaving us a trail. Once we realized one of the horses was missing we were able to find the trail and follow," Myra explained.

Tabor looked over. "I want the full story later. What's a horse, and are you really saying Henry was riding this creature?"

"It's what we used to call the long legged grazers, and yes. Apparently that's a thing Hue-mans did or do."

Tabor looked over at her again with a suspicious face. "I'd accuse you of pulling my tail, but we picked you up in the middle of nowhere." Tabor turned back to her controls. "Command, this is Trauma Ship One. We will be landing at the New Hope Trauma Center in eight minutes."

"Trauma Ship One this is Command, we've received confirmation. New Hope is ready and waiting.

The moment they were in range, Myra fired off a quick message to Jer and Marcus letting them know the others had been found, although she didn't have time to go into details, and intended to follow up after surgery. Nor did she have time to read the messages that were piling in, as moments later the ship landed. Myra followed the other Healers as they floated the stasis units out the ship and into the Trauma Bay.

Brice and Ammond were both waiting, as were several other healers. Little Flower and GrandFather's scans had already been transferred to the unit, and the surgeries prepped and ready to operate. She started to follow Little Flower into that surgery bay but Ammond stopped her and peered into her eyes. "Your instinct is still on. Turn it off," he commanded.

She blinked in surprise, having completely forgotten all about it, and quickly turned it off. She was honestly more surprised Tabor hadn't said anything about it.

Ammond sighed with relief, but placed a paw on her chest stopping her from entering when she tried to push past. "We've got this. You've had far too little sleep this past half week, and you just ran nearly fifty leagues on top of it, and yes I'm pulling rank, so don't argue, or I *will* permanently demote you. You're not fit to operate right now," he said, grabbing her arms and turning her paws to show her how raw they were. She hadn't even noticed they were bleeding. "The others will be here in a few minutes. Go take care of yourself and Hope."

She closed her eyes and sighed, but nodded her understanding. He spun and left her standing there without another word, as the surgery doors swished closed behind him. She watched for a minute and turned to walk away.

*He's right. I am too exhausted to perform that surgery,* she said to herself. She made it halfway to the outside doors when the full extent of her exhaustion, held at bay by her fear and instinct, caught up to her, and she collapsed.

# CHAPTER 35

# Marsee: The Light

Marsee bolted out of the cell, grabbed her drone, and tore off down to the end of the hall and around the corner.

Avery followed her. "Are you okay?" he asked, coming around to float in front of her when she suddenly came to a stop, and just floated there in the middle of the hallway, clenching and unclenching her uninjured paw.

"Not really, no, but I'll live," she replied, not looking at him.

Avery reached over and lifted her head, and stared into her eyes. "Are you struggling with your instinct?" he asked, pointedly.

She flicked her ears back, realizing why he was so concerned. "No, this is all me. My instinct is fully in control. *I* want to kill him, slowly, piece by tiny piece. I'm just... His voice and..." she couldn't explain how the phrase 'little kitten' now gave her a physical reaction. She could have sworn she felt him shock her again. She closed her eyes, and shuddered with the remembered pain and fear.

"Open your eyes," he demanded and she did, instantly, looking at him now in fear. His eyes softened and he let go, nodding slightly before looking over her shoulder.

She turned to see her father floating by the corner, just watching them. He was both tense and furious, but suddenly slammed his emotions behind his mask as his eyes flicked between her and Avery.

Avery backed off and returned to guard mode, and her father visibly relaxed.

"I'm fine, Papa, but I hope you roughed him up," Marsee said, nodding her head in the direction of the cell.

"Technically, I can't do any more than I already did, and that's already pushing the boundaries of the Charter, not until he's been officially found guilty. This isn't my jurisdiction, and we haven't cleared Clear Seas of tampering with the archives."

Marsee frowned, but surprisingly Avery spoke up. "The Guard will not stop you."

Her father looked at Avery, brow raised in surprise.

"It's merely a formality. Trial or not, his guilt has been established by three people, and there are other missing people, including members of the Guard, people I've known and trained with for decades. If that's not something you feel comfortable doing, just say the word, and we'll take care of it." Avery looked just as furious as her father had a moment before.

Her father stared at Avery in surprise for several moments but surprising her, he didn't answer the honor guard. Instead he turned to her. "Come on, let's find Marcus, and then hunt something down for you to eat. Are you warm enough?"

"I'm fine. The water is warm here, but I'm starving. Can we make it quick?" she asked, trying to look pathetic.

Her father snorted at her expression but nodded and they made their way up to the suite. When they arrived, he ordered her to stay outside, telling her that the fewer people in the suite the better, since it was a crime scene now, but he hadn't even placed his paw on the keypad when the door opened and Marcus and the Senior Healer swam out.

The Senior Healer looked awful and Marsee could hear a high pitched wheezing sound every time she breathed.

Marcus flicked his whiskers forward in a yes, and her father frowned but said nothing.

*I wonder what they found,* Marsee thought.

"I'll have a report to you in an hour or two," the Senior Healer signed, and swam off in a hurry, coughing hard as she swam.

Her father watched the Healer swim off until she was out of sight and then turned to Marcus. "Marsee confirmed Rip's voice, and he used the same phrase he used to mock and torment Marsee with, although he still denies involvement. Rip refused to talk further, although Avery has offered the...*services* of the Guard in that regard."

Marcus turned raised a brow at Avery.

While her father and uncle were brothers, they didn't look at all alike. Marcus favored her grandmother in appearance, while her father was nearly identical to her grandfather, but in that moment, Marcus looked exactly like her father had only a few minutes before.

"If you prefer that he receive some of what was done to Marsee, I recommend Honor Guard Tanner. Her son is one of the missing guards. I've known her and her son almost as long as I've been in the Guard and trust both of them with my life. They are not involved in this," Avery said.

"You're sure you can trust this Honor Guard?" Marcus asked. "She was in charge the day of the protest."

"On my honor and with my life, Councilor," Avery said.

Her father looked thoroughly surprised at Marcus for even considering it. Marcus turned to her father. "We have enough evidence to convict Rip for Marsee's kidnapping, but I would prefer to officially exonerate Clear Seas first or get a majority decision from the other Seniors, especially considering what Rip has accused us of doing. At a minimum, I have absolutely no problem with doing what was done to Marsee to him, if it means locating and saving the rest of our family. "

"Agreed," her father said with a growl. "Have you had any luck with the rest of your investigation?"

"Some. The Techs are still sifting through the wreckage on Temperate's shuttle. Apparently there isn't much left. We probably won't have that report back until at least tomorrow evening."

Marsee frowned. "What happened to Temperate? Is he okay?"

"He had a run in with a Leviathan. He's fine, a broken arm, but he'll make a full recovery," her father replied.

"I haven't been able to find the two members of the patrol he mentioned either, but I have people looking for them. They're at the top of my suspect list. I do have pictures of them though." Marcus scrolled through a few screens on his tablet and then handed it to Marsee. "Do either of these two look familiar?"

She tapped one of them. "He looks familiar, but he wasn't the one who brought me the note in the garden. That one had green and yellow ear fins. I'm not really sure where I've seen him though."

Marcus showed the pictures to Avery but Avery shook his head. "I've never seen either of them before," Avery replied.

Marcus took the tablet back and made a note, before reattaching it to his harness. "I have a meeting scheduled with the Senior Commander in two hours. She's out on patrol right now, taking over Temperate's shift."

"Why is she taking over his shift?" Marsee asked. "That'd be like Ellie filling in for...for me?"

"Everyone was out looking for you for two days. She's filling in so someone else can get some sleep," Marcus answered, and she nodded her understanding.

"Well in that case, I think we should find something to eat. Marsee has informed me that the food in the trauma center was revolting and she's starving" her father said.

"I could have something sent to my office," Marcus offered. "And I really should assign us a suite. I slept on the couch in my office last night, since someone bumped me out of my room," he grinned at her teasingly.

She grinned back, but then sobered and shivered slightly as she looked at the door of the suite where Ellie had been beaten and shook her head. "No, I want to stay on Ellie's ship. I don't feel safe in the suites right now."

"The ship would be a good choice," Avery said. "I can easily guard it by myself. There's only one entrance as the cargo hold can't be opened from the outside. Plus, I can enable the shields while we sleep, and if something does happen, we can fly out."

"That works for me," her father said, and turned back to Marsee. "Do you want to go there now?"

Marsee shook her head. "No, I don't know if it's been restocked yet, and I think I want to go back down to the market anyway. If that's all right?"

"Are you sure," Jer asked. "What about your missing fur? The healer says we should keep you warm and dry."

"I'm sure. I've been dreaming about some of the food I had the other day, and I'm warm enough right now." Her body decided to shiver and prove her wrong. "Well, warmer anyway. It's probably going to take me a month to feel warm again, at least not until my fur grows back. Besides, I'm either going to have to get used to people staring at me, or hide for the next several months, and there isn't time to do that. I want to visit the platforms and Habitat and see if I can figure out what Deep Current was so worried about, and there are still all the Guild meetings I need to reschedule and attend."

Her father flicked his ears back in surprise. "I'm sure they would understand if you canceled them. Especially since we haven't released that Ellie's still alive."

"I'm sure they would too, but this is all prep for the Council Meeting, which still needs to occur, and Rip was up to something more than just getting back at us for claiming too much power after the trial. I had a lot of time to think in that cave. Several of the edited items in the archives happened before the trial. Whatever's going on has been in the works for months. Ellie and I just stuck our tails in it, and made a convenient target, or possibly a distraction from whatever else is going on. If he was just after you, he wouldn't have hurt Ellie so bad. There has to be another reason why Ellie was targeted, and he inferred that people were upset that I'd been named her heir. The best way to figure out who, is to meet with the people we were going to meet with."

"It's my belief that Rip was attempting to stage a coup," her father replied. "We don't know yet if that's against Clear Sea's or if the two were working together to take out the rest of the Senior Council. The evidence that Ellie had Lowell look into show Clear Seas was the one that edited both the archives and the logs. He could have been hiding that evidence for Rip. Rip and Clear Seas are related too, second cousins or something like that. Lowell is still trying to see if she can restore the unaltered footage. Besides, we're not going to be able to go with you to those meetings, with everything else we need to investigate here, and if the Guild is involved then meeting with them could be very dangerous."

"I'm very well aware of the danger," she said with a glare. "Trust me."

"Marsee, I really don't feel comfortable leaving you out of my sight right now. If something else happened to you, your mother would kill me," her father said, only half joking.

"I feel the same way too, but I need to do something. I can't just sit around when the others are still missing. I'll take Avery with me," she replied, not backing down.

Her father continued to frown.

"Clear Seas offered to take me to the Habitat before, so I was thinking of asking him, but if you want, I can ask Temperate if he's feeling up to it. I've met him and I trust him. I suppose I could take Ellie's ship but I'm not sure if the platforms or Habitat have a dry dock. I'll have to ask. If not, I could rent a shuttle. Either way, while Clear Seas may still be a suspect I don't believe he's behind or involved in what's going on, regardless of what happened at the Trial or the evidence you found. He wasn't the one who attacked me, Rip Current was. I was pretty sure it was Rip in the cave, and now that I've confirmed his voice, I'm absolutely sure of it. I'm not sure what he was intending, but I believe Clear Seas was being targeted too, and quite likely his son. So are you, if you're looking into his accident. Besides, by the time I went out for a swim in the Arboretum, we were pretty sure someone altered the archives to make it look like Clear Seas, and were planning on telling him about it when we saw him the next day."

Her father frowned. "She didn't mention that when I spoke to her, and why didn't you mention this before?"

Marsee shrugged. "I just remembered. Anyway, the fact that Clear Seas uploaded the video to the archives and even made a change wasn't what was concerning. He could have just uploaded whatever was sent to him by someone else. The problem was, the meta data on the video itself was missing. That information states who created it and where. That's an easy change with the right tools and skills, but it wouldn't have been allowed as evidence in the archives without that information, and it can't be altered afterwards, which means someone found another way to edit it, most likely with direct access to the servers. If someone even tried editing that information after it was uploaded, the council software would have sent Ellie and everyone on the Senior Council a warning. If they had access directly to the servers then they could make any changes they wanted, I know I could, which is why access to the servers are so closely guarded, and why they're physically located in the depths of the Archives. Only the Senior Council and Ellie have access to those rooms...and the Senior Archivist, and you can't give anyone permission to access them. Access is tied directly to your position and rank as Seniors."

"Clear Seas or the Senior Archivist could have escorted someone in to make those changes," her uncle said.

Marsee shook her head and looked at her uncle with a grin. "That's what we thought at first, but that's not possible. Uncle, I'm surprised you didn't figure that out when you dropped Lowell off."

Her uncle looked at her frowning, and then a moment later his eyes widened. "It's a dry room."

Marsee nodded and turned to her father. "The whole floor is purposely designed to be inaccessible to Water Sprites. Their carts can't make it because of several sets of stairs, and it would be too far for a Sprite to crawl from the nearest water entrance to have enough time to locate the right server and make those changes. They'd never make it without passing out. The other servers, used for the general public, are in a wet room that the Sprite's techs can manage, but not the Council's servers."

"Why would the Sprites have areas in their Archives they can't access?" her father asked with a frown. If there was a problem, their archives could be down for weeks, depending on where Ellie was."

"I asked about that too. There are a number of off-world techs who live here for just that reason. Ellie has the ability to remotely open it, but only from within any of the other council archives, and she's the only one that can do that. Not even the Senior Council can, and it's both password and bio-protected. Do you remember the day she first came to the Compound to meet with Little Flower? That's why she had to leave. One of the servers went down and she had to fly back to Council City to grant them access, and then stayed there and monitored all of the changes made."

"It takes a good hour or more for communication to travel to Saber. How would she be able to monitor it from there?" Marcus asked.

"She's given priority access on the hubs due to the critical nature of the situation. It still takes time, but only a few minutes, not hours. It shuts down all other non-priority traffic, so she tries not to do that unless there's a critical problem."

All three of them looked surprised. "I didn't even realize we could communicate that quickly between the planets," Marcus said.

"The reason it's so slow is due to volume of traffic, not distance. Anyway, most of the time she flys here it's to supervise hardware up-grades, and those are usually planned well in advance. Ellie told me it was set up that way when the Sprites joined the Consortium and never changed. When she suggested moving them to a wet room, both Clear Seas and his father said they liked the added security it gave. Regardless, if they didn't have access to the servers directly then someone's figured out how to hack the system remotely without letting anyone know, and we're both pretty sure Clear Seas doesn't know how to do that."

"What makes you think that?" Marcus asked.

"Because he's not in the Tech Guild. This is all the kind of in-formation you don't get until you have a mentor because of the risk involved. If I did something illegal with this information, Ellie would be held accountable. Whoever made this change, assuming they didn't have direct access to the server, would have had to be rated a master tech level three or four to get around all of the safeguards, but it still should have set off an alert."

"That matches what Lowell told us," Marcus replied, but then looked at her with an odd expression. "How do *you* know how to alter the archives?"

"I've been taking classes in the tech guild for months now, and Ellie has been showing me what she's able to do. As Senior Guild Master some day, I would need to sign off on any changes to Senior level code. She's been focusing on it with me because it's one of the few technical requirements for the position I am, or was lacking. I'm now rated as a journeyman in the tech guild with a focus in programming as of last week. I can't get into the Archives, but I have enough training to make those changes if I did. All Ellie would have to do is make me her Acting Senior in order to access the server rooms."

"Who's Acting Senior now?" her father asked Marcus.

"Nardal, I believe," he replied, but pulled up the information to confirm and blinked in shock for several seconds. She'd never seen her uncle at a complete loss for words before. "I stand corrected," he said several moments later. "Marsee is."

"What?!" Marsee and her father both squeaked.

"According to this, Ellie changed her preference the same day you were abducted," Marcus said. "With Nardal listed afterwards. The moment you were released from the Trauma Center, you were bumped back up. Congratulations Acting Senior Guild Master."

If Marsee hadn't been floating she would have fallen over. It took her several moments to regain her composure enough to even begin forming words. "Well, that makes more sense I suppose," she muttered.

"What does?" her father asked.

"One of Rip's comments. He asked me how it felt to have control of all of the Guild's resources and not be able to do anything to use them to save my life, or something like that," Marsee said, and then scratched at her bare ears. "I thought he was just referencing the fact that Ellie made me her heir. Granted I did demote her the day before. I suppose it could have been in response, just to mess with me. I've been demoted and promoted so many times, I can't keep track."

"You did what?!" Marcus asked.

"Long story. Can we go eat first? I'm starving," she asked, purposely trying to look pitiful again, as it had worked with her father.

Her uncle snorted, but waved a paw to head out.

The silent crowd as she entered the market almost made her turn around and swim back, but she took a deep breath, lifted her head and directed the drone to the first of the food vendors she was hoping to find. It took the vendor several moments to recover from the shock of her lack of fur before signing a welcome. "Translator, Councilors, welcome! What can I offer you today?"

"Hey Opal, I was hoping you had more of that stuff you had the other day. It was delicious but I can't remember what it was called."

"The brenna berry sticks?" Opal suggested.

"Yes, that's it!" Marsee replied with a smile.

"Sadly, I'm all out of those, but if you liked them then you should really enjoy these." Opal picked up a stick with several different looking foods on them. "This is a mix of yellow tail, fire fruit, and jelly eggs," she explained. "Don't be concerned by the jelly eggs. I know your species doesn't eat meat. They're a plant that produces a fruit that looks like an egg."

"Anything with fire in the name sounds perfect. How many hours would you like in trade?" she asked.

"Oh no. These are freely given. You've given us all so much already. It's the least I can do. I'm just thankful you were found safe. If I might ask though, what happened to your fur? The news has only reported about a claw being delivered. You don't have to tell me if you don't want to," Opal added hastily.

She sighed. "It's okay, I'm sure everyone is curious about what happened to me, and I'm probably going to be asked a million times anyway. I'm honestly surprised the press hasn't pounced on me yet." She shook her head and shuddered at that thought, hoping she could get out of giving an interview but doubted it, not if she was Acting

Senior now. She refocused her attention on the question. "My paw was crushed and *two* claws ripped out." She wiggled her new claws slightly in the cast and then motioned to her lack of fur and one of the lightning bolt scars. "And I've been told this is a side effect of being electrocuted. I've been told it should have killed me."

Opal's skin flashed white, red and orange, before she managed to bring herself under control. "Forgive my emotional outburst. I just can't... The pain you must have endured, and after all you have done for us..." she trailed off, shaking her head at a complete loss for words.

"I thank you for your sympathy and concern. I'm no longer in pain, and I'm told my fur should grow back. If not, well, I guess my father's right, the lightning bolts do leave rather interesting scars." Marsee could tell there was something else she wanted to ask and guessed what it was. "Go on. Ask your question. If I can answer, I will."

"There are so many rumors floating around, I don't know who to believe anymore. We were all looking for Deep Current, then Clear Seas was arrested, but now the news is reporting that Stormy broke into the Council Meeting and accused Rip Current."

She looked over at her father for confirmation, not sure what she was allowed to say yet.

"Your information is correct. Stormy led me to a cave deep in the Trench where we found Marsee and Deep Current," her father replied. "Deep Current is dead. He gave his life trying to keep Marsee warm until we could arrive. We have enough evidence to convict Rip Current of kidnapping and torturing Marsee, but there are others we're still looking for, including someone in, or pretending to be in the Sea Patrol that was also involved in Marsee's kidnapping, and we still haven't found the other missing members of my family, and several missing honor guards and other members of the Sea Patrol. We don't know if they're involved or were taken too. Rip is refusing to talk." Her father's expression remained the same mask expected of a senior councilor, but the tone of his voice was full of fury and frustration.

"Why, that no good, bottom-dwelling, mud-sucker! I never liked him. He was always so arrogant, swimming by, taking what he wanted without even so much as a thank you. I hope you throw *him* in the Trench," Opal signed with venom.

"*That* is a very distinct possibility," her father replied without the slightest hint of humor.

"Good," Opal nodded with equal seriousness. "And Clear Seas?"

"We haven't been able to clear him of involvement yet," Marcus added. "But as Stormy's testimony has proven accurate, with regards to Deep Current and Marsee's location, I expect that it's only a matter of time. We are still offering a reward for any information leading to the location of the other missing people. If you hear of anything, even rumors, let us know."

"Of course! Oh, where are my manners? Here!" she said, handing everyone a stick to try.

Marsee took a bite and groaned. "Oh Opal! This is amazing!" she awkwardly signed as she tried to hold onto the stick and sign with only one working paw. She gave up, hoping Opal could understand Saber. "I think it might even be better than chocolate chip cookies."

Her father lifted a brow and took a bite himself, letting out a matching groan. "I think you might be right, Marsee," her father signed back. "These are incredible!"

Marsee took another bite and suddenly her insides bloomed with heat. "Oh wow! That must be the fire fruit. This is exactly what I needed. I have never been so cold in my life as I was in that cave. May I have another?" Marsee asked after finishing the rest of hers quickly.

Opal beamed her pleasure in bright blues and greens and handed her three more. "Of course! I'm glad you like them!"

Marsee purred her contentment as she ate every last bit of them, reveling in the warmth. Opal took the sticks back from them, and Marsee turned to look at the rest of the market. She saw flashes of white, red and orange travel through the market as the information they had provided Opal made its way to the other vendors, but she did her best to ignore it.

She saw the vendor with the bowls she'd admired the other day and turned back to her father. "Do we have a few minutes? There were a few items I wanted to get for the others back home, and I can see at least one of the items is still here. I don't want to take up more of your time though, so if you need to leave, Avery can stay and guard me."

"Go ahead, Marsee," her uncle answered instead. "I can work while you shop, and the distraction would do you good right now."

She beamed a smile at her uncle. "Thanks Uncle Marcus! I'll be quick." She directed her drone down to the vendor with the bowls. Thankfully none of the other vendors she stopped at questioned her or showed their shock at her appearance. Maybe she wouldn't have to repeat her story a million times after all. *Gossip has its uses, I suppose.*

Like at Opal's booth though, she was freely given whatever she asked for, and it made her uncomfortable, but hearing from so many how much of an impact she had on them helped to temper it. She guessed that they were all trying to make up for what had happened to her as well, and their kindness helped soothe the wounds to her soul and temper her fear of being around the Water Sprites.

By the time she was done, she'd picked up several new toys for Hope and the set of hanging baskets for her mother that she'd admired the other day. She'd also picked out some art supplies for Little Flower, in the hopes that she would draw again. If nothing else, the fact that they worked underwater might intrigue her enough to try. For GrandFather, she picked out a set of exquisitely crafted articulating sea creature sculptures, and she'd also picked up a large embroidered bag to carry everything in to give to her mother as well. It was far prettier than the medical bag she used, and there were several compartments to help organize everything. She just prayed she'd have an opportunity to give it to them.

Thankfully there was a hook on the front of the drone to hook the bag on. She was having a hard enough time steering the drone even with the adjustments, and talking was proving to be far more of a challenge than she'd anticipated, even after seeing how much trouble her sister had signing these past few months. It did leave her with ideas on how to modify the language for those with injuries or disabilities though, and she decided she would work on that when she returned home.

She was done with her shopping in less than half an hour, and they were just about to leave the market when both her father's and Marcus's tablets dinged simultaneously. She recognized the tone of her father's as belonging to her mother. They both flipped their tablets open, read the message and said 'thank the moons,' at exactly the same time.

"They've found the others!" her father explained and then handed her the tablet to read the message from her mother.

Her ears and whiskers went back in astonishment by the time she finished reading. "I seriously can't wait to meet this horse and I want to find something for Henry as a thank you. That was incredibly dangerous for him to attempt alone. He could have been picked off by any number of predators. Do you have any ideas?" she asked her father.

"He's apprenticing with Nazari, so maybe something to do with animals like you picked up for GrandFather, or maybe something musical to go with that beautiful voice of his?" he suggested.

"Those are great ideas! Oooh maybe I can do both!" she said, and took off back towards a booth they'd just passed, her tail spiraling in happiness at the news the other's had been found. While she was worried about their injuries, she had full confidence in her mother's ability to fix them, and her joy that they were safe made her practically bounce as she came to a stop in front of the vendor's booth.

"Translator! Welcome back!" the vendor said, flashing blue in response to her own happiness.

"Thank you! Am I correct in remembering that your name is Sea Turtle? Forgive me if I've remembered incorrectly, I've learned so many names the last few days."

"You are correct, and I am impressed and honored you even took the time to try. If I might be so bold, you seem far happier than I would expect. I hope this means you've had good news?"

"We have! We just received word that the other missing members of my family have been rescued thanks to the heroic efforts of one of the other Hue-mans, by the name of Henry Curtis. From what we've learned so far, he spent all day following after them, traveling through the uncharted Wilds surrounding New Hope on one of the Earth creatures called a horse, with nothing more than a small knife for defense."

"*Riding* on a horse? That's the long legged grazers right? They're ten times their size. You're pulling my tentacles," Sea Turtle said, flashing his disbelief and humor.

"She's not," her father said. "I've seen it for myself. Little Flower has been injured and unable to walk for months. Apparently her grandfather's horse was also rescued, and I walked into the barn to see her sitting on his back without so much as a lead rope on him. Apparently this was a thing the Hue-mans did before."

Sea Turtle flashed his surprise. "Well, if Little Flower can tame former Senior Councilor Tabor, then I suppose I shouldn't be surprised if she can ride on a horse too." After they stopped laughing, he signed. "So how can I be of service today?"

"I'm looking for something special to thank Henry. He's apprenticing to be an Animal Healer, and he has the most beautiful singing voice I've ever heard, high pitched, like that of a very young cub, but far more controlled, and I was hoping to find an instrument that would accompany it well. It would need to work on land and be high pitched, so that he could hear it. I don't know if he knows how to play an instrument either, so something easy to learn would be good too," she explained.

Sea Turtle thought for a moment and then brightened. "I have something that might work, but it's at my home. It is only a few minutes away. If you don't mind waiting, I can fetch it. Nothing I have here is remotely worthy enough to honor a person such as that."

She checked with her father and he nodded, so Sea Turtle took off at a fast swim. Not more than five or six minutes later he returned with a large object wrapped in a beautiful piece of shimmering cloth. He shoved several objects out of the way with one of his tentacles, set it down in the center of his booth, and then carefully unwrapped it to reveal an oddly shaped object with a flat base and covered in intricate jeweled carvings of strange and wonderful sea creatures. The whole thing glistened with color.

"Oh! How beautiful! What is it?" she asked, examining the carvings closely. The detail was simply astounding.

"I think the closest translation would be a story drum," he signed, then unwrapped two matching mallets and began to play. As he did the sweetest of tones came out and the water began to shimmer, making the creatures carved into the drum appear to dance and flash in a rainbow of colors that mimicked their visual language. She didn't quite get everything, but as he played, the creatures told a story of a missing mate and the efforts to find them, ending in their joyous and safe reunion. Sea Turtle was clearly a Master Musician as well, and by the time he finished the entire market had swum in behind her, and the water lit up a radiant blue with their approval.

"Oh Master Sea Turtle! I don't even have the words to express how beautiful that was. Thank you so much for the honor of hearing you play. I have never heard or seen anything even remotely close to the perfection of your performance, and all of my older siblings are master musicians."

"The honor is all mine. Will this work then?" he asked, flashing blue at her compliments.

"It's more than I could possibly hope for, but will it still work above water?" she asked.

"You won't get the same effects from the vibration of the water, but I assure you the tone will be just as clear and beautiful above water," he replied.

"Then it's absolutely perfect. What would you like in return?" she asked. This drum was likely to completely deplete her banked hours at the Guild and likely put her into debt, but it would be worth it. Then again, if her books were as popular as Ellie had said they were, then Ellie owed her some back pay.

"Wonderful! This drum belonged to my grandfather and was given to him in honor of a similar heroic deed. I don't have any children of my own to pass it along to, so it would bring me a great deal of joy to know it was given to honor the saving of another grandfather. It is freely given and I ask nothing in return," he replied.

"I can't just take a family heirloom, That's too much!" she exclaimed. Once she realized that everything was being given to her, she'd been careful not to ask for too much from any one vendor, but this drum was a masterpiece of artwork in of itself, and as a family heirloom, priceless.

"Please, I insist, but if you feel you must give something in return, perhaps you might translate another of the Adventures of Crawly Man for us, or one similar?" he asked, looking hopeful.

"Gladly!" Laughing at the surprise. She'd not expected that at all. "I'm almost done with translating another one called the Night Flyer. I'll send you a signed copy before it is distributed to anyone else," she promised. "But are you really sure you want to give up your grandfather's drum?"

"Quite sure. I will send you instructions on how to play it, and if your hero wishes, I would be honored to mentor him."

Marsee blinked hard, stunned. The offer of mentorship was worth far more than the drum. To do so, on nothing more than her word alone spoke volumes on how much he respected her. "Thank you, Master Sea Turtle. I will be sure to pass along that information. I expect it may be a few weeks before I see him to give him the drum though. Your gift and offer mean more to me than you could possibly know. I don't even have the words to begin to explain how much, and your masterful performance brought such joy to me after what has been several of the worst days of my life. For that, I can never thank you enough."

He brightened with the purest blue she'd ever seen. "*That* is all the repayment I could ever wish for. Thank you, Translator." He bowed low in respect and she returned the bow far deeper to show just how much his gift meant to her. He wrapped the drum back up and placed it in another bag along with the mallets and handed it to her. She thanked him again, fully intending to buy every one of Sea Turtle's albums once she'd tracked down her tablet.

Purchases complete, they swam back to Ellie's ship, although she did stop to grab several more of the fire sticks for later. Opal wrapped up the remainder of her supply and handed them to her with a flash of humor, and the promise that there would be more for her tomorrow.

She thanked the vendor profusely before leaving and spent the return trip wondering how much it would cost to get them shipped to New Hope. She was seriously considering begging Opal with an offer of partnership. They were *that* good.

# CHAPTER 36

# Petra: Carrie

Petra woke to the feel of someone shaking her gently, and found herself face to face with the young child that Rip Current had dangled in front of her.

"Hey there," Petra whispered. "Are you okay?"

"I am. Thank you for what you did earlier," the Sprite flashed. Thankfully, Petra's mother had insisted she learn all the languages. She couldn't sign easily with her hands bound, and it appeared that the child knew her language, even if she couldn't speak it.

Petra nodded, and winced as the motion made her wings ache but started to drift off again. She was so tired and weak that she knew she wouldn't survive much longer.

"I caught you a fish," the child said, holding up a still wiggling fish in one of her tentacles. "You need to eat."

Petra shook her head. "No, you eat it. I won't last much longer anyway."

"I know, but I don't have any other way to thank you, and no one else has done what you did to stop him from hurting me," the child replied.

Petra frowned at the child. "Why not, and why aren't you chained to a wall like everyone else?"

"Rip Current is forcing my father to work with him. He's only agreeing as long as he gets a video message from me every day and I'm not locked up. I can't fit through the bars anyway. Rip's allowing it because I catch food for everyone and I'm too small to hurt him. Please eat. Just this once?"

Petra sighed and took the proffered fish. It was tiny and she didn't even bother to chew, just swallowed it whole. "What's your name?" Petra asked afterwards.

"Carrie," the child flashed.

"It's nice to meet you, Carrie. My name is Petra." Petra winced as some other creature tried to nibble on her. Carrie bolted forward and caught the creature. "Thank you," Petra whispered, and closed her eyes, wondering briefly if she would wake up again, but Carrie shook her, harder this time.

"You need to stay awake," Carrie said. "Please eat. For me."

"No, you eat it," Petra said, and tried to go back to sleep.

"No," Carrie said and shook her again. "Wake up. You have to survive. Your people need you."

"They'll kill me anyway after my confession," Petra said.

"No, they won't," Carrie said. "Something happened and he took off swearing. If he was submitting your confession as evidence he would have killed you or dragged you off for questioning by the Seniors by now. Come on. Eat. You have to stay alive until they can find us." Carrie didn't even wait for her to answer, just shoved the fish in her mouth.

Petra snorted weakly at the child's audacity but ate the fish anyway.

Red Fin eventually woke from his abuse and Carrie started looking for anything he might be able to use to pick his restraints, but that was going poorly. Rip had made sure that the cage was clear of just about everything, but Carrie did her best to try every suggestion the guard came up with.

Over the next several hours, Petra dozed fitfully while the child fished to feed her and the others, but she knew she wasn't going to last much longer. Her injuries were infected now, and she alternated from feeling like she was freezing to burning up. The only positive to her injuries was that it attracted more fish for Carrie to catch, and helped to keep the others alive.

When night came and Carrie was too exhausted to stay awake anymore, she curled up next to Petra, wrapping one of her small tentacles around her arm to sleep and keep from floating off. She was glad to have the company, however small, thankful to have at least one friend with her at the end. Her last thought as she drifted off to sleep was to wonder if she would live to see morning.

# CHAPTER 37

# Myra: Interrogation

Myra struggled to wake. Her eyes seemed like they were glued shut, and every muscle in her body ached. She groaned and rubbed at her eyes.

"Serves you right for running fifty leagues on nothing but stimulants," her mentor said with humor.

Memories flooded her as the effects of the sedation wore off, and she bolted upright, fully wide awake, to find Ammond pacing the room, carrying a giggling Hope in the crook of his arm, tickling her.

"They're still sedated, but we've downgraded their condition from critical to serious," he told her, before she could even get the question out, and then motioned to the table beside her where she found her work tablet.

She read through the reports, growling at everything that had been done to Little Flower and GrandFather.

***Can we maim him now?*** her instinct asked. ***I've been very patient.***

*Soon,* she promised. When she was done reading, she set the tablet down and reached her paws out for Hope. Ammond handed her over and Myra practically enveloped the tiny cub in a hug, purring furiously. Hope wiggled and she looked down at the giggling cub.

"Play?" Hope signed, so Myra tickled the cub who started squealing with laughter.

"In case you're wondering, she's been having me do that for the last hour. She seems completely unfazed and unaffected by her ordeal," Ammond said. "Now as for your condition, I've treated the cuts on your paws and gave you a shot of pain reliever about an hour ago. You'll probably be walking like you're my age tomorrow, so I highly recommend spending at least an hour in the hot tub tonight before bed."

"Hot tub?" she asked, only half listening, as her brain was still processing her family's injuries.

"You know, that wonderful contraption you dragged me out of months ago, before throwing me in the pool?" he teased. She snorted and her tail curled at the memory. "The jets are fantastic for massage, and it will be good for you to relax."

She dismissed her injuries as irrelevant. They were minor and a little pain and stiffness was nothing if it meant her family was safe. "What about Marsee? Tabor said they found her."

Ammond nodded. "They did. They aren't releasing any details on her injuries yet, but she has been released from the Trauma Center. The press caught sight of her in the market a few hours ago. From what I saw she looked okay. Her hand was in a cast, and most of her fur appeared to be missing, but otherwise she seemed her normal energetic self, and get this, apparently Ellie made her Acting Senior."

Myra blinked at him. "She did not. You're pulling my tail."

He chuckled. "No, I'm not. The news is having a field day over it."

"I bet," Myra said, and reached for her tablet to see if there was news from Jer or Marcus, but Ammond stopped her.

"Now the real question I need answered before I can clear you for duty, is how's your control on your instinct? You've only just come off of your last watch, and you spent most of yesterday tracking and hunting, which would strain any of our instincts."

"Damon is unharmed is he not?" she growled.

"Aside from a few bruises and a rope burn, he arrived uninjured," Ammond said, but didn't back off.

"Then that should be your answer," she replied. "I'm fine, Ammond. Honestly. As much as I want to tear him to shreds for what he did, we need him to figure out who else is involved. And besides, I can't legally do anything to him until the Council authorizes it, and Jer and Marcus aren't here."

Her instinct grumbled at the delay, but she squashed it.

Ammond looked at her closely. "Doesn't matter. You know the drill," he said, taking Hope back from her.

She sighed, let it loose, and waited for Ammond to tell her to turn it off. The moment it was on she flinched at the sting of the antiseptic. It was far stronger than she'd expected.

"What was that flinch? Is there a problem?" Ammond asked immediately.

"No. The antiseptic stings my nose," she said, blinking furiously, and then started rubbing at her nose and making faces to keep from sneezing. He burst out laughing at her expression. She failed and let off several loud sneezes before the sting went away.

"Okay you can turn it off now," he said, and handed Hope back over to her, who she tickled immediately to hear another squeal of laughter. "You're cleared for duty, but next time, get some sleep, and take it easy on the stimulants. I shouldn't have to tell you the effects of taking too many of those back to back. You need to start trusting us to help you care for your family. You don't have to do it alone." When she nodded, he continued. "Now go check on the other two, which I know you're dying to do, and then there's something I need to show you."

"What?" she asked.

"Check on them first," he ordered, refusing to divulge any further information, so she did.

GrandFather's room was closest to hers, so she stopped there first. His face looked horrible, swollen and covered in bruises, but the broken bones in his face had all been set and healed, as had his cracked rib, and the nearly gut piercing wound to his stomach sutured. Myra shuddered at how close that had been to a fatal wound. It would take a few days for the swelling in his face and the bruises to go away, but he'd make a full recovery.

It was the fracture in his skull they were all worried about. Ammond had decided to risk using the bone knitter to repair it, which was a first for the species. So far everything was looking good. "I'm thinking he should be good to wake up this afternoon. We probably could now, but he'll be in a lot less pain if we wait a few hours."

She agreed and moved down the hall to check on Little Flower. Her condition was far worse. Damon had somehow managed to kick exactly where her rib was missing, and that had caused injury to her internal organs, in addition to the swelling on her brain from the operation. The antibiotic that GrandFather had given her had taken care of the infection, thankfully.

"I'm not seeing any new damage to her brain, possibly due to the fact that there were still active nanos, and I'm starting to see improvements in several areas. The swelling was fairly easy to treat but we needed to perform surgery to repair some of the damage caused by that kick she took. Since we were already in there, I also replaced that broken section of rib, so she has better protection in the future. You and I both know the Hue-mans seem to have a knack for getting themselves hurt. So far, I've not seen any signs of rejection, and it appears to be healing normally. We should know for sure by tomorrow and I'm thinking we should keep her sedated until then. With everything she's been through it would be best to keep her still."

Myra growled at the setback, but nodded. "The nanos were working. She was standing on her own in the barn the other day, for a few seconds anyway. She even managed to take a few steps while holding onto the stall railings. That's the best she's done since she's woken up, and her signing was significantly clearer. When I first saw her, before Damon kicked her, she couldn't even lift herself into a sitting position though. I'm worried how she'll do if there's been a setback."

"The swelling on her brain would have made her very sick, so it wouldn't surprise me at all that she had a hard time sitting up. It's clear she threw up at least once. She must have been terribly dizzy."

"Then I agree with you. Let's wait until she's fully recovered to wake her. She's been through so much lately. I don't want her to have to wake up sick, or in any pain, or at least no sicker than the sedative usually makes her. Is anyone researching her infection though? That's the first cross species infection we've had with them."

Ammond nodded. "Nerissa has a team working on a vaccine. We're both concerned about how severe it got in just a few hours, but thankfully the standard treatment appears to work quickly."

"So what is it you want to show me?"

"Come with me," he said, nodding towards the door.

She followed him out of the Trauma Center and surprisingly straight to the Tower. When she realized where they were going, she'd expected him to take her up to Little Flower's room, to show her something relating to the damage that had been there, but instead he kept going up to Marsee's room. Myra frowned as he paused, and then opened her door.

She let out a horrified gasp. Marsee's room had been utterly and completely destroyed. Everything had been broken, torn, ripped apart, and covered in paint, and, if her nose was any indication, feces. The walls had been covered in various hate symbols in both paint and actually carved into the stone in several places. Myra growled her fury.

*Can we maim him now?* her instinct asked, and she stood there for a long time considering it.

"Myra?" Ammond asked.

"I'm fine," she growled. "I'm going to carve those symbols back into his skin, but I'm fine. How did he do all of this and not wake GrandFather?"

"No idea, but I think we found your missing tablet." He pointed to a pile of broken pieces. "My guess is that he wanted to make it harder for you to call for help, to give himself more time to get away."

Myra took several pictures. "Has anyone interrogated him, or found out who the crawler belongs to?"

"No, Paxton should be here in a few minutes, and he's bringing a few master techs with him." When she raised a brow in surprise, Ammond explained. "It was late and everyone was exhausted here. We conducted a full search of the compound and performed a census of everyone to make sure no one else was missing while you were gone. In addition to Damon, two others were missing. Paul Markson and Danny Shuto. They're both presumed dead. And, since everyone else has been found, Paxton decided to wait until morning so he could take your statement and GrandFather's and Little Flower's as well. Nazari and Henry both gave theirs last night."

"Paul and Danny were involved too?" she asked.

"It certainly looks that way. The guards were apparently trying to sneak into New Hope and stumbled upon a ship containing four Ice Giants who were waiting for Damon. The Ice Giants blew their ship up rather than be captured and the guards eventually found the other crawler. It looks like a flock of harbingers got them both, although they haven't found the bodies yet. There may not be much left, if anything, but we did confirm their DNA in the blood splattered around the crawler."

She frowned. She didn't know the other two well, but Paul had been one of Brice's wards at the agency and knew she would be upset. "Where's Damon?"

Ammond rubbed the back of his ears. "Well, we didn't exactly have a good place to put him, so Nazari threw him in an unused stall in the barn, after he refused to speak, and Tabor has been guarding him since her shift on the trauma ship completed last night."

"That's far too nice of a place for him," she growled, "But why aren't the guards watching them, and for that matter, why were they trying to sneak in?"

He paused before answering.

She glared at him.

Ammond sighed. "Apparently there was a demand on the ransom note stating that if the guards came anywhere near your other children, they and Marsee would be killed."

Myra's eyes widened in horror.

"Before you ask, Kendra has the rest of your family in a secure location. She moved them as soon as Marsee and Little Flower were found. There are guards hidden in the trauma center, but they're posing as healers and flew in on one of the trauma ships. My understanding is that Kendra is waiting for permission from Jer before sending official guards to take custody of Damon."

"Jordan couldn't give that permission?" she asked.

"She could, but since it was your family being targeted, she wanted Jer's input too."

Myra growled with anger and frustration. Surprisingly Ammond didn't stop her or say anything, but she could tell he was angry too, even though he kept it well hidden behind his mask.

Before she could ask anything else, she heard the sounds of a ship approaching. "That must be Paxton," she said, as she watched it fly towards the shuttle bay. He was using Marcus's ship, which was clearly marked as belonging to the Senior Council and had their planetary sigil painted on the side. She made her way back down the ramp and cut across the courtyard. They made it to the shuttle bay moments before he and four others exited.

"Ah, Myra, just the person I was looking for. How are you feeling?" Paxton asked.

"Much recovered, and the others are doing better too," she replied.

"Oh good. Myra, this is Master Techs Haden and Resner. They're here to investigate the shuttle, and these two are Honor Guards Plinth and Wallace"

"It's nice to meet you," she said to the others. "This is my mentor Master Healer Ammond Greyfoot, and this little ball of giggles is Little Flower's cub, Hope."

"I had no idea they were so tiny," Resner said. "She's adorable though. Almost makes me want to have another litter."

"If you think this is tiny, you should see them when they're born. She's more than doubled in size already," Myra said.

"I'll show the techs to the crawler," Ammond offered. "Myra, do you want me to watch Hope while you take Paxton and the guards to the barn?"

Myra nodded, tickled Hope for a moment making her screech with laughter again, and then handed her over. As much as she didn't want to let go of Hope, she didn't want her on the same planet as Damon, much less in the same room.

"Come see Uncle Ammy, Hope," her mentor crooned.

"Uncle Ammy?" Myra snickered.

"She gets to call me that. No one else," her mentor glared at her, and then motioned for the others to follow him back into the shuttle bay.

"Come on, I'll show you to the barn," Myra said.

"Actually I'd like to see the damage to Marsee and Little Flower's rooms first. Ammond said the pictures didn't do it justice."

Myra growled. "No they wouldn't." She turned and led them back across the courtyard to the tower and up to Marsee's room.

Paxton stood dumbfounded for several moments before carefully making his way into the room. Pulling out his tablet he began recording. After recording a complete circle, he started snapping pictures of individual items. He sighed when he saw the damage to Little Flower's painting and lifted the torn pieces up.

"From what's left of this, I can tell it was a masterpiece. I'm assuming Little Flower painted this?"

"She did. And it was. I only just saw it. She must have finished it right before she had Hope. Who knows if she'll ever be able to draw again."

Paxton frowned, and continued snapping pictures. "Do you know if anything is missing?"

"No. Not a clue. Marsee would be the only one that could really determine that. That pile of rubble over there is likely to be my missing tablet. Ammond says he thinks Damon took it to make it harder for me to call for help, in order to give himself more time to get away. I'm guessing that's partly why I was sedated."

"You were sedated? Ammond didn't mention that," Paxton said, standing to look at her after snapping a picture of the tablet.

"I'd been up for almost four days straight caring for Little Flower. We'd just attempted another surgery to try and fix some of the remaining damage to her brain and hearing loss, and she had complications from the procedure, but when I tried to sleep, I couldn't. I was too worried, so I had Ammond bring me a sedative, which I took in the middle of the afternoon, maybe an hour or so after Jer left for the Water World. I was sedated again in the middle of the night just after midnight.

"Could you have dosed yourself?" Paxton asked.

"Yes, and that was my first thought. I thought I'd been sleepwalking too, and that was why I couldn't find my tablet. I distinctly remember setting it on my bedside table, because I'd used it to call Ammond, and then let GrandFather know I was taking a sedative to help me sleep. He's trained up enough now to know how to administer the correct dose of anti-sedative and Little Flower's room is stocked with that."

"How do you know when the sedative was administered?" Paxton asked as he continued to take pictures.

"There's a display on the hypo that shows the last time and dose administered," she explained.

He nodded and continued recording the damage. "If he'd been up here waiting for GrandFather to leave after dosing you, he would have had hours to do all this damage."

"It would have taken hours to do all of this," Myra agreed.

When Paxton was done with Marsee's room they moved downstairs and he recorded the broken playpen and the now moldy food. "Why didn't you sleep here?" he asked.

Myra sighed. She'd been asking herself that same question from the moment she knew they were missing. "I guess, it was a combination of confusion from my lack of sleep, and the fact that there's only one bed in here, which GrandFather was using. Plus, I thought Jer was the real target, not the others. He didn't tell me what else was on the ransom note."

He nodded and they moved down to her room, where he took an image of the timestamp on the hypo, which was still on her bedside table.

"Ammond already sent me their medical reports, but I will need a statement from GrandFather and Little Flower as to what happened," Paxton said.

"I don't feel comfortable waking Little Flower until tomorrow, and we were planning to wait until this afternoon to wake GrandFather."

"I should interview at least one of them. It would be better if I knew exactly what happened before talking with Damon, but I do need your statement too. We could do that first," Paxton suggested.

Myra nodded. "I'll allow waking GrandFather, but if he says he's in too much pain, I'm sedating him again. Where do you want to start?"

Paxton nodded his agreement with that plan. "Let's start with the poisoning," he said, and set up his tablet to record. An hour later, Paxton had exhausted all of the questions he could think of, and set his tablet down and stared at her for several moments. "Have you had any problems with your instinct?" he finally asked.

"No, I'm firmly under control, and Ammond tested me an hour ago. Outside of the smell of the antiseptic making me sneeze, I didn't have any problems."

He gave a slight smile and nodded. "I'll need to see for myself though. Turn it on please." She did, and off again, when he indicated. "Thank you, Myra. By law I have to place you on a watch, but frankly, I'm impressed that Damon came in unharmed. I'm not sure I would have been so kind."

"I'm nothing, if not patient. I can wait, assuming the others don't want a piece of him first."

That made him chuckle and they left to make their way back over to the Trauma Unit, after collecting the guards who were waiting outside for them.

She found Ammond and Brice playing with Hope by the triage desk when the entered. Ammond said nothing just handed her an already loaded hypo.

Myra snorted and led Paxton to GrandFather's room.

Paxton winced as he saw the swelling and bruising on GrandFather's face. She looked at him for confirmation she should wake GrandFather. Paxton frowned but indicated she should continue.

"Hey there, you're safe and everyone's okay," she signed once GrandFather opened his eyes. "How are you feeling?"

"I hurt. How bad is it?" he asked.

"You had multiple fractures to your face, skull, and ribs, plus a really nasty cut to your midsection, but everything is healing and you should be as good as new in a few days," she replied. "Paxton is here. He needs a statement from you about what happened. Do you feel up to that?"

"I'll manage. Have you found Marsee?"

"We have and she's safe too," Myra replied.

"Thank the moons!" he signed. Myra smiled. It was so adorable when the Hue-man's used their expressions. "Please tell me you caught Damon, roughly."

"We caught him. You can thank Henry Curtis for tracking you down on Buster. We followed the trail he left for us. We'd have never found you otherwise."

"I thought I heard his voice. Tell him thank you if you see him before I do." GrandFather looked over at Paxton. "What do you need to know?"

"Tell me everything that happened starting from when Myra left your room," Paxton replied.

It was all Myra could do to keep the beast inside her from growling as GrandFather told his tale. As it was, she ended up tucking her tail between her legs to keep it from lashing.

"Thank you GrandFather, that's all I need for now," Paxton said, and left the room.

"Do you want me to knock you out again, or leave you with a jar of nanos?" she asked him. She'd seen him clenching his fists during the statement, but she wasn't sure if that was pain, or remembered trauma.

"Sedative please," he said. "Nano's won't help this."

Myra nodded and applied the hypo. GrandFather was out almost immediately.

*Now?* her instinct asked.

*Soon,* she replied and left the room, handing the hypo to Ammond on the way out. Paxton and the guards followed behind. A few minutes later she walked into the barn and started making her way down the aisles looking for Tabor. She found Henry and Buster first. Henry was wrapping something around one of Buster's legs. Henry looked up as they walked down the aisle, but didn't stop. They waited for him to finish whatever he was doing.

"Morning Myra, Councilor," Henry said as he stood up.

"Good Morning, Henry. Is Buster injured?" she asked.

"No, a little stiff and swollen this morning, but we've dosed him with nano's. The wraps will help keep the swelling down until they can do their thing. Aside from a few small chips in his hooves, he managed remarkably well for how far we traveled and the rough terrain, and that'll grow out eventually. He's probably feeling better than I am right now. I'm not sure I could sit if I wanted to."

"Are you hurt?" Myra asked, concerned.

"No, just out of shape. I haven't ridden that long in at least two decades. The healers gave me a giant tub of nano cream, unfortunately not quite big enough to sit in though. I do intend to spend several hours in the hot tub once my shift is done," Henry signed.

Myra chuckled. "Sounds like you're feeling about as good as I am. Thank you so much for putting yourself at risk to follow and find them. If you hadn't, I'm sure we would have lost them both. GrandFather sent his thanks as well."

Henry nodded. "They'd have done the same for me."

Paxton examined the horse intently. "I've never been around a domesticated animal before. Are they always so docile?"

Henry smiled. "No, but this fella here is probably the best horse I've ever had the opportunity to know, smartest too. Would you like to pet him? He's very friendly and loves dried star fruit. If you'd like to give him some, you'd be his friend for life."

"Can I really?" Paxton asked.

Myra's tail curled. He sounded just like an excited cub, not the Acting Senior Councilor he was.

"Of course. Here," Henry reached into his pocket and pulled out a handful of star fruit and handed half to Paxton.

Buster nickered his excitement, and tossed his head up and down, almost as if he was saying yes.

"Hold your hand out flat, like this." Henry demonstrated, and then afterwards gave Buster a pat on the side of the neck.

Paxton did the same. His tail curled and his eyes lit up. "His fur is so smooth," Paxton said afterwards. "What I don't understand is how you communicate where you want to go, and why he would let you ride on him? He's so much bigger than you."

"Well there's no point in riding something smaller," Henry said with a grin.

Paxton chuckled and nodded the point. "Fair point, well made."

Henry continued. "As for how, it takes a lot of patience, practice, and trust, if you want to end up with a horse as good as this one. They speak, you just have to know their sign language, head position, ear posture, the sounds they make. Then you teach them yours. When we ride we use a combination of leg pressure, posture, and a special harness to indicate how we want the horse to move. Buster knows a few of our spoken words too, although he has no way to speak them back to us."

"How do you teach them though?" Paxton asked.

Henry thought for a moment but rather than answering, he walked up to Paxton and pressed his paw against the side of Paxton's leg.

"What are you doing?" Paxton asked.

Henry didn't reply, just kept his paw there.

They stood there for several moments, and then Paxton shifted away.

Henry immediately put his paw down, but a moment later put his paw back on Paxton's leg.

Paxton immediately moved away.

Henry then put his paw on the back of Paxtons leg.

Paxton moved forward this time, but Henry didn't remove his paw. Paxton thought for a moment and then tentatively lifted his leg.

Henry immediately removed his paw. "In a matter of a minute, without speaking, I've taught you to move away from the pressure I apply with my paw to your leg. You made the obvious adjustment to what I wanted, by moving forward when I changed where my paw was, but by not releasing pressure you realized that I wanted something else. As soon as you did what I wanted, I rewarded you by removing that pressure. I would then build on that and over time we'd have a language of sorts."

Paxton flicked his ears back in surprise. "That was an incredibly effective demonstration. Thank you. I will need a further demonstration of what this creature is capable of doing when he's feeling better, as I'm sure that others on the Council won't believe you rode him without evidence. For now, I really should interrogate Damon. Do you know where he is?"

"You're welcome. Come back when you're done with Damon. Buster is good for a demonstration. The activity will be good for him. As for Damon, you'll find him that way, all the way down at the end. Last I knew Tabor was sitting on him, unless Nazari switched places with her."

"Thank you," Paxton said, although he tilted his head at Henry's phrasing. "She's not actually sitting on him, is she?"

Henry laughed and shook his head. "Figure of speech. Myra, can I see GrandFather soon? When I went over this morning Healer Ammond said he was still sedated."

"Try later this afternoon. He should be ready for visitors by then," Myra replied.

"Will do. Thanks!" Henry said, and went back to wrapping Buster's legs.

They made their way down the barn to the very last aisle where they found Tabor sitting comfortably in the aisle outside of a stall.

"I was wondering when you would show up," Tabor said.

"Sorry to keep you waiting," Myra replied.

"Oh no worries. It's been very entertaining." Tabor stood and stretched as the two guards took up their station on either side of the stall.

"Oh, how's that?" Myra asked.

"Well for half the night, he tried digging his way out. Shame no one told him there's a solid foundation about six feet down under all that dirt. Kind of wish I spoke Hue-man. I'm pretty sure I would have learned a few new colorful swears when he figured that out. Then he tried climbing his way out, only apparently no one told him the wire mesh above the stalls were electrified to keep the crawlies out. It's really a shame I'm not very good at sign language yet either. I'm pretty sure I mixed up the signs for 'electrified' and 'cookie'. They are very similar, you know."

Myra snickered and her tail curled. The two signs were about as different as any two signs could be.

"Then this morning several of the Hue-man cubs came by, and we had a lovely conversation about how crime doesn't pay, and what the consequences of destruction of property, theft, kidnapping, and attempted murder would be. They were so very polite and asked such wonderful questions, and even taught me a few new signs. I really should spend more time with them," Tabor replied with a curl to her own tail.

Myra burst out laughing. "You know, you really should. I'd be careful though. I think my daughter is starting to rub off on you."

Tabor laughed. "One could only hope."

"Was Damon injured by the mesh?" Paxton asked with a frown.

"Sadly no. Before Nazari left last night she told me the charge is designed to cause temporary pain, not damage," Tabor answered.

"That's a shame," Myra muttered.

"What can you do? It's not like you have a proper holding cell here," Tabor replied, shaking her head.

Myra's tail curled further. Tabor had spent six weeks in self imposed isolation at the Agency following Little Flower's trial, and had been moved here to complete her sentencing with community service, as the Hue-mans had banned solitary confinement for any length of time, and no Guard Hall had been built yet. Her time was done but Tabor and her family had decided to remain.

"I am going to pretend I didn't hear any of this conversation," Paxton said with a sigh.

"I always knew there was a reason I liked you," Myra said, with a wicked glint in her eyes.

Paxton snorted in amusement, as she had sent more than one letter to Paxton back when he had been against ending quarantine, and by the last few she'd been unable to keep the snark out of her letters. "If that's the case, I'd hate to see what you write to people you don't like," he replied, which caused both her and Tabor to burst out laughing.

He brought his emotions under control and then sighed as he looked in at Damon, who was sitting against the back wall glaring up at him, and then switched his tablet on to record. "Jennette, would you mind holding this, since there isn't any place to set it up?"

Tabor took the tablet and stepped back to make sure both Damon and Paxton were in the recording.

"Damon Minor, I am Acting Senior Councilor Paxton Parner. Are you fluent in sign or will you require a translator?"

Damon glared up at Paxton for several moments without responding before signing "I understand you."

"Damon Minor, you have been charged with the kidnapping, assault, and attempted murder of GrandFather Chenzira. There's enough evidence to find you guilty on all three accounts. Do you deny these charges?"

Damon glared at Paxton. Paxton stood there patiently waiting.

It was nearly half an hour before Damon finally answered. "No."

"You have also been charged with the kidnapping, assault, and attempted murder of Little Flower Chenzira. There's enough evidence to find you guilty on all three accounts. Do you deny these charges?"

Damon glared. "Yeah, I deny those charges. I didn't try to kill her. I only kicked her once, and not even that hard."

"Do you deny being informed by a journeyman healer that Little Flower needed immediate medical attention due to swelling on her brain, and responding to that with 'if she lives or dies, so be it. They don't care one way or another'?" Paxton asked.

Damon frowned. "No, but I'm not a healer. I just thought he was lying to me, to get away."

"What was your reason for dragging her out of the shuttle?" he asked next.

"I didn't want her in the shuttle by herself if she was faking," Damon said.

"So, why didn't you just tie her back up?" Paxton asked.

Damon didn't answer for several minutes. "I needed the rope," he said finally.

"For what purpose?" Paxton asked.

Damon didn't answer.

"The statements I've taken, indicate the belief that you were going to use the rope to kill GrandFather. Do you deny this? You have already indicated that you intended to kill him."

"No, I don't deny it," he said finally.

"Who are the 'they' you referred to? Who were you waiting for and why? Why did they want Little Flower?"

"I don't know," Damon said.

Myra snarled at him.

"I'm serious, I don't know!" Damon glared back.

"Explain," Paxton said, giving Myra a warning look.

"Look, you can't do anything on this stupid planet if you're not an adult, except make baskets. I wanted to travel, see the planets, but I can't do that without 'adult supervision'. I wanted to learn to be a pilot, but I don't qualify to join the Ship's Guild. You stripped me of my freedom for almost two years of my life, and then stripped me of my adulthood for another twelve. Most of the people here won't even talk to me. I know that's because of my tattoos. I was young and stupid when I got those and we didn't have a good way to get rid of them, not easily, especially not with how many I had, and I had no way of hiding them when we were at the Agency. I tried telling people that I wasn't like that anymore, and as soon as I was able to ask, I had them removed, but it was too late. I tried to be a good citizen, tried to get people to like me, but the women won't even let me get within a hundred feet of them, and if what several of them have said to me is true, my genetic line will die off. I want children and a family again. I'm lonely. I want a say in my future and don't want to have to wait until I'm old and gray before being able to do the things I want to do. I don't have any say in what happens to me or to my surroundings. Every suggestion I've ever brought forth has been put down. Every job or task I've wanted to do I've been denied because the others don't want to work with me. But I took the worst jobs and did them without complaint, hoping someone would recognize that I was trying to prove myself. Eventually I got to the point where I just wanted out of here. I hate it here, but I couldn't leave. I tried. I asked to be allowed to move somewhere else, anywhere, but by the rules of your society, I'm not considered old enough to have my own place. I get why the women won't sponsor the men. We deserve it for the crap we put them through over the years, but that's why I tried to change the rules, find some way to make it so we could leave and do our own thing. Not a single man of my species has been granted that status except for GrandFather, and he's part of the ruling family here, who frankly already have far too much power. We should be in charge of our own destiny, not some stupid cat. At the Hallowed Eve Festival, I tried talking to everyone about how unfair it is for half of our species to not have equal representation, even you, Councilor, if I remember correctly. Most everyone dismissed me and I figured that was it. I was doomed to spend the next decade of my life by myself. But after the Council refused to even discuss it, I had a message come in wanting to talk more about it, and then eventually agreeing with me. They said if I helped them, then they'd give me adult status and I could do what I wanted, and they'd even help set me up with a new place, like we were *promised* by the Council."

"Why didn't you come to me?" Myra asked. "I would have gladly helped to find you a new home if you weren't happy here. For that matter, if you'd come to us telling us what this other person had planned and helped us catch them before anyone got hurt, I'd have gladly sponsored you for adulthood."

Damon looked angry. "I put in requests to leave with Jer. Multiple requests in fact, and they were all denied because I wasn't a legal adult yet. I tried bringing it up at the council meetings, again multiple times, and they were all denied too. You were informed. You were at all of those council meetings early on, but you didn't speak up when I asked to leave, and then you stopped caring for us."

Myra frowned at his accusation. She had gone on leave to care for Hope and Little Flower and had followed Jer's lead when it came to the men.

"If they sent you a message it would have a name associated with it. We don't allow for anonymous accounts on our worlds as those accounts are tied to our votes," Paxton stated.

"Yeah, well I tried looking the person up, but the system said they were dead, so I don't know who's behind it. They said they'd tell me who they were when they picked me up."

"What was the name on this account? Paxton asked.

"Snapper Fish, or at least that's what the translation made of it."

"Do you still have those messages?" Paxton asked.

"No, they always disappear shortly after I read them," Damon said.

"Where is your tablet?"

"In the shuttle."

"What did Snapper Fish want you to do, specifically?" Paxton asked.

Damon was silent again for a long time.

"Damon, you are also a person of interest in the kidnapping and assault of Marsee Chenzira, and the assault and attempted murder of the Senior Guild Master. The information you provide towards catching that person may help lessen the punishment you'll receive," Paxton said after a while.

Myra and Tabor both looked hard at Paxton with that statement but didn't speak. *Attempted murder?! Is Ellie still alive?* Myra wondered, praying with everything she had that it was true. *How could she be though? It was all over the news that she was dead. Had Clear Seas lied about it?*

"I didn't have anything to do with that. I swear. This is the first I've heard about it," Damon stated.

"How could you not know? It was all over the news. There was even a missing persons alert that went out," Myra hissed.

"I had everything packed in the shuttle, including my tablet, which I was told to turn off so it couldn't be tracked. By the time I got where I was supposed to meet up with them, I was out of range of everything."

Paxton glared at Myra for interrupting. "We're not saying you did. You were here and not on the Water World so you couldn't have, but we believe that the person you spoke to was."

Damon sighed. "He said that if I helped him with what he wanted, he would ensure that Councilor Chenzira stepped down."

"And what did he want?" Paxton demanded.

"He wanted Councilor Chenzira incapacitated for a few hours, and to have me bring him Little Flower."

"What did he want with Little Flower?"

"I didn't ask, but I assumed she was going to be held hostage until Chenzira stepped down."

"So why did you take GrandFather and Hope?"

"Little Flower was never left alone for more than a few minutes. I needed time to get away. Hope was leverage. Plus, I wouldn't leave a baby unattended for the hours I was hoping to get before someone figured out what happened, and well, I figured if no one was ever going to let me have a child of my own then Hope was the only chance I'd ever have. The other mothers wouldn't even let me be around their children or the orphans. I had a little girl about Hope's age, before. She was the joy of my life."

"So GrandFather was only taken because he was with Little Flower, and not for your dislike for his skin color? Why then did you try to kill him?" Paxton asked next.

Damon sighed "Initially, yeah. I knew he often took the evening shift to watch Little Flower, but when I showed up his door was locked so I went upstairs to wait. I figured he'd leave eventually, but then I saw the painting of everything this world was supposed to be for us, and I kind of lost it. It was like the past three years of grief and anger all boiled up and exploded out of me. I never intended to try and kill him, I swear. And frankly, I'd almost gotten myself back under control when GrandFather brought it all back up again and stated that Snapper Fish wasn't coming, which was probably true, because he was several hours late, and well, I guess something inside of me snapped. I figured if that's what he expected of me, if that's all I was ever going to be, and if I was going to die anyways, then I was going to take him with me."

"When was he supposed to show up?" Paxton asked next.

"I honestly expected them to be there when I arrived."

"I'm assuming by your comments that you did attempt to incapacitate Councilor Chenzira? How." Paxton asked.

Damon looked down at his feet. "I laced some brownies. Grand-Father recovered fairly quickly from his bite and Snapper Fish only wanted him sick for a few hours. He didn't say why."

"Sand Spinner venom when ingested is apparently far more deadly than a bite. Little Flower, GrandFather, and Hope nearly died, and if they hadn't already been in the Trauma Center when it happened, they probably would have," Myra stated.

"Where did you get the venom?" Paxton asked.

"From the dead Sand Spinners that ended up in the compost. I swear I didn't mean for anyone else to get hurt. I figured he'd eat one and get sick and that would be it."

"Were you involved in the Sand Spinners found in the arena and animal pastures after the Hallowed Eve Festival?" Myra interrupted again.

Paxton looked at her in confusion and then turned back to watch Damon.

"No. Never even heard of them until that day," Damon signed.

"Where did you get the ground crawler? Did you steal it?" Paxton asked next.

"No, Snapper Fish sent it the night before," Damon replied.

"How did you know it was the one Snapper Fish sent and not any one of the hundreds of shuttles around the compound?"

"He sent me the designation id, and it showed up right when he told me it would."

"What about the other shuttles?" he asked.

"What other shuttles?" Damon replied, frowning with confusion.

"There were dozens of shuttles that disappeared after you did," Paxton stated.

"I don't know anything about them," Damon answered.

"How were Paul and Danny involved in this?" Paxton asked next.

"They weren't," Damon said, a further look of confusion on his face. "I never told them anything about what I was doing."

"We found...bits of them about an hour away from the people you were supposed to meet. Based on the coordinates, it looks like you transposed a number and ended up in the wrong spot. In case you were wondering, guards overheard them say they were going to kill you as soon as you arrived," Paxton said.

"Paul and Danny are dead?" Damon asked.

"It would certainly appear that way, as we found a large amount of their blood. It looks like a flock of harbingers got them, although we haven't found anything else."

Damon let out a heavy sigh. "Well, there go the last two friends I had."

"One last question. Did you sedate Myra and take her tablet?" Paxton asked.

"Yeah, when I first showed up. I didn't want her to wake up until we were far away."

"How did you know what it was? You're not a healer?" Paxton asked.

Damon snorted and rolled his eyes. "I can read you know. Not just Saber. I've been learning all the written languages. Councilor Chenzira said that was a requirement for being able to enter the Ship's Guild."

Paxton took the tablet back and stopped recording. "Thank you, Jennette."

"Any time," Tabor replied.

They left the two guards and Tabor walked back with them, but as soon as they were out of sight, Myra dragged Paxton into an empty aisle. "You said attempted murder of Ellie. Is she still alive?" Tabor signed with a brief look of hope before containing it behind her mask. "The news reports..."

Paxton looked around and lifted his paws to sign back. "She's still alive and expected to make a full recovery. Clear Seas and the Senior Healer put out a fake death announcement to protect her from whoever had tried to kill her, until she could recover enough to give a statement. No one knows but the Senior Council and whoever they've told. Clear Seas was afraid to involve the Honor Guard because the guards he had on Ellie and Marsee are still missing, and we've since learned that someone either in or pretending to be part of the Sea Patrol was involved in Marsee's kidnapping. The only guards Marcus and Jer are trusting right now are the six they brought with them."

"Oh thank the bright blessed full moons!" Myra whispered.

Tabor looked just as relieved. Myra was surprised with the amount of emotion on Tabor's face. While she hadn't spent much time with the former Senior Councilor since her arrival, they did work together, but Tabor rarely dropped her mask.

"Did they catch Deep Current?" Myra asked.

"Deep Current is dead. He died trying to save Marsee's life. His uncle, Councilor Rip Current is the one that attempted to kill Ellie and kidnapped and...and tortured Marsee. They don't know who the second person is though, or if there are more. They're still trying to exonerate Clear Seas. Right now, Jer believes there was only one other person in the suite with Rip."

Myra growled. "What did they do to my baby?"

Paxton took a deep breath. "He..." Paxton stopped. "Are you sure you want to know?" he asked, but nodded when she just growled at him. Instead of answering though, he opened his tablet and handed her Marsee's statement.

It was all she could do to restrain herself from crushing Paxton's tablet with her grip. Her tail was lashing in fury at what had been done to her cub and Tabor looked positively sick, watching the statement with her.

*I've changed my mind. We kill* him *first.*

"Is he dead yet?" Myra growled, for the first time in her life actually struggling to contain the desire to act on her instinct's demands. It wasn't pressuring her, but she wanted to kill Rip Current just as much as it did.

"No. We have enough proof to convict him though. Marsee has confirmed his voice and the Senior Guild Healer has positively identified that he was in Ellie's room. He also threw a claw at Marsee, which the Healer has confirmed belonged to Ellie. They're still trying to figure out who else is involved and find the missing people Deep Current identified. He's locked up and guarded though."

Myra handed the tablet back to Paxton and paced, trying to control her fury. The last thing she needed to do was lose control of her instinct in front of the Acting Senior Councilor and Former Senior Councilor, especially when two honor guards were only a few aisles over. They'd kill her and ask questions later.

"He will die though. It's just a matter of when," Paxton said, trying to calm her.

Myra took several deep calming breaths, and forced her healer's mask back in place before turning back around to face Paxton with a nod, and was surprised by the expression on Tabor's face, or lack of one. Her mask was in place, but her tail was thwapping, not angryly, but more rhythmically, like the claw tapping her mentor did when he was thinking.

"What is it?" she asked Tabor.

"Regardless of who was in the suite with Ellie, there are others involved. I've never particularly liked Rip, but I always chalked it up to inexperience. His father was one of my best friends and I'd hoped with time he would settle into the role. Don't take this the wrong way, Paxton, but he's a lot like you were until right before the Trial, although more subtle about it."

Paxton snorted and Myra's tail curled slightly at the understatement. Paxton had been quite the trouble maker.

"Most new councilors are fairly vocal about their own district's needs in their first term. It's expected. You're trying to prove yourself to your people after all. He has a pretty heavy track record for voting against any projects we put forward unless they benefit the Water World in some way, but he's not the only one. Unlike you though, he was arrogant about it. The Water Sprite Council may be voted in, but it's still heavily feudal and Rip and many others believe they have a birth right to that position, rather than having earned it. Clear Seas will hold his position until he dies, is voted out, or is convicted of a crime, but his family's rise to power was not unanimous, nor was his last vote to Senior. He was voted in by the people in his district with a vast majority, but he's been slipping in the ranks of the other councilors. The other districts want their turn and it wouldn't surprise me if they're trying to change the will of the people. At the last vote for Senior, nearly a third voted against him, which was unprecedented. On top of that, what Marsee said was right. We did not go with the majority opinion against Jer and the Local Council. Just about everyone thought that Jer should have been found guilty of collusion, not just accessory, and more than half thought the entire Local Council should have been stripped of their position, except for you, Paxton. And perhaps we should have, but none of us were willing to harm the people of Saber for our mistakes. Paxton, if I were you, I'd investigate everyone who voted against Clear Seas at the last election."

Paxton frowned, "So you believe this is a coup?"

"Rip said as much, according to Marsee. Not just with the Council, but with the Guild as well, and if you haven't already, put guards around the rest of Jer and Marcus's family," Tabor said.

Paxton nodded. "Already done. More guards will be here shortly to help guard Damon and provide additional security for New Hope. I'm not sure how much you were told, Myra, but the ransom note indicated that if we had guards around your children, they would kill Marsee *and* the rest of your cubs. After what happened with Little Flower, we've decided to risk having the Guard stationed here going forward."

Myra nodded although her tail thwapped with pent up emotion. "When do they intend to release Ellie's status?" she signed.

"When she's awake enough to make that decision. They woke her briefly between surgeries, long enough to find out that she was not awake for what happened to her, and she didn't know who had hurt her," he signed back.

She nodded, grateful to find out she hadn't been awake for her beating.

They left the empty aisle they were in and made their way back to where they'd left Henry, and found Buster all tacked up and ready to go. Paxton took several pictures and asked about the various pieces of equipment and their purposes, and then Henry led them over to the arena and gave a short demonstration of what Buster could do.

"You'll have to talk to GrandFather, about how else he's been trained. I know his former partner used to use him as a workhorse, for plowing the fields, logging, and other tasks. I've only worked with him a few times but he's done everything I've ever asked for, and learns new commands very quickly." Henry said, sitting astride Buster on the other side of the gate afterwards.

"Councilor Parner," a voice called out.

"Over here!" Parner called back.

A minute later the two master techs appeared, blinked hard at Henry and Buster, before one of them found the words to speak. "We have the information from the shuttle, and we found a tablet but it's been wiped clean," she said, and handed over Damon's tablet.

"What did you find out?" Paxton asked.

"You're not going to believe it, sir. I'm not sure I do," Resner replied, rubbing the back of her head.

Paxton raised his brows, waiting.

"The shuttle belongs to the Guild in Sand Dune. It was remotely sent here by none other than Master Nardal."

"Nardal?!" Myra, Tabor, and Paxton exclaimed at the same time.

"That's what the logs say." Resner handed over her tablet so he could see. "I've sent you a copy as well."

"You're sure? This hasn't been tampered with in any way?" Paxton asked.

"No, we checked. The order definitely came from Nardal's currently registered tablet and account," Resner replied.

"Have you been able to access Damon's account remotely yet?"

"No, it's still locked, and we still have no idea why your access isn't working. As Acting Senior Councilor, you should have authorization. We have an entire team working on it."

Paxton frowned and walked away. They all followed, well except for Henry and Buster who were still in the arena. Paxton made his way back over to Damon's cell and slid the tablet through the bars in the cell. "Please log into your account."

Damon stood and took it, entered his credentials, and handed it back.

Paxton took it and handed it to the techs. "See what you can find, and find out anything you can about a person by the name of Snapper Fish. Damon indicates that is who he's been working with. Myra, let me know when you wake up Little Flower. I'll take her statement then, but it looks like I need to head back to Council City."

"Will do," Myra said, and watched as Paxton and the techs left, and then turned to look back at Damon.

*Now can we maim him?* her instinct asked.

She wasn't so sure anymore. His story was not all that different from Little Flower's. Her hatred of them had been just as intense. The only difference was that she'd been powerless to act on it. Assuming Snapper Fish was actually Rip Current, then he'd taken advantage of Damon's rage and added fuel to the fire. Rip was the one that needed to die, slowly.

"Are you okay, Myra?" Tabor asked.

She looked up at the former senior councilor. "Is what we did to Little Flower any different than what we did to Damon? Even an invisible leash is still a leash."

Tabor's ears and whiskers flicked back at the question, and then looked at Damon.

"If Little Flower had been given a weapon to use against us in the Agency, and been offered a way to escape. I think she would have done the same," Myra said, and walked away, leaving Tabor, dumbstruck, behind. Even the guards flicked their ears back in surprise.

Myra returned to the Trauma Center, and pulled Ammond into her office, and let him know about Ellie, to his immense relief. Then she made her way over to her daughter's room, fired off several messages to Jer, and read through the thousands of messages awaiting her. When she was done, she leaned back in her chair, watching her daughter sleep, and thought for a very long time.

# CHAPTER 38

# Marsee: Trust

When they arrived at the ship, Marsee hit the switch to unlock it. The door swished open and the lights inside flickered on, but Avery stopped her before she could enter. "Wait here, please," he ordered, and proceeded to enter cautiously. He examined all of the rooms on the small ship before returning and indicating it was safe for them to enter.

Marsee frowned at this, but considering everything she'd been through, she was glad Avery was taking her safety seriously. It was going to be a while before she'd feel comfortable being by herself again.

"Petra and the other's must be out still," she said, after setting the items down on one of the seats with a yawn. With the others safe, she decided she could wait until tomorrow to continue her investigation, and thought she might just take a nap instead.

Her father and Marcus looked at each other. "Marsee, do you know where they went?" her father asked.

She shook her head. "When we landed, Ellie wished them a good vacation. They never said where they were going. She didn't expect them back for a while. Ellie told me later she planned to use Guild Master Agate's shuttle and drag her with us to the other guild halls. Why?"

Her father and Marcus gave each other another look.

"What's going on?" she asked.

"We haven't been able to reach Ellie's pilots," Marcus said. "On top of that, we found one of Petra's scales in Ellie's room, and evidence that all three pilots were involved in your kidnapping, by order of Wind Rider."

"What?! That doesn't make any sense," Marsee said, sitting down hard in the nearest seat as she considered everything she knew about the pilots. "No, I don't believe it," she said eventually. "I believe you found a scale, but Petra wouldn't attack Ellie. I spent hours flying with her, and we spent a lot of time talking about the challenges of being the daughters of a Senior Councilor. She loves flying for Ellie and is really sad that she'll have to go back to Flyer soon."

"Well, that makes three people who have said the same thing," her father replied.

"Those messages are pretty damning though," Marcus stated.

Marsee frowned. "What messages?"

"On their personal accounts. They were sent a few hours after you arrived here," her uncle replied. He flipped open his tablet to show her the group chat.

She frowned at the screenshot Marcus had taken. "Can you pull this up on her account? This doesn't feel right. I want to check something out."

Her uncle raised a brow but took the tablet back, logged in, and handed it back to her. It only took her a few seconds to access the raw code, her recently added tech skills coming in very handy.

Marcus raised a brow as he watched. "I didn't know you could do that."

She ignored the comment as she scanned through the code. "That's what I thought," Marsee muttered. "There are several things wrong here. First off, none of them would have been able to type as fast as the timestamp on these messages indicate. Flyers type the slowest of all of the species due to the shape of their paws. Secondly, they all came from the same location. There's no reason why they would be texting each other when they can just talk to each other and avoid an evidence trail. For that matter, they would have had the entire ship to themselves for weeks. We had no intention of returning until after the council meeting."

"So you know where the messages were sent from?" he asked.

"Yes, no, well, not exactly. This number here points to a specific network hub and distance from that hub, but I don't know where that would be. It's the same for all the messages, which means they would have been within a foot of each other. Third, this word is wrong. It's a common mistranslation. Whoever wrote this isn't a native speaker, Petra wouldn't have made that mistake. Also, Petra said she had word from her mother to move forward with the plan, but there's nothing here from her mother to indicate that, and no record of a deleted text from her mother, or any other messages from anybody for several hours. Just the large info dump that occurred when we connected to the planet's network. She sent a message off to her mother saying they'd landed and that she was looking forward to seeing her when she arrived for the Council Meeting. The next message is from her mother several hours later, which would be about the amount of time it would take for a round trip to Flyer. Wind Rider couldn't have called either, unless she's on the planet somewhere, but this message from her mother was sent from Flyer. The first digit of the hub identifier is the planet it was on. It's based on the order in which the planets were added to the Consortium."

"How can you tell that there aren't any deleted records?" her father asked.

"It's this field here. It's a setting in the message app. You can choose to display whether or not there were deleted messages and restore them within a minute or two of deletion, in case you do it by accident. However as Senior Councilor, you can retrieve those messages for evidence. After a time though, the deleted records are moved to the archives to save on space. Most people don't realize it, but they're never actually deleted, unless someone deletes them from the servers directly. I wouldn't even know that if Ellie wasn't my mentor. That's restricted to level four knowledge."

She flipped over to Marcus's account, sent herself a message that read "I have the best niece in the world," to Marcus's amusement, deleted the record, and showed him how it looked, then flipped over to another screen, and had him enter his authorization and the message reappeared.

Both her father and Marcus flipped their ears back in astonishment. "I think we're going to need to have a conversation with Ellie when she's feeling better. I wonder why we weren't told about this?"

Marsee considered. "Probably because neither of you had a normal transition. This access is only for the Senior Council or your Acting Seniors."

"I was Tabor's Acting Senior for all four of her terms and she never once mentioned this capability," Marcus replied with a frown.

Marsee shrugged. "Maybe she didn't know?"

They flipped back to Petra's account to confirm there weren't any deleted messages when another thing popped out at her.

"Here. Her response to her mother is wrong too. It's too formal. Look at the rest of her conversation with her mother. She always uses this term, unless she's annoyed, where she uses this one. They never use this term for mother in this context. It would be like...if Mama was angry and called you by your full name. In this context, it would mean the exact opposite of what she's written here, stating that she had no intentions of visiting her mother ever again. I suppose it could be a joke, but Wind Rider wouldn't take it that way. It's too harsh even if it was sarcastic, but it's similar enough that it's commonly mistaken by off-worlders as well. I don't think Petra wrote this message. Finally, there hasn't been a single further message sent out of Petra's account although dozens of messages have come in. Something's happened to them, or to her at least. Can you log back into the other accounts?"

He did and she quickly scanned their messages. "It's the same with them. Hundreds of messages and not a single response. They haven't even been read, not even the emergency alerts from the Ship's Guild."

Marsee accidentally touched the alert as she pointed to it and it opened. She read it, and frowned at the message.

"Why would they be evacuating all off-worlders?" Marsee asked.

"It was part of the demands on the ransom note we found," Marcus replied.

Marsee's eyes narrowed. "What else was demanded?"

Rather than answer, Marcus showed her the ransom note. A low growl formed deep in her throat as she read it, and her injured claws flexed before she remembered they were injured. The pain in paw her caused her to flinch and hiss, but that was nothing compared to the turmoil she was experiencing.

When she looked up, Avery was watching her closely. She took a deep breath and tried to bring her emotions under control, but failed as everything she'd suppressed started bubbling to the surface, ready to explode.

"Are you in pain? The Senior Healer said we should bring you back if you start to hurt," her father asked worriedly.

"No," she said, handing the tablet back to Marcus, trying hard not to dig her claws into it, and shifted her gaze to her father with a glare. "*Did you step down as Senior Councilor?*" she asked, not really wanting to know the answer.

He didn't answer right away, and it was all the answer she needed.

She looked down at her injured hand. "So you chose your power over me. Just like he said you would," she said, barely above a whisper. She hadn't told her father about that part, not wanting to hurt him, or believe what Rip had said. Her father flicked his ears back in astonishment or perhaps horror, she wasn't sure. She didn't wait for an answer either and bolted out of her seat to run to her room. She didn't want to talk to him anymore.

"Marsee, wait!" her father called after her, trying to catch her on the way by, but she dodged out of the way and kept running. She slammed the door open, ran through, slammed it shut behind her, and hit the lock. Then with a sob, climbed carefully onto her bed, curled up around one of the pillows facing the wall, and started shaking. He knocked on the door. "Marsee, let me in."

"Go away!" she yelled back, but he didn't. She heard the door slide open and he walked in. *Stupid door,* she thought, *with a stupid lock, that her stupid father as a stupid Senior Councilor could override.*

She felt the bed shift as he sat down next to her. "Marsee, I would never choose my power over you."

"Oh, really?" She turned and hissed at him, shoving her bandaged paw in his face. "How many more claws would I have had to lose before you resigned?"

"None, I was about to..."

"About to!" she yelled. "One wasn't enough? You think being electrocuted was bad? Try having a claw ripped out and then having to swim for hours in salt water while you keep one paw up in the air to keep the sea creatures from finding and eating you! Try walking for hours to stay warm on three paws because you don't have the strength or energy to stand up on two feet and then try to fight back without claws in absolute darkness while every inch of you screams in pain, and then when you finally pass out because the pain is just to much, you to wake up with *another* claw missing. You had to wait until a *second* claw was delivered to make up your mind? I shouldn't be surprised. You've always chosen the Council over me. Why would this time be any different?"

Her father visibly wilted under her attack and accusations, and he closed his eyes and took several deep breaths before speaking. "I needed the authority of my position to try and find you. Without it, I have absolutely no jurisdiction here, and Marcus couldn't do it on his own. I was praying that Rip meant the interplanetary day in his ransom letter. I didn't know about the first claw until the second one arrived, and it arrived early. Sampson brought us on an experimental ship. It wasn't outfitted with long range communications. I didn't even get Clear Seas' message about the first claw until after the second one was delivered. I'd only been here for maybe an hour before the second claw arrived, and according to the Healer it had been removed hours earlier, as had your first one. I'm sorry I wasn't fast enough, but I promise you, the moment the Habitat was clear I was going to resign, publicly in front of the Council. We were just waiting for the all-clear from the Senior Healer there to give the orders to destroy it when Stormy showed up. If you don't believe me, ask Marcus."

She glared at him, trying to tell if he was being truthful.

*He waited. He waited more than an interplanetary day. We would have still lost a claw,* her instinct reasoned.

She couldn't stop herself from letting out a low growl. "Why didn't you resign before you left home or before the interplanetary day was up? Marcus would have given you temporary authority. I know he would have."

"Marsee, every one of Rip's demands were designed to be impossible to meet. There aren't enough ships to get every off-worlder off this planet at the same time and evacuate the Habitat in a day, even an interplanetary day, and he didn't even wait a full local day to remove your first claw. He wanted to hurt us both, and he would have never let you go, not alive anyway. I'm sure of it. He left Ellie for dead and he tried to kill you. I don't know if he was behind the poisoning but regardless, it was all designed to make me suffer, and make it impossible to find you or the others in time. I would have done anything to get you back safely, if I thought it would have had even the remotest chance of being successful, including giving up my life, if that's what it took."

Marsee looked at him in suspicion. *Would he have gone that far?* "I seriously doubt that," she hissed at him. "You've never once put me first!"

"That is blatantly untrue and you know it," her father snapped back.

She just snorted at him and shoved her broken paw in his face again, before turning away.

She heard him take a deep breath, almost a sigh before speaking. "Marsee, if I had honored my oath, I should have killed you that day in my office when you went non-verbal, and I should have killed you that night in the garden, but I didn't. I couldn't. I put you first. I put my life on the line and put others at risk to give you the chance I've never given anyone else. I chose to protect you at the expense of the others, at the expense of the species I swore an oath to protect *before* you. I should have stayed in New Hope and protected them, but I didn't. I came here looking for you, and the people I swore to protect have been injured and killed because of it."

She snorted at him again, but didn't turn back around. "Did you wait to step down because you thought I was already gone, lost to my psychosis?" she asked, after considering his words. He didn't answer right away and she spun around to glare at him. "You did, didn't you?"

He sighed and his ears drooped. "I knew that even if we did find you alive, there was a very good chance I would have to kill you anyway. You're strong. Stronger than anyone I've ever known. That you're alive and speaking to me right now is a miracle I can't even begin to understand, but I promise I *was* planning to step down."

She glared at him trying to decide if he was telling the truth or not. Rip had been trying to make her lose control to harm her father, or at least that's what he'd said.

"Marsee, If you need me to prove it to you, I will. No job, no amount of power or authority is more important to me than you. My oath may be to my people at the expense of myself and my family, but I never expected anyone to do *this*." He motioned towards her lack of fur and her paw. "I always thought that my oath just meant giving up time with you when my people needed me, and voting in ways that benefited my people, instead of me. I didn't realize you'd be a target. Nothing like this has happened in thousands of years, at least not on our planet."

Her father flipped open his tablet and typed in a message stating his resignation, not only as Senior Councilor but as Councilor as well, and handed it over to her. "Send it or don't send it. I don't care either way. I just want you to trust me, and believe me when I tell you that I love you, and would do anything for you. *Anything*."

She pinned her ears back in disbelief but took the tablet from him and stared at it for a long time. He'd just handed her all of his power and authority to do with as she pleased.

*Rip wanted him to resign,* her instinct said. *And Rip wanted you both to suffer, but your father has hurt us in the past. I do not trust him, but I trust him far more than Rip Current.*

She deleted the message and handed it back, and realized he looked disappointed, not relieved. *He'd wanted her to send it?* That more than anything proved his point to her.

"I believe you," she said, and he nearly collapsed with relief and pulled her in for a hug. She let him hold her for a while, before pulling away and climbing off the bed. She didn't want comfort, she wanted Rip Current dead, and she didn't really want to think about what had happened to her. She started walking towards the door and turned back to face him. "Promise me one thing though," she said.

"Anything," he replied.

"Rip dies. Painfully and slowly," she replied, letting her instinct flair with her rage.

Her father flashed his instinct too, looking absolutely feral. "Nothing would make me happier. I promise," he growled back.

She nodded and left the room. As much as she and her instinct wanted to tear Rip Current to shreds, she had her instinct back under control before she made it two steps out the door. No point in worrying Uncle Marcus, she reasoned.

Avery was dozing in the seat closest to the door but he sat up when she exited her room, and watched her closely as she walked down the hallway and over to her seat. She looked back at him wondering why he was focusing on her so intently.

Marcus was still scrolling through messages. If they'd heard her yelling at her father they gave no indication of it, and she flopped down in the seat next to Marcus.

Marcus looked up then, and reached over and gave her a one armed hug. "It's going to take a long time to get over what Rip did to you. Be patient with yourself and if you need someone to talk to, I'm always here, and before you even ask, yes, your father was planning on giving up his seat."

"Thanks, Uncle Marcus," she replied.

Her father followed her out a few minutes later and sat down across from her and looked like he was about to speak, when Avery spoke up instead.

"Marsee, did you use your instinct in the cave?"

Both her father and uncle whipped their heads up and over to stare at Avery, their bodies immediately full of tension.

Marsee swallowed hard and nodded, realizing why Avery had been watching her. *Did he see me with my instinct on?* she wondered. "I didn't have any choice. It was that or drown or freeze to death, and I couldn't fight back through the shocks without it. But I promise, it's fully under control now."

"I don't fault you for doing what you had to do to survive, but what you went through would challenge anyone's control," Avery said calmly. "and you were struggling earlier to control it, outside of Rip's cell, and again just now."

"I swear I wasn't!" Marsee replied emphatically. "Yes, I had it on just now, but I turned it on and off on purpose. I'm fully in control and I wasn't struggling earlier, not from my instinct anyway. I was struggling with the reaction I had to what Rip said. He used the phrase 'little...kitten'" She flinched involuntarily, even though she'd been the one to say it. "He used that phrase all the time when he was torturing me, and I don't know why but just the sound of it makes me feel that pain and fear all over again. That was the reaction I was trying to control. I promised my father I would tell him and Uncle Marcus immediately if I had any more issues with my control."

"Any *more* issues?" Avery asked, sitting up and tensing.

Marsee looked over at her father and then to her uncle, not sure what to say.

"Avery, Marsee is the one who was broken free of psychosis by the use of sign language," Marcus answered, raising a paw to stop the honor guard.

"I swear I haven't had any issues since that day when everything snapped into place. I can turn it on or off without difficulty," Marsee said, only half lying about the two incidents where it had turned on without her noticing. She wasn't sure if that counted.

Avery glared at her and she swallowed hard.

"We both tested her regularly for months afterwards," her father added quickly. "Since then, she's had a few episodes where she was upset and didn't know her instinct was on, but had no problems turning it off, once she was made aware of it, and had no control issues while it was on. In both situations that reaction was warranted, and what I would consider a normal reaction for someone learning to control their instinct during stressful situations, much like a young cub, not the kinds of trouble she had before. She didn't pounce on anything, or go non-verbal for example. I've spoken at length with Kendra about the issues she's had, and Kendra personally took her off the watch list."

Avery considered her father's statement but turned back to face her. "That may be, but you had difficulty turning it off after waking up in the trauma center," Avery countered. "It took several hours for you to fully regain control."

Marsee slumped and nodded. "I did, but not in the same way. For a time in the cave, I...I hid. I guess that's the best way to explain it. When we woke up in the trauma center, everything was very confusing and far too bright and loud. We didn't know where we were and we couldn't see or hear anything properly. We just knew we were trapped and underwater, and at first my instinct thought we were drowning and that the healers were attacking because we were in so much pain. I couldn't tell they were healers at first, just that they were Sprites. When my vision cleared, enough that I could recognize that you were a guard, my instinct realized the threat you were to us if I didn't come back, but *I* didn't want to come back. I couldn't think through the pain, and a large part of me wanted you to kill me, just to make it stop. I told my father earlier though."

"She did tell me," her father replied.

Avery raised a brow but eventually nodded at him. "I am fully aware of her...medical history. Even without it, we fully expected this to be a recovery and containment mission, not a rescue. Still, please come over here Marsee. I need to see for myself that you're still in control."

Marsee nodded and fully expected this. She slid off her chair to stand in front of Avery, wondering to what level he was going to take it. She hoped it was just the on/off test, not the other variations. She wasn't sure she could handle even a single swipe after everything she'd been through in the cave. She still felt raw and jagged.

"Turn your instinct on," he ordered.

She flicked it on and waited, doing her best to remain calm. Her instinct was fully in control but she was worried Avery would mistake her nervousness for a lack of control.

Avery watched her closely for several minutes before speaking. "You said you used your instinct to help you swim, how?" he finally asked.

"I had to swim for hours when the tide came in. The first time I managed on my own but the second time I was exhausted, injured, and missing a claw. I had to keep my paw above the water or the fish would go after it. I was so tired I kept falling asleep. I let it have control, and it swam for me while I dozed. When the water receded it kept me walking until I dried off. I wanted to sleep but I also knew if I did I might not wake up again. I don't remember turning it off. I think I must have passed out, but when I woke up it was off."

Avery continued to stare at her and then nodded. "You can turn it off now," he said.

She did, instantly.

"When you gave yourself over to your instinct, was it like what happened when you were dealing with your psychosis? Did you lose sense of yourself at any time, or did it fight for control?"

Marsee shook her head and then shrugged. "It wasn't anything like before. Back then I felt like I was being pushed out, and the entire time between when my sister came to live with us and that night in the garden it was like something was scratching at my brain trying to break through my defenses. In the garden that last night, I *was* pushed out, before Little Flower freed me. I didn't know who she was, couldn't understand my father, and the only thoughts we had were to hunt our prey, and escape whatever had us pinned. Since then it's felt like more of a partnership. I never lost sense of who I was the entire time I was in the cave, but there were times I couldn't turn it off, like when it was making me walk to stay warm, but I was far too exhausted and in too much pain to really even try, and as much as I wanted to stop and sleep, I knew I couldn't and didn't really fight it, but it never pushed me out, just kept me moving when I wanted to quit. At the end though, we both knew we were dying, and it was like it wrapped itself around me to protect me. I fell asleep and woke in the Trauma Center. I don't remember Stormy or Deep Current being there. If that means I was pushed out, I don't know. If anything I gave up full control to it, hoping with our last breath that it could do what I hadn't been able to do."

"Does your instinct still talk to you?" Avery asked.

Marsee opened her eyes wide in surprise. She hadn't put that in her report, not really wanting people to know she heard a voice in her head, even her family and hadn't told anyone. "How did you know?"

He looked at her sadly.

She understood and nodded. "Yes, but not like before either. It was pressuring me all the time to hunt. Now it's mostly only when I have it on and need it, like when trying to fight Rip Current."

"Mostly?" he asked, frowning with concern again.

"It's given me occasional advice when I've asked, and nudges or warnings, when I've been too frozen to move. Like when I was too surprised by Ellie's offer of mentorship and desire to have me take over the Guild to answer her. It nudged me to tell me to accept. It likes her, a lot, and it's warned me to move when there's been danger a few times."

"But it spoke in the cave?" he asked.

"All the time, but I had it on almost all the time too," she replied. "We were...trying to figure out how to kill Rip and it was trying to keep me distracted from the pain and cold. It was protecting me."

"What about since you were rescued?" he asked.

She nodded. "A few minutes ago. I was trying to figure out if I could trust my father. Rip said a lot of things in the cave that I'd rather not go into detail about. Not yet anyway. I'm still too raw, but I believe Rip was trying to make me mistrust my father so I would attack him if he found me."

"And how does it feel about your father now?" Avery asked.

She considered how to explain and looked over at her father. "Mostly the same, but wary too. Rip played on a lot of my own frustrations with my father. It's not easy being the daughter of a Councilor and we had a...an argument a few months ago, which it's still grumbly about."

Her father sighed and Avery raised a brow. "I have a feeling that was no argument. What really happened?" Avery asked.

"I tested her," her father said with a sigh. "Kendra knew about that too."

The look of astonishment on Avery's face as he looked between her and her father would have been comical, if her life didn't hang in the balance. "You're serious?" he finally spluttered. "A full test?"

Her father nodded. "Close enough to be sure. I mistook her grief over her sister's coma for loss of control and chased her out into the Wilds, knowing I couldn't contain her by myself if she was losing control, and it's pretty clear I wouldn't have been able to if she had. I said some truly awful things to her and accidentally broke her shoulder in the process too. Even with that injury, she still beat me, and walked away, *after* she had had my neck in her mouth, hard enough to break through the skin."

Avery just shook his head in astonishment. "I honestly can't believe either of you are still alive." He sat back in his chair considering.

Her father and uncle remained quiet and tense. Senior Councilors or not, if Avery said she was too unsafe to live, she would be killed. That was his right. Her instinct was thankfully quiet, almost as if realizing that even the slightest reaction would be taken badly.

"In the past, I would have brought you in for testing, but you're far more in control than I ever expected you to be, after everything that was done to you, and I'll be honest, when I saw the medical scans, I was shocked you even regained control at all. I am, however, putting you on the watch list. Do not turn your instinct on unless you're being tested or there's an emergency."

Marsee saw her father and uncle both visibly relax, which made her sigh with relief. Another watch she could handle and she'd fully expected it. She turned to walk back to her chair, when Avery indicated she could.

"Councilors, do not raise a paw to test her, even if you think there's cause for it. After what she's been through and her instinct's...grumbles, any form of physical violence could cause her to react very harshly, even if she doesn't lose control. Marsee, if you do have even the slightest issue, come see us and we can work with you, although it would probably be best if you came to see us anyways, once you're back on Saber and have had some time to heal from your trauma. If you continue to have issues with that phrase, we can help you with that too, but that should wait until you've recovered some. For now, give yourself that time and do everything you can to relax and stay as calm as possible. Craft, read, listen to music, whatever brings you peace or makes you feel safe. If you start to feel nervous or anxious at all, leave the situation, and let one of us know."

Marsee nodded, although she wondered why her father never brought her to see the Guard when she was having issues as a cub, if they had ways to help control it. She looked questioningly at her father and he seemed to understand what she was asking.

"In the past more than half who went to the Guard for training still didn't survive," her father explained. "We were considering it before the Cataclysm, but then it seemed like you finally had it under control. Once you started going non-verbal though, it was already too late for those methods to be effective."

Turning her head, she looked out the window, not that there was anything to see but a wall, and wondered if she would ever feel safe again. *Not until Rip's dead at least,* she decided. Through the reflection in the window she could see her father watching her with concern, but she didn't turn to face him.

"Jer," Marcus stated, getting her father's attention. "I sent Lowell the information on Petra and the other two pilots, to see if she could determine if their accounts were tampered with too, but I think it might be time to put out a missing persons alert on them."

Her father pursed her lips. "Marsee, how sure are you that someone other than a Flyer wrote those messages?"

"Completely," she said. "We had an entire chapter on the forty three different ways to say 'mother' in their language and all of the different connotations. As for the other word. I got that one wrong in my language guide, and my teacher spent half an hour discussing it with the *entire* class. I'm not likely to ever forget that."

Her father nodded. "In that case, I agree with you Marcus, and I think we should inform Wind Rider and the other seniors as well about the messages, and Marsee's take on it."

Marcus nodded and began typing on his tablet and then stopped and looked over at her. "Can you send me that chapter on 'mother'?"

She nodded. "Do you know where my tablet and other stuff is? Is it still in the suite?"

"Your hearing aids and harness should still be in the tube system. I sent them to my office but never retrieved them, but we didn't find your tablet or Ellie's in the suite," her father answered instead. "Marcus, did you find them?"

"No, they weren't in the tube system, and as far as Platform Operations could tell, nothing had been sent out except for what you sent this morning. Did you ask Clear Seas?"

"No, I completely forgot. I'll message him now." Clear Seas responded almost immediately. "He says he never saw them."

"Huh, then they must have been taken. I suppose it's possible the pilot's were too," Marcus replied. "Marsee, do you know if there's a way to track them down?"

"If they're active, yes. That's easy. People lose their tablets all the time, so there's a tracking program to help locate them. So can you," she said, holding her paw out for Marcus's tablet, but handed it back after a minute, shaking her head. "They're all offline. I could probably write a script to try and activate them remotely, like we do with updates, but I don't have access to deploy it on the network."

"You are Acting Senior Guild Master now," Marcus reminded her.

She shook her head. "That doesn't matter. It's based on my tech rating, not my Guild rank, and even as Acting Senior, I can't change my own rating. Another master would have to do that. I can give permission to deploy code. Lowell can, and far faster than I could too. She's the highest rated tech in the Guild, and one of the few allowed to deploy code."

"Has there been any word from Lowell yet?" her father asked.

"Yes, she says she should be done later this evening or early tomorrow morning. I told her we'd swing by first thing in the morning."

Her father nodded. "Marsee, I'll go get your hearing aids and harness now, and be right back. As for a tablet, you can have mine. I'll pick up another one at the Guild. He logged out of his account, handed it to her, and left.

She logged into her account and just stared at all the new applications she had access to as Acting Senior.

"Are you okay?" Marcus asked, hearing her gasp.

"I just can't believe Ellie made me her acting senior," Marsee said. "I shouldn't even qualify as a journeyman. That's supposed to only be for guild masters."

Marcus frowned. "I'm honestly surprised too, even if she is your mentor. Do you think that was altered too?"

"I suppose it could have been," Marsee said. "But then here on the Water World, at least according to her anyway, I already outrank her. I suppose maybe she was worried that something would happen to her, and wanted to ensure no one else took over."

"Why would she believe that, about you outranking her?" Marcus asked, so she gave him a quick rundown of her conversation with Ellie. He was silent for a long time, considering.

She turned back to the applications and opened her messages, reading the first one, which was from someone she didn't know and sighed. "I don't even know how to answer these questions," she said with an exasperated sigh.

Marcus leaned over and looked at the message. "If you're not sure, then ask questions, reach out to Nardal, or wait until Ellie is awake tomorrow to discuss it with her. You've been through a lot. No one is going to expect you to respond immediately."

Marsee nodded and closed her messages, switching over to find the information Marcus had requested, along with Master Yellow Tail's edit to her language guide as proof of the word she'd missed. Marcus thanked her and went back to typing. A minute later her father returned with her hearing aids and harness and then he and Marcus left for their meeting with the Senior Commander. Leaving just her and Avery remaining.

She made sure the door was locked behind them, turned up the heat several degrees, and then turned to Avery. "Do you want anything to eat or drink?"

"I'm quite full from the market but something to drink would be nice," he said. "Thank you."

She nodded and walked over to the kitchen to see what was currently stocked, and smiled. "Ever had bosa berry juice?" she asked.

"Can't say as I have," he replied.

*Well there's at least one benefit to not having fur,* she thought, and awkwardly grabbed them both cups and planted her most innocent expression on her face before turning back around.

# CHAPTER 39

# Marsee: Leviathan Cloak

Marsee awkwardly set the thermos and glasses down on the table in front of Avery and then poured them both a drink.

Avery looked at her with suspicion. "Are you sure this is safe to drink?" he asked.

"I've had it before. It's one of Petra's favorite drinks," Marsee said, and grabbed her glass, downing a large swallow. She was surprised that it only felt bubbly now. *I guess being shocked within an inch of your life changes your perceptions of pain,* she mused, and sat down. "There's a bit of a tang to it, but I kind of like it."

Avery picked up his glass and sniffed at it cautiously. His nose scrunched at the smell, and he glared at her again. "You're far too amused about this," he said.

"I'm just laughing because I'm pretty sure I had the exact same expression on my face when I tried it the first time. It is a rather surprising color and the bubbles make my nose twitch."

He gave her another glare and then eyed the cup dubiously.

"Avery, would I do anything to harm the guard protecting my life?" she asked, seriously. "If you don't like the smell of it, you can get something else. I won't be offended."

Avery snorted, but valiantly took a sip and immediately started spluttering. His fur poofed out everywhere and he glared at her, but then he started chuckling. "A bit of a tang huh?" He tried patting his fur down to no avail.

Marsee laughed and took another sip of her drink. "Your fur will settle after a minute." She looked at the bubbles in her glass and then sighed, her humor evaporating instantly.

"What's bothering you?" Avery asked.

She shrugged. "Everything I suppose. So much has happened in just a few days. I was a completely different person when I first tried this. It felt like being struck by a lighting bolt then. Now I don't feel anything. Emotionally I'm much the same I guess. I should be terrified, and I am, but mostly I just feel...numb."

Avery nodded his understanding. "I've been shocked by the Sprites on a number of occasions in training. I've never been able to fight back at all. I'm amazed you were able to."

"I couldn't for a long time," she said, looking down at her broken paw. "Even with my instinct's help. All I could do was scream."

"You survived. That's what matters, and you're safe here. The numbness you're feeling is normal too. I've been in more than one terrifying situation in my career. You'll have nightmares, wild mood swings, and quite likely even physical reactions to the stress you endured. That's just your body's way of trying to process everything you went through. It'll probably happen when you least expect it too."

Marsee nodded. "I know. I've been through it with Little Flower." She picked up her tablet, not wanting to talk about it anymore, but just stared at it for several long moments and looked up at Avery again, who was still watching her. "Avery, how do I walk out that door again and face people that want me dead, that could kill me with a single touch? Will I ever feel safe again?"

He sighed. "Probably not. That innocent part of you is gone now. Life is all about balancing risk, and you've been exposed to the worst of us. I wake up every day, knowing I could die in the line of duty, and it's hard to not look at everything and everyone as dangerous. All you can do is find a purpose and reason to walk out that door every day. For me, it's a sense of honor and duty to protect the people. It's why I'm a guard.

If I die saving someone's life, then it will have been worth it. If nothing else, walking out that door means monsters like Rip don't win."

She snorted and turned her head to look out the window again. "I've spent the last eight months of my life being seen as a monster by those around me. I can't even get angry about what happened to me without worrying that you or my father or uncle will put me down. I suppose it's only fair that I experience some of the fear everyone else has felt around me, but…"

"You are not a monster and you never were," he interrupted. "And you most certainly did not deserve what you went through. Even if you were fully lost to your instinct, you would be no different than any other wild animal trying to survive. That doesn't make you a monster, dangerous yes, but not a monster. You have every right to feel angry about what happened to you, and it's better to let it out, than let it fester inside you. The real monsters are those like Rip Current. The ones who find pleasure in harming others. He will die for his crimes, slowly and painfully I'm sure. Marsee, I've seen psychosis so many times I've lost count. The ones that survive the early stages, they're like you. They care about others, and don't give in to the beast inside them. Our instincts enhance what's already there. If you were going to lose control, you would have in Rip's cell, and frankly I wouldn't have blamed you. I would have just shut the door and let you eat him first before putting you down. Psychosis or otherwise, you deserved that at least."

Marsee snorted. "Thanks, I think."

He chuckled. "My job is to ensure you won't hurt anyone that doesn't deserve it, but as long as you keep fighting, and aren't actively trying to hurt anyone, I'll keep fighting with you. I'd much rather fight to save a person than put them down. What you've been brave enough to share with us has saved nearly a dozen children so far. A monster would have kept that information to themselves, not put themselves at risk to save others."

She tilted her head in acknowledgement, honestly comforted that her struggles had helped someone else, and then with a heavy sigh, re-focused on her tablet. She rescheduled the next several days of meetings to give her time for her own investigation, and then sent out a message to Guild Master Agate to see if she was still available to meet in the morning. The reply came in almost immediately that she was, but that she more than understood if Marsee wanted to take a few days off to recover from her ordeal.

The last thing Marsee wanted to do was take time off. Every time she stopped or closed her eyes she was back in that cave again, and she was worried about Petra and the others. If it weren't for them, she probably would just curl up in her room and hide, and she wanted to be so exhausted by the end of the day that she'd fall asleep the moment she laid down, hopefully without nightmares, although she was sure that was wishful thinking. She thanked the Guild Master for her concern, but indicated that she was perfectly fine, and would be there in the morning.

She then sat and stared out of the window for a long time, thinking, before making up her mind and sent Clear Seas a message asking if the tour of the Habitat was still available for the afternoon, and if he or Temperate would be available to pilot her around to some of the other sites Deep Current had mentioned. She knew it was a risk, but she honestly didn't believe he was behind this, and he might notice something she wouldn't. Clear Seas responded within a few minutes indicating yes on both accounts. She thanked him, and said that she would meet him at his house shortly after the noon meal, as she wanted to personally thank Stormy for her rescue.

She spent the rest of the afternoon digging through her backlog of messages, letting concerned friends and family know she was safe, keeping the details light. She was pretty sure her mother would expect and want her to hide out and fly straight home, but she had no intentions of letting Rip Current chase her away in fear, even if she was terrified, and while her sister had qualms about being the one to punish her attacker, she did not. Her instinct wanted blood and it would get it. She honestly didn't care if that put her over the edge. If it did, then so be it. Granted, there might not be much left of him, after Ellie got through with him anyway, and she would be just as content to watch Ellie rip him to shreds, although the idea of watching the guard Avery had mentioned, shock Rip held merit too.

***Shock him first. Make him scream for hours, and then claw him to pieces, one finger at a time,*** her instinct suggested, and she smiled wickedly at the idea.

After that, she tried digging through the backlog of messages that were coming in as part of her new responsibilities as acting senior. To her surprise, most were actually related to the upcoming council meeting, which she'd been thoroughly prepped on already, during her trip to the Water World. She responded as best she could, or sent back a message saying she would look into it and get back to them, if she didn't have an answer.

When it was time for the evening meal, her father called to check in on her and indicated they were going to be back late. She devoured the rest of the fire sticks, while Avery dug up one of the remaining meals in the kitchen. As tired as she was, she knew she wouldn't be able to sleep until her father returned, even with Avery napping by the door, so she started work on her thank you gift to Stormy. She was nearly done when her father and Marcus finally returned. Avery was awake instantly, checked to see who was entering, and then closed his eyes and went back to sleep. How he could sleep like that was beyond her.

"Did you find anything?" she asked her father as he sat down next to her.

"Nothing particularly useful. It's pretty late. Why aren't you in bed yet?" he asked.

"I couldn't sleep, so I've been working on a thank you present for Stormy." She handed him the tablet.

"I think he's going to love this!" her father said, as he read through what she'd created.

"I'm hoping to get a copy printed off and bound tomorrow morning when I'm at the Guild. I have a meeting scheduled with the Guild Master and then I'm heading over to Clear Seas home afterwards. He and Temperate are taking me to the Habitat and to some of the other platforms, so I can check out what Deep Current was worried about."

He frowned but surprisingly didn't put up another argument. "Sounds like you have a busy day ahead of you. You'd better try to get some sleep," he said. "I'm heading there myself."

Marcus had already claimed an unoccupied room. She nodded and followed. After seeing which room her father claimed, she sprawled out on her bed to wrap up the finishing touches on her gift. When she was done, she set the tablet down and tried to sleep.

She turned off the lights only to turn them back on seconds later as the dark room caused her to instantly panic, even the emergency lighting that was always on around the door, wasn't enough to keep the demons at bay. She tossed and turned, unable to find a comfortable position, and her hand was starting to ache. An hour later when she still hadn't fallen asleep, she crawled out of her bed and walked down to her father's room.

"Papa, can I come in?" she asked, knocking lightly on the door, not wanting to wake him if he was already asleep.

"Of course," came the sleepy reply. "What is it?" he asked when she'd entered and shut the door.

"I...Can I sleep with you?" she asked. "Every time I close my eyes, I'm back in that cave."

"Oh sweetheart, of course you can." He shifted over on the bed, patting the empty spot beside him. She crawled in next to him, curling herself into a tiny ball, and he wrapped his warm body around her and started to purr. Feeling safe and protected for the first time in days, wrapped in her father's strong arms, she was instantly asleep.

~~~~~

It was a very long time before Jer fell asleep. He spent hours analyzing and thinking about all of the information he'd gathered in the last several days. He'd spent most of his life in service to his people and had willingly shared his home, and had even changed his citizenship to protect and guide Little Flower's people, and yet that service had nearly cost him the lives of his family. Rip believed this had all been a power
~~~~~

grab, yet Jer had been just as shocked by the outcome of the trial as everyone else.

He'd been a councilor for nearly fifty years, and a junior councilor for decades before that. It was all he knew and he had been prepared to throw that all away just for the hope that Marsee would be returned safely. Knowing what he knew now, she would have been dead long before he'd made that decision. That she was safe and in his arms, was a miracle upon miracles, that only happened because one brave little boy saw something he'd missed, and disobeyed his father's orders.

He still didn't know the motive behind Damon's kidnapping and murder attempt, or if it was even related, or the involvement of the other two, or the Ice Giants, but Henry had risked his life traveling close to fifty leagues to rescue the others. He was supposed to be the protector, but again and again and again, he'd failed his family, failed Little Flower's people, and had to rely on the bravery of those he was supposed to protect, to protect and save his own family.

Dawn was approaching when he finally made a decision. Once this was all over, he was stepping down. He couldn't do this anymore. His family was far more important and he couldn't, wouldn't, put them at risk ever again.

<p style="text-align:center">~~~~~</p>

Her father's alarm woke them both early the next morning. Marsee stretched, and then snuggled back in against her father's warm fur. Her skin was cold where it was exposed and it was such a strange feeling.

"Did you sleep better?" her father asked.

"Much. Thank you," she said, as she wiggled in closer.

"What *are* you doing?" her father asked with a chuckle.

"I'm cold and your fur is nice and warm. I'm trying to figure out how I can wear you to the guild meeting this morning."

He laughed, but wrapped his arms around her and purred. "Sorry sweetheart. I'd share my fur with you if I could. I think I saw a blanket in one of the storage bins."

"They're not as nice as you though. Blankets don't purr. Oh well, might as well get up. If I stay here much longer I'm not going to want to leave."

"You could cancel your meeting with the Guild Master and stay here where it's safe and turn the heat up," he said, as he gave her a squeeze, refusing to let her up.

"Don't tempt me, but I have no desire to stand up the Guild Master for the second time in a row. She might think it's a habit or something."

He laughed but let go so she could climb out of the bed.

She left the room and ducked into the shared waste room and used the static shower. That was an experience. The shower tickled her skin, and the last bits of her fur shook off. There was a mirror in the room and she spent a long time examining her appearance. She didn't even recognize herself. She was checking out her tail when her father walked in.

"You've been in here for a while. Is everything okay?" he asked.

"Yeah, just trying to get used to my appearance. I look so different. My tail looks positively scrawny without any fur, and my ears look twice as big. Even my whiskers have fallen out." She leaned into the mirror to examine her face closer.

He stood behind her and gave her a hug. "That may be, but your eyes are the same, and I can see just how strong you are. Your muscles ripple when you move and your claws look ferocious."

She flexed the claws of her good paw in the mirror and snarled viciously, and decided she kind of liked the effect. Her teeth and claws did look so much bigger.

"How's your other paw?" he asked.

"It aches, but I'm planning to stop in at the Trauma Center and have it checked out on my way over to the Guild," she told him, and left the room without another word.

She grabbed her tablet from her room, had a quick bite to eat and left before her nerves got the best of her, her guard following behind. She stopped at the Trauma Center and was quickly brought back and examined by the Senior Healer again, even though there were several other people waiting.

*Rank certainly has its privileges,* she thought.

Her hand had healed up well overnight, and the Healer changed up her cast so that she had a little more mobility in her fingers and claws, and freed up her thumb entirely, making it much easier to sign and use the drone. After an injection to help with the ache, since nano cream didn't work underwater, for obvious reasons, the Healer told her to return the following afternoon to have the cast removed, and she left to make her way to the Guild. Clear Seas had pointed it out on their tour the first day, and she was pretty sure she remembered where it was. She didn't even notice the stares of the people she passed, her attention focused entirely on the coming meeting.

She had hoped that she wouldn't spend too much time at the Trauma Center, as she wanted to be able to spend time wandering around and talking with people before her meeting, like her sister had done after the trial. She'd really liked that approach as it gave her a way to meet people and see if her instinct found anything off. Thankfully news of her appearance and lack of fur must have made it to the Guild ahead of her, as no one commented. Eventually she found her way to the writers section and was directed to one of the masters.

"Translator, it's wonderful to see you safe. We were all so very worried about you and it's absolutely horrible what happened to your mentor. How can I be of assistance?" the master asked in Saber.

Marsee frowned, wishing she could tell them about Ellie. The master clearly mistook it for grief and flashed his sympathy. "I'm guessing you've heard of how I was rescued?"

"I have. The Senior Councilor's son was very brave. I heard he faced down a Leviathan," he replied, although it was clear he was asking for confirmation.

"Twice, from what my father tells me. I want to thank him for his bravery, and put together something for him last night, but I don't have any of my book binding tools here with me, or any of the special water proof paper and ink your people use. I was hoping you might be able to help print and bind this up for me." She handed him her tablet, and he swiped through, his humor bubbling across his skin.

"I would be honored to help print this out. I've read all of your books and this is by far your best work yet. He will love it, and it's a very fitting tribute. When do you need this done by?" he asked, handing the tablet back.

"Any chance you could have this done in a few hours? I'll be spending the morning with Guild Master Agate but then I'm planning to meet up with Clear Seas after the noon meal. I was hoping to be able to give it to him then."

"Easily. Swim back down when you're done and I'll have it ready for you. Are you going to publish this one as well? I know my daughter would love a copy."

"To be honest, I hadn't really considered it. I think I'll ask Stormy and see what he wants. He may not want this shared with the rest of the universe. Fame is a fickle beast," Marsee replied, not quite keeping the frustration out of her voice.

The master looked at her for several moments and then shook his head. "I am so very sorry for what has happened to you, and it disgusts me that someone would or could hurt you. As for that book, I guarantee that most of our world has probably heard the tale by now. But it is kind of you to consider his feelings on this," he said, and then looked behind her. She turned and saw the Guild Master approaching.

"Translator, I'm sorry I wasn't here to greet you when you arrived," she said.

"It's quite alright, Guild Master. I came early to discuss a special project for a young hero of mine, and please, call me Marsee."

"Of course. Please call me Agate. What project, if I might ask?"

Marsee handed Agate the tablet and showed her. Her skin radiated blues as she read it. "*Please* tell me you plan to publish this one as well," Agate said, handing the tablet back.

"Only if Stormy wants it published," she said, and then asked the other master where she should send the document. He gave her his information and once it was sent, she followed the Guild Master back to her office and asked Avery to wait outside.

Agate shut the door behind her, and then turned to face her, anguish and grief flashing on her skin. "Please, is Ellie really dead? I know what Clear Seas said, but then he was arrested, and I've been hearing rumors that there were guards posted outside multiple rooms in the Trauma Center, and that no one was allowed to go near them."

Marsee frowned and considered what to say, but her hesitation was enough apparently.

"She's not? *Please* tell me she's not!"

"On the way here Ellie told me that you were one of her closest friends..." Marsee started.

"I've known Ellie since before she earned her masters. I know your mother too, although we were never as close. I spent several years on your planet just after I became an adult, and took many classes with Ellie. I can prove it."

Agate motioned her over to look at a picture on the wall. On it was a picture of Ellie, Agate, her mother and of all people Ammond. Ammond was covered in green stain as were Ellie's feet, although it was harder to see with her black fur. Her mother and Agate were laughing hysterically at Ammond, who stood there looking at his fur in outrage, while Ellie looked positively horrified.

"I was told there wasn't a picture of this. I have to have a copy. Ammond and my mother need to see this. This is proof enough for me that you are someone who can be trusted. Yes, Ellie is still alive."

Agate was so overcome with emotion that she had to turn away for several moments. When she turned back around, she was still barely able to contain her joy.

"You can't tell anyone though. It's for her own protection. We're still trying to figure out who else is involved."

"I give you my oath, no one will hear it from me. How is she?" Agate asked.

"I haven't seen her, but my father says she was badly beaten. The healers said she should make a full recovery though. Like me, they declawed her, but my father says they took out all of her claws, and she had so many broken bones the healers lost count. She's being sedated while her injuries heal. Papa said Ellie doesn't remember any of it. I wish I could say the same." She tried hard not to flinch as she remembered the pain from her own ordeal.

Anger, relief, and then fury flashed across Agate's skin. "I just can't imagine why anyone would do that to either of you, and I'm so very sorry about the way you've been treated. Have they caught who did this to the two of you? I've heard rumors but they change every ten seconds."

"Yes and no." Agate looked confused so Marsee continued. "We've caught the person who hurt us, but there's at least one other person involved, if not more. Honestly, that's why I came to you first. You're one of the few people I can trust here, and I need your help to catch the other people involved."

"It would give me immense pleasure to catch those who hurt the two of you, but how could I possibly help?" Agate asked. "If I knew anything, I would have gone to the Council about it already. I promise."

"I believe you. While I was kept in the dark and never saw my attacker, I was able to identify his voice last night, and from what he told me, I believe that there's someone in the Guild, and likely very high up in the Guild working with him," Marsee explained.

"I can't believe it. Why would anyone in the Guild want to harm Ellie? Everyone loves her. It was a unanimous vote when we elected her to that position, and it's been that way ever since. No one has even nominated anyone else for that role or much less even indicated they wanted the position, and the last vote was less than six months ago."

"I believe the reason is because of me. As you know, when Ellie claimed the right of mentorship, she publicly announced that she wanted me to replace her. I think someone wants her position and was just waiting until she retired or died, but I changed everything. Ellie told me that in your society by stating her intentions, she essentially made me her heir, and that the guild masters here would vote for me, whether I'd earned that rank or not. But that's only one fifth of the vote. Someone with far more experience than I do would have a pretty easy job of convincing the others they should be the Senior Guild Master, and not a journeyman still in their in-between years."

"You're not. You're Acting Senior now," Agate said. "Didn't you know?"

"Yes, but that's only temporary. I'm not even sure if it's real with everything else going on. She never mentioned she was changing her preferences. I suppose it's possible she found something after I left the suite." She shrugged. "Either way, I'll do my best to help her until she's recovered."

Agate looked at her in surprise, and then thought for a while before answering. "You're right about how our society works, but we wouldn't just vote for you because Ellie made you her heir. She made you her heir, because you've earned it. You've done as much, if not more, for our people in the past year, than Ellie has done in the last hundred. There wasn't a Guild here before she arrived and while it's been slow to grow here, she's never taken that personally, and she's one of the few people that advocate for us outside of the Council, for which we are ever grateful, but you've changed our entire world. You've given us the ability to speak for ourselves. For that and that alone we would gladly vote for you, even if Ellie hadn't made you her heir, and we would vote for you over Ellie in a heartbeat if you indicated you wanted the position. I honestly wouldn't be surprised if many of my people nominate you at the next election anyway. And until proven otherwise, you *are* Acting Senior. No one here questions your right to that title. You are the Translator after all."

It was Marsee's turn to sit there in shock. Ellie had said much the same, but to hear it from someone she'd just met, somehow hit harder. And that they'd choose her over Ellie was simply unbelievable. She didn't even remotely feel like she deserved that.

"Now, as for who would want that role," Agate continued, "someone with enough tech savvy to alter the archives would be a pretty small list. I can't imagine it would be any of my people, but then I would never have thought anyone could have done what they did to you and Ellie." Agate swam over to her desk and grabbed her tablet.

"How did you know the archives were altered?" Marsee asked with suspicion. "I never mentioned that."

Agate snorted. "It's all over the news with Clear Seas arrest, but that never set well with me. He's horrible with tech. I send someone up regularly to un-mangle the latest mess he's made of his tablet. I've never known anyone as bad as he is, but he is wonderful at finding bugs in new software updates. Personally I think he missed his calling there. I've joked on a number of occasions with him that he should join our QA team, although he swears he's not doing anything he hasn't done a hundred times before."

Marsee raised a brow at that. "Could someone else be messing with his tablet?"

Agate shrugged. "I suppose it's possible. It all depends on if they're using his account to modify the archives, or have found a way to make it look like he did it. Now, if someone is trying to stage a coup within the Guild, then it would have to be someone still active and in good standing. No one who has retired or who has been kicked out would be considered for the position, and technically you'd have to be a guild master too, but that's just a formality. Any one of us could promote someone to that rank to get around that requirement. By consensus, we decided to hold off on calling for the vote until after the funeral for Ellie, and frankly everyone was just waiting to find out when and where that was going to happen to make arrangements, and waiting to see whether or not you'd be found alive."

Marsee sat there and blinked for several moments at what Agate had been implying, before finding words. "Does that happen often? Getting kicked out of the Guild, I mean?" Marsee asked.

"No, not often. Usually it's someone who never makes it past apprentice. If someone is continuing to try to improve their craft, no matter how bad they are at it, we keep working with them. We honestly don't care if it takes someone two years or two hundred to make it to their masters. If you love what you do, that's all that matters. We occasionally have some disciplinary issues with some of the younger fry, but in those situations we tell them to come back when they're older.

Some do, some don't. I can only think of a handful of people in the last hundred years that were kicked out after earning their journeyman rank, at least among my people."

"I'd like those people too. Maybe I'm wrong about someone wanting her position. Maybe it's someone who's mad at her for some other reason. Getting kicked out of the Guild would certainly make me mad after all the time I've put into it, but nothing is really stopping anyone from learning a skill or trade outside of the Guild if they really want to." Agate nodded and a few minutes later her tablet dinged. Marsee reviewed the list. It covered all five worlds and was ordered by planet, primary skill, and rank. She recognized a few names and several she knew personally. "Do any of these people live in Councilor Current's district?"

"Current? I've heard rumors, but why him?" Agate asked.

"He's the one that did this…" Marsee growled, and motioned to her lack of fur.

Agate seethed. "It would be him. I never liked him."

"Why?" Marsee asked.

"He's rude and arrogant, and I've had dozens of complaints from my crafters over the years. Nothing major enough to bring up with Ellie or the Council, but enough. He always pays but he'll just swim up, take what he wants, and swim off, without so much as a hello or a thank you. He assumes the crafters know who he is and will manage all of the effort for the transfer. I'll be honest, I've told my crafters that if he does that, then they should charge whatever they want."

"I heard much the same from one of the food vendors last night, a lovely Sprite by the name of Opal. She makes the best fire sticks. I'm pretty sure I took her entire supply yesterday, then again multiple days without real food makes a person hungry, and I'm seriously considering an offer of partnership," Marsee said with a curl of her tail.

Agate laughed. "I know Opal. She's already in a partnership, but she might just consider it, if *you* asked."

A moment later a short list dinged in, this time two active members, the Guild Master from that district, a Level Four Tech, and one person who had been kicked out nearly forty years prior. "What did this person do to get kicked out?" Marsee asked.

Agate flashed surprise as she read. "It says here he broke into the Guild's systems. Oh this is interesting. Apparently he hacked into Ellie's account and made several falsified comments impersonating her. Ooh, her report is scathing. She must have been livid. But this was decades ago. Do you think he'd hold a grudge that long?"

"It's possible. It'd be enough to make him a suspect worth looking into anyway, especially considering what he did. Send me that report please." Agate did, and Marsee sent all of that information off to her father and to Councilor Marcus, along with Agate's assessment of Clear Seas tech skills. "Is there anyone on the other list that you could think of that might have had a disagreement with Ellie or even gives you a bad vibe, like Rip?"

"Not really, no," she replied. "I mean some of these people can be grumpy at times, but no one I would think capable of hurting the two of you, and that includes the Guild Master in Rip's district. From what I know he and Rip don't get along at all."

This made Marsee's ears flick back. "I have a visit with him in a few days and I'll be curious to see what he has to say about Rip. Hypothetically, if Ellie and I had both been killed, who would you have nominated in our place?"

Agate considered for a while. "I think many would probably nominate Nardal. That's certainly been the consensus with the gossip I've heard the last few days. He's been Ellie's second for years. That would count pretty high with our people."

"But you wouldn't?" Marsee inferred.

"No, he's amazing with numbers and making sure shipments arrive on time and all of that, but when it comes to people skills...well, let's just say he wouldn't recognize a blubber fish if it sat on his face."

Marsee laughed. "I have no idea what a blubber fish is, but I can just imagine. Ellie said much the same about him to me. I've only met him a few times and he seemed quiet, but friendly enough, and very meticulous. Do you think he would or could be behind something like this?"

"I suppose it's possible," Agate said with a shrug. "If anyone, he'd probably have the biggest reason to be upset if he was hoping for her position some day, but I honestly don't think he's capable of hurting someone, unless maybe someone was targeting his family too."

Marsee flicked her ears back at that. *Could there be blackmail involved? Could that explain the missing people? Who would he be blackmailing though? The other councilors?* She wouldn't put it past Rip Current to do something like that, after what he'd done to her.

"So who would you pick?" Marsee asked again.

"Honestly, I would probably run for the position myself. But I'd also recommend that we split it back out to one Senior Guild Master for each species like Ellie originally wanted. It made sense having one Senior back in the day, when the various guilds were so fractured and disorganized. Everyone wanted Ellie's vision, and she was one of the few that could somehow bring people together and sweep them up in her passion for what the Guild could be. Now though, the Guild is stable and big enough to easily support a senior for each species."

Marsee nodded and sent her father and Marcus a message about Nardal as well, and what Agate said about splitting the role up, along with her thoughts that maybe Rip Current was blackmailing people, and that maybe the others had been taken hostage like she had. It was a long shot but at this point, ideas were all they had.

"Thank you. Now that that's out of the way. Ellie sent me a list of items you wanted to talk about. Shall we go over those?" Marsee asked.

Agate flashed her humor and surprise at the sudden change in topic, but agreed and they spent the next hour working through her list, with Marsee making notes to share with Ellie when she was better. Where she could, she made suggestions based on the conversations she'd already had with Ellie. When they were done, Agate took her on an official tour of the Guild, and the people she interacted with all asked for her opinion on their projects, including the various masters. This surprised her, but she did her best to give feedback the way she liked to get it, pointing out everything she liked, but only highlighting one or two mistakes she saw, and provided suggestions on what to do if they indicated they were stuck, or wanted her opinion on something specific. She found she enjoyed this immensely, and had several in depth discussions with the masters on their projects. For a time, she was even able to forget what had happened to her.

As Ellie had indicated, and as she'd seen in the market, everyone was talented in their chosen craft, but one very shy journeyman blew her away. She was nearly finished making one of the story drums, and it was equally as good, if not better than the one she'd been given the night before, and she wondered if this was a masters project.

"What level are you, Amber?" she asked after examining the intricate details of the drum.

"Level Three, Ma'am," Amber responded.

This surprised Marsee but she managed to keep from showing it. "Do you play at all?" she asked.

"Some, enough to tell that the tuning is right" the shy young journeyman replied. "You should hear Master Sea Turtle play if you have a chance. He can actually make the drums speak. I'm nowhere near that good. He usually has a booth in the market. This one's for him actually, a gift for his protege, or so I'm told."

"I heard Master Sea Turtle play last night, and it's something I shall never forget. May I hear you play something?"

The Journeyman flashed her nervousness, but grabbed the mallets and played a simple tune that made the engravings dance and flash with happiness and joy. The notes were pure and perfect, and while her skill at playing wasn't nearly the quality of Sea Turtle's, Marsee thoroughly enjoyed the performance, as did the others, who flashed blue and green when she was finished.

Marsee had been exposed to some of the best music on all five worlds, as her siblings regularly shared their favorite new music with her. She'd tried learning to play an instrument when she was younger, but she couldn't handle the sound of her own horrible out of tune playing long enough to stick with it, but she had a feeling Amber would be quite skilled if she kept practicing. Her craftsmanship was exemplary though. Taking a chance on what Ellie and Agate had said about her, she made a decision.

"That was beautifully performed, Amber. Thank you," she said, and Amber flashed her pleasure at the complement. "Unfortunately..." she said with an exaggerated sigh, "there's a problem, and without finding a way to fix it, there's no way this drum could ever be presented to Master Sea Turtle."

Agate looked at her with suspicion, and it was all Marsee could do to keep a straight face as Amber's body language radiated her dismay, although she managed to keep it off her skin.

"Why is that?" Amber asked sadly. This drum clearly took months to make, and she was nearly done.

"Because Master Sea Turtle is far too good of a musician to ever be presented with a drum crafted by a mere level three journeyman, no matter how exceptional it is."

Agate managed to keep her humor under control, while Amber looked both shocked and confused.

"That is a problem, Translator. Would you happen to have any suggestions on how we might fix that?" Agate asked, looking very concerned and perplexed as to how to solve the problem, and immediately playing along.

"The only thing I can think of would be to promote her," Marsee said, trying to keep from curling her tail.

"I don't know. Do you think that would be good enough?" Agate asked.

"You're probably right, level four probably isn't good enough either. I'm sure Sea Turtle's protege will be equally good, if not better than him some day." Marsee said.

"I guess there really isn't anything to do about it then. It's a shame though. This is a stunning piece. Maybe we'll be able to get someone to trade for it, at the market," Agate replied.

"Well there is one thing we might be able to do?" Marsee said, pretending to think about it.

"Oh? What's that?" Agate asked.

"I suppose I could try that thing my mentor once did to me. It might work, but I'm not sure. I've never really tried it on *purpose* before. It would be a little different, so I don't know if it would work or not. Now how did it go...Ah yes." Marsee waved her paws like Ellie had done and then frowned as if nothing had happened. "Ah, that's right, I almost forgot the important part...Poof, you're now a master with all the rights and blah blah blah." When she was done, she peered at Amber as if examining her work. "I don't know, did I do that right?" she asked Agate.

"It looks like it worked to me," Agate replied.

"Oh, good! Master Amber, let me be the first to congratulate you on your promotion," Marsee said formally, and then bowed.

Amber floated there in complete shock as Marsee swam out of the room with Agate and Avery right behind. Around them were flashes of humor, happiness, and from one, immense pride. *I'd bet my last piece of fur that that's Amber's mentor,* Marsee thought, *although it could be her mother. Maybe both?*

It was all Marsee could do to keep her tail straight until they'd made it out of the room, but the moment they did, Agate closed the door and they both burst out laughing. "If I didn't know you were Ellie's protege that little "poof" bit would have given it away. She did the same thing to me when she promoted me to Guild Master," Agate said.

"At this point I've been demoted and promoted so many times, I'm not really sure where I rank anymore," Marsee laughed. "Then again, I demoted her to apprentice the other day. I suppose I should reinstate her rank, eventually, *if* she behaves."

Agate laughed so hard she couldn't swim. "Oh, I wish I could have seen that! What did she say to that?"

Marsee rolled her eyes. "I believe the words were 'Yes! Finally!'"

Agate laughed even harder.

Marsee's tail was hurting pretty badly at that point. She tried hard to uncurl it, with little success.

"Thank you though. Amber really needed that boost of confidence. I've been trying for years to make her believe how talented she is. She's my niece, so she doesn't believe me."

"I know exactly how she feels," Marsee muttered, which Agate looked shocked to hear. Marsee ignored it and looked at her tablet, "I should really be going soon. I'm meeting up with Clear Seas in a little while," she said, and then shivered.

"Are you cold, or was that a reaction to meeting up with Clear Seas?" Agate asked.

"Cold. I firmly believe Clear Seas is innocent. We just don't have the proof to clear him yet. I'm just not used to being without fur," she admitted.

"If I may ask, what happened to your fur?"

"Rip Current happened," Marsee muttered. "Apparently this is what happens when my people get the full brunt of your electric charge."

Agate looked at her in horror, and then her skin turned fully red with rage. "He didn't! That monster! A full charge?"

Marsee nodded. "So the Senior Healer says, or close to it anyway."

"But, how did you survive? A full charge is enough to kill a juvenile leviathan, and make the adults second guess their decision to try to eat you."

"She said it's probably because he shocked Ellie too. Although it could be because...because it was spread out over several sessions. It felt like an eternity," Marsee said quietly and turned away, struggling hard to contain her reaction, and then shivered again. *I should stop and see if Opal has more of those fire sticks,* she thought absently.

Agate flashed her anger again, bright enough to light the room up a vibrant red. "Come with me," Agate insisted, and had her follow her down to a section of the Guild she hadn't made it to yet, and knocked loudly on a door.

The door opened to reveal one of the largest Sprites Marsee had ever seen, clearly someone of advanced age. He blinked in surprise to see them. "So, what brings *you* down into the depths of the Guild?" he asked, speaking her language. The lack of formality surprised her after the way everyone else had been treating her.

"Trench, the Translator is a tad chilly without her fur, and I was hoping you might have something to help keep her warm."

Trench squinted at Agate for a long time, and then burst out laughing, a rainbow of colors rippling across his skin.

"I'm not sure what's so funny about that," Marsee growled, pinning her ears back, and lashing her tail, furious that he'd laugh at her for losing her fur.

"Oh, child, forgive me. I'm not laughing at you. I would *never!* My devious little protege knows *exactly* what I have, and that's what I'm laughing about. Come on in." He swam back into his office and they followed.

Marsee had expected to see a typical crafters office, buried in half finished projects, but this looked more like a home. While there was a desk with work in progress, there was also a sleeping net and pictures of family members hanging on the walls, seating for guests, and even a small kitchen and refrigeration unit. Rather than a monitor as the main focal point of the room, which she was used to seeing in most offices and homes, there was a case with what looked like one of the garments the Hue-mans called a cloak lovingly displayed. A gentle light shone on it and the material, whatever it was, glittered in shades of purple and silver.

Trench swam over and looked at it for a minute before opening the case and reverently taking the cloak down. "Yes, I think this should fit you just fine. I didn't think I'd ever see anyone actually wear it, but this certainly fits the occasion, and I can't think of anyone more deserving."

Trench swam back, flung it around her shoulders, and buckled a clasp around her neck. He lifted the hood from behind her, gently placed it on her head and then took the sides of the garment and pulled them close and clasped several more buckles.

Warmth seeped into her, and she sighed. "Oh, this is so much better," she said, and then felt the material. The inside was soft and smooth but the outside was rock hard, like a shell, yet the tiny intricate pieces flowed and moved together seamlessly. She couldn't even tell how they were attached. "What kind of material is this?"

"This child, is from the only other creature, besides yourself, that has ever survived a full charge. It's Leviathan hide," he said with a smile, although there were hints of grief on his skin.

"What?!" she asked incredulously.

"Back when I was a small fry, not much bigger than your young rescuer, I lived in a tiny village far out in the middle of nowhere. We didn't have the Sea Patrol ships to chase away the Leviathan, or any other predator for that matter. Just our wits and our shocks. Actually killing one would require the effort of dozens of people. One day an adult Leviathan attacked my village. The adults tried to drive it off, but when it wouldn't leave, they had no choice but to kill it. Several people died in the attempt, including my older brother. Those who died defending the village were all given a cloak made out of the hide, as was our custom then. This one was given to my family on behalf of my brother. There is no greater honor among my people than risking your life to save another, so I can't think of anyone more deserving of this than *you* to pass it on to."

Marsee floated there in shock and then scratched her ears in confusion. "Master Trench, I...thank you. Clear Seas told me of this cloak and its meaning to your people, and I understand the honor your people place on those who risk their life to save another. I'm deeply touched that you want to give this to me, but I don't understand *why* you want to give it to me. I didn't fight off a Leviathan to save a village, and if any one deserves this, it's Stormy. He braved a Leviathan twice to save me. And, well, I'm not really sure how I feel about wearing the skin of another creature," she added.

"Translator, I fully understand your hesitancy. I know your people don't use other creatures the way we do, and I'll understand if you don't want to wear it and take no offense, but hear me out. I'm not sure what Rip Current was playing at when he went after you and the Guild Master, but if I had to guess, he was trying to stage a coup. Stormy is very brave, but he only saved one person. You've saved us all."

Marsee shook her head. "No. All I did was scream for hours in a dark cave."

Trench looked at her with a mix of pride and sadness. "I was there the other day when you approached the protesters. You, not Clear Seas, not Ellie, you. I knew something was going on, but I had no idea what, and I certainly never expected what happened. I didn't understand why the Council wasn't even meeting with the protesters. That's not like Clear Seas at all. The news said Clear Seas was arrested for tampering with evidence relating to the protests, but that doesn't make sense either, nor does the ransom note. I knew Deep Current and his parents. They were good people, honorable, but I've never liked Rip Current. It makes far more sense that he was trying to discredit Clear Seas and frame him for your death. If Rip had 'found' you, he would have secured the love of the people with that action and quite likely been voted in as Senior Councilor. Your father and uncle have been targeted, Wind Rider's daughter is missing, and I have a feeling Temperate's shuttle accident was no accident. You faced off against a Leviathan more than twice your size and survived a full charge that should have killed you. It certainly would have killed me. He was trying to claim power over this Council, if not the Full Council, yet all he did was show how weak he really is. This cloak not only shows your bravery, but your honor, one that every member of my society respects, and right now your family needs that. Too many in the Consortium believe that your family has too much power, which is likely why he tried to get rid of you first. This will help protect you and them, and it'll make Rip Current seethe to see you get the honor and respect he craves, and know just how badly he failed."

"How did you know I survived a full charge or about Rip Current? Agate didn't tell you," she asked, suddenly very suspicious.

"Sea Turtle is my son. He contacted me to get my blessing before giving you my father's drum, and I spoke to him at length afterwards. Frankly it's all anyone is talking about at the market today, and Rip Current's arrest has been all over the news." He shifted to show her a tentacle with a similar faded scar to the ones that now covered her body.

"Besides, accidents happen. Every member of my species will recognize that you've been shocked, and the severity."

"You really think this will help protect my family?" she asked.

He nodded. "I really do. The younger generation might not under-stand but the ones that matter will, and it will change their minds far more than anything you could say."

She nodded and thought for a while before answering. "Your son is an exceptional musician, and I thank you for the gift of this cloak, and for the drum. Is there anything I can do for you in return?"

"No. All I ask is that someday, if you have the opportunity, that you pass it along to someone equally deserving," he said. "And make Rip Current suffer for a very long time for the harm and pain he caused you and everyone else."

"Of that, I promise," she replied. Then feeling overwhelmed, she turned and swam out the door without another word.

# CHAPTER 40

# Marsee: Habitat

A gate led Marsee back to the writer's section of the Guild, so she could pick up her gift for Stormy. The cape flowed behind her like one of the Hue-man's super heroes. She didn't feel like she deserved it, but if it would make Rip seethe to see her in it, and keep her family safe, she'd wear it with pride, and it was incredibly warm.

When she arrived back at the desk of the master writer she'd met with earlier that morning, he smiled and flashed a color pattern of purple and silver that she didn't recognize.

"Trench finally passed on his cloak did he? I couldn't think of anyone more deserving," the master said afterwards.

Marsee smiled but didn't reply. Not really sure what to say.

"Anyway, here's your request. I made one change though, I hope you like it," he said, and handed her the book.

She smiled when she saw the change of title. "Oh, It's absolutely perfect! Thank you so much! May I borrow a pen?"

The Master handed her one, and she flipped open the book.

It took her a few moments to figure out what to write, but then inspiration struck.

> *To Super Stormy, the bravest superhero that ever lived,*
> *I had no idea when I asked to write your story someday,*
> *that it would start that very day, and that I would be the*
> *one you rescued. I can never thank you enough for what you*
> *did for me, but I hope that this will begin to repay that debt.*
> *- Your Greatest Fan, Translator Marsee Bet Chenzira*

The tour of the Guild had taken longer than Marsee had anticipated and she was running late, so she thanked Agate, and declined the offer of lunch with her, stating her desire not to be late for her next meeting. Agate gave her a bag to carry her gift in, so she could better use the drone with her busted paw, and she sped off for Clear Seas home with the intention of stopping at Opal's stand for a quick bite to eat along the way.

She was in a hurry, and didn't really pay attention to the few people she passed on her way, so she was not prepared for, or expecting the re-action she received when she entered Market Square. The night before had been challenging as people reacted from the shock of seeing her without fur, but she'd completely underestimated what the cloak meant to these people.

As people noticed her and what she was wearing, the market stilled. The Sprites all turned to face her, and their skin changed from the rapid colors of their conversation, to a checkered purple and silver, like the master at the Guild, and she realized that it matched her cloak. Then as one they bowed deeply.

Marsee floated there in shock for several moments, trying to process what was going on, and then bowed back, and swam up to Opal's booth.

Opal was beaming her joy at seeing her again. "Translator! What can I get for you today?"

"I was hoping you might still have those fire sticks from last night," she signed.

"As a matter of fact I do. I set these aside just for you, hoping you might swim by today. My gift," Opal signed.

"Opal, you are the absolute best!" Marsee said, taking the proffered sticks and sighing with pleasure at her first bite. "I don't know what you did, but these are even better than last night. Thank you!"

"My pleasure, Translator."

"Are you sure there isn't anything I can give you in return?" she asked.

"You already have. I sold out of everything last night within an hour of your visit, and I've had to have my son bring me more, to restock the booth twice already today. I've secured enough already to double the size of my garden and a few more days of this, and I'll be able to open a restaurant, which has always been one of my dreams."

"Well, in that case, I look forward to visiting your restaurant on a future visit," Marsee said.

"It would be my honor, Translator!" Opal signed.

Marsee smiled her thanks again and continued along her way. She'd finished the sticks by the time she'd made it across the market and tossed the remains into a recycler before taking off at full speed for Clear Seas home.

She'd barely made it within sight of Clear Seas home when the door opened and a tiny blur of bright blue came flying out of the house straight towards her, and nearly knocked her over in one of the fiercest hugs she'd ever received. She hugged Stormy back just as fiercely. Clear Seas followed his son out of the house, and swam over. He was flashing his happiness to see her as well, but kept his distance.

"Translator, are you okay? What happened to your fur?" Stormy signed with a flash of worry, and then "Is that really a Leviathan cape?" Stormy flashed purple and silver before waiting for an answer.

"I'm fine. My missing fur is apparently a side effect of being shocked, and yes, this is a Leviathan cape. It was gifted to me this morning," she signed back.

"Rip Current shocked you? Is that why you collapsed and started shaking?" Stormy asked.

"No, I was suffering from hypothermia," she signed back.

"What's hypothermia?" he asked. "I don't know that sign."

"I was really really really cold," she said.

"Oh, yeah. Your father said Deep Current died trying to keep you warm." Stormy's skin reflected his sadness.

"He did. But we both would have died if it weren't for you. You saved my life, and I'll never be able to repay you for that, but I did bring you something. I hope you like it."

"You did?!" Stormy asked, flashing his excitement.

She nodded and handed him the bag.

Stormy took it gently and pulled out the thin book inside. His skin went from white to blue at least half a dozen times as he looked at the cover, before he could speak. "The Adventures of Super Stormy? You turned me into a superhero in one of your books?!" He flashed awe and amazement as he carefully turned the pages, and started to read, and then frowned and flipped through a few more. "But, this isn't a made up story. This is what happened," he said, flashing his confusion.

"I didn't need to make up a story. I just told yours. *You* are my superhero, and you always will be," she replied.

"Is this going to be published too?" he asked with a mix of excitement and worry.

"Only if you want it to be. If you want to keep it all to yourself, you can, but I've had several of the masters ask me to post it, because they all want a copy."

"They really want to read about me?" he asked, flashing his surprise and disbelief.

"Really. They're all very impressed with what you did, and so am I. It's not every day a small fry like you braves the depths of the Trench and a Leviathan, not once, but twice in one day to save someone, or break into a Council meeting past several honor guards for that matter."

"Wow. I don't know. What do you think I should do?"

"Being famous can be really exciting at times and has its benefits, like having vendors in the market save you your favorite foods, but it can be very challenging too. When my family took in Little Flower, I had no idea what that would mean for me, or my family. I just wanted to help a sick little cub get better. The Senior Guild Master taught me that I would be a part of history and be known by everyone. Whether you like it or not, you're part of this world's history now too. People already know what you did for me. If it were me, I would want people to know what really happened. I tried to keep this as close to the truth, as it was told to me. If I have something wrong, let me know and I'll change it."

"Okay. Let me read it first and then I'll decide, but either way, thank you," he signed, and then gave her another hug.

"You're very welcome," she signed back, and he turned and swam back into the house, already reading and barely watching where he was swimming. He was so distracted, he actually bumped into the door frame on his way through, which made her chuckle remembering all the times she'd done the same, completely lost in a book.

She swam up next to Clear Seas, who had turned to watch his son as well.

"I'm worried about him. He didn't take Deep Current's death well. He blames himself for not being fast enough, even though there was nothing he could have done," he said quietly in her language.

"I know exactly how he feels."

Clear Seas looked back at her in confusion, so she explained.

"I blamed myself for not being there when Little Flower went into labor, and for not running to find my mother fast enough." She snorted. "You know, I think I finally figured out what my father was trying to teach me when he chased me halfway across the Wilds a few months ago."

"Your father attacked you?! That's a serious charge, Marsee," Clear Seas asked, flashing his surprise and horror.

"I'm not charging him." She paused and turned to look at her guard. "Avery, could I have some privacy please?"

He nodded, and swam over to chat with the guard watching Clear Seas, and they floated off a distance, far enough away that she couldn't hear them talking.

As they did, she checked that no one else was around. "Councilor, how familiar are you with psychosis? I am aware that the Seniors questioned my sister about my illness at the trial, and I want to thank you for speaking up for me."

He looked at her for nearly a minute before answering. She was curious about his lack of response, but waited, quite used to this with her father and uncle. "I have read your report, as have the other Seniors. Your father also submitted as evidence the risk that your sister took in trying to help you with your control, but I am not sure I fully under-stand this disease. None of us were familiar with the illness before the Trial. Councilor Tabor was fairly vague on the details, only that it was a brain defect that ultimately proved fatal, and would cause you to lose control and act out in violence as it progressed. I'm not a healer but I'm aware that brain tumors and traumatic injuries can cause similar be-havioral changes among any of our people. I assumed it was something similar." He paused for a second as if gathering his thoughts. "Jennette was…very uncomfortable with having you so close, or as Little Flower's translator, and stated that you were a danger multiple times. She be-lieved you would lose control at the reading of the verdict…and that day we brought your sister in for…questioning."

Marsee looked at him hard, curious if he would admit what he planned. "You intended to kill her didn't you, like she thought?"

He sighed but nodded. "And blame your illness for it. We wrongly thought the Hue-mans were too dangerous to keep around. But I see now my people are just as dangerous." His skin radiated a color pattern she didn't know, but his body language projected shame. "I am truly sorry. It was not my finest moment."

"Why didn't you?" she asked, feeling sick to her stomach, although honestly surprised he'd admit it to her.

"For a number of reasons. Your sister's intelligence in sniffing out what we had planned, for one. The guard's presence and Kendra's fore-sight assured we wouldn't have been successful anyway, but I changed my mind because of you."

"Me?! Why?" Marsee asked.

"Tabor assured us that the moment you thought your life or Little Flower's life was at risk, that you'd lose control and attack, but while it was obvious were scared, you remained calm and professional, translating her words. That was enough to make me doubt Tabor, and with the charges against her and her council, I began to wonder if she was trying to get rid of further evidence of wrongdoing. You earned my respect in that moment, and again later at the verdict when we wrongly voted to allow for your sterilization, even if it was precedent. You didn't stand up for yourself, but you did for your mother, and you honored your oath and kept translating even though we intended you harm."

Marsee snorted. "You give me far more credit than I deserve. I was trying to save my future cubs too, and Tabor wasn't wrong. It took every ounce of self control I had not to attack that day. I was so...so angry and disappointed with the Council, but I knew if I so much as made a single step towards you, I would die. I also figured that decision was made *because* of my illness. I just didn't know what to do either, and prayed my sister could figure out a way out of it, like she had with my father, or that my father or uncle would somehow be able to stop it from happening later. I knew going into the trial that Mama would likely die, and I had been prepared for that verdict the moment Tabor announced she was guilty, even though I didn't agree with it."

"You weren't wrong. The guards had orders to kill you if you showed any signs of losing control. Marsee, I have known both your uncle and father for my entire life. I know them well enough to know they would not put us in harm's way, and to deny your sister her requested translator would have been seen as tampering with the Trial, but I will admit, I voted against you because of Tabor's insistence that you were still a risk, along with your niece, and Tabor's belief that it was genetic, not just because it was precedent. I hope you can forgive me. I was very wrong about you, and offer you whatever form of reparations you would like for that decision, and for my inability to protect you since you arrived on my planet. I have failed you, and if you would like me to step down, I will."

Marsee stared at him, blinking hard in surprise that he too would offer to step down, and shook her head. "No. I don't want anything. Your apology is good enough for me. I don't blame you for the decisions you made. I understand why you made them, even if I don't agree with them. I've had a long time to think about it, and spoke with my father after the verdict, several times. It's your responsibility to look out for the safety of all our people, and both the Hue-mans and I represented a risk you needed to take seriously. I honestly respect you more for admitting you were wrong and changing your mind about it. I don't want you to step down either. Rip Current wanted to harm my father and make him suffer, and I believe he wanted to do the same to you. As for my illness, I too am worried about passing it along to my children. My mother says they don't really know what causes it. It usually only occurs in those who have had to hunt or kill for survival, or in single cubs. It's not a tumor either, but more a defect in our ability to control our instinct."

"How does one ever control instinct?" he asked, flashing his confusion.

A large fish chose that moment to swim by. "Councilor, your people eat fish and crawlies fairly regularly. Have you ever hunted or fished before?"

"Many times," he replied. "But not in years. I used to go out with my father hunting before he died. I haven't been since Temperate was younger."

She nodded. "Does a fish ever swim by and cause you to think, 'I should hunt that? It would make a wonderful meal' and kill it right then and there?"

"Not unless I'm actively hunting. Most of the time I have no need to hunt, so if I do want something, I pick it up from the market," he replied, but she could tell he was wondering where this questioning was going.

"For most of our people that's how it is too, but for me it was not. I would see something move and my instinct would take over, and I would pounce on it before I even knew what was happening. Our small cubs are that way, as you saw with my niece, but by the age of three most have it under control. I did not. I merely got better at hiding it. My parents didn't know it was still an issue until they brought Little Flower home and I almost killed her, several times in fact. I managed to hide that from them as well until about a week or so before the Trial, when I had an episode in front of everyone, including my uncle. I honestly don't think she fully understands just how close I came to killing her."

Clear Seas looked horrified and slightly scared, although he kept that off his skin. "Why was the Council not informed of this? It wasn't in your report."

"Would you have admitted to the Council that you'd almost killed someone?" she asked.

He tilted his head nodding the point.

"My mother said she reported it to our council and Healers Guild, stating that our hunting instinct had been triggered, but she didn't indicate by whom. I also didn't tell her everything that had happened and was happening to me. It wasn't the normal reflex I'd always struggled with. It was far more, and I was too afraid to tell her. My mother thought I'd just pounce on her leash to try and keep her from escaping, which was a valid response at the time, but it was far more than that."

"Tabor indicated that this was always a fatal illness. Are you still sick?"

She shrugged. "I have no idea. I couldn't control it at all before. I can now, but we don't know what causes it. It's not fatal because of the illness, but because those afflicted with it are executed before they can harm anyone."

Clear Seas flashed shock with that statement. "You're serious?"

"I am. There was no cure before. They would have been right to do so too. That day in the garden, before Little Flower broke me out of it, I was nothing more than a wild animal and her my prey. Somehow sign language cut through and helped me remember who I was and who she was. As far as I know, I am the first person to ever be allowed to live, the first to ever regain control, or to be able to stop before hurting someone. Whether we have a cure or not, still remains to be seen." Marsee's gaze drifted over to the two guards who were watching them, and sighed. "I may always be seen as a risk and that's something I've had to learn to deal with."

"Should I be worried for Stormy's safety or my people's?" he asked.

"I'd like to tell you no. I feel like I'm in control, but Avery put me back on the watch list last night, and I suppose he's right to do so."

Clear Seas looked at her with confusion. "Back? I was not informed of you being on a watch, past or present, and I should have been, especially after what you just admitted, and why would you be placed on a watch for what Rip Current did to you, if you're in control now?"

"My uncle put me on the watch list after he witnessed that incident, but rescinded it the same day. My father said he spoke to Kendra at Trial and that she was still keeping me on an informal watch. Even after Kendra removed me from the watch, the guard has still watched me. I've seen them occasionally, glimpses mostly, when I've been in Council City with Ellie. Kendra followed my father and I once when we went out for a run during the last Full Council. I have a feeling I'll always be watched. As for why I'm officially back on a watch, it's because I had to use my instinct to stay alive in the cave. I was always told that the more we use it, the harder it is to control. My experience has been very different though. The more I tried to avoid using it the harder it was to resist. I didn't gain control until I started using it. It has grown a little stronger every time, but since that day in the garden, I've never lost sense of who I am. I can now give as little or as much control as I want. I practice regularly to make sure. I don't want to hurt anyone."

"How do you practice using your instinct?" he asked.

She considered how to explain it for a moment. "I don't really know how to explain it. Mostly I just turn it on and off again, and make sure there's no urge to hunt, but sometimes I draw with it on or go for a run. I've never allowed myself to hunt anything on purpose, but sometimes I will sit and watch a creature and make sure I can think about doing so without losing control. Your people are born knowing how to use your electric shock defenses, correct?"

"Yes. Young children will often shock someone by accident if they're scared or startled. They're too small to hurt anyone though."

"I guess it's much the same for us then, just a different instinct. We're born knowing how to hunt and kill. If I were lost out in the Wilds as a cub, it would give me a chance for survival."

"You're born knowing how to kill?" he asked, flashing his surprise and a hint of worry.

She shrugged. "Knowing and doing are two different things. I never managed more than a glancing blow against Rip in the cave."

"I'm impressed you managed to do that at all, especially without being able to see him, or survive your other injuries, but what does all of this have to do with your father attacking you?"

"He thought I was losing control again, like I had before, and perhaps I was. I was upset about my sister and all the changes in New Hope and my instinct felt like our territory had been invaded. We decided to go for a run and find someplace we could go to when we needed space to be alone. He saw me with my instinct on and marking a tree in my anger and grief, and chased me away from New Hope so I wouldn't hurt anyone. Eventually I stood my ground and fought back. I didn't understand what he was doing, or why at the time, but for what it's worth, I won. He explained afterwards and promised he wouldn't do it again. He's never raised a paw to me since."

"You beat your father in a fight?" Clear Seas looked very skeptical, although he kept it off his skin.

"I did. I thought he was trying to kill me. I gave full control over to my instinct and we managed to pin him. I had his throat in my mouth and could have easily killed him. If I hadn't been in control, he would be dead now. Both Marcus and Kendra are aware of the incident, and Avery as of last night."

He was silent for a while, his skin dark, but she could sniff out a range of emotions, anger being the strongest, and she wondered what he was angry about, but he didn't say and she didn't ask.

"You said since. Has your father raised a paw to you before?"

"Only once. That too was a test. A single swipe, to ensure I could shut my instinct off afterwards. I blocked it."

"If you can control it, why are you back on the watch now?"

"Because we still don't know why I can control it now, or if this is just a reprieve. At the end, I knew I was dying and gave up full control to my instinct in the cave for one last chance at Rip, and hid in a dark corner of my mind. I don't remember Stormy coming to rescue me and if I hadn't been behind a shield when I woke up in the Trauma Center I would have attacked the healers. It took me a long time to come back or even dare to turn off my instinct once I had. I'm honestly surprised Avery even gave me that chance. I still feel in control, but…" She looked down at her paws and the scars and cast that were there. "I'm still very jagged. My thoughts where my father is concerned is still a tangled mess because of what Rip did and said and part of me fears your people the same way you now fear me. I think perhaps the only person I don't fear is your son. I can't even begin to explain how hard it was to leave the ship this morning."

"I don't fear you," he said. "But I fully understand why you fear me, and my people after what was done to you."

"You do. I can smell it," she replied.

He flashed surprise but quickly brought it back under control. "You can smell my fear?"

"Even without my instinct on. With it on, it's even stronger. I don't know if that's normal for my species or not. No one has ever told me they could do the same, and I've never mentioned that to anyone, not even my father. Councilor, I'm not even sure why I trust you enough to tell you all this, but, I think it's important you know. There was a lot I left out of my statement, much I don't know if I will ever be able to talk about. I don't want people to know about my illness, but I think you should know Rip Current was trying to make me lose control. I think he wanted me to attack my father or whoever rescued me, or perhaps he intended to let me loose somewhere, once I was fully feral. He said as much." She winced at the memory.

"Are you all right?" he asked.

She snorted. "I doubt I'll ever be all right again, but that's something I'm going to have to learn to live with too." She took a deep breath, trying to control the panic of her memories before continuing. "During one of the…sessions, he spent the time talking about all the possible things he might do with me once I was feral. He knew about my illness, knew things he shouldn't have, things I haven't told anyone. He hates my people, not just my family. I'm honestly not sure what would happen if people found out, but it would be bad, not just for me but for my people. They would fear us just as you fear me."

"Is that why this illness has been hidden?" he asked.

"No. Well, part of it. It's rare from what I understand, but just like you hid your history, we've hid our own. Before the Great Awakening, psychosis was common. We destroyed our former world in a war that lasted nearly fifty years because of it. I didn't even realize psychosis was still a problem, or that I was suffering from it until it was too late, but using your instinct outside of a self defense situation would be as crass as eating with your fingers would be to you, only more so. As an adult, if someone saw me pounce on something, I would be reported to the guard and likely never trusted again, if not killed outright. Imagine if one of your people never learned how to control their shocks, how people would feel around them?"

Clear Seas tilted his head and considered, but again said nothing about it. "You mentioned that your father was trying to teach you something when he attacked you?"

She nodded. "After he tested my control, I left and spent several weeks with Ellie. It took me a long time to realize the risk he'd taken during that test, but what I realized a moment ago, was that he was also trying to teach me that no matter how fast I am or how strong, there will always be someone faster or stronger than me, that there will be times in my life where I won't be good enough, where I won't be fast enough, and that's okay. What matters is that I tried. Life has a way of finding us, even when we're hiding out in a tower in the middle of a remote desert. It's those challenges that make us who we are, that define our character, that make us smarter and give us the skills to survive the next one, if we can. I honestly don't think I would have survived in the cave if it wasn't for what I learned that day, even if part of me is still mad at him."

"Those challenges are never easy, are they?" Clear Seas asked.

"No, they're not, but I don't think you have to worry about Stormy. He'll pull through this. He has courage that far exceeds his small size, selflessness, and a kind heart, but more importantly, a real desire to help people. Those are all the things that will make him an amazing Senior Councilor someday, but then that's not surprising, considering who his father is."

Clear Seas flashed his surprise and then gratitude. "Thank you, Translator. I am honored by your kind words and your trust in me. I have no right to them. I should have done more to protect you, and I am so very sorry for what happened to you."

She raised a paw to stop him. "Rip Current was targeting both our families, and very likely the Guild. Ellie and I may have just been a convenient target to discredit you, but he wanted to destroy my father and my people, just as much as he wanted to hurt you, and it certainly wasn't your fault. You tried to protect us, placed guards around us, put locks on the doors, and I seem to recall you even recommended against me talking with the protesters. Neither of us knew the Sea Patrol had been compromised, or had any idea that Rip was attempting a coup. How could we have? I neither need nor want your apology for what Rip did to me. You did nothing wrong to apologize for. What matters now, is that we figure out who else is involved, and what else Rip was up to before the people he's working with have a chance to try again, and we need to find all those other missing people."

Clear Seas looked at her with astonishment and then confusion. "What other missing people? Are you referring to Petra and the other missing pilot?"

"Other missing pilot? Did they find Leaf or Willow?" Marsee asked with confusion of her own, and listened as Clear Seas filled her in with what Marcus and her father had told him.

She frowned, hearing that Leaf was dead. "I just can't believe Petra's involved. I think she's been taken and is being held hostage too. Whoever wrote those messages is not a native speaker. I'm sure of it. I'm surprised there hasn't been a ransom note yet though. Or perhaps there has been, if Wind Rider is already on her way here. But no, I was referring to the missing honor guards that were watching me, and the missing people that Deep Current was trying to find. The ones that all went missing after they were arrested."

"There are *more* missing people?!" Clear Seas asked, shocked by this information.

Marsee nodded, unhooked her tablet, and pulled up the information Deep Current had provided her, and showed it to Clear Seas.

He was solid red in anger by the time he handed her tablet back. "Why was I not informed there were more missing people, or an alert sent out?"

"Probably, because you're still the primary suspect. The footage of their arrests have all been altered and we frankly had no way of knowing if they were actually missing or not. That's why I wanted access to the archives and didn't tell you what their demands were, although we intended to the next morning. I was trying to find out what happened to the people who were arrested. I personally don't believe you had anything to do with that."

"Thank you for your trust. However, Marcus cleared me an hour or so ago. You're more than welcome to reach out to him to confirm. I won't take offense. Apparently they found evidence that Snapper Fish is behind the edited archives, like you suspected." Clear Seas was silent as he considered what she'd just shared with him. "Most of the arrests occurred in Rip Current's district so he would have been the one to charge and punish them, except in the case where the two deaths occurred. In those situations, I had to witness their punishment, and they were executed for their crimes. I honestly don't know what happened to the others. I knew arrests were happening with the protests, but this is a far greater list than I was informed of. It certainly would explain why there have been so many protests."

He let out a heavy sigh and skin rippled with regret and shame. "It seems I was wrong once again. I should have spoken with the protesters myself instead of taking the word of others. If the rest of what I have been told is fake, then I quite likely sentenced two people to death for crimes they didn't commit. These other claims are all legitimate as well, and certainly worthy of discussion and investigation by the Council."

"That's what I intend to do today. I want to figure out what he was up to with the Habitat and the platforms, assuming it wasn't just a ploy to further discredit you. Deep Current wanted to show me several things, but unfortunately he's not here to ask, so we're going to have to figure it out for ourselves."

"Well then, let's not waste another minute," he said.

She followed him back into his house where they found Temperate waiting, his arm still in a cast that matched hers, but otherwise looking good. "How are you feeling?" she asked him.

"Much better. There's hardly any pain now, just a little ache if I try to move it too much. I should be able to have the cast removed tomorrow," he replied.

"That's wonderful news! Same with mine. I'm very glad you weren't hurt worse," Marsee said.

"I appreciate your concern, Translator. Thank you," he replied.

"Marsee, please. And that goes for everyone else too," she insisted, and he nodded.

"Are you ready to go?" Clear Seas asked her.

"Where are you going, Papa?" Stormy asked.

"I'm going to give Marsee a tour of the Habitat and a few of the new platforms under construction," he replied.

"Can I come too?" Stormy asked. "Please please please please pleeeeeease?"

Clear Seas hesitated in replying and then looked at his partner before his eyes flicked to the guards waiting outside.

"I need to go to the market, Clear. We're low on supplies, and I'd feel much safer if I picked them out rather than having them delivered. And honestly, I'd feel a lot happier if Stormy was out of Council City for a while too," she said.

Clear Seas looked at her for confirmation that it was okay, since she'd requested the tour.

"I don't see why not. An extra set of superhero eyes could be useful, and help us spot what we miss," Marsee replied.

"What are you looking for?" Stormy asked.

"I don't know. Something odd or out of place, anything that might tell us what Rip was planning, and help us figure out who else is involved," she replied.

"I can do that!" Stormy said. "I'm really good at finding hidden things."

Marsee smiled. "That you are. Well then, I guess it's settled. Habitat first or one of the platforms?"

"The Habitat is the closest. I was planning to start there," Clear Seas replied.

"The Habitat it is then." Marsee motioned for Avery to follow her, leaving the other guard to protect Jewel. Temperate led them to their shuttle bay and the shuttle inside. She'd been expecting to see the same ship her father and uncle had, but this was a much smaller, personal shuttle.

"I'm a bit hesitant about using my ship and pilots right now," Clear Seas said at her look of surprise. "Between what's going on with Ellie's pilots and Temperate's accident, I'd feel safer take my shuttle. Temperate and Aris gave it a full inspection this morning. Plus, Temperate received the report from the techs regarding his accident, a few minutes before you arrived. They believe the proximity sensors were tampered with."

She pinned her ears back and lashed her tail in anger. "So you were a target too?" she asked Temperate.

"It would appear that way," Temperate replied. "I honestly don't know how I feel about it. I'm glad to know it wasn't caused by my exhaustion, but..."

She nodded her understanding and followed them into the shuttle.

Clear Seas showed her how the safety net worked since there weren't seats, and made sure she was securely fastened. In the smaller shuttle it would take about an hour to arrive at the Habitat. Clear Seas pointed out the Trench when they passed, and Marsee swallowed hard at the dark void below her, but she was even more amazed at how far Stormy had swum to find her. Stormy read the entire way. It wasn't a very long book, mostly drawings, but Marsee noticed that he read it several times.

"So what do you think? Did I get everything right?" she asked him, after about the fifth or sixth time through.

"It's perfect, but...it makes me seem a lot braver than I felt. I was scared the whole time," he replied.

"No one ever feels brave. Bravery is what you do when you're scared. Do you run and hide from danger, or do you face the Leviathan to save your village?" She looked over at Avery who was smiling at her. "If it helps, I had much the same conversation with Avery yesterday."

"You did?" he asked, "Why?"

"Because I was terrified to leave the safety of my ship after what happened, but there are people missing, my friends, and your people, and no matter how scared I am, I'll keep fighting to find them, even if it means I'm putting my own life at risk to do so. Just like you did for me. I don't feel brave either, just scared and worried."

He nodded. "Then, I guess it would be okay if you published this. Maybe it will give someone else the courage they need to fight the Darkness, just like your other books did for me."

Clear Seas' skin radiated his pride at his son's words, but the moment his son looked away, she caught a hint of sadness and regret too. She made eye contact with him and nodded her understanding. Stormy was having to grow up far too quickly.

Marsee flipped out her tablet and sent a message off to Agate. A message came back almost immediately from her, and she chuckled. "Guild Master Agate wants to know if you'll sign her copy," she told Stormy.

He was so surprised he didn't even flash it on his skin, just looked at her completely dumbfounded, and eventually nodded.

She replied and a moment later another response came in. "She said she'll bring physical copies over tomorrow, and she wants to know how many more you want."

Stormy couldn't answer. "I...I don't know."

Marsee replied, saying he didn't have a clue. "She says she'll send over the normal amount for a new release. Whatever that is."

Stormy just nodded.

Marsee wondered what the normal amount was too. Outside of the assistance with the Hallowed Eve Festival, she'd not asked for assistance in printing copies, choosing to bind them herself because she enjoyed giving them each a personal touch. She'd have to ask about that later and wondered if Ellie would be awake when she returned that evening.

When the Habitat appeared it was her turn to be dumbfounded. She'd seen footage of the place, but nothing prepared her for how big it really was. The Habitat was several orders of magnitude larger than Council Platform. Instead of one tower there were dozens, each surrounded by tanks that were so big, she found it hard to fully grasp the size of them.

"How did you even make something so big?" Marsee asked.

"The center access towers were built much like we do any other platform, but the tanks are all solid static shields, and they're layered with three separate and independently powered shields, so that if one fails we won't lose containment of the species. This allows us to reconfigure the platforms as needed. The outer shield is charged to protect against predators, much like we do with the other platforms and ships."

"How are you powering them? Ours are all solar powered since we're in the desert and we have backup systems, but one of the biggest challenges we've had with expansion has been expanding the shields. We're running them full time as well, to protect the Hue-mans and other species from predators, but we can barely manage one shield, let alone three."

"We actually have multiple systems in place. The primary system is based on an underground geo-thermal vent, but we have wave generators and wind turbines on top of each of the towers, and in an emergency we can ship in batteries. In the event of a major storm, we can compress the size of the tanks to conserve energy and bring the tanks below the surface."

"Why are there tanks above the surface?" Marsee asked.

"Several of the species are air breathing. We can generate the air they need in an emergency, but we're trying to replicate their natural environment as much as possible," Clear Seas explained.

"Air breathing creatures that live in the water? From an evolutionary perspective that seems rather...well, stupid," Marsee replied.

Clear Seas chuckled. "I've been told that the Hue-mans believe that these species once lived on land, and then eventually transitioned back to live in the water. They contain many similar characteristics of the Hue-mans and many of the other land creatures, including giving live birth and nursing their young."

Temperate maneuvered the shuttle slowly around several towers so she could have time to observe. Marsee started recording and zoomed in on one of the tanks to show creatures swimming slowly along.

"Deep Current told me he was worried that the Habitat had been built too quickly, and that this was not the first choice of location. Do you know why this location was chosen and not the others?"

"Yes. Proximity to Council City and the other surrounding communities for the most part," he replied. "We wanted this place to be a learning center, not just a Habitat for the creatures, and the proximity made the build significantly easier. The other areas proposed were well out into the wilds and would have required far more infrastructure and resources to even start. We still plan to use those locations when we outgrow this area but that won't be for many years. This location was riskier as there is an old ground fault nearby, but we took that into consideration when the designs for the habitat were created. Just like all of the landing platforms, the Habitat is rated to withstand both hurricane force winds and waves as well as potential quakes, and there is already significant monitoring of that fault due to the other communities in the area."

Temperate set them down near one of the towers. Dozens of shuttles and ships were scattered about, with people swimming in and out, carrying smaller tanks with creatures in them from the shuttles back to the various habitats.

Marsee followed Clear Seas and Stormy out of the shuttle. Stormy still carried his treasured book with him, even though his father had suggested that he leave it behind on the ship. Stormy had flat out refused. Smiling in amusement, his father had relented. Temperate and Avery followed after her. They were met by a single Sprite who flashed the same purple and silver pattern and bowed low as they approached.

"Welcome to the Habitat, Translator. My name is Sand Sweeper. I'm the Senior Healer in charge of the Habitat. Senior Councilor Clear Seas said you wanted a tour of the facility. It would be my greatest honor to show you around. I do apologize for the absence of others to greet you, and the general chaos you will see today. My healers are still busy returning the creatures hastily evacuated these past few days back in their habitats."

"There's nothing to apologize for. I was heartbroken to learn the terms of my release, and how so many were affected. I can't even begin to express my gratitude towards the effort it must have taken to even attempt to evacuate this place. It's so much larger than New Hope by several orders of magnitude, and its loss would have been devastating."

"I am thankful that we were able to save it, but I am far more relieved to know you were found alive, although clearly we were not fast enough, and I am so very sorry for the pain you had to endure because of it," Sand Sweeper replied.

Marsee nodded. "Thank you, but I have no doubt that no matter what you did, I would not have been released, not alive anyway. The Senior Healer at the Council Platform Trauma Center said I'd have only made it another fifteen minutes or so from the hypothermia, and well," she motioned to her injuries. "He apparently came close to killing me on a number of occasions."

"A number?" Sand Sweeper flashed her shock briefly before bringing herself under control. "Forgive my outburst," she said. "I should have realized that from your scars and lack of fur."

"There's nothing to forgive, but please forgive *my* lack of manners. Let me introduce you to everyone. Obviously you know the Senior Councilor, but this is Stormy, Councilor Clear Seas' youngest son, and the person we have to thank for my rescue and saving of the Habitat."

Sand Sweeper flashed the purple and silver and bowed to Stormy as well. "I have heard that you faced a Leviathan twice in order to save the Translator. Thank you for your bravery."

Stormy nodded back, completely overwhelmed by her display of respect.

"This is Master Pilot Temperate, the Councilor's eldest son, and Honor Guard Avery Hunt."

Sand Sweeper looked uncomfortable, although she kept it off her skin, and glanced towards Clear Seas, so Marsee explained, realizing that Sand Sweeper must not be able to read her language as Avery's rank and position were clearly indicated on his badge.

"While we've caught the person who harmed me, he was not the person who originally kidnapped me. Avery is here as a precaution. Clear Seas has been cleared of involvement and restored to his rank."

Sand Sweeper nodded her understanding. "Of course. Shall we begin the tour?"

Marsee nodded and they followed after the Healer into the nearest tower.

"Each tank contains anywhere from one to ten separate levels, each designed for the species it contains. From within here we can access each level or ring as we call them, and secure a creature for care in these smaller tanks. Eventually we will be able to connect the levels in each tank as we determine which species are able to cohabitate safely. Several of the rings are already self-sufficient at this time as we've been able to balance the needs of the creatures and the needs of their food sources."

Scattered around the viewing platform, there were tablets with images of the creature or creatures contained in the ring. Marsee clicked on one and it brought up images and information they'd learned about the selected creature.

"Our goal is to make this a learning environment, and open it up to the public, bring children on school field trips and educate people, not just on the species of the Hue-man world, but our own too."

"So the Habitat is not open to the public now?" Marsee asked.

"No, only the healers and staff needed to run the place, scientists, construction crews, and special guests like yourself. We're still building and enriching many of the habitats. Most of that work should be done in another month or two, although I expect that we will continue to enrich as we learn more about each creature."

"Have you had many special guests besides myself?" she asked.

"Oh sure, councilors, guild masters, and their families, as well as the families of those who have worked on the habitats," she replied.

"Did Councilor Current ever visit?"

"Many times. This is in his district after all, or was anyway."

"Did he seem especially interested in any particular aspect of the Habitat? We're trying to figure out why he targeted this structure, since he requested it be built here in the first place," Clear Seas asked.

Sand Sweeper thought for a moment. "Usually he's here to discuss requisition requirements, but he did spend a significant amount of time around the dolphin tanks, although the last time he was here he visited one of the smaller tanks."

"Will you show us?" Marsee asked. Sand Sweeper nodded, and they left the habitat they were in and swam past several others.

"What's that?" Stormy asked as they passed a ring, and a very sad melody vibrated through the water.

"That is the song of a creature the Hue-man's call a whale. I've been told they had much larger species of whale, but we never found any during the rescue and frankly, they wouldn't have fit on the ships anyway. Sadly, we only found one of this species, but we're trying to figure out if we can bioengineer a viable embryo based on a few of the other species of whale we saved. Thankfully she seems to have made friends with the others, so she's not lonely. They travel in family groups called pods."

Sand Sweeper swam into a nearby platform. "This platform houses several species of fish and is one of the habitats where we've started to co-mingle species together. Each of the twenty species in this platform are also housed separately in other platforms, but we are trying to build a self-sustaining micro environment for those species that are no longer critically endangered. The tuna, for example, was a primary food source for the Hue-mans, and several of the larger species we rescued, like the three species of shark, and they can lay millions of eggs in its spawning season but they rely on other fish such as the herring and mackerel for its own food source. The last spawning season was so successful that we were starting to prepare a shipment of tuna to be sent to New Hope, before the evacuation order occurred."

"Chef Jordan will be thrilled to hear that. I was told the other day that the fish you're currently sending them can only be found in the nesting grounds of the Leviathan, and that several people have died hunting for them? Is that true? And will this shipment be enough to allow you to stop putting people at risk?" Marsee asked.

"Yes and thankfully also yes. We will actually have far more than the Hue-mans currently need, and if the next spawning cycle goes as well, we may actually have a problem with having too many, which was one of the things I last spoke to Rip Current about. Several of these fish are also safe for all of our species to eat, and I was recommending that we consider the possibility of farming these species rather than potentially upsetting the balance of our ecosystem by releasing them, or to at least begin the discussion of how and when we planned on trying to start releasing them into the wild."

"When was Rip last here?" Clear Seas asked.

"The afternoon the Translator was taken and you found the ransom note. That visit was entirely focused on what was needed to evacuate the species and dismantle the habitat. Before that, about a week before. That's when we discussed farming," Sand Sweeper replied.

"He must have come to the cave where I was being held afterwards," Marsee said. "He woke me by throwing some sort of slimy worm-like creature at me and said it was a rare delicacy since there were only a few left. I'm not really sure what it looked like since I was kept in the dark the whole time, but it was about this long and absolutely covered in sticky slime, and it took a long time to get it out of my fur. It was still alive when he left so I ended up letting it go on the off chance it could survive. Is that really something the Hue-mans ate?"

"That must have been what they call a slime-eel."

Marsee laughed. "That's an appropriate name for it alright."

Sand Sweeper flashed her humor and floated over to the display and pulled up an image of a creature. "They appear to be carrion eaters and burrow into the ground. We have some but not many, and it's one of the stranger creatures we rescued, and one of the few we've not been able to reproduce. We haven't even been able to identify the sex of the individuals to know if their failure to reproduce is because we didn't get a male and a female, or if these are juveniles and haven't matured enough to reproduce, or if they reproduce some other way. We believe the slime you mentioned is a defense mechanism. The Hue-mans mentioned that this was a popular food source in parts of their world, but not for those that were rescued."

"Yuck. No offense but I've tried many of their foods out of curiosity and there is no way I would eat that!" Marsee shuddered. "I can still feel the slime, even without any fur!"

The others chuckled at her expression.

"They are rather messy," Sand Sweeper agreed, "But they tend to burrow in the sand, so you don't often see them."

"So how did Rip get ahold of one? Would he have been able to access the rings?" Marsee asked.

"That's a good question." Sand Sweeper swam over to the nearest access port and pointed to the keypad. "All of the access ports are keyed to authorized personnel only, which should only be the healers. We wouldn't want someone opening the port by accident and getting in with a dangerous creature, or letting them out, but I suppose as a Councilor he might have access."

"Would you be able to find out if anyone accessed their habitat around the time he was here and if so, who?" Clear Seas asked.

"It's possible, but I'm not a tech. I can bring you back to the main office after we go to the dolphin habitat, if you'd like. Frothy Waves might be able to find that information for you."

"Thank you. It's interesting, Rip never brought up your concerns or suggestions about farming in our last committee meeting. I wonder why," Clear Seas mused.

"Not enough time, perhaps?" Marsee suggested.

"No, we had a planning meeting the morning you arrived, in preparation for the requisition meeting, and we spent quite a bit of time discussing the Habitat, so there was ample opportunity to bring it up. In fact, he made it sound more like efforts were not going well, and we certainly had no indication that they were preparing a shipment for New Hope," he explained.

"How very odd," Sand Sweeper said, and then motioned for them to follow her again. They exited that ring and swam about fifteen minutes to another platform along one edge of the Habitat, and then all the way to the top ring that actually opened above the surface of the water. "This is the dolphin ring. They breathe air through the hole on the top of their body, not water, and need to surface every few minutes. There's a static shield above the ring to keep them from leaping out and to keep something else from leaping in. "

Several small gray creatures swam up to the viewing window and looked back at them.

*No,* Marsee realized, *They're looking at me.* She floated away from the group a little and the pod followed her and stopped when she did.

"They're very curious creatures, and tend to appear when we're in the area, although it is getting to be their meal time," Sand Sweeper said as she watched.

Marsee put her paw on the viewing window and one of the creatures swam up and touched it with its nose, and then bobbed its head up and down and started making a high pitched clicking noise that made her ears hurt. She winced and rubbed at her ears.

"Is your ear bothering you, Translator?" The Healer asked, concerned.

"Yes and no. It's the noise they're making. It hurts my ears," she replied.

As she shook her head, the dolphin shook its head too.

Marsee froze. *Are they trying to communicate with us?* she wondered, *or mimicking me?*

"What noise?" the Healer asked.

"It's a very high pitched clicking noise. The Hue-man's vocal range is much higher than ours, so it wouldn't be surprising if that was the same for other creatures from their world," Marsee said absently, not even realizing she was speaking and not signing.

She raised one of her arms. The dolphin raised its flipper on the same side. Marsee switched hands and the dolphin did too.

"Is it trying to communicate with us?" Marsee finally asked out loud as they all watched her. Marsee spun around and the creature copied her.

"The Hue-man's said they were smart and capable of being trained, but didn't say anything about being able to communicate. Their healer never mentioned them doing anything like this. She's told me they liked to watch her while she works, and swim with her when she's out in the ring," Sand Sweeper said.

"Maybe it's because the Translator looks kind of like a Hue-man without her fur. Maybe it thinks she's one of them?" Stormy suggested.

"I suppose that's possible," the Healer replied as they all watched the dolphin and Marsee interact.

This time the dolphin did a flip and Marsee copied it. It made a burst of several different clicking noises that made Marsee flinch, and then it leapt out of the water and came crashing back down, spun around and faced her again. Marsee couldn't leap out of the water, since the viewing port was enclosed, but she did her best to follow the motions. Then to everyone's surprise it repeated the motions, first by putting its nose to the viewing port. Marsee put her paw up to touch it. Then the dolphin raised its flipper like she had before. She copied it and the other one, and then the spin.

"It's remembered the same order you did before!" Stormy exclaimed.

"So it did," Marsee said, amazed. "The next move should be me doing a flip. I wonder what it would do if I did something different," she said, and then raised a paw.

The dolphin let out a noise that made Marsee pin her ears and cover them with her paws, and then it did the flip she was supposed to do next. It kept making that noise until Marsee repeated the flip, and then let out the other set of clicks from before.

"That was painful, but I'm pretty sure it just corrected me," Marsee said, and then followed up with the leap and spin at the end, which the creature copied.

Marsee turned to face Clear Seas. "Councilor, I think we should consider the possibility that we have another sentient species on our paws."

Clear Seas looked at her in astonishment and then swam up to the viewing window to take a closer look at the creature.

Marsee's dolphin turned and swam over to him.

"It's making the same sound it did at the beginning, like a rhythmic clicking noise," she told him.

Clear Seas put his webbed hand on the platform window and they repeated the entire series again. When it was done it let out the same noise it did when she'd done the pattern right, and then they all swam to the surface to breathe.

He watched them for a moment and then turned back to her. "I think you may be right, Translator. This would be a big shift in our way of thinking about sentience. We've always assumed that tool usage would be a primary indicator of the possibility of sentience, but this creature would not have any way to make those tools since it doesn't have prehensile fingers. It wouldn't be able to sign like the Hue-mans either."

"We had a similar conversation before the trial. Did my father ever show the Council the flicker flyer video?"

"Not that I'm aware of," Clear Seas said. "At least it never made it to me."

So she took out her tablet and brought up the video and handed it over, with everyone crowding around.

When Clear Seas handed it back in astonishment, she continued. "GrandFather said there were many creatures on their world that could be trained to use tools, and even one that had learned their sign language. I think the question he asked my father was whether or not we deemed sentience based on the same level of technology or *our* ability to communicate. My sister could only sign a few words for the first several weeks after she came out of her coma, and her normal speech is still affected by the damage to her brain. She mixes up words all the time or says the wrong ones. She still can't walk and it took weeks before she could feed herself without assistance or even sit to use the waste facilities on her own, but she was very much aware of everything that was going on around her. Her injuries and lack of physical abilities didn't make her any less sentient. In the course of the last ten minutes, this creature taught me three of its words, yes, no, and happy. I'm not sure what the rhythmic clicks are, although they remind me of the tapping I used in the cave to see, but even if it only has a rudimentary language we should make an attempt to learn it. I'll send off a message to GrandFather and see what he knows about this creature. If they were trainable, then that would at least put them on par with several of the other domestic creatures the Hue-mans have."

Clear Seas nodded his agreement and Sand Sweeper wanted to know what she meant about the cave. Avery however looked at her oddly. His face was a careful mask, but she still had the sense he was unhappy.

She shrugged and decided to do her best to blow it off. "My sister said that some of the Hue-man creatures could echo-locate, or tell where things were by bouncing sound off of them. I'm almost done translating another one of the Hue-man legends called the Night Flyer, which is based on a creature that could do that. I've never experienced absolute darkness before. We have two suns and three moons and it's almost never truly dark out. That was honestly more terrifying at times than what else was happening to me. I don't know if I was hallucinating or if it was just wishful thinking, or even if there was some sort of bioluminescent creature in the cave with me, but at times it seemed like I could see by tapping my claw on the stone. Whatever the case, I have absolutely no desire to ever experience darkness again to find out."

The healer nodded. "I've seen and heard of stranger things before, especially by people who have been electrocuted. That can cause all sorts of unusual symptoms, including mood changes, memory loss, and hallucinations. It can really mess up a person's senses, sometimes permanently depending on how bad. I know of one person who was electrocuted accidentally and now hears music whenever she reads. Have you had any issues since?"

"When I first woke up in the Trauma Center everything was a jumbled mess, far too bright and loud, and very confusing, but I also had a severe case of hypothermia, and had difficulty speaking," Marsee replied and shrugged. "Since then, no. Not that I'm aware of anyway."

The healer nodded. "Then you should probably be fine, but if you do experience anything odd, you might want to get checked out, as it could indicate an injury that might have been missed."

"I'll keep that in mind. Thanks," she replied, and turned back to Clear Seas, who flickered sadness briefly before hiding it, and returning to the prior topic.

"If there's even the possibility that this species is sentient, we need to start treating them that way," Clear Seas ordered. "I want a full team of scientists and techs assigned to study them. Let's find out what sounds they're making, and we might want to consider moving them into one of the bigger habitats or at least opening up another ring or two for them. Translator, do you have any suggestions on how we should proceed with regards to learning their language?"

"We could try building a version of my sister's pictionary for them. We started with the basics, yes, no, different kinds of foods, that kind of thing, so my sister could tell us her preferences. Maybe put pictures up with images of the different foods you feed them, and if they touch it like they did my paw, give them that food."

Clear Seas nodded and the Senior Healer indicated they would begin just as soon as the rest of the creatures were back in their habitats.

Marsee took out her tablet and took some video of the creatures who were back to watching them again, and sent it off to her father and GrandFather, and they continued on with their tour.

After the official tour was over, they decided to split up. She, Avery, Temperate, and Stormy wandered, looking for anything out of the ordinary, while Clear Seas returned to the office to find out which tanks Rip had accessed.

# CHAPTER 41

# Jer: Wild Doba Chase

Jer watched his daughter leave the ship, both incredibly proud of her, and terrified for her at the same time.

"She'll be fine, Jer," Marcus said.

"She'd better be," he said, turning to face his mentor. "If something else happens to her, you'd probably better kill me before Myra gets her paws on me."

Marcus looked at him. "I like you, cub, but not that much. There is no way I'm getting between Myra and anyone she's after. I still have nightmares from the last time, thank you very much."

Jer laughed. "Fair. So, where do we start today? Send Rip to Myra for questioning?"

"Ha! Sadly, I have a feeling *that* would break a few too many Charter edicts," Marcus replied.

"Are you sure? I seem to have misplaced my copy of the Charter," Jer replied dryly. He he picked up his tray as if looking for it.

Marcus snorted as his tail curled. "I'm sure. But don't worry, you'll have your chance at Rip, assuming Ellie and Marsee leave anything left to him. Speaking of which, I haven't heard back from the other Seniors yet, which is honestly surprising. I would have expected something from Wind Rider at least by now."

Jer frowned and checked the current time in Council Weyr and then pulled up the news from there, to see if anything had happened, and raised a brow.

"What's wrong now?" Marcus asked with a heavy sigh.

"It's good news for a change. Wind Rider just laid two female eggs. According to this news article, the last time that happened was over a thousand years ago."

"That is good news, especially in light of what we've learned about their birth rate decline, but that doesn't explain why Wind Rider isn't responding."

Jer shook his head. "No, it might. She's probably still sleeping if she just finished clutching. I don't know what kind of recovery Wind Rider needs, but Myra was exhausted after her two litters."

Marcus nodded the point and changed the subject. "Have you heard from the Senior Healer to see if she's been able to identify the other person in the suite yet?"

Jer checked his messages and shook his head. "Nothing yet. It doesn't make sense. How could nothing come up in the census, if she had a good scan?"

"If they've figured out how to alter the archives, and keep us out of Rip and Damon's accounts, who knows what else they've changed. Lowell says she has something to show us. I figure we should start there and focus on exonerating Clear Seas so we can execute Rip. We have to do this by the book, or it will just add fuel to the fire Rip has already started. We really need to know if the two incidents are related," Marcus said, and resumed eating his breakfast.

"Rip said as much to Marsee."

"No, he said they'd be dead, by her people's own hands. That would account for the poisoning. It doesn't account for them being kidnapped and dragged fifty leagues out into the wilds, or the involvement of the Ice Giants."

"So you think there's someone else at New Hope we have to worry about?"

"Possibly. Someone had to have provided Damon with that ground crawler and taught him how to use it."

"He could have stolen it and learned on his own. There are hundreds of them parked around the compound on any given day."

"True. Have you heard anything from Myra yet?" Marcus asked.

Jer frowned. "Honestly, no. At least, I haven't heard her ding." He opened his tablet again and filtered his messages. "Nope. Nothing since yesterday."

"Same here," Marcus said.

Jer frowned with worry, removed the filter, and started scrolling, and realized he had one from Ammond. He took another swallow of his drink as he read through the message.

"What is it now?" Marcus asked, his voice weary.

Jer didn't answer, just forwarded the message to Marcus and kept reading.

Marcus hesitantly picked up his own tablet at the ding and started reading. "I'm honestly impressed Damon came away unscathed," Marcus said eventually, setting his tablet back down.

"Myra is nothing if not patient, when she needs to be. I wonder how long Ammond is going to keep her sedated though," Jer mused.

"Probably just long enough to keep the hide on Damon for questioning," Marcus replied.

"Fair." Jer checked the time. "It's still early there too, so I'm guessing we won't know more for a few hours."

They spent the next hour reviewing all of the information they'd uncovered so far, making sure they hadn't missed anything, and then made their way to the archives. Marcus led him down to the server rooms. It didn't take him long to see why Clear Seas couldn't have accessed the server room directly as they walked down a long hallway. "So be honest with me. How long after you were promoted did you wait to check out the Ancient Archives?"

"Honestly? That's where I was when you called about Tabor's little visit to the Agency," Marcus replied sheepishly.

Jer burst out laughing. "That's what I thought. You seemed very preoccupied, and totally uninterested in what Tabor had done."

"Can you blame me? It had been a rather eventful month, and I needed to relax. Besides, Little Flower's tail lashing on your behalf was more than enough punishment for me."

"You always were the master of understatement," Jer replied dryly. "So, was it everything you always dreamed it would be?"

"And then some! Jer, I've found books that are from before, nearly two thousand years before, if I've done my math right. I didn't even know we had history that went back that far. I can't even explain what it's like to hold a piece of history like that in your hands. To wonder if we'd become the society and people that they envisioned, and what people ten thousand years from now will think of our story."

"After everything that's happened, I'll be happy if I pass into obscurity at this point," Jer mumbled.

"Sorry, my boy. You're going to be remembered for eternity. I'm surprised no one has turned Little Flower's trial into a play yet. Even I didn't see that ending, and very little surprises me these days."

Jer frowned. "Marcus...Hold up for a second."

Marcus turned to face him. "What is it?"

"I thought you should know. When this is all done, I'm stepping down. I can't keep putting my family at risk like this."

"No. You're not," Marcus said.

"Marcus..."

"Listen very carefully to me. If you step down, Rip wins, and not only that but you put every other councilor and their families lives at risk because you'll show people like Rip, that they can succeed at intimidating their way into power, and besides Little Flower's people need you."

"Marcus, I've failed them. Every time I turn around, I'm failing them. Little Flower and GrandFather both warned me about Damon. Grand-Father even told me that if anything happened to him, Damon would be the primary suspect. I should have had him arrested the moment GrandFather was poisoned, but I didn't. If I had, then GrandFather and Little Flower wouldn't be in the Trauma Center fighting for their lives right now. I got so distracted by Marsee, that I completely forgot about caring for Little Flower and the rest of her people. I took an oath to protect them even over my own family and species."

Marcus slapped him, hard enough to nearly knock him over. "Enough! You can wallow in self pity later but right now, you need to focus on finding everyone else involved in this little coup of Rip's, and then you're going to keep fighting for Little Flower's people until *they* vote you out of office. Not one second before."

"But I've broken my oath, Marcus."

"No you haven't. You've done exactly what you've needed to. You're protecting your people and the people of the Consortium by finding out who's behind this coup. As awful as it is, that's more important than one life or several, even if that life happens to be a member of your family. Little Flower chose you to protect her people, because you're the best person on all five worlds who can do that. That little spitfire of a cub took on the Senior Council and won. She took your sacrifice and Myra's, and turned them into victories. She managed to do what we couldn't figure out a way to do. She saved your entire family, and then turned around and told the entire universe that you're the best person to lead her people, because she knew she couldn't protect them from themselves or the rest of the Consortium, but you can and you have. She knew this wouldn't be easy, that it would be downright impossible at times, and yet she put her faith in you. Don't you even think about disappointing her, and don't you even dare let Rip Current and others like him win. He wanted you to step down because he knew you'd be a threat. Don't you dare give him what he wanted. You keep fighting to protect your people, just like Marsee did. She was willing to give up her very soul for one last attempt to stop him. Can you do any less?" Marcus turned and stormed off without even waiting for a reply.

Jer rubbed at his sore jaw. *Well, that went better than I expected,* he thought, sighed, and followed after his mentor. They passed through several access points where Marcus needed to enter his clearance to enter before they finally made it into the actual server rooms.

"Lowell?" Marcus called out.

"Over here!" came her reply. They made their way in the direction of her voice, weaving through tightly packed racks of servers, and eventually found her in the far back corner of the room with wires connecting from her tablet to one of the servers.

"Good morning," Jer said, carefully making his way around multiple cables.

"Is it?" Lowell looked down at her tablet. "Ah, so it is. I take it you received my message."

"We did. What have you found for us?" Marcus asked.

"One, Clear Seas did not tamper with the evidence, nor did the Senior Archivist. Two, I'm not sure who did. Three, I've recovered the unaltered footage of the protest the other day which matches what Deep Current said happened, although it would appear that the rest of the footage was altered before it was uploaded. Four, as far as I can tell, no record of the disciplinary action for the missing people has ever been entered into official evidence except for two people that Clear Seas executed, and five, I can't find any evidence of tampering in those messages you sent me to look into, but Marsee was right. They were all sent from the same location."

"How did you determine all of that?" Marcus asked.

"With regards to editing of the footage, the logs were altered to make it appear as if Clear Seas had made those changes, but the backups show the actual account, timestamps and locations when those changes were made." Lowell explained.

"So you know who did it?" Jer asked.

"Yes and no. According to the systems, they died nearly thirty years ago," Lowell said.

"How could a dead person alter the logs? Their account would have been deactivated with their death," Marcus stated.

"I haven't figured that out yet," Lowell replied.

"What's their name?" Marcus asked.

"Snapper Fish."

"So how did they gain access to the archives to make the changes?" Jer asked.

"Haven't figured that out yet, either. There is nothing about that account that should give them access to make the changes, and outside of the backups, I'm not seeing any record of any use of that account since his death. Nor can I find any record that anyone physically accessed the server room in the past month. What I do have for you though, is a list of every addition or change made by that account in the backups, as well as what was there before, if there was something, and a list of everyone who has accessed this room in the last six months. I also have every edit either Clear Seas or the Archivist made for the last ten years, which is as far back as these backups go. I was just about to send you my report when you showed up." Lowell tapped at her tablet and Marcus's dinged.

Jer leaned over Marcus's shoulder to review. "That's a lot of changes."

"Fifty three over the last two local years by our dead guy. Most of those changes match with the dates Deep Current provided, give or take a few days. Clear Seas has made a whopping two edits, the last one nearly five years ago, and as far as I can tell he only changed the spelling on a name, and the time before that a birth date which had been transposed. The Archivist has made far more but most of those were related to a document restoration project in ancient archives, and nothing related to these events as far as I can tell."

"Well that matches with what Clear Seas told me," Jer said.

"And what the Archivist told me," Marcus added. "Looks like we have some information to dig through, Jer."

Jer nodded. "Have you been able to access Rip Current's account yet?"

"No, sir, and I don't know why you can't either. I have my best programmers scouring the code to look into that, but I've not heard anything from them."

"See if you can find out if Rip or Snapper Fish had any communication with the Hue-mans by the name of Damon Minor, Paul Markson, and Danny Shuto. I'd also like to have a list of everyone they've had contact with. Damon kidnapped Little Flower, GrandFather and Hope. They've been found, but the other two, Paul and Danny, are missing and presumed dead. We need to confirm this is related to Marsee's kidnapping."

Lowell nodded. "That *should* be easy enough. Give me a minute." Several minutes later though, she frowned. "I can't access any of their accounts either. I'll have my team look into them too."

Jer frowned, but Marcus spoke before he could ask his next question. "Do you know where those messages from Ellie's pilots were sent?"

"Yes, that's in my report. I haven't finished looking for the missing tablets yet, but I was able to activate Marsee and Ellie's. Their current location is in that report as well. My bots are still looking for the three other tablets."

"Would you know where they've been in the last few days too? Jer asked.

"Yeah that's easy but I would need your clearance to access that information."

"Can anyone access that?" Marcus asked.

"Anyone can access their own location data, but for someone else to access that information, I believe that's protected information that's only available to the Council and maybe Senior Honor Guards. All you'd have to do is log into their account. Like everything else, that access would be logged, or should be."

Lowell opened up her tablet and showed them how to access that information and display it on a map, and have the specified device start dinging.

"Are you telling me we could have pulled this information all along?" Jer rubbed at the back of his scruff. "The amount of time lost looking for Marsee or those involved..."

She frowned. "Sorry, sir. I figured you know that, and that the guards had already checked for that."

"Or they have and they've chosen to ignore it. I think I need to have another conversation with Stinger," Marcus replied.

"Ellie's and Marsee's tablet were taken. What kind of access to the systems would that give someone?" Jer asked.

"They'd only be able to log into the systems when Ellie was attacked. She has the same level of security in her tablet as you do, and would require a bio-scan to login, both to the tablet, and into any of the other systems. I don't know about Marsee, but the moment she was bumped up to Acting Senior, she wouldn't have been able to log in with a tablet that didn't have that security. Their access is all logged, just like yours."

"Ellies claw's were all removed, as were two of Marsee's," Marcus stated.

Lowell flinched and looked down at her own paws. "Yeah, that would do it."

"At this point, we should consider both Ellie and Marsee's accounts compromised," Jer stated. "I want to know everything either of them have accessed since 9 pm the night Marsee was taken."

"We do have both of Marsee's claws back though," Marcus replied.

"But not Ellie's. The healers printed replacements from a full medical scan she had of Ellie and from the recovered claws we had of Marsee's. Would those replacements have the same fingerprints?" Jer asked.

"Not a clue," Lowell said. "But the bio-scans use a number of different biometrics to confirm identity, including finger-prints and DNA. If they're using the claws log in with, that would only work for a few days tops before they degraded too much. Granted now that Ellie's dead, her account would be locked. However if they do match when reprinted, I suppose they could just keep printing new claws if they had a med printer. I'll look into that too."

Jer wished he could tell Lowell about Ellie.

Marcus grunted as he considered Lowell's information. "Send us what location data you have for all of those tablets since they arrived on the Water World, and Rip Current and Clear Sea's too," Marcus ordered.

"Of course." Lowell did a few things and then handed her tablet over for Marcus to enter his authorization. She tapped away for several minutes and then Marcus's tablet dinged. "I've organized the information by person, tablet, and location, in fifteen minute increments, however I can't access either Rip Current's or the Hue-man's location information. I'll let you know as soon as my bots are able to activate the other tablets. I don't have records since those messages were sent, so they were probably manually shut down."

"Thanks, Lowell," Marcus said, and started making his way towards the door.

Jer nodded, thanked Lowell as well, and followed after. "Where do we start?" Jer asked. "Do we bring in the councilors involved in the protest for further questioning or talk with Stinger first?"

Marcus stopped and considered, and then pulled up the recording of the protest. Jer watched over Marcus's shoulder and sighed when the recording was done.

"This is ample evidence to charge them with lying under oath, which is more than enough to remove them from office at the very least," Marcus said. "I think we should have Stinger bring them in for further questioning."

"Can we trust him to do that without supervision?" Jer asked.

Marcus frowned and shook his head with a sigh. "I haven't had a chance to confirm his story yet. Let's see if we can find those missing tablets first. We'll start with Marsee's tablet. It's the closest, but I'm thinking we should bring some backup with us before we go."

"Who? They're all busy. We've got a guard with Ellie, Marsee, Clear Seas, Clear Seas' daughter, and two guarding Rip, and we can't trust anyone within the Sea Patrol or local Honor Guard right now because we don't know who actually kidnapped Marsee, and frankly the guards we brought with us are likely to be exhausted right now anyway, at least Ellie's Guard and Rip's will be. The others might have been able to get some sleep, since they were in secure locations. We're going to have to figure out how to relieve them safely pretty soon. The other guards Kendra sent won't be here for a while."

Marcus stopped and turned to look back at Jer, and tapped a claw against his leg as he considered. "There's the guard Avery mentioned, Tanner."

Jer shook his head. "He might trust her, but she could just be trying to protect her son from being caught, if he's involved. I wouldn't feel comfortable having her around unless one of our guards were with us too."

"What about Sampson and the other pilots? They should be safe."

Jer considered and nodded, so Marcus called Sampson.

He answered immediately. "Yes, sir?"

"Sampson, did you and the two other pilots get any sleep last night?" Marcus asked.

"Yes, sir. Are you ready to head out?"

"No, We need some backup. The guards we brought with us are likely to be needing relief at this point and we have a fix on the missing tablets, but we don't want to go in alone. Can you join us and send one of the pilots down to swap out one of the guards on Rip's Cell and the other to the Trauma Center to spell Ellie's guard? I'll let them know you're coming."

"Ellie's guard? But I thought..."

"Long story, but yes she's still alive," Marcus said, "but you can't tell anyone."

"Oh, thank the moons! Yes, sir, on all accounts. Where should I meet you?"

"We'll meet you at the terminal exit," Marcus stated.

"On our way," Sampson said, and hung up.

A few minutes later, they met up with Sampson and they took off after Marsee's tablet and found themselves in the middle of Market Square.

"How are we possibly going to find it here, Marcus?" Jer asked.

Marcus thought for a moment and then bellowed, "CAN I HAVE EVERYONE'S ATTENTION PLEASE!"

Within moments the entire square was still and facing them.

"Thank you. In case you don't know, I'm Senior Councilor Surellis. I need everyone to be very quiet for a few minutes and if you hear a sound, buzzing, or dinging, please let us know," he said, switching to sign.

Marcus pulled out his tablet and did something and suddenly someone yelled out "over here!" They swam over, and as they approached, they too could hear the dinging. Others nearby were swarming to look for it too. "Found it!" another person yelled and they swam over. "It was in these bushes."

"Thank you. Your name and title if you have any, please?" Marcus asked, taking the tablet from the Flyer who found it.

"My name is Summer Breeze, sir, and I'm a journeyman healer, level three."

"Do you work in the Trauma Center?" Marcus asked.

"No sir, I'm here visiting a friend. I work in a clinic on my home world in the town of Wind Ridge. It's in the East Mountain District," Summer Breeze stated.

"Thank you, Summer Breeze," Marcus said, after recording the name and address of his friend as well, and turned to the crowd who was still being quiet and watching. "That was all we needed. Thank you!" The crowd dispersed, and Marcus handed the tablet to him.

Jer used his access to confirm that Marsee's account was still loaded on it. "I guess it was water proof after all," Jer said, seeing as it still worked. "I'm not seeing anything out of the ordinary. We'll bring this to Lowell and see if she can find anything on it. The last time this tablet moved was before Marsee was rescued. Do we continue the trail back and see where else it's been, or look for Ellie's?"

"Let's follow this one first and see what we can find." Marcus said, so they started following the trail back. It took them half the morning to track all of the data points as they were led on a wild doba chase that took them throughout the city and crisscrossed multiple times, ultimately ending back at the suite.

"Well it's not a complete failure," Marcus said. "At least now we know exactly when the tablet was taken from the room. We might as well start from here and work our way out to where Ellie's tablet is now. Based on the timestamps they both left here at the same time."

They were about to head out to follow the other trail when Marcus's tablet dinged. He read the message and frowned. "Wind Rider said the last she knew Petra was planning to check out the Jeweled Caverns in the Blue Fern District. She also says she had a feeling something was wrong and is already on her way via emergency jump on one of the Earth delegation ships. She left as soon as she was done clutching. She'll be here late this evening. That explains why she didn't answer. I wonder if the others are on the way too. I don't like that we haven't heard from Apakna or Sammianna."

"I suppose that's possible. I'm more worried about not hearing from Sammianna to be honest. We are really far from the Ice Planet here. It takes a good four hours to send a message and it would have been night by the time your message arrived." Jer pulled out his tablet and looked up the Jeweled Caverns. "That's on the other side of the planet. I'm surprised they'd go so far away, even if they were on vacation. I'm calling them."

Moments later a Water Sprite answered. "Councilor, how can I be of assistance?" the Sprite who answered asked in rough sign language.

"I'm calling to see if a purple Flyer by the name of Petra has been there to visit or is still there," Jer asked.

"A Flyer? No sir. As far as I know we've never had a Flyer visit. The adults wouldn't fit through the cave system and we don't allow children to go in unsupervised. We have that well posted on our public page but we barely have anyone outside of our own species visit. We're too far away from any of the platforms."

Jer frowned. "If she does show up, have her contact me."

"Of course, sir," the Sprite signed, and Jer hung up.

Marcus grunted in frustration after confirming the information on the cave's public page. "Well at least we know they're not there. Not that I expected it. Come on."

A few minutes later Marcus's tablet dinged again. "It's from Lowell. She's accessed the Flyers tablets," he said, and put the latest location on the map and they both frowned. One appeared to be at Clear Seas' home, another in the trench several leagues down from where they'd found Marsee, and the third on the east side of the city. Marcus tapped that one. "We start here first. I don't like it."

"Why?" Jer asked. He'd been expecting them to go to Clear Seas first.

"Because this is only a few blocks from where Temperate's shuttle accident happened," Marcus replied.

Ten minutes later, they were outside of a small nondescript home on the outskirts of the city. There was no answer when he knocked so he cautiously opened the door. His nose flared the moment he did, and he recoiled in disgust. "Something's dead inside."

"That much is obvious," Marcus muttered. They had Sampson wait outside and they cautiously entered and followed the scent to a small door in the floor of the home. Marcus opened it and swallowed hard as he tried to keep from throwing up. He used his tablet to shine light down in the room and they found the decomposing remains of several bodies. Two Water Sprites and a green Flyer, from what they could see. Marcus shut the door and quickly swam out. Jer followed as Marcus swam off some distance breathing hard.

"You okay, big brother?" Jer asked, not used to seeing his brother like this.

"I think I might be sick," he groaned. "I understand what you meant yesterday about the smell though."

Jer swam over. "You aren't having issues with *your* control are you?"

"No, just control of my stomach," Marcus muttered. "That smell was revolting." He recovered after a few minutes, thankfully without losing his breakfast, and called Command.

With bodies found, there was little choice but to involve the local Honor Guard. A trauma ship followed by two Honor Guard ships appeared a few minutes later. Jer recognized the first Sprite to exit, Senior Honor Guard Stinger. The second Honor Guard ship began patrolling. With the smell as strong as it was, there was an increased risk of predators approaching.

"We found several bodies. At least two Sprites and a Flyer," Jer told Stinger as he led everyone back into the home and opened the trap door. Marcus remained outside, still looking a little sick. It took them a good hour to retrieve the bodies and confirm they were the two guards Temperate had mentioned, and one of Ellie's pilots. They also located the tablet. Further scans of the home once the bodies had been secured, found no evidence tying anyone else to the crime scene and current registration showed the home was unoccupied. There was every indication that the bodies had just been dumped.

As they exited the house, Stinger looked out into the wilds. "Well, at least now we know why the Leviathan has been pestering this part of the city. I'll talk to the Commander about increasing patrols for the next few days and get a cleaning crew sent over. Left as it is, it would be a danger to the rest of the city. How did you find the bodies?"

Marcus tapped his nose. "We were heading over to check the sight of Temperate's shuttle accident," Marcus lied. Jer kept his face hidden under his mask. "I want to know who searched this home. These bodies have been here for a few days."

Stinger opened his tablet and a few moments later that information dinged.

"I want these guards available for questioning later," Marcus said.

Stinger nodded and flew off, while the other ship continued its patrol.

After watching the ships fly off, Jer turned to Marcus. "I'm assuming you didn't tell Stinger about the tablet location information for a reason."

"You know me too well. Thank you for following my lead on that. Yes. I want to track down the other tablets first. He'll be busy processing the bodies which will keep him out of our hair for a little bit anyway."

They decided to check on the tablet that appeared to be at Clear Seas home next. When they arrived, they found Clear Seas watching the news, which was already reporting on the bodies found. Clear Seas flashed his concern to see them there but they ignored it, and Marcus did the same trick he did for locating Marsee's tablet. It was Aris that found it and brought it to them.

"I found this ringing in the flower bed outside," Aris said after finding them in the house.

Clear Seas frowned. "Who's tablet is that?"

"Petra's," Marcus said.

Clear Seas flashed concern. "I saw the alert go out. I swear I have no idea how that got outside."

Before either of them could say anything, their tablets dinged with a message from Marsee.

Jer pulled it up and raised a brow at what she'd sent, and he wondered just who this Snapper Fish was. He forwarded the information on to Lowell as there was detailed information on the hack Snapper Fish had made, figuring that might help her locate the breach. He didn't understand any of it.

"Do you know anyone by the name of Snapper Fish?" Marcus asked, beating him to the question.

Clear Seas shook his head. "No, I've never heard that name before."

"I have," Temperate said, swimming into the room. "He's a pilot in the Sea Patrol. One of the best pilots I've worked with anyway. He was stationed in Rip Current's district until about six months ago when he transferred here."

"Do you know why he transferred?" Marcus asked.

"He told me he was trying to get into the Honor Guard," Temperate said.

"Can you describe what he looks like?" Jer asked.

"I can do better than that. Let me get my tablet. I'll be right back." Temperate swam off and returned, tablet in hand, and held it over to him.

"It certainly looks like our mystery dead guy," Marcus muttered.

"Snapper Fish is dead?" Temperate asked, flashing grief.

"That's the million credit question. Damon was apparently talking with someone with the same name, and Marsee found someone who was kicked out of the guild, by the same name, for hacking into Ellie's account. But that Snapper Fish apparently died thirty years ago," Marcus explained.

Both Clear Seas and Temperate flashed their confusion.

"Oh, before I forget, you're no longer a suspect," Marcus said. "We found proof that you didn't alter the archives. Our dead guy did."

"What about the tablet being outside of Clear Sea's home?" Jer asked.

Marcus shook his head. "Anyone could have put it there. Frankly, we have far more evidence against Petra at this point. I'll restore your access, Clear, but I'm keeping the guard here, for your family's protection. Also, Wind Rider says she'll be here later this evening."

Clear Seas frowned. "I find it very hard to believe Petra is involved. I've met her on more than one occasion and she never seemed all that interested in being in the Council."

"Not just Petra. Wind Rider too," Marcus showed Clear Seas the messages they'd found. "The dead Flyer we just found is this one, Leaf. We also found the two guards Temperate indicated the other day. They've all been dead for days, according to the healers we spoke to, and Stinger believes that's why the Leviathan has been pestering that part of the city."

"I figured as much when I saw the news report," Clear Seas said. "But I still don't believe Petra or Wind Rider are behind this mess."

"Neither does Marsee," Jer said. "I believe her, but their innocence is hanging on a couple of odd word choices, which Marsee believes Petra wouldn't use. She thinks whoever wrote this wasn't a native speaker."

"She's the Translator. That's proof enough for me," Clear Seas replied.

Jer raised a brow but before he could speak, Temperate spoke up.

"I agree with my father. Petra's a lot like me. She just wants to be a pilot. I've gone flying with her a few times. She's never mentioned any ambitions for being in the Council. We've talked about it. She's okay with being a nest mother as she doesn't really have any choice there, but she doesn't want to give up being a pilot, and fully intends to work part time as a pilot between clutches. The last time I spoke to her, she'd been signed up as a part time delivery pilot. The Ship's Guild was just waiting to find out where she was being assigned by the Council."

Marcus shrugged. "That may be, but she's still missing, and still a suspect until we can prove otherwise. Come on Jer. Let's see if we can track down one of the other tablets."

"Do you want me to come with you?" Clear Seas asked.

Jer shook his head. "Marsee should be here shortly. Stay here and help her figure out what Deep Current wanted to show her."

Clear Seas nodded. "Gladly."

Jer nodded and he and Marcus left, deciding to try and find Ellie's tablet next. They both had a feeling the other tablet was somewhere in the depths of the trench, and they would need a shuttle and probably an escort to safely find that one. They started back at the suite and followed the trail, and when the trail went through the market again, they stopped for a bite to eat and continued on. They finally reached the end of the trail that had them floating outside of another small house, one that they had passed several times before.

Jer swam up and tried the door but it was locked. He banged on the door. When no one answered he called out. "This is Senior Councilor Chenzira, open up!"

There was no answer.

"Do we break in, or contact Lowell to see if she has updated location information. What she sent you is a few hours old by now," Jer asked, but before Marcus could answer, his tablet dinged again.

"Dark moons," Marcus swore.

Jer's heart stopped and he turned to look back at his mentor. "Now what?" Jer said, terrified to even ask.

"Rip Current has escaped."

# CHAPTER 42

# Marsee: Cursed by the Deep

It took them nearly an hour to make a loop of the Habitat and examine the nearby environment. While many of the platforms still showed the signs of development, with nearby construction material, the first few showed significant landscaping efforts to repair the damage done by construction.

They stopped and spoke with the Master Builder, who was in the process of surveying the site for next planned tower and discussed what they did to preserve the local habitat, all of which was what she expected based on her experiences building out New Hope, and what Ellie had informed her was standard procedure.

Eventually, they made their way back to the main tower to meet up with Clear Seas.

"Any luck?" Clear Seas asked.

"Not that we could find. This place is incredible though, and the creatures themselves are fascinating. How about you?" she asked.

"There's nothing in logs that show anything out of the ordinary. However the Senior Healer did inform me that there's a tracking device embedded in all of the creatures that were rescued, and one of those eels is missing. They're going to send a team over to the cave where we found you, to see if they can find the missing one."

"So if the logs look normal, could that mean one of the healers is or was working with Rip Current," Avery asked.

They all turned to look at him. He was so good at blending into the background that they kept forgetting he was there.

"That's entirely possible," Clear Seas replied. "We know who accessed the tank that day. Sand Sweeper just left to track them down so we can question them."

Fifteen minutes later the Senior Healer returned with two other healers, and they spent a good half hour questioning them. They'd seen Rip Current around the habitat but they never spoke to him outside of a greeting. They'd been busy rounding up the animals and the tanks would have been unlocked at that time and they figured it was possible that he snuck in while they were distracted, or simply took one out of the smaller transport tanks when they weren't around.

With nothing else to glean from the Habitat, Marsee thanked the healers for their time, and they all piled back into the shuttle and took off for the nearest platform. As they traveled, Marsee sent Little Flower some of the footage that she took, as well as one to her father letting him know they'd left the Habitat and were on their way to one of the towers. She also mentioned the good news about the tuna population and the possibility of sentience with the dolphins. As she was typing it though, she had a thought.

"When I was in the cave, Rip said he was trying to save this planet from an invasive species, but he implied that we were the invasive species. I wonder if he was also thinking about the tuna. The healer indicated that one tuna could lay millions of eggs in a spawning season. In the wild they'd be picked off by bigger creatures but protected, that could be a problem, more so than just dealing with a lack of space to manage them properly," Marsee told the group.

"That's a possibility, although I imagine that our creatures would eat them just the same, of course that assumes that they wouldn't be poisonous to our species. That is something we're studying, but having an easy to manage food source like that would be very valuable for our people, and could possibly take the strain off of other species, depending on how good they taste. Just because we could safely eat them, doesn't mean anyone would," Clear Seas replied.

"True, whatever creature Rip gave me to eat the second time he showed up was revolting, but it was eat that or starve," she said.

She frowned as she looked at her message list and confirmed that she had a signal. She'd not received a message from anyone outside of Agate since she'd left that morning, and she fully expected her father to check in or at least respond to the other messages. *He did say he would be busy today,* she thought and shrugged.

"So what platform are we going to next and what's its purpose?" she asked Clear Seas.

"We're heading to the new shipyard, where we're planning to build new public transport ships. It's also where most of the protests have occurred, including the one that turned violent," he told her. She leaned forward in fascination as they approached to examine the half built platform. Construction crews swarmed the structure.

"How long will it take to complete?" she asked. She knew the answer, but was curious if he had the same information.

"Another month or so for the main platform where the ships will be assembled, and then another several months to complete the various support buildings where the individual parts will be manufactured," he replied. The information matched with what she had from Ellie and the Master Builder.

"Do you know why this location was chosen?" This she didn't know.

"Easy access to the materials needed for the manufacturing process primarily, although distance from the local community was considered as well. The process is both noisy and time consuming and delivery ships will be landing constantly to bring those materials we can't mine here," he replied.

"Is this the one where Deep indicated the endangered species were harmed?" she asked.

"According to the information you showed me earlier, yes," he replied.

"According?" she asked.

"The information he provided you is the first I've heard about any endangered species habitating in this area, or being harmed by construction," he explained. "That was certainly never brought up when I reviewed their case."

"Why wasn't Ellie informed about the deaths?" she asked. "As a guild project she should have been informed."

He sighed. "Rip Current said he'd informed her, so I didn't bother. I figured the Master Builder would as well."

She tilted her head, acknowledging the point. It certainly was reasonable enough of an explanation, although she did wonder why the Master Builder hadn't informed them.

It didn't take them long to make their way to the shipyard but as they approached, two Sea Patrol ships intercepted and hailed them. "Shuttle, this is a closed construction site, please state your authorization."

"Sea Patrol, this is Senior Councilor Clear Seas. I am here with Translator Chenzira to tour the construction site," Clear Seas responded.

"I'm sorry, sir, but your access has been revoked," the Sea Patrol replied after a few moments.

"Revoked?" Marsee asked, surprised.

"Marcus said he restored my access," Clear Seas said, and pulled out his tablet. "It looks like it's been restored. They knew what we were planning too."

Marsee nodded. "I told my father last night and again this morning, and sent him a message saying we were on our way. I can call him to authorize it," she said, and tried calling him. "That's odd. He's not answering." After everything she'd been through, she fully expected he would pick up if she called. She tried Marcus as well, but he didn't answer either. "They must be in the middle of something. Put me on with the Sea Patrol."

Temperate nodded that she was on. "Sea Patrol, this is Translator Marsee Chenzira. My father is Senior Councilor Jeran Chenzira, and we are here on official Council business regarding the investigation into my kidnapping and the murder of Senior Guild Master Kihar. This is a Guild site and as Acting Senior Guild Master, I authorize his access.

A member of the Sea Patrol was involved in my kidnapping, so if you don't allow us to land and tour the facility, then I will report you to the Senior Council for obstructing an official investigation."

There was a long pause before the member of the Sea Patrol answered. "My forgiveness, Translator. I have spoken to the Squadron Commander. *You* have clearance to access this facility, but the Councilor does not. Our records indicate he's been specifically prevented from accessing a number of locations, including this construction site, by orders of the Senior Council. If you proceed to the following location, you may disembark and tour the facility, but Councilor Clear Seas will need to remain on the shuttle."

"Sea Patrol, I can personally vouch for Clear Seas. He was not involved in my kidnapping and his access as Senior Councilor has been restored. I request permission to bring him with me."

"I'm sorry, Translator. I am aware of that, but without authorization from someone else on the Senior Council directly, I can't override those specific orders," the Sea Patrol pilot replied.

Clear Seas sighed. "It's okay, go on ahead without me. I'll see what I can do to reach your father or Marcus and clear this up."

Marsee nodded, so Temperate flew the shuttle down to their designated landing spot as Clear Seas tried to get ahold of Marcus or her father. They didn't answer for him either.

"I don't like it," Clear Seas said. "They could just be busy or have their notifications turned off. I'll try again in a few minutes. Be careful."

Marsee unhooked herself from the safety netting. "So who's coming with me?" she asked.

Avery of course. She couldn't go anywhere without her shadow.

Temperate indicated he wished to remain with the shuttle. His arm was starting to bother him and he wanted to give it a rest.

Stormy was bouncing with enthusiasm to go with them. "Please?" he asked.

"Well, without your father, I could really use that extra set of super eyes," she replied.

Clear Seas chuckled. "You can go, but make sure you do exactly what the Translator and Honor Guard say."

"I promise, Papa!" Stormy said, and swam out with them.

They didn't have a guide show up this time, so she made for the platform, and spoke to the first person they found. That person led them to the Master Builder, who immediately flashed pure white at the sight of her and Avery.

Avery immediately tensed but she raised a paw to stop him.

"I take it you know who I am?"

He shook himself out of his shock and immediately flashed the silver and purple. "Translator! It's an honor...I... Forgive me, I wasn't expecting you."

"This is Guild site and people have died here, a fact which you did not inform Ellie. After everything that's happened, I find that hard to believe."

He flashed regret, embarrassment, and fear, and nearly went catatonic again but eventually managed to speak. "Please. I meant today. I wasn't expecting you today. You were just released from the Trauma Center, and as for what happened, Rip Current said he would inform the Senior Guild Master. I had no idea she didn't know."

She glared at the Master Builder for several long moments and he wilted under her gaze. "If that's the case, why are you reacting so afraid of me?"

He flashed embarrassment again and struggled to bring his emotions under control. "I...You're the Translator and you brought the Guard with you and...I thought I was being arrested for working with...for...bottomless depths. I thought you were going to arrest me for association with Rip Current."

"Is there reason I should arrest you?" Avery signed, his face a cold mask.

"No, of course not!" The Master Builder flashed, his words tinged in fear again.

"Master Builder please, we didn't not come here to arrest you. Would you be able to tell me specifically what parts of this build they were protesting and where those deaths occurred?"

"I...uh...yes..um...this way please," he finally flashed out.

They followed after, swimming away from the platform, which surprised her and put Avery on high alert. Several minutes later they swam into a rocky canyon. "We were starting to drill for the main mining tunnel," he said, pointing to a large hole in the ground, "when our crews were attacked. Since then, none of the crews will dig here, saying the area is now cursed by the Deep, so we had to relocate to a new site."

"Why would they think it's cursed?" Marsee asked.

"It's an old superstition," he replied, flashing embarrassment and apology. "They think the ghosts of the two dead crew are haunting the place. Any time a tool is misplaced or a piece of equipment breaks, they blame it on their ghosts. Some even claim they've heard screaming, but we've not found anything. Eventually, it just wasn't worth continuing to drill here," he replied.

"Thank you Master Builder. Do you know why they attacked your crew?"

"No ma'am. I do not. They were protesting the platform for weeks, but hadn't caused damage or harm, so we mostly ignored them. Then one day they attacked the three people that were working here. Two were killed, one managed to get away. The Sea Patrol was already here because of the protesters, but weren't engaging. They were able to catch a few of the protesters due to the fact that they were boxed in, and left. We've had patrol ever since, but we haven't had a single protester show up since that day.

"Is that third crew member here?" she asked.

"No, ma'am. He quit the next day," he replied.

"Send me his information please. I'll come find you later once I'm done having a look around here."

"Yes, ma'am," he said, and bolted.

She snorted as he took off, then shaking her head turned back around, considered, and then swam over to the hole and peered down.

It wasn't a very big hole, all things considered. Wide enough that any of the species could easily swim down, but it was dark, and she shuddered at the memory of her dark cave. Flipping out her tablet, she turned on the flashlight and tried to look down, but she couldn't see more than ten or fifteen feet.

"You aren't planning on going down there are you?" Avery asked, peering over her shoulder to look down the hole too, and unclipped his own flashlight to peer down. It was far stronger than hers, but didn't reveal anything but more of the hole.

"Not if I don't have to," she spoke back. "It would really help if we had a better light. Do you think you could get one from the platform, or maybe a rope we can attach your flashlight to?"

"I'm not supposed to leave you alone," Avery said, clipping his light back on his harness.

"You wouldn't be. I have Super Stormy to protect me," she replied, still peering down the hole.

"A six year old fry is not protection," he replied.

Marsee turned to face him. "Look around you, Avery. There's nothing and no one here. You'll be gone for what? Ten, fifteen minutes? Besides, the Master Builder said the rest of the crew won't even come over here anymore. Petra, Willow, and those protesters are missing. I need to know what happened. What was so important they were willing to kill and die for? Would you be willing to kill someone over a fish, even if it was endangered? Something else happened here. I'm sure of it."

Avery frowned. "You do not leave this canyon without me, and if you so much as suspect something is off, you call me. Understood?"

She nodded, and he swam off as fast as his drone could go.

"Where's the guard going?" Stormy asked.

"To find a light we can drop down the shaft," she replied.

"You don't need a light, I could do that," he said, lighting up super bright and making her blink.

"No need to blind me," she said with a chuckle. "I know you can light up, but I'm not sending you down there without being able to see what we're up against first. I doubt it's been shored up to make it safe, and it could collapse at any time. Nor do we know what's chosen to swim in there since they stopped drilling. No, while he's gone, we need to look for a nearby cave. Deep Current said they were trying to stop the nesting ground of some endangered species from being drilled through. There's nothing here, so there must be a cave below, which means another entrance around here. Why don't you take one side of the canyon and I'll take the other," she suggested.

He agreed and bolted over to the far wall. She made her way to her side, and started looking behind the seaweed that lined the rocky canyon.

It wasn't five minutes later before a bright flashing light caught her attention and she looked up to see Stormy waving her over. "I found something!" he flashed.

She swam over and peered behind the tall grasses and sure enough there was a small cave entrance. She couldn't see very far though. Stormy lit up his skin so they could see further. What she could see was an empty rocky cave. She and Stormy could fit, along with younger adults within the Water Sprites, as they were far more flexible and narrow than her species, but Avery would not be able to, and she wasn't sure if Clear Seas could.

"It looks like another old lava tube," Stormy signed, and then ducked inside.

"Stormy wait!" she called out. He turned around. "Stay where I can see you," she signed, and watched as he slowly made his way down the sloping tube and paused, looking down.

"It looks like it drops down from here and heads back towards you," Stormy signed, and then dove down out of sight.

"Stormy! Get back here!" she yelled, but he didn't return. Frantic with worry now, she debated heading into the tube or waiting for Avery to return. She was just about to duck inside when she heard something behind her and spun around, expecting it to be Avery, and froze.

"Hello, Little Kitten. It's so lovely to see you again."

LAURA NAPOLI

Laura Napoli was born and raised in northern Vermont and continues to make the area her home. When not spending her time on the warm clicky box (computer), she is the caregiver to four heating cats who provide her with heat, massage, acu-paw-ture, and purr-therapy in exchange for pets and catnip treaties. For more information, visit https://www.heatingcats.com

*Publications*

Book 1: The Tails of Little Flower

Book 2: The Pride of Little Flower

Book 3: The Whiskers of Hope

Book 4: The Paws of Hope

*Coming Soon*

Book 5: Saber's Instinct

HUE-MAN (LITTLE EARTH)

- **2A84**
  - Alias: Nazari's Cub
- **Aaron Delaney**
- **Anne Harding**
  - *Rank:* Councilor
- **Ben**
- **Danny Shuto**
- **Damon Minor**
  - *Partner:* Amanda Minor *
  - *Children:* Sarah Minor *
- **Ezra Borovik**
- **Henry Curtis**
- **Irene**
  - *Rank:* Councilor
- **James O'Neil**
  - *Rank:* Councilor
  - *Partner:* Ben O'Neil *
  - *Grandchildren:* Jessica O'Neil
  - *Aliases:* GrandFather, Uncle James
- **Janet**
  - *Rank:* Councilor
  - *Alias:* 1A102
- **Jenny Rousseau**
  - *Rank:* Councilor

- **Jeran Frederick Chenzira**
  - *Rank:* Senior Councilor
  - *Mentor:* Marcus Surellis
  - *Partner:* Myra Chenzira
  - *Parents:* Frederick Surellis, Grammy Surellis
  - *Children:* Marsee, Jenny, Thomas, three others
- **Jordan Ross**
  - *Rank:* Councilor
- **Kai Nez**
  - *Rank:* Councilor
- **Little Flower Chenzira**
  - *Rank:* Councilor
  - *Parents:* Jeran Chenzira, Myra Chenzira, Alice O'Neil *, David O'Neil *
  - *Grandparents:* Frederick Chenzira, Grammy Chenzira, James O'Neil, Ben O'Neil *
  - *Aliases:* Jessica O'Neil, 1A1
- **Margaret**
  - *Rank:* Councilor
  - *Alias:* 4A35
- **Mary Shepard**
  - *Rank:* Councilor
- **Mitch ***
  - Alias: 3A236
- **Paul Markson**
- **Rachael Hoffsteader**
  - *Rank:* Councilor
- **Vera Scott**
  - *Rank:* Councilor


SABER

- **Ammond Greyfoot**
  - *Rank:* Master Healer - Hearing Specialist

- ○ *Partner:* Theresa Greyfoot
- **Alyx Taton**
  - ○ *Rank:* Senior Guard - North Plains district
- **Avery Hunt**
  - ○ *Rank:* Honor Guard
  - ○ *Mentor:* Kendra Hunt
- **Aris Zatara**
  - ○ *Rank:* Honor Guard
  - ○ *Mentor:* Avery Hunt
- **Brice Morningstar**
  - ○ *Rank:* Senior Healer - Agency
  - ○ *Mentor:* Myra Chenzira
- **Cynthia Lowell**
  - ○ *Rank:* Master Tech - Tech Guild
- **Elliana Reighly Khihar**
  - ○ *Rank:* Senior Guild Master
- **Gregory**
  - ○ *Rank:* Master - Builder's Guild
- **Gentry Fartooth**
  - ○ *Rank:* Master - Writer's Guild
- **Hallie**
  - ○ *Rank:* Honor Guard
  - ○ *Mentor:* Avery Hunt
- **Hayden**
  - ○ *Rank*: Master Tech
- **Jennette Tabor**
  - ○ *Rank:* Senior Councilor
- **Keeta**
  - ○ *Rank:* Honor Guard
  - ○ *Mentor:* Avery Hunt
- **Kendra Hunt**
  - ○ *Rank:* Senior Honor Guard
- **Kelly Goodwind**
  - ○ *Rank:* Master Healer

- *Mentor:* Myra Chenzira
- **Layton Reheem**
  - *Rank:* Broadcaster - Press Guild
- **Lark**
  - *Rank:* Honor Guard
  - *Mentor:* Avery Hunt
- **Maggie Chenzira**
  - *Parents:* Thomas Chenzira, Jenny Chenzira
- **Marcus Surellis**
  - *Rank:* Councilor - South Plains District
  - *Parents:* Frederick Surellis, Grammy Surellis
- **Marsee Bet Chenzira**
  - *Rank:* Journeyman - Artist's Guild, Journeyman - Crafter's Guild, Apprentice - Writer's Guild, Translator - Council
  - *Parents:* Myra Chenzira, Jeran Chenzira
- **Mattis Lawson**
  - *Rank:* Guild Senior - Primary School Guild
- **Myra Beth Chenzira**
  - *Rank:* Master Healer, Master Animal Healer
  - *Partner:* Jeran Chenzira
  - *Mentors:* Ammond Greyfoot, Nazari Jabri
  - *Children:* Marsee, Jenny, Thomas, three others
- **Nazari Jabri**
  - *Rank:* Master Healer, Master Animal Healer
- **Ned Griffith**
  - *Rank:* Councilor - North Plains District
- **Nerissa Witherspoon**
  - *Rank:* Senior Guild Healer
- **Nichola Sampson**
  - *Rank:* Oscar Rynhold
  - *Mentor: Oscar Rynhold*
- **Paxton Parner**
  - *Rank:* Councilor - Jandolf Square District
- **Plynth**

- *Rank:* Honor Guard
- **Oscar Rynhold**
    - *Rank:* Commander - Ship's Guild
- **Quinn Bluestone**
    - *Rank:* District Senior - Council City - Honor Guard
    - *Mentor:* Kendra Hunt
- **Resner**
    - *Rank:* Master Tech
- **Rowan**
    - *Rank:* Journeyman Healer
- **Tamarin Fields**
    - *Rank:* Honor Guard
    - *Mentor:* Avery Hunt
- **Theresa Greyfoot**
    - *Partner:* Ammond Greyfoot
- **Thomas Chenzira**
    - *Rank:* Master - Musician's Guild
- **Wallace**
    - *Rank:* Honor Guard

## WATER SPRITE (WATER WORLD)

- **Amber**
    - *Rank:* Journeyman Crafter
- **Agate**
    - *Rank:* Guild Master
    - *Mentor:* Trench
- **Carrie**
    - *Parents:* Snapper Fish
- **Clear Seas**
    - *Rank:* Senior Councilor
    - *Partner:* Jewel
    - *Children:* Temperate Seas, Stormy Seas, and Jade
- **Crystal Cove**

- *Rank:* Councilor
- **Coral**
- **Deep Current**
  - *Rank:* Master Tech
  - *Parents:* Gentle Current, Fast Current
- **Gentile Current**
  - *Rank:* Master Fisherman
  - *Children:* Deep Current
- **Jade**
  - *Rank:* Master Healer
  - *Parents:* Clear Seas, Jewel
- **Jelly**
  - *Rank:* Senior Staffer
- **Jewel**
  - *Rank:* Master Historian
  - *Partner:* Clear Seas
  - *Children:* Temperate Seas, Stormy Seas, and Jade
- **Hyacinth**
  - *Rank:* Senior Guild Healer
- **Opal**
  - *Rank:* Food Vendor
- **Rainbow Scales**
  - *Rank:* Translator
- **Red Fin**
  - *Rank:* Honor Guard
  - *Parents:* Tanner
- **Rip Current**
  - *Rank:* Councilor - East Sea District
  - *Protege:* Tall Grass
- **Rock Face**
- **Sand Sweeper**
  - *Rank:* Senior Healer (Habitat)
- **Sea Turtle**
  - *Rank:* Master Musician

- **Snapper Fish**
    - ◦ *Rank:* Master Pilot
- **Snapping Turtle**
    - ◦ *Rank:* Councilor
- **Spotted Trout**
    - ◦ *Rank:* Councilor
- **Stinger**
    - ◦ *Rank:* Senior Honor Guard
- **Stormy Seas**
    - ◦ *Parents:* Clear Seas, Jewel
- **Tall Grass**
    - ◦ *Rank:* Junior Councilor
    - ◦ *Mentor:* Rip Current
- **Tanner**
    - ◦ *Rank:* Honor Guard
    - ◦ *Children:* Red Fin
- **Temperate Seas**
    - ◦ *Rank:* Master Pilot
    - ◦ *Parents:* Clear Seas, Jewel
- **Trench**
    - ◦ *Rank:* Guild Master (Retired)
    - ◦ *Protege:* Agate

## DIGGER

- **Sammianna**
    - ◦ *Rank:* Senior Councilor
- **Nardal**
    - ◦ *Rank:* Guild Master - Staffer's Guild

## FLYER

- **Petra**
    - ◦ *Rank:* Ship Master

- *Parents:* Wind Rider
- **Summer Breeze**
  - *Rank: Journeyman Healer*
- **Wind Rider**
  - *Rank:* Senior Councilor
- **Yellow Tail**
  - *Rank:* Master - Writer's Guild

## ICE GIANT (ICE PLANET)

- **Apakna**
  - *Rank:* Senior Councilor
- **Brack**
- **Eenowk**

## HUMAN (EARTH)

- **Alice O'Neil ***
  - *Occupation:* Baker, Business Owner
  - *Partner:* David O'Neil
  - *Children:* Jessica O'Neil
- **Amanda Minor ***
  - *Occupation:* Social Worker
  - *Partner:* Damon Minor
  - *Children:* Sarah Minor
- **Ben O'Neil ***
  - *Occupation:* Farmer
  - *Partner:* James O'Neil
  - *Children:* David O'Neil
  - *Grandchildren:* Jessica O'Neil
- **David O'Neil ***
  - *Occupation:* Lieutenant Marines - Retired, Business Owner
  - *Partner:* Alice O'Neil
  - *Children:* Jessica O'Neil

- **Ms. Walters** *
    - *Occupation:* High school Spanish Teacher
- **Susie Thomson** *
    - *Occupation:* High school student
    - *Other:* Jessica's best friend
- **Joey** *
    - *Occupation:* High school student
    - *Other:* Jessica's Classmate
- **Mark** *
    - *Occupation:* High school student
    - *Other:* Jessica's Classmate
- **Sarah Minor** *
    - *Parents:* Amanda Minor, Damon Minor


* Deceased

Note: All ranks, species, and guild affiliations listed are those at the time they were first introduced in this book or at the time of their death.